Cruel SUMMER

C.W. FARNSWORTH

The Kensingtons

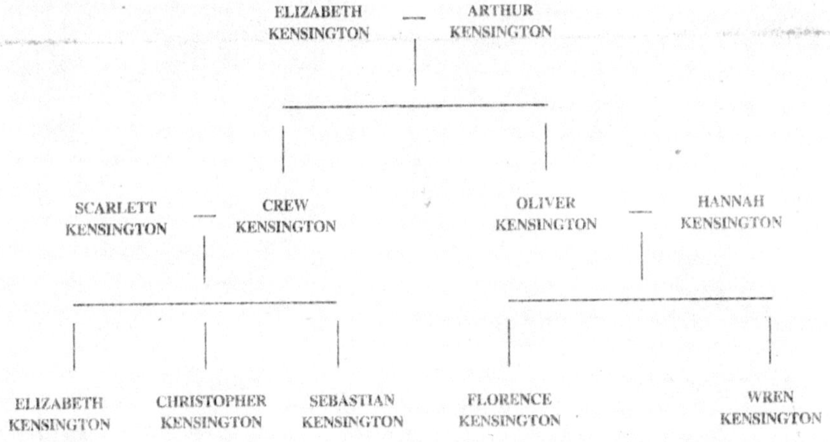

Playlist

Vertigo | Griff

I Of The Storm | Of Monsters and Men

I Told You Things | Gracie Abrams

Love Like This | Kodaline

My Boy Only Breaks His Favorite Toys | Taylor Swift

Lonely Island | Amble

The Cut That Always Bleeds | Conan Gray

Lost Cause | Beck

What I Do | Sons Of The East

The Night We Met | Lord Huron

Seventeen | Sharon Van Etten

Closing Time | Semisonic

ocean eyes | Billie Eilish

CHAPTER 1

Wren

The muffled crash of surf slamming into rock isn't nearly loud enough to drown out the persistent buzzing as my phone vibrates in the cupholder. Gia probably. I was supposed to meet her and the rest of my friends—I check the clock on the dash—five minutes ago.

When I glance at the screen, it's Rory calling instead.

I sigh and answer. "*Beep.* You've reached Wren Kensington. Leave a message, and I'll get back to you in an hour. Or in three days."

My older sister huffs. "Since you hardly ever pick up, I listen to your voicemail almost every time I call you. You never set up a personalized message, Wren. It just reads off your number in a robotic voice."

"How was I supposed to know that? I never call myself."

Her exhale is pure exasperation.

Poor Rory. She's one of those annoyingly perfect people you can't even resent for being perfect because they're also kind and thoughtful, and she got stuck with *me* as a younger sibling.

Rory is sophisticated and dependable, and I'm … well, I'm detoured next to a bluff because it's been a boring Thursday so far.

"Where are you, Wren?" Rory asks wearily.

"Driving to get ice cream with friends."

"It doesn't sound like you're driving."

I drum my fingers against the steering wheel. "I pulled over to talk to you. I can't hear anything in the convertible."

Rather than commend me on my responsibility, Rory wonders, "What's *ice cream* code for?"

"Want me to bring you back a scoop of cookie dough?" I offer innocently.

Another sigh from my sister. "Hanson invited us out on his boat tomorrow. We're leaving Scarlett and Crew's place at eight a.m. Mom wanted me to tell you, and you weren't replying to my texts."

"Eight?" I groan. "It's *summer*, Rory."

"Come home and argue with Mom and Dad about it," Rory states. "Don't eat too much *ice cream*."

She hangs up before I can refute her heavy skepticism.

To be fair, she's right. Ice cream isn't on tonight's itinerary.

I huff, tossing my phone on the passenger seat before stepping out of my car. Briny wind whips through my hair, blowing strands across my face and obstructing my vision with a snarl of pink. Dyeing the bottom half of my blonde hair felt like a fun idea last week, but I'm already sick of it. Maybe I can squeeze in a trip to the salon after going out on Aunt Scarlett's parents' yacht in the morning.

My dress gets dropped on top of my phone. After a second of deliberation, I decide to leave my sandals behind too. They're my favorite pair, and I don't want to hike back up to retrieve them.

The rough asphalt feels strange beneath my bare feet. Cool, thanks to the branches shading this section of street, and scratchy. The cheerful pink from my latest pedicure is bright against the drab gray backdrop.

The road ends, transitioning to trampled grass. At least I know I'm probably in the right place based on the amount of foot traffic. The lifeguard made this spot sound like a local secret, but the worn path looks like it was recently trod by a traveling circus. Can't be *that* covert.

Leafy green foliage surrounds both sides of the path and stretches high, creating a labyrinth effect. So far, the path ahead is perfectly straight. I can't see the ocean yet, but I can hear it. Taste it, the tang of salt in the air coating my face and hair with stickiness.

My steps slow when I hear voices ahead.

I wasn't expecting company, based on the lack of other cars where I parked, and I'm suddenly very aware I'm alone, wearing nothing except a swimsuit, with no phone. Even for me, that's reckless.

A dozen feet ahead, the path veers left. I approach the curve carefully, a surge of adrenaline ratcheting my heart rate up to a rapid, concerning rhythm.

One of the voices sounds female, which reassures me a little. And there *is* one woman, I discover, rounding the bend, but the rest are all men. Boys really. I'd guess they're close to my age, in high school or possibly college. Their faces are unfamiliar. Their standard uniform is board shorts and baggy, sleeveless tees. A few are shirtless. Most are smoking.

Locals.

A guy with shaggy blond hair spots me first. He smiles, eyes scanning my exposed skin appreciatively, but there's nothing lascivious in his expression. My instincts aren't screaming, *Run*.

Other heads turn my way. I spot curiosity and surprise, but no creepiness. In my experience, the most dangerous people tend to appear innocuous at first. These guys might be unkempt and stoned—sweet smoke swirls in the air—but not threatening.

"Hey." Shaggy speaks first, raising a hand to shade his eyes from the setting sun as he squints at me.

"Hey," I reply, scanning the small clearing they're standing in and spotting the start of stone that must lead to the rocky outcrop I'm planning to leap from.

"Country club is in the other direction, princess," another guy calls out, prompting scattered laughter among the group.

My molars grind. Not because I'm bothered by his childish comment. More annoyed he can tell I'm not a year-round resident based on my appearance and one word. What about a navy one-piece announces *I'm rich*?

"I'm not lost," I state, then continue toward the ledge.

More wild growth surrounds it, aside from an opening a few feet wide that's been cut or kept open by use. Once I'm through it, I'll be out of sight. It shouldn't take me more than ten minutes to swim back to shore, then walk to my car. I'll be late to meet everyone, but none of them will be surprised by my tardiness. My mom refers to my schedule as its own time zone.

"That's a dead end," Shaggy calls out.

"*That's*"—I hook a thumb over one shoulder toward the opening—"why I'm here."

Watching shock blanch across a few faces is somewhat satisfying.

"If she wants to jump, let her," the woman says.

I think she's older than me, but it's hard to tell for sure. Her face is scrubbed free of any makeup, freckled nose pink from too much sun recently.

I'm not sure if I should be grateful for her intervention. Her tone is dismissive, more *I don't give a shit* than *You go, girl! Be independent.*

Whatever. I don't need—or want—permission.

I turn back toward the opening, right as two more guys trample through the shrubbery, coming from the direction I'm headed in.

I spare the newcomers a quick glance. One's shorter, stocky, and smiling. And the other ... the other requires a longer look.

Most people are easy to read. A cursory scan is usually enough to form a solid opinion. Since Third, I've become almost obsessive about it, trying to train myself not to miss whatever I missed with him.

But this guy? Every time I tell myself to look away, to stop staring, I notice something else. His appearance filters in slowly, each new observation catching my attention all over again.

He's wearing a pair of green swim trunks, so saturated with water that they're still dripping. A few tattoos are scattered across his bare chest, a couple more on his left arm. I can't decipher shapes from this distance or what's hanging from the silver chain around his neck.

His face is especially captivating, a contrast of precise angles and imperfections. A white scar splits the center of his chin. There's a bump on the bridge of his straight nose, like it's been broken at least once before. His eyebrows are dark, angry slashes, interrupting a carefully controlled expression.

I force my eyes to look away, annoyed by my own fascination.

He's hot. So what? So was the lifeguard I flirted with this morning who told me about this spot.

"Cap!" Shaggy shouts, loud enough for anyone in a mile radius to hear.

Shaggy and the entire group he's part of have gravitated closer to the new arrivals. Like they were waiting for them. Which, I realize, watching a towel get tossed to the shorter guy, was *exactly* what they were doing.

Shaggy's talking to the guy I was staring at—Cap—who has his head bent to listen.

Turns out, the guy wrapping a towel around his waist isn't that short. Cap is just really tall.

With a shake of my head, I pick up my pace across the clearing.

No more distractions.

Since I left my phone behind, I have no idea how long the walk up here took. I still have a decent drive to the bar where I'm supposed to meet my friends. If I take too long to show and I'm not answering my cell, someone might call the house. If Rory—or worse, one of my parents—answers, I'll wind up grounded for the foreseeable future.

"Wait."

I'm not in the habit of taking orders. Actually, if you ask anyone who knows me, they'd tell you I lack basic listening skills. By choice.

But something about the smooth command—maybe how I know who said it, even before I turn around—makes me pause.

When I spin on my heel, they're all watching. Shaggy looks concerned. The fellow female appears peeved I'm still in near proximity. Most of the guys are checking out my cleavage.

Not *him*. He's focused on my face, a lofty, irritated expression on his.

"What, *Cap*?" I ask, then smirk and glance at the towel-wearing guy slouched beside him. "Is your buddy Bottle?"

His friend grins.

Cap doesn't. He crosses his arms, biceps bulging in a way that's intimidating and, unfortunately, a little impressive. He has the lean build of a swimmer—broad shoulders and a tapered waist—but the confrontational stance of a boxer.

"That's a fifteen-foot drop," Shaggy states. "Then a couple hundred meters to swim back to shore."

"I know."

I *didn't* know that. All I knew about this place was its general location. But I'm sure as hell not going to admit that.

Well, if it were just Shaggy here, I might have. He gives off friendly golden-retriever energy. But the scowling, tattooed Cap, who's radiating disapproval and can't appreciate a joke? No chance.

"It's dangerous. You shouldn't risk it, especially alone." Shaggy glances around, like he's hoping I'll have a friend magically show up.

I have friends. I have lots of friends. But not one of them would do this, which is why I'm here solo. Gia's idea of swimming is floating in a heated pool with a frozen margarita in hand.

Today isn't very hot, and the sinking sun isn't warming anything. The waning daylight adds a sense of urgency. Soon, this *will* be dangerous.

"I'll be fine," I say confidently.

"Idiotic, is what you are."

My gaze snaps to Cap, like it's been hoping for a reason to. I refuse to admit, even to myself, that's probably the case. "You're kind of an asshole."

"You can drop the *kind of*," he tells me, unsmiling and completely serious.

"Where did you jump from?" I ask, glancing pointedly at his wet trunks.

"The edge," he drawls.

I look at Shaggy. "See? He just did it, and he's fine. Aside from the asshole thing, of course."

"I've been bluffing since I was ten. How many times have you jumped off a cliff, princess?"

I scowl at Cap. I wasn't talking to *him*. "None of your business, asshole."

"That means none," one of the other guys says unhelpfully.

"She's a rich brat," the girl comments. "They'll send out the Coast Guard if she gets into trouble. Not our problem."

"Nice, Cammie," Shaggy tells her, shaking his head.

"What? If—" Cammie glances at me. "What's your name?"

"Wren Kensington," I state icily. For some reason, my eyes dart to Cap as I say it.

The furrow in his forehead deepens as a few of his friends mutter to each other, recognizing my last name.

My family's well known in the Hamptons—well known everywhere. And they *would* send a search party after me. Probably several.

But I'm not incapable. Or *idiotic*. I wouldn't be doing this if I wasn't sure I could.

Deciding I've humored Shaggy's genuine concern and the others' mocking for long enough, I spin and stride toward the opening. No one follows or calls after me, which is a relief.

The rock's surface is fairly flat, the few grooved indentations easy to step around. It extends about twenty feet before I reach the edge.

I stand there, staring down at the churning water. Fifteen feet looks like fifty from here.

But I never intended to look, then turn back, and it's absolutely not an option now. The one upside to running into that crowd is, I know this is the right spot and that someone—two someones—jumped successfully today.

I glance left, at the beach that I'll need to swim toward, mentally plotting my route to safety.

"You're stubborn."

The gruff statement startles me—something you *don't* want to happen while standing near the edge of a cliff. An unattractive squeak sneaks out as I hop closer to solid ground and away from the approaching fall.

"You good?" Still husky, but there's a softer note to his tone as he stops beside me.

"Yes. To both."

I'm not sure because he's looking at the horizon ahead, but I think Cap rolls his eyes at my answer.

"You going again?" I ask.

"No. I'm supervising."

It takes a second for his meaning to sink in. Once it does …

"Like *fuck* you are," I growl.

He looks mildly amused by my annoyance. "Kitten's got claws."

I cross my arms and glower. "First *princess*, now *kitten*? Are you president of the Stupid Nickname Club, *Cap*?"

He rubs a palm along his jaw. I have a sneaking suspicion it might be to cover a smile, and I'm aggravated by how badly I wish I could see it.

"You can stop saying it like that," he tells me.

"Like what?" I sass.

"Like it's the dumbest word you've ever heard. And it has nothing to do with bottles. It's short for Captain. I like boats."

"You like boats," I repeat.

"Uh-huh."

He's glancing down at the water, scrutinizing the choppy surface closely. *Supervising*, I guess, although I have no clue what he thinks he'll be able to do once I jump. Control the current with his mind?

"What's your real name?" I ask.

"Sawyer. How well can you swim?"

"*Really* well."

He looks at me then, lifting an eyebrow with obvious skepticism.

I hold his gaze. "I'm not modest, but I'm not a liar either. I also hate failing at things. I'm only doing this because I want to—and I'm certain I can. So, you can *go*."

Sawyer's chin jerks toward the clearing. "Boys are worried you'll drown."

Not the snide brunette, I note.

"And you're not?"

"Birds can fly. Right, *Wren*?"

I snort, attempting to ignore the silly flip that appeared when he said my name like a lilting taunt. Whenever I get home tonight, I know I'm going to lie in bed and replay the sound on repeat.

"What are you, some kind of ornithologist?"

"At least insult me with words I understand."

I tilt my head as I study him. "You get underestimated a lot?"

There's a brief flash of ... something before his expression shutters back to neutrality. Enough of a reaction to tell me I hit a nerve.

"You're stalling," he states flatly.

"You're deflecting," I retort. "Or do you not know what that means either?"

"I see it happen all the time," Sawyer continues like I said nothing. "Tourists looking for a little thrill, sick of sitting around while their staff does all the work. They take a boat out during a storm or drive too fast, and *we* wind up having to risk our own necks or the cops get a 'donation' to look the other way." He shakes his head, jaw clenched. "Fucking idiots."

"Sounds like you have some issues," I inform him.

"Just a short fuse for people with a lot of money," he replies.

"I have a lot of money."

"I know," he says, dark and sardonic.

I spin and poke the center of his chest with one finger. It's solid muscle. Sawyer doesn't shift back a single inch.

"That doesn't mean you know a damn thing about me."

"You jumping or not, Wren?"

I like the way he frames it, like it's my choice.

I love the way he says my name. Softer, missing the sharp, mocking edge from before. I'm unsteady again, and the vertigo has nothing to do with uneven footing or surprise.

I reach for the silver chain around Sawyer's neck to anchor myself, using it to yank his head down closer to my height. Still, I have to rise up on my tippy-toes to reach his mouth.

My lips collide with a pair that is warm and soft. I run my tongue along the length of his lower lip, inhaling his startled exhale. Smile proudly because my initial impression of Sawyer is, he's not someone who gets caught off guard often or easily.

"In case I'm about to die," I explain, releasing his chain and patting his hot, firm chest.

Then I turn, run, and jump off the edge.

The plummeting fall from the bluff lasts just long enough for me to second-guess my decision.

Cool water closes around my head as I sink beneath the surface of the sea. I savor the silence and darkness and weightlessness for a few seconds, then kick hard to the surface to inhale a deep breath. Shout my success at the pastel sky overhead, the exalted sound getting lost in the whipping wind and splashing surf.

Another head breaks through the waves, about ten feet away, startling me. I blink rapidly at Sawyer as my limbs churn to keep me afloat, my eyes stinging with saltiness.

He jumped in after me.

I don't know how I should feel about that, if it was a nonvote of confidence in my abilities, but I know how I *do* feel about it. Warmth spreads through my chest and into my extremities, chasing the ocean's chill away as I tread water.

"Try to keep up," Sawyer calls out, already starting toward the shore with swift, precise strokes.

I jumped. I plummeted. I landed.

But watching him swim away is the strangest feeling.

Like I just started falling.

CHAPTER 2

Sawyer

The brim of my baseball hat gets knocked up, forcing me to squint at the sun.

"I'd say you look like shit. But frankly, that's offensive to shit."

I scowl at Gus. Yawning ruins the effect of my annoyance some. "Your shirt is on inside out."

Gus rolls his eyes before glancing down. He laughs. "Woke up late. Thanks for saving my ass with Dusty."

I grunt an acknowledgment.

Augustus Griffin is the most cheerful, genuine person I know. Anyone who's met the two of us wonders how we possibly ended up best friends. Wonders why *he* is best friends with *me*, rather.

Gus fixes his shirt, runs a hand through his shaggy blond hair, and then takes a seat on the opposite side of the picnic table. "All good, Cap?"

I scratch my forehead, then tug the brim of my hat down more

securely. "Yeah. You?"

"Uh-huh."

I feel Gus's eyes on me, but I keep mine aimed at the horizon.

The view is the main reason I stick with this job. I could make more money caddying, and lifeguarding would be a lot less work. But I don't want to be stuck staring at the ocean on the green with a bunch of boring rich guys or beyond swarms of screaming kids. I want to admire it like this, interrupted by nothing except the occasional mast. The way the sea is supposed to be admired. On a clear day, like this one, you can see the stripes of the lighthouse located past the breakwater.

"She made it to shore okay?"

Gus's question is more of a fishing expedition than a simple query, but it's subtler than the other ways I've gotten asked about this topic. Like Cammie's all-caps *WHAT THE FUCK?* text waiting when I remembered to charge my phone late last night.

"You'd have heard about it if she hadn't." I reach for my mug, covering the Atlantic Yacht Club logo printed on the ceramic with my thumb.

Wren Kensington's disappearance would have made national news.

If I'd sunk beneath the waves, it would have been a very different local headline.

"You talk to her after?" Gus's tone falls far short of casual.

I clocked his interest in Wren the second I stepped into that clearing. Gus is a good guy, but he's not normally *that* concerned with a stranger's safety.

"Not really." I sip more coffee.

"Bennett! Griffin! The Ellsworth boat is headed out today. Make sure it's ready." Dusty, the marina manager, hurries past, appearing more stressed than usual.

Monday's the Fourth of July, also known as our busiest day of the season.

"Now!" he adds loudly, without glancing back to check if either of us has moved. "Pratt and Quincy are already down there."

I have two theories about why Dusty insists on referring to marina employees only by their last names. One, it saves him the trouble of learning our first names. Two, it makes him feel more important. Like a lieutenant commanding troops during battle, not a fifty-something-year-old man in charge of a horde of hungover teens and a fleet of very expensive boats.

I stand with a sigh and stretch, downing the rest of my coffee before heading toward the gangplank. Heavy footfalls tell me Gus is following.

The Ellsworth yacht is impossible to miss. It's the biggest boat in the yard, sleek and shiny and fast. The younger guys always argue over who gets to service it, wanting their chance to check the bilge and fuel levels and other regular maintenance simply for a chance to get close to the vessel.

Four guys are three too many for a standard safety check, but it means we'll be finished in record time. And I get why Dusty wanted it completed so quickly when he approaches with a large group behind him right as we're wrapping up. He's talking animatedly to the silver-haired man who's walking in front.

I kneel and squeeze a fender, double-checking its inflation, before glancing at Gus. He's chatting with Mike Quincy, a sophomore who started this summer, oblivious to what I immediately noticed—Wren Kensington is part of the group headed this way.

I don't pay close attention to gossip about the Hamptons' elite. I make an effort to purposefully ignore it as much as possible actually. I could not care less who's having an affair with whom or whose company just went public for a bajillion dollars. But I dimly recall Ellsworth's daughter is married to a Kensington.

Hanson Ellsworth is a chatty, boastful sort, especially when he has a captive audience counting on tips. I'm not sure where Wren is located on the family tree, but it's close enough to Hanson to receive a coveted invitation out on his pride and joy.

Her golden-and-pink hair is pulled up in a ponytail today, showing off the perfect symmetry of her face. If she needed more money, Wren Kensington could make a lot off her looks.

I think she's noticed me, too, although I can't tell for sure since her sunglasses shield the direction of her gaze. I have this sense she has, which sounds stupid to even think.

"Who's *that*?" Ricky Pratt mutters under his breath to my left.

"Dunno," I reply, pretending my eyes weren't focused on the same spot a second ago.

"Cap! Gimme a hand here?"

I turn, spotting Wade Greene steering a pontoon boat in a few slips down. I head Wade's way, catching the line he tosses me. I secure it around the cleat, then do the same at the stern.

"Smooth ride?" I ask, grinning.

Wade flips me off before vaulting over the gate.

Pontoon boats are tricky in the ocean. They're not as seaworthy as deep-V hulls—equipped to handle moderate choppiness and short coastal trips in good conditions, but not much else. Dusty keeps a couple around because tourists sometimes request them.

"Hey, isn't that the chick from last night?" Wade asks, glancing in the direction I came from.

I don't turn to look before shrugging.

The feigned nonchalance feels foreign. I've never had to *act* oblivious before; I genuinely haven't cared.

"Probably."

"Wren Kensington, right? Why'd you go after her? Cammie was pissed." Wade chuckles at the memory.

Yeah, got that vibe from her text.

"None of her business," I say. *Or yours.*

"C'mon, man. You know she wants it to be."

I do know. Which is why I haven't touched Cammie since last summer. I might be an asshole, but I'm not one who intentionally hurts his friends.

"Hey, *Cap.*"

My heart does this silly somersault in my chest when I recognize her voice.

I turn slowly, making a show of lowering my gaze to make eye contact.

Wren isn't especially tall, but I wouldn't describe her as short either. Partially because I don't *have* to crane my neck—I'm just enjoying the view down her shirt—but mostly because she carries a confidence that adds to her height.

"Hey." I don't use her name, even though I remember it. It fits her. A little wild. Unusual. Intriguing.

She pushes her sunglasses to the top of her head, nose scrunching as she glances around the marina. "You work here?"

"Yes," I answer shortly.

Her family is busy making themselves comfortable on the yacht, but Gus is looking this way. I watch him swipe a hand through his shaggy blond hair, a resigned smile appearing on his face before he turns to fuel the rentals that were recently returned.

I'm a dick for liking that she approached me and not him.

"Still an asshole, huh?" she asks.

Her blue eyes are exploring the ink on my left arm, specifically the script on the inside of my wrist. I resist the urge to rub at the spot. Whenever people stare there, I'm tempted to cover it. Which leads to guilt, then grief, followed by self-loathing.

"What do you want, Wren?"

A small smile plays across her lips, like she finds my short fuse amusing rather than the warning most people take it as. "Want? Nothing. Just being friendly." She glances at Wade, who's doing a shitty job pretending he's not eavesdropping on our conversation. Takes a step to the left, holding out a palm toward him. "Hi. I'm Wren."

Her elbow brushes against my forearm as they shake hands. I fight the impulse to scrub at that spot too.

"Wade," he says eagerly. "We sort of met last night."

"I remember," Wren replies sweetly. She plays with the end of her ponytail, twirling the mixed strands around one finger as she aims a pleasant, practiced smile Wade's way.

If Wade wasn't a buddy, I'd blurt out the, *Bullshit*, I'm dying to say. But Wade is lapping up the attention, the lie, adjusting his polo so he has an excuse to flex.

She's flirting with him to irritate me, I think, and I'm pissed it's working.

I jerk my chin toward the idling yacht. "They might leave without you."

Wren smiles ruefully. "Tried that already. They waited while I got ready. This"—she waves toward the water—"was not my idea. So far, summer here has sucked."

I'm certain Wren Kensington and I have two very different definitions of life sucking. It's tough to summon any sympathy for someone who sees spending the day sunning on a three-million-dollar yacht as a hardship.

"If you're free tomorrow night, you should come by our party," Wade suggests. "We all have to work the Fourth, so we're celebrating early. Address is 53 Maple."

I scowl, then quickly school my expression. My guess is, if she thinks I don't want her to show up, Wren will be much more likely to.

"Tomorrow, 53 Maple," Wren repeats. "Yeah, maybe."

"Wren!" A blonde woman is leaning over the railing of the yacht, waving. "Let's go!"

Based on the close resemblance between them, I'm certain it's her mother.

Wren steps back, meeting my gaze as she executes a crisp salute. "See ya, Cap."

Despite my best effort to remain expressionless, one corner of my mouth curves up. "Wear a life jacket."

"Because I beat you to shore?" She spins and skips away before I can reply that it was a tie.

"Think she'll show?" Wade wonders, staring after Wren with goddamn hearts reflected in his eyes.

I sigh heavily, shaking my head. "Doubt it. You good here? I gotta go finish the dock repair."

"Yeah, I'm good."

I nod, then head for the ramp.

I don't think Wren will show.

But I do think there's a small part of me that wants her to.

CHAPTER 3

Wren

The narrow house located at 53 Maple isn't much. Three levels tall, it's painted a faded yellow, with a raised deck that wraps around the entire exterior of the second floor. An empty boat trailer sits in the yard, next to three older cars, one of which is propped on wooden blocks instead of having tires.

Close proximity to the ocean appears to be the only obvious selling point. There's an access point to the beach directly across the street.

I check my reflection in the rearview mirror one final time, then climb out of my convertible and lock it.

I pick my way around the clumped weeds carefully, glad I opted for sneakers over sandals. I thought it'd make my dress look more casual, and I got the sense this would be a laid-back affair.

The correct sense, I confirm when climbing the stairs and stepping inside the open sliding door of the deck. The interior of the house isn't any nicer than the exterior. The only furniture in what I think is the

living room is a stained floral-print couch and a coffee table so covered with cans that I can't tell the color.

As I shoulder through the crowd, I get a lot of double takes. I haven't spent enough time in the Hamptons for any of them to recognize me as a Kensington, but they can all tell I don't belong here. Not wearing a designer dress with a full face of makeup.

Whatever.

I like looking good. And I had time to kill, waiting for the rest of the house to go to bed, before sneaking out.

Amid a sea of ripped denim and faded shirts, plus a few swimsuits, my outfit stands out.

I scan the unfriendly, surprised faces, looking for someone I recognize. The woman from the clearing is across the room. She looks younger tonight, with her hair down, and happier, laughing loudly at something the girl next to her said. Then she sees me and immediately sobers.

I wave, and she glowers.

What is her problem?

I push ahead rather than wait to find out.

The kitchen is next. Linoleum floor, white appliances. Cheap bottles of alcohol and used plastic cups litter the counter.

"Wren! You came!"

I turn, finally spotting another semi-familiar face. It's the guy who invited me. Will? Wes? Neither sounds right. I nod and smile and try to recall his name as he approaches, a beer bottle in one hand and a wide smile aimed my way.

"Cool party," I say.

He smiles. Sips some beer. "Probably not what you're used to, huh?"

I shrug a shoulder. "Variety is good." Glance around the kitchen. "Is this your place?"

"Not just mine. But I live here, yeah."

"Great location," is the only honest compliment I can come up with.

What's his name lights up. "Right? That's what sold me on this place. Do you surf?"

"Uh, no. Not really big on the ocean. I prefer a pool."

He tilts his head. "Why'd you go bluffing, then?"

"I wanted to. I'm not *afraid* of the ocean."

"Huh." He still seems confused. Or maybe I've offended my only ally. "You want a drink?"

"Just water. I drove."

"Oh. Okay. Well, we usually just take it from the tap." He nods toward the sink.

I clear my throat. "Anything flavored? Sparkling?"

He shrugs a shoulder, not appearing optimistic. "I'll check the fridge."

The door swings open, revealing the contents. Several cases of beer sit on the shelf, all but one ripped open. Aside from that, all that's inside is a random assortment of condiments.

I should have brought a seltzer.

"Tap it is," I say, spinning toward the sink.

Immediately, my eyes latch on Sawyer. He's standing just through the doorway that connects to a hallway, talking to a guy with a shaved head. I can't tell if Sawyer has noticed I'm here, much less cares. But he's here, and that realization ratchets up my heart rate.

He's just a guy.

A guy I hardly know.

A guy who seems to be an asshole most of the time.

A guy I'm not even sure likes me.

A guy who has Skylar tattooed on the inside of his wrist.

And also, the main reason I'm here.

"Here you go."

A plastic cup of water is handed to me by the guy whose name I still can't remember. I thought it was a W, but maybe it was a D? Dale?

Shit. I'm going to have to ask soon. It'll be more awkward, the longer I wait.

I was distracted by Sawyer at the marina. Just like I'm distracted by him now. He's still talking to Buzz Cut, but his eyes have shifted to me. He's noticed I'm here, but I can't glean any reaction from his expression. Not if he's surprised or disappointed or annoyed or pleased to see me. *Nothing.* It's as thrilling as standing at the edge of a cliff with him was.

Most guys are obvious. They leer or smirk or look at my boobs. For the most part, I don't care what people think of me. But I've always— until now—had some idea.

"So, you staying the whole summer or …"

"Just a few more days," I answer. "My dad's work trip got canceled, so we came to stay with my aunt and uncle. My aunt's mom throws this big Fourth of July party every year."

"Oh yeah. The Red, White, and Blue thing. My sister was part of the catering staff at a couple of those. Said the food was gross. Oysters and caviar and shit."

"Sounds right," I say, sipping some water and hoping I'm imagining the rusty aftertaste.

"Where are you spending the rest of the summer?"

"New York mostly. I'm teaching a tennis camp. And I'll probably take a trip to California to visit my grandparents. Next weekend, I'm going to Marseille for a friend's eighteenth birthday."

"Oh. Uh, cool."

"What about you? Any summer plans?"

"Pretty much just this." He waves a vague hand around. "Surfing and working, you know. Hanging with the crew."

"The crew?"

"Guys at the marina and—hey, Cap!"

A flat, "Hey," comes from behind me.

I fight the urge to look in every muscle, counting down from ten until I allow my head to slowly turn his way.

When I do, his eyes are on me.

"You showed," Sawyer states with no intonation.

He would seriously clean up at poker.

"Yep," I say cheerfully. "Since"—I glance at the guy I was talking to, then quickly away—"you guys made it sound fun."

What's his name smiles, but there's a crease of confusion on his forehead. Sawyer didn't encourage his invitation in any way.

He hasn't realized I forgot his name yet.

But I think Sawyer might have come to that correct conclusion. He taps a finger against the rim of his plastic cup, scrutinizing me. Judging me, it feels like.

I hold his gaze, refusing to be the one who looks away first. Yeah, it was rude of me to forget the name of the guy who invited me, but it's not a crime. He's acting like I committed a felony.

"What are *you* doing here?" a snide voice asks.

The brunette is approaching. I forget her name, too, but I don't feel badly about that.

I deliberate not answering, then decide saying, "I was invited," is more satisfying. So, I do.

"Who invited you?"

One second passes. Two. Three.

"Me," a male voice says. Not the one I'm expecting, but the one I instantly recognize and can connect to a name.

Her snideness wavers, hurt appearing instead. "Seriously, Cap? The fuck?"

"Leave it, Cammie," Sawyer says, then strides past me and out of the kitchen.

"The deck cooler is out of ice, Wade," Cammie comments cooly, then follows after Sawyer.

Wade. *Wade, Wade, Wade,* I chant silently, determined not to forget his name again.

"On it," Wade replies. He glances at me, curiosity evident in his expression. He's the only other person here who knows what Sawyer just said was a lie. "I'll be back in a bit."

"Sounds good," I say, raising my glass in a silent *cheers*.

Wade smiles, then leaves me standing alone in the kitchen.

CHAPTER 4

Sawyer

I should head home. I couldn't fall asleep last night, so I drove to the secluded inlet I found a few years ago. It's probably private property, but no one's ever bothered to tell me so. Then I went to the field, threw until my shoulder was screaming. By the time I collapsed into bed, it was well after three a.m. Tomorrow, the Fourth of July, will be an early morning and a busy day at work.

Yet I don't move from my truck's hood. I continue to stare up at the clear, dark sky, scattered with stars, wishing I hadn't bothered to show up. If I hadn't, I wouldn't have known she had too. Wouldn't have been stuck with this awareness, left wondering what she's doing inside. Wondering who she's talking to. Wondering why she bothered to come.

It wasn't for Wade; she didn't even remember his name.

With a frustrated exhale, I slide off the hood and trek toward the house. Tonight was supposed to be simple—a cold beer and fooling around with Macie, a new waitress at the yacht club's restaurant. Instead,

I'm sober, and I've been too busy avoiding looking at Wren to notice if Macie is here or not.

Wade is leaning against the railing, smoking a joint, a melting bag of ice propped against the post to his left. "Thanks," he says as I approach.

"Don't mention it."

I mean that literally. The last thing I want is misplaced gratitude from Wade. I didn't lie to spare him Cammie's wrath. I lied because I had seen how all the guys were looking at Wren, and I knew they'd be less obvious about checking her out if they thought I was interested in her.

I leave Wade smoking on the deck and head inside. The air-conditioning has never worked well in this house, and having a few dozen people crammed inside isn't helping, but at least the living room is less humid than outside. The kitchen is my current destination, but I only make it a few steps before I hear my name called.

Gus beckons me over when I glance his way, shouting, "Cap!" again.

I wish I could discreetly inquire what the hell he's thinking. Wren is standing next to him, and I have no clue why Gus is calling me over to join them.

You got the girl, idiot. Fucking hoard her. Make a damn move. Don't create competition.

Not that I'm competing.

"Oh, look. It's my personal lifeguard," Wren drawls as I approach.

"Thought you didn't need one," I say, stopping a few feet away.

She acts like I said nothing, glancing at Gus. "Sawyer invited me," she informs him.

My molars grind. I should have anticipated Wren would make a bigger deal about my kitchen comment than Cammie or Wade.

"He did, huh?"

My best friend sounds surprised, but it's not because of the invitation. It's because very few people know my first name. Even fewer use it.

"You remembered my name?" I gasp in mock shock.

Wren rolls her eyes. I doubt Wade even noticed her memory lapse; he was too busy ogling her.

"How long have you guys worked at the marina?" she asks.

Gus answers for us both. "Since the start of high school."

"Which was … when?"

"Three years ago."

"You're my age, then." She looks at me, not Gus, as she says it.

So, I say, "I prefer older women."

"Like Cammie?" Wren's tone makes it clear the dislike is two-sided.

I know what Cammie's issue with Wren is. Wren is a member— an esteemed member—of the group of entitled, privileged people who consider summer a verb, not a season. Snobs who descend on our hometown like locusts for three months, acting like we're the interlopers, expecting to be catered to and accommodated and prioritized.

But I don't know what Wren's issue with Cammie is. Yeah, Cammie wasn't welcoming, but Wren doesn't seem that thin-skinned.

I shrug rather than answer her question. I regret what happened with Cammie, and I have no interest in explaining it.

Wren flicks her hair over one shoulder. "What about you, Gus?" she asks, glancing at him. "You prefer older women too?"

He chuckles nervously, swiping some hair out of his eyes. "Eh, I'm not too picky." His eyes widen. "Not like—I mean, I'm open to anyone. In-in a, uh, inclusive way. Not like I think girls—women—are easy."

"I can be easy," Wren says, then winks.

Gus's ears go red. "Oh. I, uh … cool." He takes a long swig from his beer.

I don't laugh because Gus is uncomfortable. But I want to. I would have if she'd said that to me.

I can't picture her and Gus together. Wren pushes because she wants to be challenged back, and Gus is too polite. Too worried about offending.

But he needs to recognize that incompatibility for himself. Maybe he has, and that's why I was called over.

"Gotta take a piss," I say. "See you later, man."

I glance at Wren rather than including her in the goodbye, and it's a mistake. Far less of a dismissal than I meant it to be.

I walk away as fast as I can in the crowded living room.

There's a line for the half bath off the kitchen, so I head upstairs. Moans coming from Cammie's bedroom suggest at least one couple has already headed to bed. I haven't seen her since she chewed me out earlier for inviting a "spoiled princess" to her home, so maybe it's Cammie in there. I hope it is. Our friendship would be less tense if she met a new guy.

I pee, wash my hands, and then rake a wet hand through my hair, trying to come up with a game plan for downstairs. I don't want to be here, but I don't want to not be here either. If I head home, I'll lie awake and stare at the ceiling.

Maybe I'll walk to the beach. Being near the water always clears my head.

I open the door, my eyes taking a second to adjust to the dimmer light in the hallway. They still locate her immediately.

Wren's leaning a shoulder against the wall across from the bathroom, inspecting her nails. Her cup is gone. Her chin lifts to meet my gaze as I enter the hallway.

We stare at each other for a few seconds, the babble of overlapping voices downstairs suddenly muted.

"All yours," I state, stepping toward the stairs.

"I didn't come up here to 'take a piss.' " Her imitation of my voice isn't very accurate. At least, I hope it's not. Or else I sound like a douche.

I glance back. She's given me the perfect opening to ask, "Why did you come, then?"

I'm no longer talking about upstairs. I'm wondering why she's here, period.

Wren doesn't reply. She closes the distance between us in a couple of rapid strides, colliding our mouths together.

Kissing me—again.

Catching me off guard—again.

She doesn't taste like alcohol. She tastes like mint and watermelon. Her lips are soft and warm, moving against mine in a demanding rhythm that's impossible to ignore.

I get caught up in matching it for longer than I'd like to admit. Lack of oxygen is the main reason I step back, sucking in a hasty breath. "Stop kissing me."

"Because you hate it?" Wren's smirk is knowing as she glances at my crotch.

I exhale heavily, fists clenched, urging my dick to deflate. Her staring isn't helping. I've been less turned on during blow jobs than I am by her gaze lingering on the bulge of my erection.

Wren has this infuriating talent for teasing. A skill of manipulating people exactly where she wants them. I know it, I've seen it, and yet I'm still susceptible.

She doesn't need to know that though.

"You're not my type," I tell her, which is absolutely true.

"You know I can see you're hard, right?"

I scowl. "I get hard watching porn too. Don't take it personally."

She scoffs. "You have a high opinion of your hand, if you think jerking off is the same as sex with me."

I grudgingly admire her confidence. Wren isn't the only one who enjoys a challenge, and there aren't many people who push back at me.

"You want to fuck?" I ask bluntly.

I'm expecting her to laugh. Or act offended. Or do anything really, other than reply, "Yes," equally frank.

"It won't be what you're used to," I warn. "I don't do sweet or romantic. Just fast and hard."

This time, I predict her reaction correctly.

Her chin juts defiantly. "I told you, you don't know me. Or what I'm used to."

"We can use Wade's room." I start that way, the opposite direction from the stairs.

Most—maybe all—of me isn't expecting her to follow, but she does. I've been propositioned at parties in the past, but hooking up at one has never unfolded like this before. I'm sober since I never made it back to the kitchen for a beer, and I'm starting to suspect Wren is, too, which is also an anomaly.

That must be why this feels different, I decide, as I flick on a lamp to rummage through Wade's bedside table for a condom. Once I find one, I turn the lamp back off. Enough moonlight is coming through the open window to illuminate shapes, and I want this to feel as impersonal as possible. Hard and fast, just like I told her.

I'm already wondering what she looks like naked, imagining what her tits look like bare, with no swimsuit in the way. Picturing how perfectly they'd fit in my hands. I kind of want to kiss her again. Getting a girl fully naked and making out are not things I normally think about.

I unzip my jeans before ripping the condom open with my teeth. Releasing my throbbing cock from its denim prison is a temporary relief. I pinch the tip of the condom and roll it on, glancing at Wren. She's watching me, her profile silhouetted by the mirror as she leans against the wall beside Wade's dresser. There's something sexy about her stillness. About how intentional this all feels, like she showed up tonight with the sole purpose of this happening and is waiting for me to follow through.

I walk over to her, battling an unexpected barrage of uncertainty, not stopping until our bodies are pressed together. I can hear her breathing. Feel her body heat. Smell her shampoo or perfume—some floral, expensive scent that doesn't belong in Wade's messy room.

I rest my left hand on the wall next to her head, cupping my right around her throat. I can feel the steady thrum of her pulse pressed against my palm. She swallows once, her neck muscles contracting quickly. Her expression is shadowed by my head, and I suddenly wish I'd left the lamp on. I can't tell if she's anxious I'll hurt her or aroused by the possessive grip. I doubt the one percent spends their summer parties whispering about townie scandals—I never told her my last name, even if they do— but it's possible she's heard the rumors about my father. If she has, she'd be afraid.

My grip relaxes. My hand slides lower, cupping her left breast. I was right—the curve fits my palm perfectly.

"Fast and hard, huh?"

I nearly smile, hiding it with a scowl as I drop my hand to the hem of her dress. I fist the fabric roughly, shoving it up to her hip before moving my hand to the heat between her legs. She's soaking wet, the strip of lace clinging to her pussy.

She's as affected by me as I am by her. Reassuring. Also loosens my grip on control.

"Impatient?" I taunt back. "Those rich boys really can't do anything right. Do you always have to fake it?"

"You're an—"

She gasps when I locate her clit, pinching the swell of swollen nerves.

"Call me an asshole one more time, Wren."

"You started it," she mutters.

It's bad for both of us that I find her impertinence so intriguing.

I finger her through the lace for a minute, conflicted between teasing her longer and ending the torture I'm inflicting on myself. Once a breathy moan slips out, the decision is made for me. All the blood in my body must be in my dick by now. I was planning to just tug her underwear to one side, but I yank the lace down to her knees for better access. Gravity pulls them lower.

"Move," Wren says, planting her hands on my chest and giving me a light shove.

I'm surprised enough to step back because I'm always the one issuing orders in these situations.

She bends down, lifting one foot and then the other, freeing her thong. I'm unreasonably relieved she hasn't changed her mind about this. Ridiculously aroused by the sight of her blonde head bobbing so close to my crotch.

When she straightens, I kiss her roughly, breaking my own rule. This is the only time we'll do this—might as well indulge more. She's already kissed me twice. Initiating it once is just about evening the score. Her tongue twines around mine, and I imagine it caressing the crown of my cock. If I wasn't already painfully hard, I would be now.

Wren bites my bottom lip, hard enough to sting, but not rough enough to draw blood, and my dick jerks.

I reach between us, guiding my erection between her legs. She feels it, rubs against it, and the room suddenly smells like sex.

"Wrap your legs around my waist," I urge. "Like—yeah."

When she *wants* to be, Wren's compliant.

I palm her ass with one hand, guiding my cock to her entrance with the other, scowling when I realize I'm showing off. That I'm more focused on this being memorable for her than on getting off.

"Mother*fucker*," she hisses.

I still, a Herculean task, considering Wren has the tightest pussy I've ever felt and I'm only a couple of inches in.

"You okay?" I manage to ask between deep breaths.

I could come from the warm clench of her cunt around the tip of my cock, but I don't want to. I want to be buried inside her when it happens, and I want her to come too.

In answer, Wren winds an arm around my neck and pulls my mouth back to hers. The kiss is softer and slower this time, not nearly as desperate. Vulnerable almost.

"Keep going," she whispers, then kisses me again.

I do, pressing deeper at the same leisurely pace we're making out to. I'm bigger than the other guys she's been with, I'm guessing, which inflates my chest with some primal pride. But I don't want to hurt her. I'm *not* my father.

I thumb her clit a few times, feeling how tight she's stretched around me, hoping the friction will help. She's plenty wet, her arousal soaking my fingers as I rub them around.

I pull back enough to see her face, wishing again that I'd left a light on. I can't do anything about that now though, so I ask, "Still good?"

Her fingers play with the short strands of hair at the base of my neck. It feels fucking incredible. I fight a groan, quite certain she can feel my dick jerk inside of her. I'm desperate to pump—to fuck.

"I have a theory," Wren tells me, tilting her head. Some blonde strands brush my biceps. "I think the asshole thing is a front to cover the fact that you're secretly a decent guy."

This is why I don't kiss girls or talk during sex. Because they start to see what they want, not what I'm showing them.

"Your theory is wrong," I tell her. "I'm an asshole, pretending to be a decent guy for a few minutes since you're used to tiny dicks and rose-petal sheets."

Rather than appear insulted or annoyed, Wren laughs. I feel the vibrations against me. Around me. We're so intimately connected. Joined in a way I've never experienced during sex before because I'm normally thrusting, not lingering.

"I won't break," she tells me. "Don't treat me like crystal."

I suppress the snort that wants to slip out. Crystal. She's so goddamn rich. I grew up drinking out of plastic cups. Glass *does* break and is expensive to replace.

Her legs tighten around my waist, shifting the angle slightly. I slip a little deeper, and Wren moans, nails sinking into my shoulders. I take it as a signal to keep moving, pulling out and pushing in with only slightly less effort. She's still so tight. I move my thumb to her clit again, rubbing slow circles. Her mouth lands on my neck, sucking gently. Her teeth graze the skin, followed by the slick flick of her tongue. My control is slipping, base instincts fighting to emerge.

"You feel good," Wren murmurs.

I adjust my grip on her hips. My hold is firm enough that I'm probably leaving marks.

I want this to last, but it's not going to be physically possible for much longer. Fire is licking up my spine, feeding the distinctive tightening in my balls.

Wren makes this sexy whimper, and I let go, flooding the condom with cum. The release is longer and fiercer than I'm used to, blurring the edges of my vision. Robbing my ability to breathe. To move even as it rips through me with unexpected intensity.

Breathing heavily, I pull out and set her on the floor. Wren's face dips, hair falling forward as she grabs her underwear, then adjusts her dress around her thighs.

When her chin lifts, her expression is serene and unreadable in the moonlight. "I'd say see you around, but I probably won't."

"You probably won't," I agree, amused by her parroting my parting comment when we reached the shore the other night.

I like that she remembers what I said. Like that she tossed it back in my face even more. And I wish it weren't true—that I would see her around again.

"Bye, Sawyer."

She's walking out of Wade's bedroom before I can muster any reply.

I stare at the door she left ajar for a few seconds, inhaling floral-and-sex-scented air and enjoying the lingering endorphins, then walk over to Wade's bedside table to grab a tissue. When I can't find one, I turn the lamp back on. There's a small stack of napkins from a local pizza place that will work.

I grab a couple, go to peel off the condom, and freeze, staring at the dark streaks on the latex.

CHAPTER 5

Wren

No sign of Rory or Dad when I stumble downstairs. Just Mom, perched in a dining room chair with a cup of green tea, flipping through a cooking magazine.

"Happy Fourth," I say weakly, walking into the kitchen.

We're staying at Aunt Scarlett and Uncle Crew's house while they're at my aunt's parents' place. The Ellsworths are hosting today's famous party. We don't normally attend it, but my dad had a work trip get canceled and suggested it would be fun—mandatory—for our family to spend the holiday weekend in the Hamptons. A decision I'm decreasingly resentful of.

"Good morning." Mom leans back in her chair, grabbing her cup of tea and blowing at the steam. "Where were you last night?"

I knew this interrogation was coming. "Drove to Boston," I answer. "Dumped some tea in the harbor to be patriotic."

Mom shakes her head, unamused. "You're grounded, Wren."

I figured. I opted for the front door rather than attempting to sneak

through the window last night and triggered the alarm, waking up the whole house. My parents aren't overly strict, but they're not the type to ignore what sounded like a screeching cat competing with a siren. Or that their teenage daughter wasn't fast asleep in bed at two a.m.

I reach for an empty mug, filling it to the brim with coffee as I slump into a chair across from Mom.

"Where were you last night?"

I exhale, then admit, "A party."

Mom sighs too. "Whose party?"

"I'm … not … actually … sure." I swallow a large sip of coffee right after, avoiding her gaze.

Mom and Dad are masters of the *we're not mad, just disappointed* shtick. It works on Rory.

"Wren, that is unacceptable. I understand wanting to have fun and spend time with your friends, but we need to know where you are and who you are with. It's not—"

"Safe?" I supply bitterly.

Mom moves her tea aside and leans closer. "I'm always here to talk, sweetheart. And so is Dr. Hurts. I can call, set up an appointment—"

I shake my head immediately. I didn't dislike Dr. Hurts, but I didn't find our sessions helpful past a certain point. I mostly spent them pondering the irony of a therapist having the last name *Hurts*.

"I'm fine. If anything, going to a party with strangers shows how well I'm doing."

Mom frowns. "Honey, you don't have to prove anything."

"I know. I'm good, Mom. Promise."

I reach for the plate piled high with croissants, grabbing one and then helping myself to jam and butter.

"Did you drink at this party?"

I swallow a bite. "No."

"Drugs?"

"No."

"Am I going to be a grandmother in nine months?"

"Mom! *No.*" I grab my coffee and down half of it.

She reclines back in her seat, flipping a glossy page of her magazine, seeming mollified I wasn't too irresponsible. "You're still grounded."

I nod, spreading more butter on my croissant.

The front door opens and closes, followed by the sound of my dad's deep voice as he converses with one of the staff. He appears in the doorway a minute later, wearing running clothes and a wide smile as he approaches the table.

"It's so peaceful, entering a house during normal waking hours," he comments, snagging a cup of coffee for himself.

Mom nods. "I was thinking the same thing."

Dad glances at me. "How is my favorite burglar this morning?"

I roll my eyes. "It's not considered breaking and entering if you have permission to be on the premises, Dad. If Rory were here, she'd back me up."

For as long as I can remember, my sister has known she wanted to be an attorney. It's what I admire most about her, more than her propensity to always say or do the right thing. I've never been that certain—about anything. I keep waiting for some assuredness to kick in as I get older, but so far … nothing.

"I'm sure she'd also agree courts take second offenses far more seriously. *No car keys or trip to Marseilles* seriously. Understood?"

I nod. "Understood."

Lots of people consider Oliver Kensington intimidating. But I rarely see it. Around Mom and Rory and me, Dad is attentive and loving. But that doesn't mean he's not capable of switching to his important CEO persona in some situations.

"Good." He kisses Mom—I make a face and grab another croissant—then heads upstairs to shower.

"Is Rory sleeping in?" I ask.

Mom shakes her head, picking up her phone and typing. "She's out by the pool. Carson called."

I make a face again. I am not a fan of my sister's boyfriend. But Rory and I have never had similar tastes in guys. One of our many differences.

"Wren," Mom warns, noticing my expression.

I know she's not a huge fan of Carson's either, but my mom has mastered the art of keeping certain opinions to herself. One I have yet to attempt.

"I said nothing," I remind her, then stuff my mouth with more croissant.

CHAPTER 6

Sawyer

I shove my hands deeper in my pockets, ignoring my buzzing phone as I walk toward the illuminated tent ahead. The *massive* tent. For shade earlier, I guess? Not a single drop of rain fell today.

Everyone knows where the annual Red, White, and Blue party takes place.

Few people know about the cove around the corner from the Ellsworth compound. If more did, I'm guessing they'd have a security guard stationed there.

I trample through the last of the undergrowth and finally reach sand. The first guy I see is wearing a suit. Full suit, tie and everything.

I swapped my marina polo for a plain T-shirt before driving here, thinking the khaki shorts would pass for a beach party.

I was wrong. The next group of guys I see have tuxedos on. I might as well be wearing a neon sign advertising *does not belong*.

My jaw clenches as I continue trekking through the sand. A few people glance my way, trading whispers behind glasses of champagne.

Showing up here was stupid. My buzzing phone is likely evidence Gus or some of my other friends are questioning the vague *I've got something to take care of* text I sent to the group in response to their shared plans to watch the fireworks down by the pier. Depending how long this takes, I might miss it entirely.

But this is the only place I could think of to track her down. And possibly my last chance to, if she's leaving right after the holiday.

So, here I am.

The closer I get to the tent, the more I comprehend the scale of this party. Up closer to the house is the main event. The crowd down on the private beach is undoubtedly younger. Most are luxuriously dressed, but a few closer to the shoreline have stripped down to swimwear.

I recognize no one. I'm sure some have been to the Atlantic Yacht Club to go out on parents' or grandparents' boats, but they all tend to blend together in my mind. Except for one, of course, who's nowhere to be seen.

Shouts draw my attention to the far side of the private beach, opposite from the end I trespassed from.

She changed her hair. It's shorter, the pink gone, the new length falling just past her shoulders. But I'm certain it's her, even before she turns and volleys an inflated, striped ball at a giggling brunette.

I head that way, tucking my hands into my pockets and hovering at the edge of the tent as I watch the chaotic game that appears to be a mix of volleyball and soccer.

Wren is wearing a strapless red dress and no shoes. She's also the most dedicated player on the makeshift court, tackling the role of referee and player. She declares out of bounds, even though there are no obvious lines on the ground, and no one argues with the assessment.

Watching her, I'm tempted to turn and leave before she spots me. She's laughing and vibrant, unbothered. I'm not even sure what I came here to say. I was annoyed she had shown up last night, and she had technically been invited. I'm undeniably crashing.

But I linger too long, watching her compete. The teams drift apart, like time expired, even though there's no visible clock. Most players head for the open bar under the tent.

Except for one.

Wren walks straight to me, pausing a few feet away with an expectant expression and windblown hair.

"Wren Kensington." I drawl her full name, partly to cover for the fact that I looked too long before talking.

Her beauty is blinding. Something you stare at, even knowing you shouldn't. Also, I had no clue she'd seen me. I certainly hadn't expected her to stride over here.

"Captain." She mimics my tone, extending each syllable. "What are you doing here?"

"I came to talk to you."

"I'm busy."

"I'll wait."

She raises one eyebrow, but she doesn't look surprised. More scheming. "Have fun," she says cheerfully, then sashays away.

A group of four guys call her over as soon as she enters the tent. All four are wearing suits, signifying they're invited guests. Another commonality: they're all staring at her with obvious interest.

I turn, joining the line for the open bar.

My guess is, Wren is going to be "busy" for a while. Might as well enjoy a free drink in the meantime.

Three hours later, a lone figure strolls my way, swinging a pair of heels in one hand.

I've been reclined in the same spot on the dunes for the past hour, since the fireworks ended, nursing a beer that's now warm. Watching the party lights reflect off the waves' choppy surface. Occasionally surveying the festivities. I'll say this much for rich people: they're entertaining. One girl was bragging about buying a new mattress for her rental this weekend—to ensure she wasn't sleeping on a bed someone else had used. Another guy was loudly discussing getting a new Porsche because he didn't like the color of his current one anymore. I've heard similar stories from Cammie, but firsthand, they sound even more outrageous.

Wren sinks on the sand to my left. She leans back on her palms, then glances at me. Tucks a shorter strand of hair behind one ear, revealing a twinkling diamond earring. She smells the same as last night, mixed with salty air and smoke. "You stayed."

"Why didn't you tell me?" I ask abruptly. I've been sitting here forever, so my interest in small talk is nonexistent.

Her nose scrunches. "Tell you what?"

"That it was your first time."

Wren stares at me, and I can't gain the slightest sense of what she's thinking.

"There was … blood on the condom," I add awkwardly, wishing for the thousandth time that Wade had tissues handy and I'd never turned that light on. She hadn't wanted me to know, obviously, and I spent all day trying to forget. Ended up here anyway.

"So?" she finally says. "I thought my period had ended. Guess it hadn't. Did you want a calendar of my menstrual cycle, or does that cover it?"

Now it's my turn to assess and stay quiet. It's a reasonable explanation, so why don't I believe her?

"You're … okay, then? I didn't, uh, hurt you?"

I'm so uncomfortable; it feels like ants are crawling all over my skin. Sex is a physical act. It's never involved talking after—at least for me—and I'm very aware of why I've always avoided this. It's weird as hell.

But I can't stand and walk away. Not yet. I need to know she's okay first.

And there's some part of me that simply wanted to see her one final time.

"You didn't hurt me," Wren answers. She's turned her face toward the water, so all I can see is her profile.

"Okay." For some fucking idiotic reason, I don't leave it there. I ask, "Did you come?"

"No."

"I'm sorry," I say. "I thought you had."

"It's fine. Doesn't usually happen for me."

My jaw tightens. Maybe she wasn't a virgin. That thought should relieve me, not piss me off more. Some part of me liked that she'd trusted me with something special. I should be glad I was just a rich-girl rebellion she'll go home and laugh with her friends about. That's not messy or meaningful.

"It should."

"Cool. I'll let the next guy know." She's drawing circles in the sand between us with one finger, meaningless loops that look like a challenge.

I huff what's meant to be a laugh, but it comes out more as a regular old scoff. I can't figure Wren out. She keeps surprising me.

She glances up, finger pausing. For a few—or maybe a lot of—

seconds, we stare at each other. I'm annoyed with her. More annoyed with myself. I don't know what to say. I'm not going to admit I came so hard that I couldn't tell if she had. That I lasted for as long as possible.

Wren smirks at my disgruntled expression. "You asked."

"I know."

We both hear the irritation in my tone, and Wren's smile widens before her gaze drops to the sand. The circles resume.

"You free tomorrow night?" I say, topping the list of dumb things I've done tonight.

"No." The circles have stopped, but she doesn't look up. "That's our last night here. There's a big family dinner. But"—the drawing resumes—"I could sneak out after it."

"You know how to get to the marina?" I hope my voice doesn't betray the irregular thud in my chest.

"Yes."

"I'll meet you there. Midnight."

Wren salutes me. "Aye, aye, Captain."

I snort as I stand. "Happy Fourth."

She calls, "You too," after me.

The entire trek back to my truck, I have to battle the urge to look back. But if I did, there's a chance someone would see the grin stuck on my face.

CHAPTER 7

Wren

This could end badly, I decide, dangling from the trellis like one of the wild roses.

Dinner at the country club took forever. Everyone there came over to our table at some point. I would have expired from boredom if not for Kit cracking jokes the whole time or Lili talking about her upcoming trip to London for a friend's wedding.

We only got back to the house an hour ago. I think my parents are asleep, but I wasn't willing to risk running into one or both of them. Sneaking out my window again seemed like the only option.

I swear under my breath as the painted wood creaks. I'm halfway to the ground. A fall from this height wouldn't kill me, but it could do some damage. Equally concerning, I'd probably bring the trellis down with me, wake up the whole house, and wind up grounded for the rest of high school.

Thirty stressful seconds later, my foot connects with solid ground. I release a long, relieved breath.

"What are you doing?"

I whirl, hand pressed against my pounding heart, as if I can physically slow the rate. "*Shit*, you scared me," I say, a nervous giggle slipping out.

Rory doesn't appear amused. She crosses her arms across her chest. "That didn't answer my question."

"Snack run?"

My sister shakes her head. "The kitchen is fully stocked."

"What are *you* doing?" I attempt offense as a defensive strategy.

Amusement flickers across her face. "You think you're the only one allowed to stay up late or keep secrets?" Her gaze drops, surveying my outfit. "You're going to meet Marina Guy?"

I gape at her. "How did you know?"

Rory rolls her eyes. "I saw you talking to him before we went out on Hanson's boat. On the beach last night. And I'm assuming he was at the party you snuck out to?"

"Maybe," I admit, impressed by her deductive skills.

Rory's brilliant, but I didn't think my summer fling would rate on her radar.

"You're meeting him alone?"

"I trust him," I say simply. Trusted him before he waited three hours to have a conversation he clearly didn't want to have, but even more so now. "He's nothing like …" I hate saying his name, but that's not why I hesitate. I pause because I'm struck by a different word that fits better. "Anyone. He's nothing like anyone I've ever met."

"It won't end well, Wren," Rory warns.

I wave her caution away. "It'll end after tonight. We're leaving tomorrow."

My sister sighs and heads for the front door. "Mom changed the alarm code," she calls over one shoulder. "It's Dad's birthday now."

"You're my favorite sister!" I say, then skip to my waiting car.

I parked it as far down the driveway as possible earlier, *and* I remember to turn off my lights before rolling through the open gate. I'd make an awesome spy.

I slept during the last trip to the marina, so I start the GPS after flicking on the headlights. I'm relieved to see the arrival time estimated at 11:52, then wince at my own eagerness. If I hadn't run into Rory, I'd have been even earlier.

I feel a little better when I see the truck parked in the marina's lot. I doubt anyone else is hanging around at this hour. Also, it's exactly what I picture Sawyer driving. Sturdy and practical and a little rough around the edges. The bumper's a lighter shade of blue than the navy paint, like it was replaced more recently, but it's otherwise in decent condition. No dings or rust marks.

I park one spot over from the truck, then glance left. Sawyer is slouched in the driver's seat, ball cap pulled low and fingers drumming on the steering wheel.

I climb out of my car, waiting for him to do the same.

He doesn't. Sawyer glances at me, the closer corner of his mouth curving up. I still have yet to see a full smile from him, but his little smirks give me heart palpitations, so that's better for my cardiac health.

"You're early," he comments.

"So are you," I retort, resting my elbows on his open window.

Sawyer straightens, turning the key in the ignition. His truck rumbles to life, the engine's vibration sending reverberations up my arms. "Get in."

"Where are we going?"

"You'll see."

"Why don't we take my car?"

"Because you don't know where we're going."

I consider that, then open the door.

"Finally," Sawyer mutters.

I ignore his impatience, focused on surveying the interior of the truck. The leather seat is worn, duct-taped in a couple of spots, and there's sand in the footwell. But it's pretty clean overall. No trash or smelly sneakers.

I hoist myself up, shut the door, snap on the seat belt, and glance at Sawyer expectantly.

His jaw's a perfectly straight line as he studies me, settled in the passenger seat.

"I've never ridden in a truck before," I tell him.

"Why does that not surprise me?"

I roll my eyes. "For that comment, I'm not going to compliment your choice of vehicle."

"The limo is getting serviced," Sawyer mutters as he reverses out of the spot.

The window's still rolled down, so I stick a hand out, letting the wind sift through my fingers as he turns onto the main road and accelerates. A minute later, we fly past the country club where I ate dinner earlier.

The cab has a bench seat. The lack of separation makes the front section feel larger.

I shift my knee a little to the left, closer to the gearshift, getting more comfortable. "I like your truck," I tell him.

Sawyer glances over, only one hand on the wheel. Still, I feel safe.

Maybe because the road is otherwise empty. Maybe because this truck seems so solid, one step removed from a tank. Maybe because of

… him.

He scans my face like he's looking for a lie, and I squash the urge to squirm. Funny, since I didn't flinch when I actually lied to him.

"What do you like about it?"

I slip one foot out of a sandal and slide it under me. Rest an arm on the window and recline against it. "It's … spacious."

Sawyer snorts, refocusing on the road. "Subtle."

Warmth floods my cheeks. "That wasn't what I meant."

I assumed we'd hook up tonight. The expectation is there, and my lingerie was carefully chosen, assuming he'd see it. I'm as prepared as possible. But I'm not the experienced seductress I pretend to be, and I'm worried Sawyer is going to realize that. He already has suspicions.

He takes a left, turning the truck off the asphalt street we were on and rolling along a gravel road instead.

I peer through the windshield, looking for any clues about our destination. Waiting for some flicker of apprehension to appear when there are no signs of civilization ahead.

I never thought Third was capable of what he did. But there were moments I felt uneasy around him. I'm not sure what to make of the fact that nothing Sawyer does incites fear in me. That my instincts are screaming *stay* when, rationally, they should be telling me to run from any scenario involving being alone with a stranger in an unfamiliar place.

The road curves. Sawyer brakes for the bend, then even more once we're around it. Headlights sweep across an open stretch of sand, water lapping the shoreline a dozen feet from where he stops.

"What is this place?" I ask.

"Somewhere I like to come sometimes."

Metal creaks as Sawyer opens his door. He shucks his shirt, tossing it on the seat, then walks toward the water.

I'm not wearing a bikini. I spent the past hour styling my hair and applying a careful layer of makeup to make it seem like I was wearing none.

But I know, watching Sawyer wade in, I'll be swimming tonight.

CHAPTER 8

Wren

I squeal as he dives for me, inhaling a lungful of salt water when a wave closes over my head. I surface with a burning throat, splashing Sawyer between hacking coughs. "You *asshole*."

"Get some new insults, Kensington," he says, swimming away.

I huff and twist onto my back, floating along the surface as I stare up at the sky. It's almost a full moon, bathing everything with a silvery glow that's ethereal. I can't remember the last time I felt this light, and it has nothing to do with buoyancy.

I feel *normal*, swimming late at night with a boy I really like. No envy-inducing trust fund, no pending college decision, no polite answers to formulate.

My fingers and toes are pruned by the time we finally head ashore. Sand sticks to my feet as I step out of the shallows, the crunch of dried seaweed uncomfortable. At first, I think that's what the sharp prick is. But it's followed by a burst of pain and a warm trickle I'm concerned is blood.

"Shit," I hiss, pausing.

"What?" Sawyer asks, stopping too.

"My foot. I stepped on—"

He's already bent down to inspect it. I don't look. Blood makes me queasy.

"It's not bad," he says.

I grimace, keeping my gaze on his truck ahead. "I think you and I have different definitions of *not bad.*"

Sawyer's smirking when he stands. "I promise you'll live."

"That's not very reassur—*oof.*"

He's scooped me up, carrying me back toward the water.

"I can walk," I add awkwardly.

My cheeks are hot, and I hope he can't tell I'm blushing. I feel … unsteady, in a way that has nothing to do with my injured foot.

He doesn't reply. Or set me down. Not until we reach the shoreline.

"Stick your foot in the water," he tells me. "The salt will sanitize it."

"What advanced medical training you have," I tease, but I do as he said, suppressing a wince as the cool water stings the cut.

As soon as Sawyer is satisfied by the submersion, he picks me up again.

This time, I don't protest. I tuck my head under his chin, enjoying the feel of his arms around me and the steady rocking of his steps. It's like riding bareback, except better.

When we reach his truck, Sawyer sets me on the open tailgate. "I've got a first aid kit in the cab," he tells me, walking off.

I stay in place, tilting my head back to stare up at the stars overhead. For everything Manhattan has to offer, this is one view it lacks. The city lights are too bright for any astronomy.

Crunching gravel announces Sawyer's return.

I risk a quick peek at my foot. He was right; it's not bad. Blood has welled again, but it's more of a scrape than a cut. Probably from a rock.

"You're prepared," I comment, as he opens a white square box with a red cross printed on the top.

"Yeah, I—" He suddenly stops talking.

I lean back on one palm, watching him spray some antiseptic on the wound, then cover it with two overlapping Band-Aids.

"Thanks," I say softly.

"No problem," he answers.

I lean forward. My wet bra and panties weren't hiding a whole lot anyway, but it's an invitation to look. I want him to look.

"Any suggestions for how else I could thank you?" I nudge his thigh with my knee.

He steps away, not meeting my gaze as he shuts the box. "We should go. I've gotta work in the morning."

I sigh. "I didn't think you were supposed to say anything, okay?"

He glances at me, expression unreadable. But he's listening.

I swing my feet forward and back, not looking at him, but not, *not* looking at him either. "All my friends … I thought it was some unwritten rule unless you'd been dating the guy since, like, elementary school. No guy really wants to know, even if he asks. And you didn't ask, so …" I shrug a shoulder, swallowing rapidly. "It was my decision, how I lost my virginity. Not really any of your business."

Sawyer still looks serious. But the left corner of his mouth has crept up, just a little. "None of my business?"

"I didn't think it … mattered. Didn't think I'd ever see you again."

I stare down at the Band-Aids he carefully applied. I don't believe Sawyer—about the asshole thing. How someone acts says a lot more than what they share aloud. My gut says he's a good guy.

A callous thumb tips my chin up, forcing me to meet his gaze. "You didn't lose anything, Wren. And you should have told me."

"Would you have stopped?" I ask, holding his gaze.

He exhales. "Probably."

"Then I'm glad I didn't tell you."

Sawyer scoffs, but his mouth is still turned up a tiny bit. Like he wants to smile but is fighting it. "It had to have hurt. I was rough, and you didn't come." He raises a brow, challenging me to argue.

I can't disagree. It did hurt, and I didn't come. But I don't regret it, not at all. In fact, I want to do it again.

Bluntness worked last time. So, I ask, no hedging, "Can we do it again?"

He studies me. And I force myself to hold eye contact as I internally squirm from the foreign sensation of vulnerability. Being at a disadvantage? Needing something from someone? Both unfamiliar. Two things I normally avoid at all costs.

I can't tell why he's conflicted, which makes this more difficult. If it's that I lied, or that I was a virgin, or that he's already lost interest.

What I *do* know? "An asshole would already have a condom on."

"Or he'd tell you he doesn't do repeats," Sawyer says.

I tilt my head. "Is that your final answer?"

He exhales, and I'm surprised to hear it's a little unsteady.

"It was a yes-or-no question, Captain."

Sawyer takes another step. Closer this time, not away.

As soon as he's near enough, I wrap my legs around his waist, anchoring him to me. His skin is still damp, boxers dripping seawater. He's solid. Warm. Firm. Stable. And his abs are ridiculous. Until I saw him shirtless by the cliff, I thought guys my age were incapable of being so built. I trail my fingers over the miniature mountain range, lingering in each valley between ridges.

He watches me touch him, his mouth quirking in another almost smile.

"You're really hot," I tell him honestly.

Sawyer laughs, making the muscles under my fingers flex from the vibrations. "You're not so ugly yourself."

"That is, by far, the worst compliment anyone has ever given me."

His hands slide under my ass, and I'm suddenly airborne. Being carried for a third time tonight.

He walks us over to the driver's side, setting me down on the edge of the seat. I would have been really impressed if he'd opened the door while carrying me, but it was already ajar. Probably from him grabbing the first aid kit.

"Lie back," he tells me.

I unclasp my arms from around his neck, missing the heat of his body as I recline on the seat. It's not that cold out, but it's not warm either. I'm not wearing much, especially since Sawyer is tugging my underwear down, and the bra I'm left wearing is flimsy and wet.

A rush of anticipation chases away most of the cold as his hands grip the inside of my thighs, parting them wide. I startle when night air gusts *there*. Again when his hot tongue replaces it.

This is another new experience. After a few fumbling fingering attempts, having a guy lapping down there sounded really unappealing. I was missing out, or maybe Sawyer's skill is just superior because the rush of arousal is so rapid that it's dizzying. A lightning bolt of lust, immediate and devastating. I try to lift my hips for more, silently begging. But his hold on my thighs is firm, allowing me only what he decides to give. There's something arousing about that, too, having to cede all control to him.

I'm going to come.

I'm stunned, suddenly sensing it hovering ahead, my muscles trembling and tingling as I brace for the incoming wave of pleasure. I'm so thrilled about it, so relieved that my body is cooperating the way I want it to, that I forget about being cold or self-conscious or apprehensive. I let go, relaxing into the pleasure as it washes over me in steady pulses. I'm not quiet. I'm not sure I could stay silent, even if I had to. It's too much to bottle inside. Too intense and too consuming. That's never happened before either.

The bliss fades slowly, like an undertow receding from the shore. I can feel my heartbeat everywhere, loud and steady. I'm energized and sleepy, and I don't know how I'll continue to exist without craving that sensation every second.

Sawyer straightens to his full height, tossing my underwear onto my stomach.

I sit up slowly. I don't think I'll ever be able to call him an asshole and mean it again. Because he looks smug—deservedly so—but his eyes are soft as he surveys my likely dazed expression.

"Thanks," I say.

He smiles, one shoulder propped against the doorframe. I was right; it's bad for my heart health.

"I owed you one," he says simply.

My gaze drops to the big bulge in his boxers. I didn't get a good look in the dark bedroom, but I got the gist of his dick's dimensions during sex. I'm not sore anymore, but that's a very recent development.

"Do you have a condom?"

"Glove compartment," he replies.

I scoot back until it's in reach, twisting the knob I assume opens it. Mixed in with gas receipts and packs of gum, he doesn't have *a* condom.

There are several strips of them and a few wrappers. There's a strange spasm in my chest when I picture this exact scene, but with Cammie or a faceless girl in my position. A weird and unwelcome reaction, considering I'm leaving tomorrow morning and this will probably be the last time I ever see him. Probably just because I don't have anyone else to picture in his position yet.

I tear one condom off, shut the glove compartment, and toss the packet to Sawyer. He catches it one-handed, climbing into the truck and shutting the door.

I fold my underwear and set them on top of the dress I pulled off before swimming, watching Sawyer tug his boxers down out of the corner of my eye. I can feel my heart banging against my rib cage; it's beating so fast. It's very intimate, sitting in here with him. The radio isn't on. Checking my phone would be odd. People always act as if sex just happens, and I've never given much thought to the logistical process of getting naked with someone.

After some crinkling, his voice is the next sound to break the silence. "C'mere."

I crawl onto his lap, relieved that things are progressing. Eager when his erection grazes sensitive, swollen skin, and I'm reminded of how incredible I felt a few minutes ago.

Last time, I could focus on keeping a confident facade. On suppressing the pain. This time, there's no act. No pretenses. It's easier … and harder. Less terrifying and scarier at the same time.

His hands slide up my back, one rough palm tracing the bumps of my spine, until they reach the clasp of my bra. One deft flick, and the lace lets go. Sawyer flings it away, toward my other clothes, and then his hands are cupping my boobs.

"You have amazing tits," he tells me, thumbs teasing the stiff peaks to painful points. His tone is matter-of-fact, more of a statement than true flattery.

"Gee—*mmm*—thanks." The moan that slipped out steals some of the sarcasm.

He smirks. "I'm working on my compliments."

"Work hard—*oh*."

His tongue has replaced his thumb, and it feels almost as good as it did between my thighs.

The throbbing there is getting more insistent. My muscles clench around emptiness, and I realize I'm craving something there. I reach between us, fisting his dick and guiding it to where I need it, too impatient to wait any longer. And then I start to sink down.

At first, it's as bad as before. Sudden pressure, followed by a pinching sting as my body stretches in a way it's unaccustomed to. I keep going, pushing through the flare of discomfort.

"*Fuck*, Wren," he hisses.

Sawyer's expression is pained, almost, but I'm the only one of us experiencing actual discomfort. So unfair.

"Holy shit," he adds, sounding a little stunned.

Some pride sparks in response, even though gravity is doing most of the work right now.

Sawyer is still cupping my *amazing tits*, but he's not looking at my boobs anymore. His attention is lower, on his lap. I look down, too, sucking in a startled breath as I watch his cock disappear inside of me. It's—well, it's hormones and pheromones and biology, but it's also dizzyingly intimate. Way more so than waiting for him to roll a condom on.

The world outside this truck has ceased to exist for me. There's just me and him and the sudden fullness that feels more natural with each passing second.

He tilts his head back, eyes closed, the tendons of his neck straining as his jaw clenches to a sharp, straight angle. His shoulders and arms are tense too. I can feel his thighs bunch beneath mine. I'm worried if I move, he might crack in half.

"Am I doing something wrong?" I whisper.

His eyes open. "No." He huffs a rueful laugh. "I'm trying to make this last longer than thirty seconds."

Something about the way he says it, half disgruntled and half awed, makes me feel special. I assumed he wasn't a virgin when we hooked up before—and the glove box basically confirmed it—but I like that some part of this is unique for him. Again, I can't pinpoint why I care, but I sort of do.

I lift my hips, then sink down again. It's easier, smoother, this time, the slow drag stimulating a flicker of heat low in my pelvis. It's deeper, stronger, than when I came before. More powerful, too, the building enormity of it startling me. This was supposed to be for him. I wasn't expecting to come twice.

One of Sawyer's hands is in my hair, tugging gently on the loose strands. The other brushes just above the spot where he's spreading me, circling my clit.

My hips move faster, chasing pleasure in earnest. I know it'll be the best orgasm I've ever experienced long before it rips through me, stealing my breath from my lungs and erasing any thoughts from my head.

I want to live in this thoughtless, weightless moment forever.

I don't want to move, but I have to. The clock on the dashboard reads three thirty, and my dad usually gets up at five. The correct alarm code won't matter if he's waiting in the kitchen when I sneak in.

I pull away, shifting back to the passenger side, tugging my clothes back on while Sawyer deals with the condom.

He leaves his shirt off, pulling his shorts on without bothering with boxers beneath. How little he's wearing is more distracting than it should be, considering we *just* had sex.

I speak first once we're rolling along the gravel road, headed back the same way we came. "Is it always like that?"

As soon as the question is out, I regret it. I blame the dopamine rush drugging my system and lowering my usual defenses.

Sawyer is silent. He'll pretend to have not heard me, which is per—

"No." That's all he says, then turns on the radio.

I thought I could rely on myself to stay detached. To treat this like exactly what it was—a summer fling.

And I *really* thought I could rely on him to say yes.

CHAPTER 9

Sawyer

Gus holds a joint out to me.

I shake my head, lifting the plastic cup of vodka. "I'm good with this."

We're at work, but we're not working. Post–Labor Day, Atlantic Yacht Club is pretty quiet. One of the reasons it's my favorite time of year. The temperature is still balmy, the water warmer than ever, but there's no traffic. The marina is practically deserted, just me, Gus, and a few other guys who are still in high school sticking around to help with winterizing. All the college guys are gone, same with most of the boats' owners.

"More for us," Wade says, reaching for the lit joint eagerly.

I slouch lower in the lawn chair, swallowing another sip. The bar in the yacht club's restaurant is completely shut down now, leaving the liquor unattended. It'll reopen around the holidays, for the members in town that time of year, but no one will remember the exact inventory

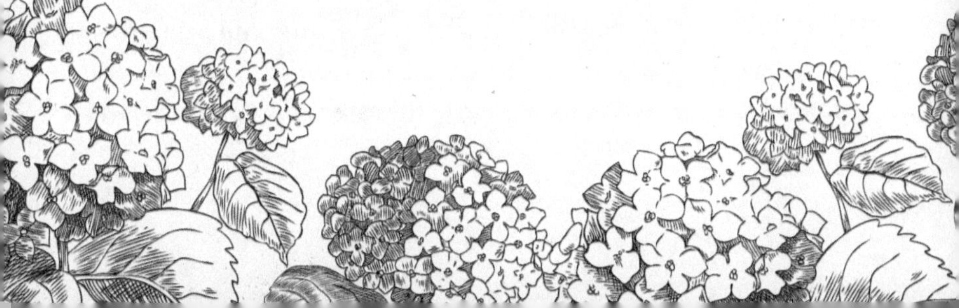

by then. And Macie, one of the summer waitresses who's since returned to college, said she fudged the numbers a little. She told me at the end-of-the-year party, paired with a sly smile. It was an invitation to filch a bottle and sneak off. An offer I pretended not to notice, and I wish I had no clue why the prospect lacked appeal.

"How's it been with your mom?" Gus asks, nudging my arm with his elbow.

"Fine," I say, which is an accurate summary.

It's nice, having her home, but it never lasts long enough for us to settle into a real routine. The house feels emptier when it's the two of us versus just me, her company making the other absences more obvious. Closer to normal … but not.

Gus nods, knowing me well enough not to push for more details. I guess the only upside of my family's dirty laundry being so public is that there's little space for speculation. Everyone just knows already and are mostly too polite to mention it to my face.

I swig the remainder of my drink and stand, tossing the cup toward the nearest trash can. It lands on target, and Ricky whoops in approval.

"Still don't get why you quit baseball, man," he tells me.

"Pratt," Gus snaps.

"What?" Ricky says. "Sports have nothing to do with …" He reaches for the joint Wade offers like it's a life preserver, letting his voice trail.

I fold my chair and add it to the stack in the corner. "See you guys on Monday."

"Bye, man," and, "See you, Cap," echo behind me as I walk toward the nearest exit, mixed with Wade saying, "You know Cap doesn't …"

I'm out of earshot for the rest. For the best probably. Gus means well, but he has no idea what it's like to be a Bennett. For people to have no idea what to say to you. For your whole life to twist into a tragedy and for you to wind up as collateral damage.

It feels warmer outside than it did in the cavernous warehouse, where some of the plastic-wrapped boats are stored for the winter. I pull a piece of gum out, shoving the silver wrapper back in my pocket and popping the spearmint in my mouth. I didn't drink much since I'd have to drive home, and the mentions of my mom and baseball basically chased away any buzz, but I've got to stop by Dusty's office to grab my latest paycheck. He's more laid-back in the fall than during the busy summer, but he wouldn't look the other way if he knew we were stealing alcohol.

I find Dusty bent over his desk, flipping through a maritime magazine. I think, not for the first time, that I'm probably staring at my own future. Dusty has worked at Atlantic Yacht Club longer than the rest of us combined. I remember him from the years my dad would launch our small dory off the ramp for father-son fishing trips. That was a good ten years ago, and Dusty had already been working here for decades.

I don't just miss baseball—it was my best shot at college.

I knock lightly on the open door, and Dusty's head jerks up.

"Bennett." He glances at the clock on the wall. "You're here late."

"Had a few things to finish up," I say, hoping he can't smell the sweet smoke clinging to my clothes.

"I can't pay overtime this late in the year."

I shove my hands in my pockets. "I know. It's fine."

Dusty studies me for a few more seconds, and I think he'll say something else. Something well intentioned but ultimately empty, like the motivational phrases in the guidance counselor's office. *It's never too late*, and, *You can make a difference*, and, *Believe in yourself*—all that blah bullshit.

Ultimately, he picks two envelopes up and holds them out to me. "Here."

I glance at the first—my paycheck—then flip to the second. "What's—" The question dies on my tongue as the written words register.

"Direct your personal mail to your house, Bennett."

I manage a nod, then turn for the door. I make it back outside without tripping once. A feat since I keep glancing at the return address, a snarl of curiosity and concern writhing around in my chest. I can't think of a single reason why Wren Kensington would have mailed me anything. I haven't seen or heard from her since early July, when I dropped her off in this exact parking lot. We didn't exchange phone numbers, and we didn't make a plan to see each other again—pretty pointless since she'd said her family was leaving. Yeah, she's popped in my head a few times— mostly when other girls hit on me—but I figured that was some random fascination that would fade any day.

The only personalized mail I've ever received are college recruitment letters, and those stopped arriving a while ago.

I reach my truck, leaning against the tailgate and ripping the sealed flap open as quickly as possible while being careful not to tear the envelope's contents.

Her handwriting looks fancy. Intricate curls and exaggerated loops. I read the neat lines in her voice, a sound I didn't even realize I'd memorized.

Sawyer,

Hi. You'll probably never read this. I'm addressing it to the marina, but I'm not sure if you work there after summer ends. Maybe you're reading this next year, and it's even stranger I sent you this because it's been forever since we saw each other.

My new English teacher thinks she came up with the concept of pen pals over the summer. And that writing letters is a "lost art" since texting was invented. I argued it was an improvement since it was way more efficient, but Ms. Plemmons (my English teacher) said we had to complete the assignment anyway. We could get randomly paired with another senior or write to someone we know. Not that I know you, but you fulfill the senior who doesn't go to Dalton requirement, so …

How was the rest of your summer? Did you go bluffing again? Crash any good parties? What's it like, living there yearround? You probably prefer it without all the tourists, but doesn't it feel empty too? Manhattan is always crowded and loud, so I guess I just can't picture living somewhere that's quiet.

~~If you do get this, you don't have to write back.~~

Another reason texting is superior. I could have just deleted that. But I don't feel like starting this letter all over again, even though you can still tell what I wrote. I just realized, after I had, that you wouldn't write me back unless you wanted to. I got used to people sucking up to me again, I guess. And I get why (I'm a ton of fun to hang out with). I just get sick of it too.

Anyway, since we're "almost adults," Mrs. Plemmons said she won't be checking if we receive letters or reading the ones we send to make sure we are actually writing and mailing them. So, if you don't write back, I won't flunk English.

There's a lot of space left, and I'm not sure what else to write, so here's a sailboat drawing I did in art earlier. You know, since you like boats.

    —Wren

CHAPTER 10

Wren

om walks into the kitchen while I'm rifling through the fridge. "Don't ruin your dinner, Wren, please."

"I won't be home for dinner," I say, grabbing a yogurt, shutting the door with my hip, and reaching for the drawer of silverware. "I'm going shopping for Halloween costumes with Gia and Josie."

"It's not even October."

"It's almost October," I counter, snagging a spoon. "And we need multiple outfits apiece. There's no such thing as too early."

Truthfully, our shopping probably will stray from Halloween. There's no reason to limit an outing to one occasion. But I know my parents are struggling with the idea I'm nearing adulthood. It's in everyone's interest that my parents picture me browsing for a cute costume, not at the new lingerie store that opened on Fifth Avenue. Gia met a freshman at Columbia last weekend, and she wants a new bra for their first hookup. And I can't wear my favorite set without thinking about Sawyer Bennett, so I'll probably pick out something new too.

I'm halfway to the doorway when my mom speaks again.

"Did you finish the draft of your personal statement?"

I turn slowly, forcing my fist to relax around the spoon. *Just stress*, I tell myself. Everyone gets stressed about college. "Almost. I'll get the rest completed this weekend."

Mom sighs my name, followed by, "You need to take this seriously."

"I am."

I really am. If I wasn't, I wouldn't have written a statement to start with. But no amount of seriousness can disguise my lackluster interest in college. Four more years of classes and homework assignments and mandatory attendance, away from my favorite city and familiar people? No part of that appeals to me. It took me a while to distill my friend group down to those who possessed genuine loyalty—or to those I thought did—and starting from scratch with strangers sounds exhausting.

Whenever I've expressed uncertainty about college, my parents have responded with resounding variations of, "You'll love it once you're there!" or, "Nerves are normal," or, "We'll find the perfect school for you."

Worse, they worry my hesitation stems from what happened sophomore year. But Third didn't destroy my university fantasy. It never existed to begin with. And no one—not my parents or my sister or my friends—understands that. Gia already applied early action to Yale, and Josie is currently planning the color scheme for her dorm room at Stanford.

"Is everything okay, honey?"

I'm not much of a people pleaser. I'm too strong willed for capitulation to come easily. But there is a short list of people whose feelings and opinions I care about, and my parents are at the top of that list. I can't tell my mom that my reservations about college are multiplying, the closer application deadlines creep, rather than dissipating, like she and Dad said they would. At least not until I've come up with an alternate plan to pitch them.

"Everything's great," I reply. "Just tired from tennis practice."

"Okay," Mom responds, heading back toward the dining room. She likes to spread out her massive building plans on the big table in there. "I'll probably meet your dad at the office, and we'll go out for dinner, if you're not going to be home."

"Sounds good," I say, strolling toward the stairs.

"Grab your mail," Mom calls from the next room. "It's sorted by the espresso machine."

I sigh, shifting my yogurt into the same hand as my spoon as I walk over to the neat piles on the counter. "If this is Princeton again, they're starting to give desperate."

Especially since I'm not Ivy material. The only impressive grades I earn consistently are in art class. The rest of my report cards offer some variety—mostly *B*s, but the occasional *C* has snuck in. And yet a famously selective college will recruit and accept me simply because they're correctly assuming—or they have carefully researched—that my last name is Kensington, as in *those Kensingtons*, so my enrollment will coincide with an eight-figure check.

The preferential treatment annoyed Rory—because my sister *was* Ivy material. She could have applied as Florence Garner—Mom's maiden name—and had her pick of elite institutions, plus an academic scholarship. Rory wanted to earn her way into college on her own merit. Me? I don't want it, no matter how it's delivered.

There is a glossy college mailer—UPenn, not Princeton, as if I would move to Pennsylvania—and a white envelope that looks drab alongside the colorful paper. Until I flip it over to read the return address and my stomach somersaults.

He wrote back.

I hadn't been sure he would.

Became certain he wouldn't after one week and then two passed since I dropped the letter on Ms. Plemmons's desk on my way to lunch the second day of senior year. I convinced myself I'd written the marina's address wrong—Dalton has a strict no-tech policy during school hours, so I'd had to sneak an internet search in, then scribble it as quickly as possible—or that boating didn't extend past Labor Day, and if the letter had arrived to the right place, it'd been tossed or lost.

But *he wrote back.*

Mom's out of sight, focused on work in the dining room, and unable to question it, so I allow a wide smile to spread across my face as I practically skip toward the stairs.

I question it though as I reach the landing and continue down the hallway toward my bedroom.

I'm more cynical than the average seventeen-year-old. Money can solve a lot of problems, but it also creates some. The more you have, the more obvious a target that wealth becomes. What happened with Third didn't help, but I'd already leaned toward believing ill intentions in most people. To questioning friendliness and being suspicious of seeming sincerity.

So, I have no explanation for why holding a letter from a boy I barely know has a whole acrobatic routine happening in my chest. I can't explain Sawyer. Not the enigma himself or the compelling interest that began before I knew him at all. That formed the second I saw him scowling, unimpressed by my boobs or my bravery. Well—I recall his *amazing tits* comment—he was a little impressed, I guess. Just excellent at acting otherwise. With a letter, he didn't even need to act. He could have just ignored it.

I drop my backpack by the foot of my bed before sitting on the upholstered bench and carefully sliding my finger under the flap of the envelope. I'm impatient enough to tear it open, but I don't want to risk ripping the return address on the off chance he didn't send me a blank page or a curt, *Don't contact me again.*

I slide the folded sheet out as carefully as I opened the envelope, my heart doing a tiny stutter, like the beat equivalent of a jump for joy, when I note there are many lines of writing, not just none or one. His handwriting is neat and deliberate. All uppercase. Like his truck, it fits him—solid and decisive.

WREN,

HI BACK.

NOT MANY PEOPLE TAKE THEIR BOATS OUT AFTER LABOR DAY, BUT I WORK AT THE MARINA THROUGH OCTOBER. THERE'S A LOT OF WORK TO BE DONE IN THE FALL, STORING BOATS AND DOCKS SO THAT EVERYTHING IS ALL SET FOR THE WINTER. YOU'RE RIGHT. I PREFER IT THIS TIME OF YEAR. GUS, WADE (BROWN HAIR, HE INVITED YOU TO THE PARTY), AND A FEW OTHER GUYS ARE STILL WORKING TOO. IT'S FUN BUT QUIET. I GUESS I'M JUST USED TO IT. SORT OF THE CALM AFTER THE STORM, AS THE SAYING GOES.

I WENT BLUFFING LAST WEEKEND. THE WATER IS WARMEST NOW, BUT THE WAVES WERE ROUGH. IT FELT LIKE I WAS SWIMMING AGAINST THE CURRENT, HEADING TO SHORE, BUT I MADE IT IN FINE. I'LL PROBABLY GO A COUPLE MORE TIMES BEFORE IT GETS TOO COLD.

I GOT MY FILL OF RICH-PEOPLE PARTIES ON THE FOURTH, BUT WADE AND CAMMIE HOSTED A COUPLE MORE NORMAL ONES IN AUGUST.

FOR SOMEONE WHO KNOWS SHIT ABOUT BOATS, YOU'RE REALLY GOOD AT DRAWING. IF THAT WAS FROM MEMORY, I'M FUCKING IMPRESSED. ACTUALLY, I'M IMPRESSED EITHER WAY.

IF YOU WANT TO PASS ENGLISH WITH A CLEAR CONSCIENCE, TELL ME MORE
ABOUT NEW YORK AND ALL THE SUCK-UPS YOU KNOW.
  SAWYER

SAWYER BENNETT
23 CHURCH ST.
MONTAUK, NY 11937

I didn't have to save the envelope. He made sure I could write him back regardless of how carelessly I opened it.

And I don't realize, until my cheeks start aching, that I haven't stopped smiling since I read his name.

CHAPTER 11

Sawyer

"Yo, Cap! You home?"

I drop Wren's letter into an open drawer on my desk, sliding it shut with my knee seconds before Gus fills the doorway.

"No," I drawl, leaning back in the chair until the first two legs lift off the ground. "Someone kidnapped me and left my truck outside for the cops to fight over."

They wouldn't spend much time searching for a Bennett.

"If you got kidnapped and—I'm presuming—murdered, wouldn't you gift your truck to your best friend?"

Gus's mode of transportation is a bike. He's earned as much at the marina as I have, but unlike me, he plans to go to college. Every cent he earns gets deposited into a fund that should get him through a couple of

semesters at the local community college Cammie attends. Unless you want to pile the expense of room and board on top of tuition fees, it's the best option around here.

"Sure, after I haunted you for being happy I was murdered since you got a free car out of it."

We share a quick grin before Gus's attention shifts to my desk. "You're doing homework? For real?"

I'm what teachers like to refer to as "wasted potential." I'm smart. School has always come easily. I can ace tests based on paying attention in class, even if I never bother to study the material at home. But right when grades started to really matter, it felt like nothing in life made sense, and my scores on everything skydived. Sympathy and pity only stretch so far before people stop making excuses, and my GPA was unsalvageable by then anyway. I do enough to ensure I'll graduate, and that's about it. I doubt Gus or my other friends even remember the days when I wouldn't skip occasionally or was the sole student to make High Honor Roll each semester.

When I shrug a shoulder and say, "Not really," Gus doesn't look the least bit surprised.

He would look shocked if I mentioned what I was doing—reading Wren's latest letter.

We've been writing back and forth for weeks—months. Before September, I hadn't written a letter since the final Christmas I believed in Santa Claus.

I could have included my number in any one of the dozen or so letters I'd written Wren, but I haven't. She hasn't sent me hers either. If we want to communicate with each other, we have to write it and rely on postal workers to transport it between my house and her penthouse, which is weird and rather ridiculous and also strangely fun. I like watching the ink shimmer and dry on the paper as I scrawl out random thoughts. Like covering the page with a stream of consciousness rather than typing a one-worded text between classes or at a red light. Like decoding where Wren was when she wrote me based on the paper she used. Lined paper means school; pink stationery is from home.

If I mentioned any of that to Gus, he'd be incredulous or laugh uproariously. Probably both. He hasn't mentioned Wren since she left in July, and while I'm glad he's over his crush, I'm unsure how he'll react to mine.

And that's all this interest in Wren Kensington is. Attraction, mixed with a little intrigue, because our lives are so fundamentally different from each other. Talking to her is like reading a book or watching a movie—escapism into another world. Do I roll my eyes when Wren mentions attending premieres for TV shows my classmates at school talk about? Yes. Or when she goes to concerts for artists who sing the songs my truck's crappy radio occasionally picks up? Yes. Or how she spent a weekend shopping for the perfect Thanksgiving outfit—whatever that means—when I'd bet my savings that she has a clothing collection that would make most department stores envious? Yes. But I'm entertained by it all, too, so I keep writing back, and although I don't know what Wren finds the least bit interesting about *my* life, so does she.

Something hard hits my left arm.

"The fuck?" I glower at Gus, the only baseball-throwing possibility in the room.

My best friend just grins. He knows me too well to shrink from the glare most people would look alarmed by. "What's with you tonight? I asked three times if you wanted to hit Lucky's."

"You mean, if I'll be your chauffeur to Lucky's," I correct, avoiding his question.

Lucky's—the only bar in the area with reasonable prices and no fancy cocktail menu, plus a lax carding policy, even if you can't afford a bad fake—is outside Gus's biking range. Especially this time of year. It hasn't snowed yet, but the temperature has been hovering around freezing, so it's just a matter of time.

"Everyone's going?" I lean down, retrieving the baseball from the floor and running a thumb along the knitted seam on the worn leather.

"Yep," Gus confirms.

"Yeah. Sure." I set the baseball down by my laptop. Stand. Stretch. Better than spending the evening reading a letter from a girl who's probably getting hit on by a bunch of surfers right now.

Wren is spending Thanksgiving with her mom's family, who live in Los Angeles. An insignificant detail I shouldn't even know.

"Just gonna change," I say, heading for the closet.

Gus nods. "Cool. Do you have food?"

"Have at the fridge," I tell him, knowing there's not much to have at. Because I haven't bothered grocery shopping lately—not because I'm the oldest of four boys, like Gus is. My mom left last week for a monthlong deployment, and I haven't readjusted to being fully responsible for food again.

I swap my wrinkled T-shirt for a navy henley that smells clean, then pull an old windbreaker from baseball on over it. Move Wren's latest letter from the desk drawer to the old shoebox, replacing it on the shelf in my closet before grabbing my phone, keys, and wallet.

I find Gus in the kitchen, munching on a jar of pickles.

I make a face as the smell of vinegar burns my nostrils. "*That's* what you're eating before we go to Lucky's?"

"All you had," is what I think Gus mumbles around a mouthful, capping the jar and sticking it back in the fridge. He walks over to the sink, flipping on the faucet and drinking straight from the tap.

I roll my eyes. "I'll be in the truck. Lock up."

My parents swapped keys with the couple down the street when they moved into this house fifteen years ago. Now, it's how Gus solicits rides and how I let Gus's family's dog out after school since both his parents work and he and his younger brothers participate in just about every activity the local school system offers.

Once I'm in the truck, I roll the windows down as a preemptive necessity, certain water isn't going to do much to diminish Gus's pickle breath. I'm not sure the gauge on the dashboard is entirely accurate—it reads *41*—but it doesn't feel inaccurate either. Midday on Thursday nearly reached fifty; Gus's youngest brother suggested we eat our turkey outside.

Sure enough, I smell salty brine when Gus climbs in. But the evidence of his snack fades—or I just become used to it—as I drive toward Lucky's, groaning when I spot the crowded parking lot ahead.

The busyness is predictable—there's not much to do here in the winter, and it's a holiday weekend to boot, but still annoying. I have to park a half mile down the road, right before a guardrail, and I wish I'd worn more layers, as my windbreaker does nothing to block the chilly gusts.

Then, as soon as we enter the bar, I rip it off and shove my sleeves up. The air in here is humid and sticky, sweetened by sweat and smoke. Like most of the bar's rules, *no smoking* isn't strictly enforced.

Lots of familiar faces surround us, but Cammie's is the first I spare more than a passing glance. This is the first year we haven't attended the same school, and it's felt weird, not having her be part of our everyday crew. Between driving back and forth to her classes and working part-time at the hotel by the country club, I've hardly seen her all fall.

Cammie glances this way a few seconds later. She spots Gus first, smiling, then sees me, and it grows wider.

My stomach caves in, and my steps slow automatically. *Shit.* I was hoping some distance would help our friendship return to normal.

I glance at Gus, but he didn't notice. He's striding toward Wade, hand outstretched to slap his back.

I exhale, hoping I'm misreading.

I greet Ricky first, who's growing out his buzz cut for the winter, ribbing him about the spiky strands.

I hug Cammie next, my, "Good to see you," genuine. We've been friends since elementary school.

After greeting everyone, I announce I'm grabbing a beer. "Want one?" I ask Gus, who's looking at something on Wade's phone. The Knicks game, I think.

"Yeah," he replies, pulling a ten out of his pocket and holding it out to me.

I shake my head. "Don't worry about it."

I know he's stressed about money for next year. I made a decent amount at the marina this summer, and I'm saving up for … nothing.

"Gas money at least," Gus says, holding the bill closer to me. "Or your chauffeuring tip." He glances at Wade. "Do drivers get tips?"

Wade doesn't take his eyes off the game. "Dunno."

Wren would know. The thought is random and unwelcome.

She's literally on the opposite side of the country. I haven't seen her since July. We're fucking pen pals, not normal friends, and she's definitely not my girlfriend. It's ridiculous that I'm out at a bar with my closest buddies and I'm thinking about her.

I stride toward the bar, resolved to keep my thoughts Wren-free. I order from Owen, one of the usual bartenders, who doesn't even bother to ask for my fake.

While I'm waiting for the beers, Emily Stone sidles over.

And my ban on thinking about a certain blonde becomes a spectacular failure. Because I'm sure not focused on the girl beside me as she asks how my Thanksgiving break has been, "accidentally" brushing her boobs against my right bicep.

I'm relieved when Owen returns with the beers, ignoring his amused smirk when he notices I'm no longer standing alone.

"Want to come over to my table for a bit?" Emily asks, twirling a strand of hair around one finger. "We could hang out, then head out …"

"Can't tonight," I tell her. "It's guys' night."

Emily glances at my table. "Cammie's there."

"She's friends with the guys."

"Please." She rolls her eyes. "Everyone knows you two hooked up."

"Bye, Emily," I say, then walk off.

When I make it back to the table, everyone except Cammie is grinning.

"Careful drinking that, man," Wade comments as I hand Gus his beer. "Emily might have spit in it."

"You should just fuck her, Cap," Ricky tells me. "Then she'll probably lose interest."

I flip him off as I slide onto the open stool, hoping the guys will be the ones who lose interest and move on to another topic.

"What about you, Cammie?" Wade asks. "College guys treating you okay?"

Cammie nods. "I'm dating this guy from my business class. Luke. He's great. I was hoping you guys could meet this weekend, but he headed home for the holiday."

Relief spreads through me. At least one good thing came from tonight. She has moved on.

"That's great, Cam," I say quickly.

Too quickly.

Her head swivels to me. "I didn't know it was so easy to get on your good side, Cap. You don't want to meet him first? Ask a few threatening questions about his intentions? *Any* guy is good enough for me?"

The table is suddenly silent, a few of the guys exchanging awkward glances.

My grip tightens around the beer bottle. There's a good chance the glass might crack. "Of course not. But you have good judgment, so if you like him ..."

An uncomfortable silence lingers around the table as we all wait for Cammie's response. She scoffs softly, then takes a sip of her drink.

I look at Gus. He shrugs a shoulder, not knowing what to do about the awkwardness either.

"I'm going to the restroom," Cammie mutters, sliding off her stool and heading toward the back of the bar.

I sigh heavily. "Fuck."

No one asks. They all know—like Emily said. I wasn't just making bad decisions back then. I didn't bother to hide a single one.

Wade clears his throat. "She'll get over it."

Will she? It's been over a year.

I take a swig of beer, then stand and follow Cammie. There's a small stage back here that sometimes gets used for live music or karaoke—a couple is currently making out against it—and a pool table.

A few minutes later, Cammie reappears. She sighs when she sees me waiting, approaching slowly.

"Can we talk outside?" I ask.

She nods, heading for the door. I trail behind, dreading the approaching conversation.

"I'm sorry," I say once we're outside.

She exhales, wrapping her arms around herself. "No. I am. I overreacted."

"If you're happy, then I'm happy for you. That's all I was trying to say."

"I know." Cammie swallows, glancing at the ground. "I've been … I've been waiting for you to change your mind. About us. Are you ever going to?"

I swallow, too, delaying the honest answer. "No."

I said it softly, but she still flinches.

"I'm sorry," I repeat. "I never should have—"

"It wasn't you. I wanted to. I knew you were hurting, that you'd been drinking that night. I'm not even sure you knew it was me for most of it." She rubs the toe of her shoe in the dirt. "I don't want you to keep apologizing. Just … I thought you'd finally see me differently after it happened. And then I told myself you needed more time to come to terms with … everything. But now … I guess I needed to hear you say it. To tell me to stop waiting."

"It's not you, Cammie. I'm fucked up after everything that happened. I can't—I'm not capable of—"

"Lovers' quarrel, Bennett?"

I stiffen, recognizing the voice. Spin slowly to face a smirking Brett Nichols.

He looks the same as the last time I saw him a year ago. He's good-looking, I guess. The guy always gets plenty of female attention since he can be charming on the rare occasion he's not acting like a prick.

"Just a private conversation, Nichols," I reply evenly.

Brett glances past me. "Hey, Cammie. I didn't recognize you at first. Figured you'd have stopped hanging around, begging for scraps of Bennett's attention, by now."

I clench and unclench my fists slowly, trying to rein in my temper.

"Fuck off, Brett," Cammie retorts.

"I'd treat you a lot better than the so-called Captain ever did, sweetheart."

"Did your new town toss you out too?" I snap.

Brett sneers, no longer looking so nonchalant. "Just visiting. *I* don't stay where I'm not wanted, unlike some people."

"Then go away because you're not wanted here," I tell him, turning away.

"Cap!" Cammie shouts.

But I'm ready, smiling wide as Brett shoves me against the side of the building. His right fist is already raised and cocked. Mine are by my sides. He wants a reaction. Wants to prove I'm exactly like my father— who ruined his. He can take as many cheap shots as he wants. I won't hit him back.

"How's the shoulder, Nichols? Still pitching softballs?"

"Heard you're pitching *nothing* these days. That golden arm isn't looking so good, Bennett." Brett shoves me again, then steps away.

He's here with two buddies, neither of whom I recognize. Probably new friends. According to rumors, he moved upstate with his mom after his parents divorced.

Brett stares at me, that maddening smirk still on his face. "You used to be more fun. Still too much of a pussy to punch, huh?"

"Let's go, Cap." Cammie appears beside me, glaring at Brett.

I step closer to Brett, effectively blocking her. I know I won't swing, but he's unpredictable. I don't want Cammie to get caught in the fray.

"You're not worth it, Nichols," I say, then follow an anxious Cammie back inside.

I'm half expecting to get jumped from behind. But it never happens.

About damn time tonight improved.

CHAPTER 12

DECEMBER

"What about your place?" Ricky asks Wade.

Wade nods. "Cool with me. I'll check with Cammie when she gets here. Anyone know where—"

"Cap." Gus nudges my arm.

"What?" I tug on the constrictive collar of my dress shirt.

The only reason I came to this holiday party was because Gus had begged for a ride, and I've been ready to leave since we arrived. Hopefully, he's finally come to the same conclusion.

"Isn't that Wren Kensington?"

My head whips left, following the direction of his nod. I don't have to look for long or very hard. Wren is impossible to miss. Her hair is longer, the blonde strands falling in a cascade of golden curls. Her dress is short and shimmering, black with glints of silver. She's wearing heels, and her legs look endless.

I walk that way without saying a word.

Wren is talking to a girl I don't recognize, who appears to be roughly our age.

"… Kit won't care," she says. "You know the house?"

"Of course I do," the girl says eagerly.

"Perfect." Wren glances my way, holding my gaze. "See you there."

I grab Wren's hand as soon as it's within reach, tugging her down the hallway, past the bar, and toward the kitchen. Even in her heels, she keeps up with me easily.

There's a small stockroom tucked around the corner, where nonperishables and extra supplies get stored.

I pull Wren in there, flip on a light, close the door, and face her. "I thought you were in Paris."

Weeks ago, one of her letters mentioned that she was spending the holidays in France. That's not what I intended to say to her first, but … I'm shocked. She was supposed to be on the opposite side of the Atlantic.

Wren shrugs a slim shoulder, the strap of her dress sparkling under the fluorescent lights. She looks wildly out of place in front of the shelves lined with takeout containers and soda cans. "Plans changed. My cousin Kit is having a party here tonight, so Rory and I drove down earlier. You said you'd be at this, so …" Her head tilts, studying me—way too intently.

Because … fuck. She just showed up here. To see me, it seems, because Hanson Ellsworth is a member of the Atlantic Yacht Club, but no Kensington is.

Wren hasn't been that far away. Same state. Manhattan is roughly a hundred miles from here. She's been untouchable during the months we've been exchanging letters though.

She's suddenly touchable. Talking and breathing and near and so goddamn gorgeous that my chest burns.

I can't summon a single reasonable reaction to her proximity, which unnerves me because nonchalance has never been hard for me to find before.

"Kind of a lame party out there," she adds, nodding toward the door.

"Tell me about it. Gus wanted to come."

Wren leans back against a shelf. My guess is those ridiculously high heels are hurting her feet.

"The *Captain* only does what he wants. Right?"

I'm not sure we're talking about my plans for tonight all of a sudden.

I battle the urge to unbutton my collar. "Right."

"I came to invite you to Kit's, if you're free after this rager wraps up. Your friends can come too. There will be tons of food and free booze, and they're setting off fireworks at midnight …"

Part of me wants to go. The rest knows it's a terrible idea. Our worlds don't overlap. Pretending they do, even for one night, is foolish.

We were a summer fling. Summer is over.

"Yeah, okay." She shoves away from the shelf and steps closer, a familiar scent surrounding me.

I know nothing about perfume, but I could pick this particular smell out of thousands. The floral scent lingered in my truck for weeks after the night we went swimming together. If I could think of a casual way to, I'd ask what flower it is.

"That was the second, less important reason I came," Wren continues. "I mostly came … because I wanted to come."

She smirks, proud of the double entendre. My lips twitch as I fight smiling back.

Wren on paper is compelling. In person, she's dangerously charismatic. I'm watching her walk closer, entirely aware that I should probably stop this and utterly powerless to.

I want her. I've wanted her for months, replaying that night in my truck on repeat.

I'm not sure who moves first—probably me—but we're kissing. She moans into my mouth as my tongue invades hers, hands already working my belt.

This shouldn't feel so familiar—we haven't hooked up since July.

This shouldn't be so exciting—it's already happened twice.

Somehow, it's both.

Logically, I'm not sure this is a good idea. But I'm really lacking in logic right now. I fumble for a condom while she strokes my erection, both of us breathing heavily between kisses. I can hear the distant murmur of voices and holiday music, but the party might as well be happening on another planet.

"Bend over," I say once I'm covered.

"Don't mess up my dress," Wren warns, spinning and gripping the nearest shelf. "It's Oscar de la Renta."

I don't know—or care—what that means. But I do tell her, "That's why I told you to bend over."

"Or you're just impa—*fuck*."

I swear too. I didn't forget how fucking her had felt, but I doubted my recollection. She couldn't have been that tight and responsive and— she is.

It's heaven and hell, being buried inside of her. It feels so good, and it won't last, and I'm not sure I'll last, yet I'm determined for this to not be a repeat of our first time.

I think about breaking my arm as a kid. Recite my freshman year stats.

And then she's spasming, the clench of her pussy making it impossible for me not to fill the condom. Still embarrassingly fast, but at least she came first this time.

I catch my breath, then pull out, ripping open a new package of napkins to clean up the mess.

"So, are you coming?" Wren asks, carefully fixing her dress.

"I just did." I toss the condom and napkins into the trash can. Nothing but net. My future might be fucked, but I've still got a good arm.

She rolls her eyes. "To the party."

I zip up my pants. "I can't. I already made plans with the guys."

Truthfully, they'd probably be thrilled to go to a Kensington party. Wade's house has lukewarm beer and not much else. Definitely no caviar or champagne or fireworks. But they don't have to know about the invitation.

Wren nods. "Okay."

She doesn't sound disappointed. It makes me feel better—and annoyed—about lying. She *shouldn't* care if I go or not. No doubt there will be plenty of guys there, thrilled to keep Wren company.

"Are you free to hang out tomorrow? I'll probably sleep in since it's going to be a late night, but we could meet later?"

Fuck. I want to tell her yes, and that's … what is up with that? I don't do—I need out, to end whatever this is.

So, I force myself to hold her gaze as I reply, "Why?"

I watch that rude response detonate between us. Watch the word hit her. Watch Wren's composure falter, then harden. She's accustomed to people accommodating her. And I'm not trying to be the outlier. I'm just calling it quits before she can. Being left behind sucks less when you retreat first. At least, that's what I'm trying to convince myself of.

Seconds of silence pass, but they stretch like hours. Like lengthy letters, filled with inside jokes and … I never should have written her back.

Wren lifts her chin, her eyes never wavering from mine. "Nice of you to say something *before* you got laid."

She sounds annoyed more than anything else. I was right—this meant nothing to her. I've just bruised her pride.

"Don't act like you didn't want it," I drawl, irritated she's acting like I lured her here.

She showed up. She told me she was here for sex.

Wren stiffens. "I'm not—I never said that. I just forgot what an *asshole* you are."

So, she's given up on her theory I'm secretly a decent guy. Good.

"I told you I was."

"Yeah." She scoffs. "You sure did. Thanks for the reminder."

We stare at each other. I don't know what else to say. I figured, after the pity invitation, she'd waltz out of here to get to her non-lame party.

"What do you want from me, Wren?" I ask because I truly don't know.

She doesn't know everything about me—I've never mentioned my family in any letters, for instance—but she knows enough to realize I'm a dead end. No trust fund, no college plans, no exciting future.

"Nothing." Wren shakes her head once. "I mean, we already … so there's … nothing." Finally, she heads for the door. "Bye, Captain."

My nickname sounds different this time. An insult instead of a tease. I sort of hate it.

I also hate how I'm realizing my future mail will only be bills and junk mailers. No way will Wren write me again, not after I rejected her twice. She'll go to her cousin's fancy party—laugh and dance and drink and kiss another guy at midnight. Return to her penthouse. Take vacations to places I've only ever heard of. Have her pick of colleges. If I see her again, it'll probably be from a distance, if she ever returns to the marina.

And … it sucks.

The door opens and closes, and I'm alone in a glorified pantry. Just me and the temper I inherited.

I'm a lost cause.

Everyone knows it.

About time Wren realized it too.

It shouldn't bother me so much that she finally has.

CHAPTER 13

Wren

There's nothing fun about attending a party while holding back tears. If Kit hadn't texted me earlier, asking where I was—or if I had anywhere else in this town to go—I wouldn't be here. And to think, I'd considered driving separately from Rory because I thought I'd want to stay in the Hamptons for *longer* than my sister. If ditching Rory wouldn't raise lots of questions in my family that I have no interest in answering, I'd be halfway back to Manhattan by now.

I glance at Gia, who's happily chatting with some guy, then edge my way out of the living room. It's packed in here, loud pop music and even louder voices reverberating off the walls. The kitchen is just as crowded. I don't even stop; I just continue down the back hallway. There's something intensely isolating about being surrounded by laughter and merriment while you're secretly miserable. Especially when you have a reputation for being unbothered and outgoing and fun. I don't sulk at parties; I flirt and dance.

Gia has asked me what's wrong twice. I lied and said I had cramps. If she notices I left the living room, she'll probably assume I had to use the restroom.

Finally, I find a room that is empty and likely to stay so. I flip on the light, shut the door, and press my forehead against it, forcing myself to take deep, even breaths. The stinging in my nose is getting worse, not better, and my feet are killing me.

I move away from the door, shoes wobbling on the slate floor, then step out of the heels. Take a seat, barefoot, on the cold ground, my back to the washing machine, half trying to avoid wrinkling my dress and half not really giving a shit anymore. I'll never be able to wear this outfit again without thinking about how long I spent picking it out.

God, I was so *excited* about tonight. I thought I'd be flirting and dancing with him right now, not sitting in my aunt and uncle's laundry room, alone. I can't even be mad at Sawyer. I mean, I can—I am—but he was right; he'd warned me. I was the one who got confused, who couldn't keep it casual. Who showed up, unannounced, expecting him to act like a boyfriend.

The sobs start a few seconds later. And once they start, they're impossible to stop.

I can't recall the last time I cried. I'm overdue, I guess. I was numb after what happened with Third. Furious and scared once the shock wore off, but never sad.

Tears continue streaming down my cheeks in salty streaks. I swipe them away before they can drip onto my dress, wishing I had a tissue.

"… swore I saw her headed this way," a male voice says, followed by one I immediately recognize.

"That'd be useful knowledge, if you were ever reliable."

Rory.

The door opens a few seconds later, revealing my sister. Flynn Parks is right behind her. Flynn is Kit's best friend, so I'm unsurprised he's here.

I do wish he weren't here, in this room, seeing this. Flynn is hot. In a perfect male-model sort of way, not in the rugged bad-boy way Sawyer is, but attractive enough that I care he's seeing me crying on the floor. He also might mention this to my cousin, and I really don't need Kit coming in here, all concerned. I want to grieve my stupidity alone.

"What happened, Wren?" My sister's expression is creased with worry as she kneels down next to me. She doesn't even hesitate to lower to the floor, appearing unconcerned about wrinkling her silk dress.

I tease Rory for being so straitlaced and proper, but I can't imagine a better sister.

I shake my head, still crying. My eyes are like two leaky faucets, and I'm focused on figuring out how to shut them off. I don't want to talk. I'm not sure what I'd say.

Retreating footsteps announce Flynn's departure. No doubt I freaked him out, but I'm too depressed to really care.

I release a watery sigh. Sniff. "Ugh."

Rory rubs my thigh reassuringly. She looks awfully concerned, which is the equivalent of freaking out for my poised sister.

I feel like I lost something, which is absurd. I never had him to begin with.

"Here." Flynn has returned, and he's holding a full glass of champagne out to me. "Waiters aren't serving back here."

I manage a wobbly smile before accepting the drink. I gulp the contents in one go, the bubbles burning my throat.

"She's *seventeen*," Rory hisses.

"And already a pro," Flynn says, taking the empty glass from me.

"You are so immature. And irresponsible."

"Let me guess. You downed Shirley Temples to take the edge off in high school?"

"Of course *you* would think teenage drinking is some sort of accomplishment—"

"Is there more champagne?" I ask, avoiding Rory's reproachful expression.

Usually, I enjoy listening to her bicker with Flynn since Rory rarely talks back to anyone. But alcohol will cheer me up more than their arguing.

"Tons," Flynn replies cheerfully. "Kit's party planner ordered about a hundred cases. But before you get drunk"—he crouches down next to Rory—"what happened?"

I blow out a long breath. "Bad night."

Rory shifts closer, away from Flynn. "Are you … okay? Should I call Mom? Or … someone else?"

She means Dr. Hurts, but is considerate enough not to mention my therapist by name in front of Flynn.

"No. I'm not—I'll be fine." I sigh again, attempting to focus on the warm buzz of alcohol settling in my empty stomach instead of the sharp ache in my chest. "You were … you were right."

"Happens to broken clocks twice a day," Flynn comments.

My lips twitch in response.

"Shut up, Parks," Rory snaps. "I know it's a foreign concept, but not every situation requires your idiotic commentary."

"Shutting up." Flynn shifts, moving to the spot on my other side.

We would look ridiculous to anyone who walked into the laundry room now, reclined on the floor, but I'm still too heartbroken to care about appearances. Plus, we're about as removed from the party as possible. I doubt anyone else is going to wander in here.

"What was I right about?" Rory asks softly.

"That it wouldn't end well with him."

It takes her a minute. "Oh. This is about Marina Guy?"

"Who is Marina Guy?" Flynn wonders.

"Go get more champagne," Rory instructs him.

"Oh, *now* you support underage drinking?"

"Just *go*, Parks."

Flynn sighs, lumbering to his feet.

As soon as the door shuts, Rory spins so she's facing me. "Two glasses—that's it, okay?"

I'm not sure it's a promise I'll keep since oblivion sounds pretty great right now, but I agree. "Okay."

"Did he hurt you, Wren?"

"Yes," I whisper. "But not the way that you mean. I thought he—I thought *we* were something real. He just wanted to get laid."

The bitter words leave an acrid taste on my tongue. Because I know they're not true—not entirely. Sawyer didn't write me letters for months on the off chance I'd show up tonight. He didn't invite me, had no idea I would be there, and I was the one who instigated sex earlier. But I'd rather convince myself he never cared at all than deal with the reality he cared some—just not enough.

I was the one who chased him. Who followed him upstairs. Who sent the first letter. Who got stupidly swept up in the possibility he might be mine because I felt like his.

Rory strokes my hair the same way Mom does. "I'm so sorry, Wren."

"It's fine. I knew better."

"You were safe? You used protection?"

"Yes, *Mom*," I reply, rolling my eyes.

I say it partly to lighten the mood. Partly because I've never discussed sex with my sister and it's a little weird that it's happening now. She mostly treats me like a little kid, and I mostly let her. That's shifting all of a sudden, and too much has already changed tonight.

Rory doesn't smile. "It's important, Wren. Not only for pregnancy, but also for sexually transmitted—"

My cheeks are flaming. "Oh my God, Rory. *Stop.* Just because I didn't get an A-plus in health class, like you did, doesn't mean I'm an idiot."

"Of course you're not an idiot, Wren. But if you're too embarrassed to discuss sex, you're not old enough to be having it."

"I'm not *embarrassed* to discuss it. It's just weird to talk about it with you. It's not like you told me about your first time."

Her smile is sad. "He was your first?"

I wriggle my toes, enjoying the freedom of not having them crammed into heels, and admit, "Yeah."

She moves, mirroring my position against the dryer. "My first time wasn't that special. I went out on a few dates with a guy in my Political Philosophy class freshman year. We went back to his dorm room after grabbing pizza. It lasted about two minutes while his roommate kept texting, complaining about how he needed to get his soccer ball out of the room. Mostly, I just remember the endless buzzing being annoying. The second time was a little better."

"What was his name?"

"Calvin."

"Did he wear—"

"I *knew* you were going to ask that. They were a different brand."

I giggle. Rory does too, reluctantly.

"Thanks for telling me," I tell her.

There's a knock on the door.

"Okay if I come in?" Flynn calls.

Rory glances at me.

I nod. I spent forever on my makeup earlier, and I'm sure I look like a raccoon by now. At least I've stopped crying.

"Okay," Rory answers.

Flynn enters a few seconds later. His arms are full, so he shuts the door with his foot. He hands Rory a bottle of Pellegrino, me a bottle of Dom Pérignon, and selected a bottle of Grey Goose for himself.

He takes his former seat beside me, knocking our bottles together. "Cheers, Wren. If you want me to beat him up, just say the word."

"Thanks, Flynn." I lean forward, letting the cork fly. It hits the ceiling, then bounces into a corner. I suck the foam off before it can spill down the neck, then wash it down with a hearty swallow. "He could take you though."

I guarantee Flynn has never thrown a punch. He's too easygoing and carefree. Whereas Sawyer possesses a raw intensity that makes me think he'd win any brawl, no matter his opponent.

Rory coughs, but it doesn't really cover her laugh.

Flynn frowns. "How old is he?"

"My age," I reply. "He's … scrappy."

"I'll start training now. By next year, I should be ready to kick his ass." Flynn checks his watch. "That gives me ten minutes."

"Thanks for offering," I say sincerely. "You guys should go grab good spots to watch the fireworks." I glance at Rory. "Did Carson end up coming? Go kiss him."

Rory shakes her head. "He couldn't make it."

Flynn scoffs lightly, then sips more vodka. I don't like Rory's boyfriend because he's bland and predictable. I wonder what Flynn's issue with him is.

"But as long as you're sure you're good"—I nod in response—"I will go grab a *real* drink." Rory stands slowly, careful not to step on the hem of her dress.

"I thought you'd started Dry January early," Flynn tells her.

Rory ignores him. "If you need anything, Wren, let me know."

"Thanks, Rory."

My sister leaves, and Flynn stands a second later.

"I should check in with Kit. I couldn't find him earlier, and the caterers had some questions."

I nod. "Thanks for being my personal bartender."

"Anytime. As long as you don't tell your sister."

I smile. "What's your issue with Carson?"

"Who?"

"Rory's boyfriend. You scoffed when I mentioned him."

"I think I swallowed some lint."

I glance around the spotless laundry room. Raise a disbelieving eyebrow. "Okay. If that's your story."

"Speaking of douchebags—"

"Were we?" I interject.

Flynn ignores me. "He'll regret tonight, Wren. Take it from someone who was a high-school guy once—we take too long to figure some important shit out."

I nod. I figured I was too dehydrated by now, but more tears threaten. At least I'm about to be alone again.

Flynn flashes me one final sympathetic smile, then leaves.

I reach for the bottle of champagne.

CHAPTER 14

Sawyer

One problem with living in a small town and having the same friends since kindergarten? When you want to escape, it's hard to find some privacy.

"What the fuck, dude?" Gus shouts, striding toward me with his hands outstretched. "We were supposed to go to Wade's, then you just take off?"

"Wasn't feeling well," I say, tossing another ball in the air and slamming the bat against it with a satisfying smack.

"That won't help." Gus nods toward the half-empty bottle propped against home plate.

It's the only thing helping actually.

I don't reply, just pick up another ball and send it flying into right field.

"We playing pickup?" Wade asks, approaching. "I missed trying to hit off you, man."

"Sweet. You broke into the equipment shed?" Ricky's here now too.

I didn't break in. They haven't changed the code since I stopped playing. Which will probably make me a prime suspect, if anyone reports the mystery of a bucket of baseballs going from being neatly stored to scattered across the frozen field, but I really don't give a shit.

"Why don't you guys go grab the balls?" Gus suggests.

"Leave 'em," I say, reaching into the bucket again.

Gus steps closer. "What's going on, Cap?"

I drop the ball and reach for the bottle instead. Gus watches me take another swig, judgment and concern written all over his face. I don't know why he doesn't just give up on me like everyone else. He has plenty of other friends. He has a dad. He's headed to college in the fall.

I wait, but he doesn't walk away. I sigh. "Just in a bad mood. Needed some time alone."

"You were fine before … this have something to do with her?"

I scoff, dropping the bottle. "Dunno who you're talking about."

Most people would take the note of warning in my tone seriously.

Gus calls out my evasiveness. "I'm talking about Wren Kensington."

I glower at Gus, who's staring steadily at me. We both knew exactly who he was talking about—that was his cue to drop it.

"You guys disappeared for a while at Wade's party," Gus continues. "Your truck smelled like fancy perfume for a few weeks after the Fourth. And she sure didn't come to the yacht club because we had the superior party—Cammie said the Kensington place was crazy."

"What the fuck was Cammie doing there?"

Gus shrugs. "I dunno. She came to the marina when we couldn't find you and mentioned she'd been there."

I grab another baseball, tossing and catching it as I watch Ricky and Wade collect the many I've already hit. It's annoying—I wanted to leave a mess behind.

"So … Wren Kensington?"

"Drop it, Gus. And get over your stupid crush on her. She won't be back."

Gus doesn't even flinch. "Fuck. You really like her."

"I liked fucking her, is all." I slam another ball.

"Home run!" Wade yells from the outfield.

Gus shakes his head. "Yeah, right. You're out here, drunk and playing baseball by yourself because you 'liked fucking' a girl you hadn't seen in months? I mean, I haven't seen you this low since …"

I laugh. Once. Humorlessly. "It's not the fucking same."

For many reasons, including that I'm at fault for this fuckup.

I drop the bat I'm holding, picking up the bottle with both hands instead.

Gus reaches for it, too, yanking it from my grasp. He flips it, letting the remaining liquor spill out to soak the strike zone. "Where's your truck?"

I scowl, annoyed by his intervention, but also too drained to really summon any annoyance. "Home. I walked here."

"I'll walk back with you. Just let me tell the guys." Gus jogs toward where Wade and Ricky are still collecting balls, pausing to pick up the bucket that's nearly empty.

I turn, shoving my hands in my pockets and heading toward the sidewalk. I make it about halfway down the block before Gus catches up to me. He doesn't chastise me for walking off, and the guilt makes me feel even worse.

"Sorry," I mutter as a blanket apology for this entire night.

I'm pretty sure it's past midnight, but I'm not sure. I left my phone in my truck when I got back from the marina. No matter what time it is, this was a shitty way to start the new year.

"You're better than this, Cap," Gus tells me.

"I'm not. Obviously."

He nudges my arm with his elbow. "You are. You're just having a bad night."

I blink rapidly, a deluge of exhaustion hitting me as I trudge along. My muscles feel leaden, soaked with rum and weighed down with self-loathing. "I'm like my dad."

Gus grabs the sleeve of my coat, pulling me to a halt. "You're nothing like that piece of shit, Cap. *Nothing.* You got a good arm from him, and that is it. You care about other people, not just yourself, and your dad never did."

I shake my head. "He did. He loved Skylar. He let it all fall apart after losing her, you know?"

There's so much pity on my best friend's face. It makes me feel sick. The contents of my stomach are spinning like a washing machine.

I pull my arm away and continue walking. Gus does too.

"I'm always here to talk, Cap," he tells me quietly. "I know it all sucks and nothing I say will fix it, but I'm always here."

"I know," I say thickly. "Thank you."

We walk another ten minutes, past the library and Dunkin' and the gas station.

"I did like her. She was … it was different."

Out of the corner of my eye, I see Gus has turned his head to look at me.

Before he can say anything, I add, "I don't want to talk about it. Just … yeah, you were right."

"I'm sorry, man."

"S'okay," I slur. "Was never gonna work out."

We walk another block.

"Want me to come in with you?" Gus asks once we reach our neighborhood.

I shake my head, glancing at my house and noting the light on in a downstairs window. I don't know how Mom can sleep in that room. She doesn't, I guess.

"What time is it?"

Gus checks his phone. "Little after two."

I sigh. "Happy New Year."

"Drink some water, Cap," he calls after me.

I wave a hand, acknowledging the suggestion, as I head up the front walk. The door is unlocked, so I don't have to locate my key.

It swings open before I have a chance to push, my mom jumping back with a startled, "Oh," as I enter the front hall.

I shut the door against the cold air sneaking inside, and she flinches. It's dark and late, and I suddenly feel like I'm being suffocated by ghosts. How many times did she intercept Dad here while I slept down the hall, oblivious?

"I'm not gonna break anything," I tell her.

She frowns, assessing my disheveled state. "Of course you're not, Sawyer."

I laugh darkly, resting my head back against the door. "You sure? I'm half him after all."

"You're *drunk*, is what you are." Her voice is full of recrimination.

"Yep." I pop the *P* obnoxiously.

Mom's face softens. "Did someone say something to you about ..."

"No one has to *say* anything, Mom. They all know. Everyone fucking knows! How can you stand to stay in this town? In this house? You can't, right? That's why you're always gone, leaving me here."

"It is my job, Sawyer. I am doing the best I can to hold things together. You want to leave your friends? The marina? The house where your sister lived? Start over somewhere else? If that's what you want, what you really want, tell me, and I'll call a realtor tomorrow."

I close my eyes. "I don't know what I want."

"Go to bed, Sawyer. We can talk tomorrow."

I open my eyes in time to see her turn toward the kitchen. "Why didn't you tell me, Mom?"

Mom stills. "It wasn't something I ever wanted you to know, Sawyer. Do you know how humiliating it would have been to tell my son something so ugly about his father?"

"More humiliating than me finding out with everyone else?"

"I never thought that would happen, honey. I got blindsided too."

I blow out a long breath. "I hate him. I really, really hate him. He fucked up *everything*, even worse than it already was."

"I know."

I shove away from the door, slipping off my shoes and hanging up my jacket.

"Hey." Mom walks closer.

She's not short, but I tower over her. I inherited Dad's height. I might even have a couple of inches on him by now.

"We will get through this, Sawyer, you and me. Okay?"

I nod, too tired to summon more of a response.

Her worried eyes scan my face. "I'll see if I can change some trips—"

"No. Don't change your schedule. I'm hardly ever here anyway."

She sighs. "We can discuss it more when you're sober. Tell me how you're feeling all the time, not just drunk in the middle of the night, yeah?"

I nod again, even though I probably won't. I already said too much tonight.

Mom reaches up, brushing some hair off my forehead. "I love you, Sawyer."

"I love you too," I say, then start down the hallway.

"No more drinking!" she calls after me.

"I'll drink less."

"I mean it, Sawyer. Or Uncle Carl will be coming to stay with you whenever I'm out of town."

I grimace. My mom's older brother lives in the same town Mom grew up in. He works remotely in some software job, and he has three cats that he brings every time he visits, which has thankfully not been frequently.

"And have some water before bed. I need your help taking down the Christmas lights tomorrow, and I don't want to hear you complaining about your hangover all day."

"I will."

I swerve into the bathroom, down about a gallon of water straight from the tap, strip off my clothes, and then face-plant on my bed in my boxers, sinking into a sweet oblivion where nothing that happened earlier exists.

CHAPTER 15

Wren

The guy groans, "God, you're so hot."

I don't return the compliment. He's cute, but I doubt I could pick him out of a lineup. He's a sophomore in college, visiting friends at Columbia this weekend. I stopped paying attention after that, so I can't recall where he goes to school or where he's from originally. He is taller than me in heels, wears a Rolex, and hasn't mentioned a stock portfolio or fraternity once. We wound up on the dance floor after he bought me a drink. I was the one who suggested coming in here, and he looked like he'd won the lottery, which was flattering.

He didn't drawl that this wouldn't be what I was used to. He opened the door for me on the way in here. He's been respectful and very obviously interested, and there must be something seriously wrong with me—because I sort of hate it. I can't even remember his name, and I think he mentioned it multiple times.

I guide his hand to my thigh, and he gets the hint, slipping under the hem and then starting to finger me. It's not an easy glide. We both realize the truth—I'm not turned on.

He chuckles awkwardly. "Guess I have more work to do."

His other hand migrates to my left boob, like that's a magical button that will immediately get me wet.

"Kiss me," I suggest, and he complies, but it doesn't help.

Rather than getting lost in sensation, I'm too aware of everything. The rasp of my dress rubbing skin as he grinds against me. The pinch in my pinkie toes as my feet protest standing in my heels after an hour of dancing. The distant thump of the bass, muffled through the wall. It sounds like a giant heartbeat. Like my heartbeat, steady and slow and … bored.

I'm bored, kissing him. There are no tingles. No butterflies. And definitely no orgasm, even though he's rubbing between my thighs again.

He's hard, his erection pressed against my hip, and that's disappointing too. I'm jealous of his obvious arousal. I wish I were experiencing it. But I'm not. I'm really not. It's getting worse actually, like there's a set amount of lust allotted between us and his enthusiasm is shorting my share.

"Stop," I say, but it's muffled against his eager mouth.

A heavy dose of panic and adrenaline streams through my veins, chilling my blood. I fight to stay present, stay here, forcing my hands between our bodies and shoving his chest hard.

"Stop!" This time, my airway is clear. My shout echoes off the dark green tiles covering the walls. I hate the loud, scared sound. "I—too many martinis. I'm going to throw up."

I mime gagging, and the guy takes another step away, so rapidly that he nearly trips.

I almost laugh.

"I'll, uh, I'll let you deal with that," he says quickly.

"And then you'll be back, right?" I flutter my eyelashes, glancing at the bulge of his crotch. It's not that impressive, but maybe he's not fully hard yet. At worst, it'll hurt less.

Something I hate more than my weak yell? Sawyer Bennett's huge, beautiful dick. I'd rather drink cheap vodka, *then* upgrade to premium champagne. I don't want to compare other guys to him. Yet it's all I've done since we met last summer.

I thought the prospect of fucking me post-vomit would be the final nail in this failed attempt at a hookup.

Instead, the guy nods, shoving his phone in my direction eagerly. "Text me."

I clap a hand over my mouth, groaning.

"Er, just find me out there. I'll be by the bar." He backs away slowly. Faster as I beeline toward the toilet.

I hear the door open, then close, and I halt, spinning on one heel to head for the sink. Second-guess, detouring to flip the lock on the door in case he realizes ditching me in my moment of need isn't the best strategy to get laid.

Without warning, my mind fixates on being carried to a truck tailgate. To the warm press of slick skin and salty air and the absolute certainty I would be fine. Sawyer took care of me without a single grimace or complaint.

I slip my right foot out of one Prada slingback, twisting my foot and staring at the white line by my heel.

It's the only scar I have. It'd probably be my favorite, even if I had dozens.

Sawyer would have stayed to watch me vomit. If I *were* sick. I'm sure of that, despite the careless way he dismissed me on New Year's Eve. The same way he'd jumped after me. The same way he had taken care of me when I got injured.

I think that's why he's lingered in my head the past three months. Because he hurt me, but I'm not sure he meant to. I was a fling for a guy who never wanted more than that. He didn't want me to get too attached while he was still floating free. Some small part of me respects him for being honest. Most guys would have agreed in the moment and then ghosted later.

I wash my hands, dry them with one of the plush towels from the basket, and release a long exhale while staring at my reflection in the gilded mirror.

I look good. I put extra effort into my appearance tonight. But I don't look happy.

I was so sure I could do this, and I was wrong. Not because I was scared to be alone with a guy, but because that guy wasn't Sawyer. He was supposed to help fix what Third had damaged. Instead, I feel more broken than before.

My flawless makeup doesn't make me miss him less.

While I was styling my hair, I kept glancing at the drawer I kept all of his letters stashed in.

As I was selecting my outfit, I was thinking about all the different dresses I could have worn the night of his friend's party. I'd only packed a few for that long weekend, my options far more limited than with access to my entire closet. There are others I wish he'd seen me wear.

I toss the towel in the hamper, fix a smile on my face—glancing in the mirror to confirm it appears unbothered—and then walk out of the restroom.

"*Finally.*" The woman waiting in line hurries inside past me.

I stride toward the nearest exit, pulling my phone out of my clutch and texting my friends, letting them know I'm leaving. Then message my driver, Miles, letting him know too. There's no sign of the guy I was with earlier, and I'm relieved. Hopefully, he found someone else to have a considerate one-night stand with.

I retrieve my faux-fur jacket from the coat check and continue out onto the sidewalk. My upper half is warm, but my bare legs are already numb from the cold. It's so unfair that guys' outfits are weather-appropriate this time of year while wearing a dress requires freezing. I should have stayed inside until my car pulled up, but I'm breathing easier in the brisk air.

I pull my phone out again as a distraction, ignoring the replies from my friends, and search Sawyer's address. I don't know what I'm looking for—a photo of his house? proof he exists?—but the fourth result is unexpected. A phone number. I tap it and raise my phone to my ear, fully expecting a *this number is no longer in service* recording.

Someone picks up, which is a surprise.

But that's nothing compared to the shock of recognizing the voice that says, "Hello?"

I sway in my heels, too stunned to speak. My mouth has forgotten how to form words, and my throat feels too tight for any to exit anyway. It's so bizarre, hearing Sawyer's voice on a busy sidewalk outside a club when I've only ever heard it in the Hamptons.

"Hi," slips out.

Immediately, I regret it. I should have just hung up as soon as he answered. How can I explain this without sounding insane? *Sorry, I accidentally called you while looking up your address. My bad.*

He never gave me his number, and I'm sure he's happy about that now. I've now shown up at his work without being invited and randomly called his home phone like a deranged stalker.

Seconds of silence pass as I frantically try to decide what to do next.

Just when I'm about to hang up and hope he doesn't bother to look up this number, he asks, "Is everything okay, Wren?"

He recognized my voice from a single syllable.

I'm abruptly furious about that. Never mind that I wouldn't know that if I hadn't called him.

"Yeah. You?"

I miss him. Not just sex—although I haven't forgotten how incredible it felt and am very disappointed tonight didn't include that high. I miss his letters. I miss hearing about his life. I wanted more, from him, and I wound up with nothing.

"I'm fine," he replies.

A familiar SUV pulls up to the curb. I hold a finger up to the driver, letting Miles know I see him.

"Good."

I can't think of anything else to say. Nothing funny or witty or cutting. I want closure, and I have no clue how to get it.

"You bored?" His voice has changed. There's a lilt to it, a taunt, and I seize the challenge.

"Hardly," I say loftily. "I'm at Proof." The name of the exclusive club would impress most people I know. But I realize it likely won't mean anything to Sawyer, so I add, "With my boyfriend."

There's a pause that allots plenty of time to regret the lie that just left my mouth.

"That's why you called? To tell me you're dating some douche?" He sounds amused. Distant and detached.

I'm relieved. At least, I tell myself I'm relieved, that his disinterest is exactly what I needed to hear. That's the reason I made this call—

because I wanted him to know that I don't care either. That I don't care that he doesn't want me. That I don't care that he exists, nearby and out of reach.

"He's not a douche."

"You left him to call me. He's a douche."

I inhale sharply. He doesn't even exist, but I'm offended on my boyfriend's behalf. Irritated on mine because he couldn't just say, *Good for you*, or some meaningless bullshit like that.

"I really called to thank you," I say. "You were right, on New Year's, about us. If we'd continued our … whatever, I wouldn't have met"—a bus with a sneaker ad on the side rumbles past—"Jordan."

"Bye, Wren." Sawyer hangs up.

I lower my phone, staring at the time—12:01.

Happy birthday to me.

Two weeks after my eighteenth birthday, Mom lets me know she accepted a project in Montauk. My parents already rented a house near Scarlett and Crew's.

Meaning I'm expected to spend the summer in the Hamptons.

CHAPTER 16

MAY

At first, I think I'm hallucinating. I see Skylar sometimes, which makes me sound crazy. But in those moments, I don't forget that my sister is dead. I know that seeing her is an anomaly. A mirage that will fade and no reality can replace.

Wren, sitting on my secret beach, isn't as easy of an image to shake. Because it could be a hallucination, or it could be real, and the only way to find out for sure is to talk to the seated form. She's wearing a fancy, full-length dress, most of the fabric strewn across the sand. That's the most compelling evidence this is really happening—I doubt my imagination could conjure the design details of her dress.

Still, I walk slowly down the beach, blinking rapidly, expecting her to disappear at any second.

If it wasn't for the salt-saturated air sticking to my skin, the constant crash of surf against shore, the breeze playing with my hair, I would have

already dismissed this. But those all feel very real, same as every time I walk along this stretch, and Wren is still sitting ahead.

When she glances this way, her eyes that same shade that knocks me senseless every time, I stop hoping—fearing—she'll disappear.

I sink down beside her without saying a word, leaving a good foot of sand between us.

Wren says nothing either. No explanation, no indictment. She turns her head back to the water, staring at the waves again.

I lean back on my palms, burrowing my fingers deep in the sand. In the summer, it's a relief. The sun warms the top layer to a temperature that's almost painful to touch, so digging deep enough means more comfort. This time of year, it makes no difference. The sun never came out today. All the sand feels the same.

"Tonight was my senior prom."

I don't look over at her. I fix my eyes on the horizon, too, pretending we're not close enough that I could reach out and touch her. "That's not how you dress every Friday night?"

"I mean, most."

I *almost* smile. "Bad DJ?"

"There was a band. I left before the dancing."

Out of the corner of my eye, I watch her pull her knees tight to her chest. She's probably cold. If I were wearing a hoodie, I'd offer it to her.

"Sophomore year, I started dating this guy. He was new, which never happened at my school. His dad was a hotshot lawyer who transferred to his firm's Manhattan office. Most of the guys I knew, I'd known since kindergarten, which got boring. All the girls had crushes on him, but he only really paid attention to … me." She drops her chin to her knees, still focused on the water.

"He asked me to a school dance—Fall Fling. After, we all went to a friend's to raid her parents' liquor. We ended up alone in a bedroom. I'd said—I'd told him I was ready for sex. But when it was actually going to happen, I panicked. I told him no, and he got … mad. Then super apologetic. Asked what he did wrong, how he could fix it. I left as quickly as I could, told my friends I wasn't feeling well. I didn't tell anyone what had happened because I was embarrassed. I thought he'd be embarrassed.

"I texted him the next morning, saying we were done. He called me. Messaged me incessantly. I blocked his number, but he used an app that kept generating different ones. He started showing up when I was out with friends. They thought I still liked him. They liked him. And he acted so normal all those times. I started wondering if I'd made it all up in my head. Or overreacted. We'd both been drinking that night."

She sucks in a ragged breath.

At some point while she was talking, my fingers curled into fists. I don't remember it happening. But the tendons in my hands are protesting, pulled taut and tight for too long. I ignore them. There's more. I know it, even before Wren continues.

"That spring, I stayed late after tennis practice. I had a big match the next week—I remember I was trying to adjust my backhand. He must have been watching me. He followed me into the locker room when I finished practicing and tried to … force me. Said I owed it to him and … other stuff."

I barely hear her shaky inhale over the sound of blood roaring in my ears.

"A janitor heard me screaming. My parents came to the school. So did his. My dad—I'd never seen him like that. He was going to sue. Call the police. Press charges. And I … I wanted to pretend it'd never happened. Not deal with two years of whispers and gossip and speculation and be the girl who got assaulted for the rest of high school. His dad was an attorney. They would have fought it. Dug up all the messages I'd sent him. Everyone knew we'd dated, had seen me flirting with him.

"He got expelled. His parents said they'd send him to a private treatment facility, get him help. They disappeared overnight, no explanation, and I acted like I had no idea why Third had stopped showing up to school. And then, earlier tonight, I overheard some of the guys saying they'd been talking to him recently. Over video games, I guess, or maybe on social media. And I … I froze. I thought I'd fixed—"

I pull a hand out of the sand. Slowly so I don't startle her, but quickly enough that I can capture her chin and turn it toward me, giving her no choice except to meet my gaze. "There's nothing to *fix*, Wren."

"There is," she whispers. "I'm—I was never good at intimacy, I guess, but now I'm really fucked up."

"It was him, Wren. You did nothing wrong. None of it's your fault."

"What if he hurts someone else?"

"That will also be *his* fault."

"But if I'd pressed charges—"

"As a minor, if he'd been convicted, how much time would he have served? Assuming he had no prior record."

Her mouth twists. "I don't know. Probably not much. He didn't … there wasn't any physical evidence. Just my word against his."

I exhale, trying to release the rage in my body at the same time. It doesn't accomplish much.

Wren sighs, too, running a hand through hair that's tangled in the wind.

"How'd you get here?" I ask. There weren't any other cars when I parked.

"Cab." Her hand falls back to the sand. Her fingers are painted the exact same shade of pink as her prom dress. It's such a small *Wren* detail. "You don't—I didn't know you'd be here. I didn't come here for you to, like, comfort me. I just needed … this was the first place I thought of to get away from everything."

"How long have you been here?"

"What time is it?"

I check my phone. "After midnight."

"About an hour." She sighs. "I'll go to a hotel. I was supposed to spend the night at a friend's—at Gia's. My parents aren't expecting me back until tomorrow afternoon. If I come back early, they'll ask questions."

"Doesn't your family have a house here?"

She shakes her head. "My aunt and uncle do. I doubt anyone has been there since … since New Year's. Who knows what the alarm code is now."

"They paranoid about security?" I joke, not wanting to touch the topic of the last time we saw each other.

"Not really. They were trying to keep me from sneaking out last summer."

She's standing before I can decide how to respond to that comment. Does her family know about me? How strongly do they disapprove? Strongly, I'm assuming, if they were essentially locking her in.

Wren reaches down to pick up a bag I didn't notice in the sand, glancing over as I climb to my feet too.

"Let me give you a ride," I say.

"Why?" She faces me, handle clutched between both hands.

"Why should you let me?"

"Why are you offering?"

I shove my hands into my pockets. "I want to."

She holds my gaze for a few seconds, then shakes her head.

There's this weird dip of disappointment in my stomach, followed by a pinch in my chest that only eases when she adds a sighed, "Okay."

I scratch my jaw, hoping my hand will hide how relieved I am, then jerk my chin left. "My truck's there."

It's a stupid comment. Wren knows what my truck looks like. Even if she didn't, there's only one vehicle in sight.

I forgot how fucking nervous Wren Kensington makes me. How she evaporates all the ease that usually inhabits my body, strips me down to second-guessing, and spins me around in circles.

She glances where I nodded. I catch the tiny divot in her cheek, the indicator that her next words are going to be a tease before, "Almost missed it," leaves her mouth.

I roll my eyes, at myself more than her, then head that way. Wren follows, tossing her undoubtedly expensive bag into the bed of my truck without a second glance to check where it landed.

That's one thing about Wren. I have this strange sense of connection, almost kinship with her, because she's as unpredictable as I am. She'll turn her nose up at a marina's stench, then have sex in a dusty supply room. She'll match her nails to her prom dress, then leave her fancy luggage to fend for itself in the bed of my truck, which has been cleaned … never since I bought it. She'll share a traumatic, terrifying experience, then treat me like a hired driver she's never met before.

Wren texts for most of the trip, the ceaseless buzzing of her phone proof that plenty of people have noticed her absence.

I'm about ten minutes from my house when she glances up and says, "You missed the turn into town about fifty turns ago," making me think she wasn't as absorbed in her phone as she was acting.

"You can stay at my place tonight."

I keep my eyes on the road, ensuring I miss her reaction.

"Won't your parents mind?" Wren asks quietly.

I nearly snort, stifling the sound at the last possible second. "No."

"They're used to you having girls over?"

I brake at a red light, drumming my thumbs against the steering wheel. "My dad is in prison, and my mom won't be back from deployment for another three weeks. They won't mind."

Wren doesn't say, *Sorry*, in the tragic tone people like to use to talk about my family. Or, even worse, ask what crimes my father committed.

Her next question is, "Will Skylar mind?"

I know she's noticed the tattoo on my wrist; I've seen her stare at it. But telling her about my parents was enough. I'm not in the mood—or the right mindset—to discuss my sister.

"What would she mind?" I ask, lifting an eyebrow.

"Nothing," she says quickly.

I want to push her—want Wren to admit that she thought something might happen between us because it always had when we were alone—but I don't.

I feel guilty about letting her believe my dead sister is a girl I can't get over. And my mind is now stuck on a loop of all the things we *could* do when we reach my empty house.

I wonder if Wren is still dating someone. Wonder if he knows she called me while they were out together. Wonder if Wren realized what she did—she was thinking about me, not him, that night. I doubt she called another guy to brag after we fucked. Only unhappy people boast about how happy they are.

Bringing her to my house was supposed to be an altruistic decision. Dumping her off at a hotel, knowing she was upset, didn't feel right. She had a chance to demand I turn around, and she didn't take it. She still hasn't suggested I take her somewhere else. I think, maybe, that means she's glimpsed the partial apology this is meant to be. Somehow, it feels like too much and not enough simultaneously.

Wren clears her throat, and I think *this is it*. Again, my reaction is mixed. Some relief, some disappointment.

But she doesn't direct me to the nearest four-star hotel. She says, "That sucks, about your parents."

I nod so she knows I heard her.

What doesn't suck? The way Wren grasps that I told her that so she knows, not because I wanted to have a conversation about it.

Neither of us says another word the rest of the drive.

CHAPTER 17
Wren

I've pictured what Sawyer's home looks like an embarrassing number of times. When I imagined him sitting and writing me back, it wasn't in a house terribly different from this one. The interior is more spacious than the exterior suggested, extra rooms jutting off from the back that aren't visible from the street. The total silence, the encompassing emptiness, makes the space seem larger too.

I follow Sawyer down a narrow hallway, swallowing all the questions I doubt he'd answer. The house—white walls, worn hardwood floors, small rooms—might be typical to most people not born with the last name Kensington, but I think the quiet would be abnormal to anyone. When I thought about him writing me, I assumed siblings were barging into his room. That his mom was cooking dinner and his dad was in the yard, raking leaves. All those stereotypes I've never experienced. Rory is too principled to invade my privacy. Mom cooks occasionally, but our private chef manages most meals. And our penthouse doesn't have a yard for Dad to maintain, just a private terrace.

Sawyer shoves the door at the end of the hallway open, entering what I'm assuming is his room.

I glance around at the three other doors. Two are closed. One is open, the shadowed outline of a sink and toilet barely visible.

When I walk into his room, Sawyer is yanking the comforter off the mattress.

I drop my bag next to his desk, the *thud* announcing my presence.

He says nothing though, until I ask, "What are you doing?"

"Changing the sheets."

"You don't have to do that," I say, actually meaning it.

Sleeping on someone else's sheets would normally bother me. But it doesn't bother me with Sawyer. We've had sex. He knows about Third. Lying on the same fabric he has doesn't seem so intimate by comparison.

"It's fine. There's a clean set in the closet. It won't take long." He balls up the linens, heads into the hallway, then returns with a folded set.

"Can I help?"

He glances at me. Smirks, and my stomach pitches like the floor is tilting. "Is this your first time?"

My breath keeps getting caught in my chest, making a regular rhythm impossible. "It can't be that hard to figure out."

His grin widens while I hunt for a corner. "It is. Damn. Wonder how many times I can take your virginity, Kensington."

I pause sorting through the sheets so I can flip him off. "Don't flatter yourself, Bennett."

"I don't have to," he says, rounding the foot of the bed and coming up behind me. I stiffen as he reaches for the pile on the mattress. "You keep doing it for me."

I scowl, even though he can't see my expression, watching him quickly find a corner. Our housekeeper, Martha, changes the sheets once a week. I make my bed every morning—I'm not *that* spoiled—but I'm guessing Sawyer will laugh if I say so. And he probably should.

"Once you finish the fitted sheet, the pillowcases go on." Sawyer narrates his actions, visibly entertained by himself, while I watch with my arms crossed. "Last, the top sheet. Pull it up here, tuck here and here, and then you fold the ends like this." He demonstrates.

It's a more complex process than I would have assumed, almost like origami.

"Can't you, you know, just do this?" I make a shoving motion with my hands.

"Sure, if you want them to fall out." He nods toward the other corner. "You do that one."

At no point in my life did I ever think I'd be spending my senior prom night—historically when I planned I'd have sex for the first time— with the guy I did have sex with for the first time while he taught me how to properly tuck sheets. I'm going to have to check under the comforter when I get home to see if Martha uses the same fancy folding method. I'm probably going to check every bed I sleep in from now on and think of Sawyer fucking Bennett every damn time.

My edges aren't as crisp as his, but the overhanging sheet doesn't fall back out after I jam it under the mattress, so I consider it a success. "You can sleep on that side," I say, nodding toward the corner he did. "In case mine falls out."

Rather than laugh or make fun, Sawyer sobers. "I'll take the couch," he tells me.

"Oh." Sleeping in bed with a guy would normally freak me out. I never have before. But I'm disappointed more than anything. And I feel guilty for putting him out. "You don't—I'll take the couch."

That makes him grin. "You'd last five minutes."

Most of the time, I enjoy being accommodated. Prioritized. My last name means I get waved to the front of lines. Served first. Told yes when others would get told no.

But I do not like Sawyer seeing me as spoiled and helpless, and I think he might.

"No, that was you," I say sweetly.

The amusement remains on his face, but it transforms. Smolders, sending a shiver down my spine.

"Wouldn't your boyfriend mind?"

It takes me several seconds to realize what he's talking about. I suppressed that humiliating phone call as deep as possible. Plus, I feel drugged, even though I left Manhattan totally sober. I'm drunk on him, on sudden exposure to an addiction that elicits bouts of insanity—like lying about dating someone so I seem less pathetic. Which is, undoubtedly, way *more* pathetic.

"I don't have a boyfriend," I tell him. "And I"—I hate apologizing, but I owe him this one—"I shouldn't have called you that night. It was … I'm sorry."

I almost add that it was a lie. But that would be even more mortifying. Not to mention ruining everything calling him was supposed to accomplish.

I want Sawyer to think I'm over him. That I'm unaffected by being in his room, by the prospect of sleeping in his bed. That this is just another Friday night to me.

"It's fine." He heads for the door. "Glad you had fun."

I scoff, but he's already in the hallway, so I'm not sure he hears me.

I walk over to his desk, picking up and unzipping the bag I packed for the after-party. I thought, at some point, I'd regret missing most of the evening I'd planned meticulously, but it still doesn't hit as I unpack.

I set my toiletry bag on Sawyer's desk, pulling out both sets of pajamas as I debate which to wear. I'm not sure if Sawyer is coming back or if he's taken up residence on the couch.

And I don't care, I tell myself sternly.

I'll leave tomorrow morning, spend as little time as possible in the Hamptons all summer, and fly to LA at the end of August.

I settle on the pink silk pair, toss the blue set back, and then reach for my overstuffed toiletry bag. My hand slows midair, my attention caught on the edge of an envelope holding the top desk drawer open an inch. I look over my shoulder. No sign of Sawyer in the doorway. So, I slide the drawer open carefully, heart somersaulting with the realization that he kept my letters. One of them at least.

It's not until I slide the envelope out and see the neatly typed address that I realize this letter isn't from me. My heart stills, but curiosity builds. The letter is from Cornell University. And it's open, so I don't think it's illegal to read the contents of mail addressed to someone else without their permission. Just extremely unethical.

I'm too intrigued to care. I peer inside and scan the lines of text quickly, aware I could get caught at any second. If I'm going to get busted, I at least want to know what I'm looking at. After his address and a generic greeting, it reads:

Congratulations on your outstanding academic success!

Using information obtained from college testing services, the admissions office at Cornell has identified you as a student who may be an excellent candidate for our institution. Your strong performance on the SAT demonstrates a high level of academic potential and the kind of intellectual curiosity we look for in prospective students.

We encourage you to consider Cornell as you begin your college search. Our university offers a vibrant academic community and unique opportunities—

I stop reading, stuffing the letter back in its envelope. There are more envelopes under the first one. Hastily, I peek in another. This one begins with:

Dear Sawyer,

My name is Dean Martin and I am the head baseball coach at Vanderbilt University. I am writing to express our interest in—

I glance up, thinking I heard a creak in the hallway, and my gaze snags on a poster attached to the back of the bedroom door. It's of a player captured mid-pitch.

I flip through a few more envelopes. The return addresses include nearly every school my classmates are expecting their parents to buy their way into.

As carefully as I can, I replace the envelopes where I found them and head into the bathroom with my toiletry bag.

While I run through my ten-step skin-care routine, I speculate. Why isn't Sawyer going to college? He never offered any explanation in his letters. Money must be the reason? I'm not well versed in scholarships or how financial aid works, but I know both exist. College is considered expensive to plenty of people, but they find ways to make it work. If Sawyer is smart enough to ace a standardized test to the extent that schools with single-digit acceptance rates are recruiting him, he could figure it out. So, why?

Not my problem. And not something I can ask him about without admitting I was snooping.

I finish in the bathroom and return to the bedroom. Still empty, no sign of Sawyer. I drape my prom dress over the back of his desk chair, casting one last curious look at the drawer where I discovered the college letters, then flip out the lights and climb into bed. The mattress is comfortable. The sheets aren't too stiff or too soft, infused with the familiar fragrance of detergent. There's a masculine undertone that I can taste in the back of my throat. A relentless reminder of where I am, coupled with the unfamiliar soundtrack of silence that never exists in bustling Manhattan.

I'm wide awake when the door opens, hinges squeaking softly.

I recognize his outline. His steady breathing. And it's so much more intimate than remembering someone's eye color or an outfit they wore.

"I lasted longer than five minutes," he says, flipping the comforter back and then flopping down beside me.

"If you say so," I tell him pertly.

Sawyer sighs, but I think I hear a trace of laughter.

It's weird—good weird—having him in bed with me. Rather than be stifled by the close proximity, I feel secure. His body heat is bleeding into my side of the bed, the warmth relaxing my muscles and making me feel sleepy. I can hear his even exhales rather than the haunting quiet when I was alone.

A small part of me—okay, a large part—is tempted to roll over. To kiss him and run a hand down his abs and into his boxers and see how he reacts. To beg him for a final time, one that's not rushed. That includes a bed, not a hard wall or a cramped truck or a dusty shelf. To fulfill one part of my prom fantasy.

But I'm not brave enough to set myself up for rejection again. Or as cavalier as I'm trying to act. I'll fall a little more if I literally let him in, and I should be clawing my way back to casual. He doesn't know my family is spending the summer here, and while our paths are unlikely to cross, they could. If we see each other, I don't want it to be weird.

"Can I ask you something?"

"Sure." He's tense beside me, awareness thrumming beneath the tucked sheets. It doesn't feel like my side has fallen out yet, so I must have done something semi-right.

"What branch of the military is your mom in?"

Sawyer relaxes. That's not a question he was concerned about answering. "Coast Guard."

"Is that why you 'like boats'?"

"It probably factored."

I roll onto my stomach, tucking both hands under my pillow. "Good night, Sawyer."

"Night, Wren."

It's the fastest I've ever fallen asleep.

CHAPTER 18

Wren

When I wake up, I'm alone in bed. I sit up, stretch, and look around for a clock. Nothing. Once I'm out of bed, I hunt down my phone. It's 9:09 a.m.

I do a quick scan of my notifications, confirming they're complaints about my disappearance and nothing urgent. Then tiptoe into the bathroom to run through my eight-step morning routine.

I doubt it was his intention, but I'm glad Sawyer gave me a chance to brush my hair and teeth before facing him. Yes, I'm that vain.

Back in the bedroom, I change into the outfit I packed for what was supposed to be brunch at my favorite spot in Greenwich Village. Then I follow the sound of sizzling oil into the kitchen.

Sawyer's standing at the stove, shirtless. He's barefoot, too, wearing nothing except a pair of gray sweatpants, slung so low that I'm concerned—hopeful—they won't stay up, and a backward baseball hat.

I hate him. I really, really do. It should be illegal to look that good.

He glances up, catches me staring at his six-pack, and grins.

"Morning, sunshine."

I grunt. "Do you have coffee?"

"Help yourself." He nods toward a bag on the counter. "I'd love a cup too."

Another test, I realize, when his smile stays fixed in place. I'm guessing he doesn't have an espresso machine that makes a cappuccino with the press of a button.

I step into the kitchen, rolling the sleeves of my Chanel blouse up. I pick up the bag he nodded toward, scanning the text on the back and hoping they're instructions.

"You're a coffee-making virgin too?" His voice is thick with feigned surprise.

I flip him off with my free hand, a low chuckle confirming he caught it.

The front door opens, then slams closed, followed by a voice I'm surprised sounds familiar. "Cap!"

Sawyer sighs, glancing at me. "Watch the eggs?"

I focus on the pan. "Uh … like, actually just look at them, or do I—"

"Why aren't you replying to my texts—oh. Shit. Hi." A guy with shaggy blond hair has appeared in the doorway, head rotating rapidly between me and Sawyer.

Gus. I come up with his name, pretty proud of myself for recalling. "Hi, Gus."

"Hey, Wren. Hey." His gaze is still bouncing between me and Sawyer. He doesn't seem to know what to make of my presence.

I have no idea what Sawyer has shared about us with his friends. Not much, it seems. Not that there is—or was—an us.

"Nice knocking," Sawyer comments, measuring ground coffee.

Gus rubs the back of his neck. "Well, you're never …" His voice trails, leaving me even more confused. Never *what*? "Okay, I should, um, just call me when—"

"What's taking forever?" A woman's voice echoes down the hallway. Both Sawyer and Gus stiffen.

"Seriously?" Sawyer snaps.

Gus gestures helplessly. "I had no idea, Cap."

I'm focused on the doorway, waiting for the woman to appear. Is this Skylar? If so, how awkward will this get? Nothing happened last night, which I'll happily testify to, but I'd be pissed about him spending the night in bed with anyone else if we were together.

It's not Skylar.

I know because I recognize Cammie right away. She's cut her hair into a long bob that barely brushes her shoulders, and she's wearing some makeup, but the frown when she spots me? Identical to the annoyed expression I've seen several times before.

I smile at her, then sniff, glancing at the pan of eggs. "Sawyer, what am I—"

"Stir," he says, ambling over. He sticks a spatula in my hand. "Just move them around so they don't burn."

"Cute," Cammie comments as he returns to the coffee. "I didn't know you were offering cooking lessons now, Cap."

"I didn't know you were finished with finals," he replies.

"Last one was yesterday afternoon. Texted you to meet us at Lucky's, but you never answered. You were busy, apparently."

Is Lucky another nickname? I don't ask the question aloud. I'm the outlier here. Gus likes me—I think—but Cammie definitely doesn't. My best strategy seems to be to keep my mouth shut and let Sawyer handle his friends.

Except he says nothing, too, so the awkward silence in the kitchen just expands.

"We'll catch up lat—" Gus starts.

Only to be interrupted by Cammie's, "I'd love some coffee."

"It's not ready yet," Sawyer says.

"We can wait," Cammie says, propping a hip against the counter.

Behind her, Gus sighs.

"You can finish making it, then," Sawyer tells her, walking over to me and taking over the eggs. "I'll bring them over when they're ready," he adds quietly.

"Thanks," I reply, heading for the kitchen table and taking a seat.

"So, how've you been, Wren?" Gus asks, joining me.

"Good, thanks. You?"

"Great. Only a few weeks left of high school. And then all summer at the marina. When do you graduate?"

"Next weekend. You?"

"Two weeks."

I nod. "Nice."

I don't know Gus very well. It's been almost a year since we talked at Wade's party, and that was mostly me fishing for information about Sawyer. He's Sawyer's best friend, and I want him to like me for that reason alone. But I'm unusually shy. Entirely out of my element.

"Here you go." Sawyer sets a steaming plate of eggs down in front of me, then takes the seat next to me.

His knee bumps my thigh, and his arm brushes mine, and I forget for a few seconds that we're not alone.

Cammie loudly setting a pot of coffee and some mugs on the table is an unwelcome reminder.

"So," she says, pouring herself a cup and then taking the last remaining seat, "I had no idea outsiders remembered this place existed before Memorial Day."

Gus sighs.

I reach for the pot, pouring myself a cup too. I've never drunk coffee black before, but I'm not about to ask for vanilla creamer.

"Your hair looks nice, Cammie. I've been thinking about cutting mine shorter for summer." I stab some eggs, taking a big bite.

Cammie stares at me. Unsure if I'm messing with her, I guess. "Thanks," she finally mutters, leaning back in her chair.

Gus jumps in. "We were thinking Hither Hills today."

Beside me, Sawyer perks up. "Yeah?"

Gus nods. "Guys said they were all in for hiking last night, but no one was answering phones yet. You were the first stop, and then we were planning to pick up everyone else. Cammie's got her Suburban."

"Want to come, Wren?" Cammie asks sweetly. "It's only eight miles."

"Sounds fun, but shopping is my only cardio. What's the point of exercising, really, if you don't get cute clothes out of it?" I aim my best ditzy smile at her, then swallow a huge gulp of coffee. It tastes awful on its own.

I tried to be nice. This is me being nice. But Cammie *really* does not like me, and I don't think anything I say is going to shift her opinion of me at this point.

"That's one way to look at it," Cammie comments.

I finish my breakfast in silence while Gus and Sawyer talk about a dock project at the marina. I didn't realize they'd already started prep for the summer, but I suppose it makes sense. Summer isn't that far away, which means I need to commit to a plan. Either stay here with my parents or make other arrangements. Following my catastrophic last visit, I couldn't imagine spending any more time here than absolutely necessary. Now … after last night … I'm conflicted. I could have Apollo, my mare, trailered to a barn here. Play tennis at the club. Maybe even get a summer job. I have limited access to my trust fund now that I'm eighteen, but earning my own money is appealing. It would be a different, final summer before heading to college.

"I should get going," I say during a lull in the conversation.

Cammie looks thrilled. Gus, unsure. Sawyer? I can't get a read. He just nods, reaching for my empty plate.

"Thanks for breakfast," I add awkwardly.

He nods again.

I stand and head down the hallway, releasing a sigh of relief when I'm out of earshot from the low voices that are no doubt discussing me.

It doesn't take me long to grab all my stuff. The hardest task is folding up my prom dress, but I manage to fit it in my bag, along with everything else. My gaze sweeps around the room, and I tell myself it's to make sure I'm not forgetting anything. But really, I'm trying to memorize this space. The odds I'm ever back in Sawyer Bennett's bedroom seem extremely low.

I order a car—the nearest is five minutes away—then walk back down the hallway. I can hear the clatter of dishes and rumble of laughter. I should have offered to help clean up. I would have, if it didn't feel like every action was being scrutinized under a microscope. Even Gus's friendliness didn't manage to hide how unexpected my presence was. I don't belong here.

I poke my head inside the kitchen, and all commotion comes to a screeching halt. If I had a pin, I could hear it drop.

"I'm headed out," I say, keeping my voice cheery. "Bye, Gus. Cammie."

I glance at Sawyer last. He's drying his hands with a towel.

"I'll walk you out," he says, and I nod.

"Bye, Wren," Gus calls after me.

Cammie, unsurprisingly, says nothing.

Sawyer is silent, too, following me out onto the front porch.

It's not that warm yet, but it's turning into a beautiful day. There's not a single cloud in the clear sky overhead. Birds chirp, flitting from spot to spot on the lush grass.

"Nice weather for hiking," I comment.

"Yeah." Sawyer props a hip against the railing, studying me. "I know Cammie was being … you could come with us, if you want."

For a few seconds, I allow myself to picture it. Most of my time around friends is spent shopping, sneaking alcohol, or talking about boys. I don't have friends who go hiking on a Saturday morning. Or who want nothing from me except my company. They expect me to have exclusive, unlimited access to everything, and that's part of the appeal of my friendship. That's simply my life, and there are so many upsides that it feels silly to complain about the pitfalls.

"I can't," I say. "I've got to get home, and I—well, I'm not much of a hiker."

"Okay."

I can't tell if he's indifferent or happy or bothered that I turned down his invitation.

"I never know what you're thinking," I blurt.

One corner of his mouth lifts a centimeter. I pay close attention to his micro-expressions and still can't tell what he's thinking.

"You can read other people's minds?"

I roll my eyes. "Of course not. But I'm better at … I can guess at least. You're really hard to read."

"You want to know what I'm thinking?"

"Yes?" I say cautiously because he's maybe the one person outside of my family who's never tried to flatter me for some personal gain. Cammie is on that list too, I guess. Unfortunately.

"Don't cut your hair."

"What?" I blink rapidly, like that will clear my ears from anything making me mishear.

"It looks good long. Don't cut it."

I wasn't sure he was even paying attention at breakfast when I complimented Cammie's bob. And I certainly wasn't expecting him to have an opinion on my hair's length. If any other guy said that to me, I'd probably trim it out of spite.

"I'll, uh—thanks."

He smirks.

I'm *good* at flirting. I've successfully flirted with Sawyer. But right now, I can't think of a single worthwhile, much less remotely seductive, thing to say.

My phone buzzes right as a black SUV pulls up alongside the curb.

Sawyer glances at it too.

"My ride," I say unnecessarily.

I was planning to mention I might be in the Hamptons this summer, gauge his reaction to the possibility. But I can't think of a casual way to bring it up, and I'm out of time.

I clear my throat. "Thank you. For … for everything. Really. I'm— last night was the last time I'll bother you with anything."

He doesn't say it wasn't a bother. He doesn't say he enjoyed our sleepover. He just nods.

I force a smile, picking up my bag and starting down the front walk toward the waiting car.

"Good luck at UCLA," he calls after me.

I glance back, but his front door is already swinging shut.

It's not until I reach the curb and am greeting my driver that I realize I never told Sawyer where I was going to college.

CHAPTER 19

Sawyer

They're not paying attention. Not a single one and especially not Aaron Gibson, who's been sneaking looks at his phone all morning. Asking him a direct question means a solid ten seconds of him staring at me before providing a wrong answer.

As I'm the most experienced member of the marina staff, training the three new summer hires is my responsibility. Meaning it will reflect badly on me if any of them mess up. I don't care about many things, but one is this job. Since I don't have any plans, past working here ending, it's pretty much all I care about at the moment.

"What did I just say?" I question.

All three jump, and Aaron nearly drops his phone.

One raises his hand tentatively. "Make sure fueling happens first?"

"Before fueling. A renter returns a boat, and you …"

Three blank looks.

I swear under my breath, then start explaining the process all over again.

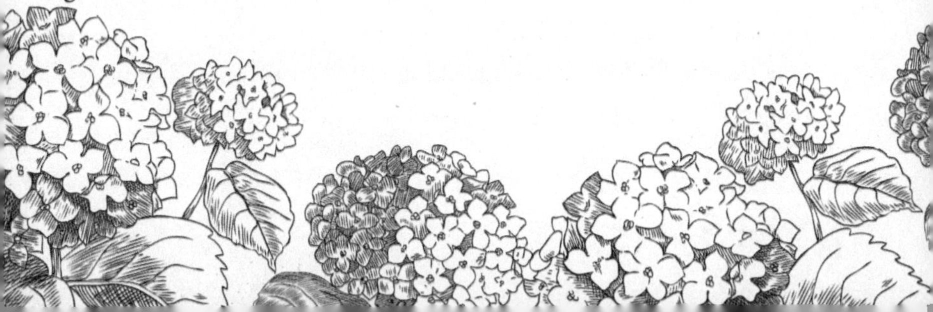

By the time lunch rolls around, I'm exhausted. I dismiss the guys for their allotted break and walk down to the very end of the main dock so I can stare at the water, unobstructed. I judge most of the wealthy who store boats here, but I'm jealous of all of them. I wish I owned one of these expensive boats so I could climb aboard and sail away. Nothing but sea and sky and peace.

"Rough morning?"

"They're idiots," I inform Gus, who's stopped beside me. "All three of them."

"They're young."

"Aaron is a year older than us," I remind him. "All morning, they've been gossiping about a new waitress. Or on their phones. Or asking pointless questions."

"I assume you've ruled out teaching as a future career path."

"I've ruled out *all* career paths," I remind him.

"No one our age has it figured out, Cap. Going to college isn't any guarantee of a great future."

"Yeah, I know." My stomach rumbles. "Have you eaten lunch yet? I'm starving."

"Uh … about that."

I groan. "Do we have to wait until one for leftovers again? I'm going to tell Dusty that—"

"No, the kitchen is open. I went in there earlier to grab some coffee."

"Great. Thanks for the life update. C'mon." I turn to head for the ramp.

"Wait, Cap. Just … she's here. Wren is the new waitress."

I spin back around. "What?"

Gus shrugs. "I don't know anything else. I just—I saw her when I grabbed coffee. Macie was training her."

Nothing about what Gus is saying makes any sense. But he's not a jokester. He wouldn't make this up.

I huff an incredulous laugh. "Huh."

I haven't seen or spoken to Wren since she left my house last month. I figured that chances were I'd never see her again. And I wasn't thrilled about that, but I accepted it.

Her parents are billionaires. What the fuck is she doing, working for minimum wage?

Gus is studying me cautiously, like I'm a volcano that could erupt at any moment. I've flat-out refused to discuss Wren since New Year's. All I told him and Cammie about Wren's prom night was that she "needed a place to crash." Which also made little sense, but Gus was considerate enough not to push for more of an explanation, and Cammie was happy to never discuss it.

"Let's go," I say, continuing toward the ramp.

Gus trails behind me.

Wade is lounging at my favorite picnic table, the one with a clear view of the lighthouse, scrolling on his phone. Ricky switched to caddying at the country club this summer, which is part of why Dusty hired the three new idiots.

"Hey," Wade says, glancing up as we approach. "Are you calling dibs on Wren Kensington, Cap, or is she fair game?"

Thank fuck for Gus because this would have been a hell of a way to find out she's here.

"Kinda confused where that all landed," Wade continues. "Cammie said she was at your house a few weeks ago?"

I ignore Wade and continue toward the main yacht club building, which contains the restaurant, taking the back stairs up to the second floor, where the kitchen is located. Food for employees gets set out in chafing dishes in a far corner, away from most of the commotion in the main area. White-clad staff is bustling around the prep stations, but I don't see any waitresses.

I pick up a plate to serve myself lunch.

"Hey, Cap!"

I glance over my shoulder. Macie is approaching, a wide smile stretched across her face. She's alone.

"Hey, Macie," I reply. "How's it going?"

"Good! Busy."

I nod.

"How are the new guys working out?"

I grimace, and she laughs.

"Can't relate. The new waitresses are awesome."

"Oh, yeah?" My tone isn't super casual, but Macie's distracted, looking left.

"Wren! Over here."

My stomach swoops. I'm—fuck. Why am I nervous? This is my town. My job. She thinks she can just show up here and—

"Cap, this is Wren. One of the new waitresses."

Wren's smile is polite, but her blue eyes are glinting with amusement. I owe Gus (and Wade, I guess) big-time. If *this* were how I found out Wren was working here, I don't think I'd be able to act this nonchalant. I've seen waitresses wear the same uniform—white polo, navy skirt—for the past four years, and it's never really struck me as a sexy outfit. Wren manages to make it one.

"What's Cap short for?" she asks innocently.

I roll my eyes, uninterested in playing this game. "What are you doing here?"

"Oh." Macie is glancing between us, forehead wrinkled with

confusion. "You guys know each other?"

"Not really," Wren replies.

I say, "Sort of," simultaneously.

Then we stare at each other.

"Did your trust fund run out?"

"Still an asshole, I see."

"Wren!" Wade enters the kitchen. "So good to see you."

"You too, Wade," Wren replies.

So, she finally remembered his name. I scoff under my breath, then turn back toward the food, attempting to tune out the chatter as Gus and then the new hires join in the conversation with the waitresses.

Forgetting Wren exists was a challenge when I wasn't seeing her every day. I doubt constant exposure is going to improve my attempts.

Wren doesn't appear surprised to find me leaning against the bumper of her convertible. She's changed out of her waitressing uniform into a light-blue dress and pulled her hair out of its bun.

She hasn't cut it.

"Need a ride?" she asks, spinning her key ring around one finger. "I owe you one."

I straighten. "What are you doing?"

"Right now? Leaving work."

"What are you doing, working *here*?"

She holds my gaze. "I stopped by last week and saw the restaurant was hiring. I thought it'd be fun to waitress."

"Fun," I repeat flatly.

"I'm here for the summer, so ..."

"You're here for the summer."

"Stop repeating everything I say."

"Start telling me the truth, Wren. This car"—I gesture toward her convertible—"cost more than the membership fee here. We both know you don't need the money. Why aren't you flying around on a private jet or doing whatever else you've done every other summer?"

She crosses her arms. "That's what you think of me? That I'm a spoiled princess who doesn't deign to fly commercial? My *parents* are rich, so I should never get a job?"

I hold her gaze. "You could have worked somewhere else."

"What do you care where I work?"

"I don't. I just—"

"Abby started today too. Are you stopping her next to check why she isn't scooping ice cream or lifeguarding?"

I scowl.

Wren scowls back.

"You could have told me," I say. "We saw each other a few weeks ago, and you didn't mention ..."

"I didn't know what my plans were then. And"—her chin lifts—"I didn't think we were on that sort of basis. Or did I misunderstand our last conversation here?"

She's talking about New Year's Eve. Would I have handled that differently if I'd known she'd be here all of this summer? Probably. I'm just not sure how. I'm never sure around Wren.

"Would be a real pain if I had to update every guy I've hooked up with about every little thing happening in my life," she continues.

I fight another scowl. Of course there have been other guys since me. It's fucking ridiculous that it bothers me. As Wren just pointed out, I was the one who ended whatever we were starting to become.

"You're right," I say, and her eyes momentarily widen with surprise. "Forget I said anything."

Then I straighten and head for my truck.

CHAPTER 20

Wren

Five, four, three, two, one, up!

I rise into two-point position at the perfect moment, shoving my hands higher. The rough gray strands of Apollo's braided mane rasp against my knuckles as she soars over the combination, that addictive dip appearing as we remain airborne for a few thrilling seconds. Hooves hit sand footing as Apollo clears the jump, cantering toward the final crossbar, and I sink back down into the saddle.

We clear the final hurdle with inches to spare, and Alice shouts praise as I tug Apollo to a trot. I've only ridden at this stable a few times before, never spending long enough in the Hamptons to make it a regular recurrence. Apollo arrived yesterday from the Connecticut stable she normally stays at. I figured, if I was going to commit to a summer here, I might as well go all in.

I tug on the reins, and Apollo slows to a walk. I kick my feet out of the stirrups, crossing the leather straps over the saddle's pommel, letting my legs relax and my toes flex.

"All good?" Alice calls.

I flash the head trainer a thumbs-up. She nods, smiles, then heads back into the barn.

I push the brim of my helmet up so I can swipe the sweat off my forehead, then pat Apollo's damp neck. I only get to ride her a couple of days a week at home, and I might not have the chance to come here that much more frequently now that I'm working at the yacht club. I'm still glad that I applied for the waitressing job. I like the other waitresses, and I like the satisfaction of completing a task that has purpose.

I like looking for Sawyer every time I step into the kitchen, although I'd never admit it. This silly fascination with him has lingered for eleven months. Now, surely, it's close to disappearing? Until it does, I've had plenty of practice at pretending it has. He thinks I dated someone else, and most of the other marina guys—particularly Aaron—flirt with me every chance they get. There's no way that Sawyer suspects I'm not over our fling.

Once Apollo has cooled down, I lead her back into the barn, untacking and then deciding to hose her off. I get soaked in the process, too, and one of the grooms graciously offers to turn Apollo out for me. I kiss her muzzle, change into shorts in one of the restrooms off the tack room, and head for my car.

Gia calls as I'm pulling out of the stable's parking lot.

"You're still coming to Leah's, right?"

"Yeah, I—" I check the time on the dash. "I got caught up at the barn. I just have to swing home and change. Twenty minutes. Thirty, tops."

Gia sighs. "Hurry! Everyone's asking where you are."

Dad is outside, fiddling with the sprinkler settings, when I park in front of the house my parents rented for this summer. It's nice, not as big as Scarlett and Crew's, but also located directly on the water. Waking up to views of the ocean didn't take any getting used to.

I climb out of my convertible, and Dad raises his eyebrows, glancing up at the clear sky.

"Passing shower?"

"Apollo needed a bath," I explain. "And I'm late to meet friends, so …" I spin toward the house.

"I had an interesting talk with Hanson Ellsworth earlier," Dad calls after me.

My steps slow.

"He wanted to let me know it was an 'unfortunate look' for my daughter to be staff at a 'preeminent establishment.' "

I wince before spinning to face my father. "What did you say?"

"That it was none of his business how or where you spend your time. If I'd had any idea you were waitressing at the yacht club, I could have come up with a better response."

"I'm sorry," I say. "I was going to tell you."

"Why didn't you?"

"I didn't—I wasn't sure what you and Mom would think."

Dad exhales, walking past me and taking a seat in one of the rocking chairs that line the front porch. After a moment of hesitation, I do too.

"What made you decide to work there?"

"I don't like that people might see me as … helpless. As inept because we have so much money and because of all the advantages that go along with that. It's one thing back home, where all my friends have similar backgrounds. Or when I was younger. But as an adult, heading to college in the fall? I don't want to be the sheltered rich girl who has never changed her sheets or ridden in an older car or cooked for herself. I figured this summer was my last chance to change that, so I'm trying to … branch out. I didn't want you or Mom to think I was ungrateful, or—"

"We would have been proud, Wren. I *am* proud. Your mom will be too."

"Yeah?"

"Of course. I know what it's like for people to make assumptions. I grew up with the last name Kensington too. I know it can be a burden more than anything else. It took me too long to exert some autonomy over it, but you've never been afraid to break away from the expected." Dad smiles. "Maybe too unafraid at times, but this isn't one of them. If you want a summer job, I think it's fantastic."

"Thanks, Dad."

"Anything else you want to tell me?"

I think, then shake my head. "Nope. We're good."

Dad stands. "I'm going to pretend that pause didn't terrify me. You still have a curfew, Wren. Don't think your latest birthday changed that."

I roll my eyes, then head inside to change. Truthfully, I don't hate that my parents are constantly checking in. They've always been that way. And I know a lot of peers whose parents let them do whatever they want, which sounds appealing but actually sort of sucks.

I change, braid my hair so that it's not flying in my face while I'm driving, and head back downstairs. There's no sign of Dad. I'm guessing he snuck into the room that's been designated as his office, even though he told Mom he wouldn't be working on weekends while we were here. Not that Mom's much better—she's currently *at* work, overseeing the construction site.

Driving to the Rausings' place—Leah is hosting this afternoon's pool party—takes about twenty minutes. I park at the end of the row of cars, swinging my bag over my shoulder and whistling as I walk along the gravel driveway. Some bits get stuck in my sandals, so I walk over the grass edge instead.

"You finally made it, huh?"

I glance left, at Tanner Whitney. He's leaning against a silver Range Rover, smoking a cigarette.

"Aw," I say, pausing. "Were you waiting for me?"

"Nah, just noticed you weren't here. Party was boring."

"Are you leaving?"

"Not unless you want to."

"I *just* got here," I remind him.

"We see these people all the time, Wren. Literally, it's just the same people. Don't you ever get bored?"

Yes, I think. *All the time.*

But I get bored around Tanner too. His dad works for mine, and we've gone to school together since kindergarten. He's attractive and occasionally charming, but that's about all I can list as his positive attributes.

"I don't like the smell of smoke," I say, then keep walking.

Leah's house is unlocked and empty. Screeches and splashes echo from the backyard pool, so I follow the sounds through the first floor and outside.

"WREN!" Gia greets me with an overeager hug, nearly splashing me with the contents of her cup. *"Finally."*

"I'm only"—I check my phone—"two hours late. That's practically a record for me."

Gia grabs my wrist, pulling me over to the outdoor kitchen. "Strawberry margarita?"

"How sweet are they?"

"Sweeter than you," she teases.

I take the cup offered by Maya Lauren, another former—that's still weird to say—classmate, and sip. The cocktail is sweet, but the lime juice and salt rim cut it some. It's delicious, the burn of alcohol barely there.

"Are you really *working* this summer, Wren?" Mabel Stewart asks, strolling over.

"Yep," I reply, swallowing more margarita.

"You are?" Gia asks, sounding stunned. "Since when? Where?"

"This was my first week. I'm waitressing at the yacht club restaurant." I shrug a shoulder. "My mom's project is going to last all summer. Wanted to stay busy."

"Busy *waitressing*?" Gia says, her tone thick with disbelief.

"I can't believe your parents let you pick UCLA and ..." Leah's voice trails off as I glare at her.

Some hostess she is turning out to be.

I arch an eyebrow. "And?"

Wisely, she reaches for her drink, adding nothing.

I know everyone was surprised by my choice of college. It's a good school, but it's not an Ivy. It's not where I was expected to go because I could have gone anywhere.

"My parents support me," I tell Leah. "Sorry if yours don't."

Her lips purse, but her mouth stays shut.

"What's working at the yacht club like?" Mabel asks me. "My parents rented a boat there last summer, and the guys who worked there were really cute. There was one with dark hair who was super broody and not very friendly, but he was so *hot*." She pretends to fan herself, making Gia laugh.

"I don't see the marina guys much," I say. "The restaurant is separate from the boat stuff."

"Maybe Dad will want to rent a boat again," Mabel muses. "I'll have to ask."

God, I hope not. Not only would it be weird, waiting on a friend, but I'm ninety percent sure the hot guy she's talking about is Sawyer. And watching Mabel flirt with him, no matter his level of interest in her, would be … awful.

"I hate boats," I announce, prompting scattered laughter.

"It wasn't that much fun," Mabel admits. "Sort of boring."

"Right?" I say. "Nothing to do, and you're literally stuck in the middle of a giant puddle. What if the motor breaks down? Or there's a storm and you're getting tossed around like a toy ship?"

"We went sailing, so there wasn't even an engine," Mabel says, laughing. "Maybe I won't say anything to Dad."

I shrug, like it makes absolutely no difference to me, then resume sipping my margarita.

CHAPTER 21

Sawyer

"**M**om?" I call out, shutting the door behind me.

Her muffled reply comes a minute later. "In here!"

I follow her voice down the hallway and into the bedroom that used to belong to my parents'. I avoid entering it. Last time I did, it looked the same as always.

Now? It's unrecognizable. All of the furniture—queen-size bed, dresser, and a rocking chair that Mom's dad carved himself—has been pushed to the center of the room and covered with clear plastic. Mom is crouching in one corner, a roll of blue tape on either wrist, measuring the baseboard.

"Uh, what's going on?" I ask.

"Write down sixty-four inches," she instructs.

"Write? Where?"

"There's a notepad over there." She nods to the other corner.

I walk over, picking up the pad of paper and pencil, and write down

the measurement. I drop both and glance around again. "You're ... renovating?"

"Only painting for now. We can paint yours too, if you want. No dorm room to decorate."

"No one paints their dorm room, Mom."

"I know that because I went to college. How do you know that?"

I sigh. "Can we not do this tonight? Please? I had a long day."

"It's not too late for second semester, Sawyer. Or for next year."

I hold her gaze, saying nothing, and she exhales.

"Fine. You know how I feel about it."

"Do you have the paint already?"

She nods. "It's in the closet. I needed it out of the way while I moved the furniture around."

I walk over to the closet and open the door, bending down to look at the cans. Spin one to see the sample smeared on the side. "Pink?"

"It's my favorite color."

"It is?" I straighten, surprised, as I glance over one shoulder.

Mom's nod is decisive.

Pink is not a color I associate with my mom. She's more of a deep green or a vibrant blue. A bold shade that camouflages bruises and shadows grief. Not quite black. Not too dark, but close.

I glance at the nearest wall. I always thought the paint in here was white, but it isn't really. More of a very light gray, like some of my athletic socks that I've accidentally washed with darker clothing a few times.

"Pink it is," I say. "Dad would hate it."

"He would." Mom's tone is vehement. A little gleeful too.

My father had very traditional views when it came to gender roles. He hated Mom's job—resented how people thanked her for her service, same as they thanked him—and I think the only reason he never insisted on her changing careers was her deployments. When she was gone, there was no interference with me practicing pitching for hours. With him spoiling Skylar, ensuring he was her favorite parent.

It was also one of the reasons Mom never left him, I think. Dad would have fought for sole custody, and there's a decent chance he would have gotten it.

Watching the pale pink cover the old color is oddly soothing. We work in silence, until Mom drags an old radio out of the hall closet and plugs it into the wall. The song playing isn't one I recognize, but Mom hums along. It's more static than music, but that pairs well with the glide of paint.

It takes us two hours to get a first coat on and clean up. Mom makes dinner while I take a shower.

I've only taken one bite of my pasta when she tells me, "I boxed up Skylar's room."

I freeze mid-chew. Force myself to swallow.

"You were right; this house holds a lot of hard memories. Neither of them is coming back."

"*I* know that."

"I'm sorry it took me so long, honey."

"Don't … don't *apologize*."

She doesn't have anything to apologize for, least of all grieving.

We eat in silence for a few minutes.

"Do you have plans tonight?"

"Wade wanted to do a bonfire. But if you want to do more painting, I can—"

"No, no. Go have fun with your friends. I'm wiped."

I nod, polishing off the rest of my dinner. I help load the dishwasher, pull on a hoodie, and head out to my truck. Gus is waiting, sitting on the tailgate.

"Why are your hands … pink?" he asks as I start the engine.

I scrubbed at them in the shower, but some of the streaks wouldn't come off.

"My mom is painting her bedroom. I assisted."

"That's cool," Gus says, leaning forward to flip on the radio and then slouching back against the seat. "FYI … Wade invited everyone."

"Yeah. I saw he texted the whole group."

"Not just our group. Everyone … from work."

This time, I understand his meaning.

"Whatever," I say dismissively, taking the next left. "Want to go fishing in the morning?"

"Hell yeah. Off the breakwater?"

"That's what I was thinking."

"I've got bait from last summer stashed in the garage freezer. My mom's been begging me to get rid of it. Remind me to grab it."

"What kind?" I ask as I park.

"I dunno," Gus replies, hopping out. "Worms probably?"

I shut my truck door, stuffing my hands in the hoodie pocket as we trek toward the stone circle ahead. Salty wind whips through my hair, making me wish I'd worn a hat. I pull up my sweatshirt's hood.

The tension in my shoulders disappears when Gus and I reach the group, dispelling my theory it was soreness from painting. Worse is the way the apprehension is replaced with disappointment. Worst is the way the emptiness of it lingers.

I wish she were here, and I really wish I hadn't even noticed she wasn't.

I try to distract myself, but I mostly stare at the flickering flames, listening to overlapping conversations. Macie tells me about a tennis tournament at the country club she's entered. Wade pulls out a vintage guitar, plucking notes to a country song that he knows about half the words to. The rest he makes up. The resulting melody is underwhelming. Everyone talking and the crash of surf drown most of it out, thankfully.

"I'm craving ice cream," Ricky announces once the fire has smoldered down to embers. "Anyone else?"

"Me!" Macie says. "How late is What's the Scoop open?"

"Eleven in the summers, I think," Gus replies.

"It's ten thirty," Abby says, standing. "Let's go."

Everyone collects shoes and phones, Wade douses the ashes from the fire, and then we migrate over to the cars.

Gus and I are the first ones to arrive at the ice cream shop. It's crowded with families and teenagers. Mostly tourists, but a few faces I recognize. Gus stops to chat with one of his younger brothers, Nate. I say hi to him, then scan the list of flavors.

Over the communal ruckus, I'm not sure how I hear it. But I do, glancing at the clustered picnic tables with renewed interest. I already know what the sound means, but I want to see it for myself.

Her. Laugh.

I recognize her fucking laugh.

Wren is sitting on the edge of the table, not the attached bench, head tipped back as she reacts to whatever a wildly gesticulating brunette told her.

I stare for a few seconds too many, and she glances this way. Randomly at first, and then her gaze lingers.

Our eyes collide. Remain connected.

I wondered, when she wasn't at the bonfire, where she was. I have an answer, and I still feel unsatisfied. I didn't want to know where she was. I wanted to see her. Be near her. Talk to her. We haven't spoken since I confronted her at her car, and … *fuck*. I miss her.

Wren looks away first, slipping off the table and turning to face her friends, back to me. Whatever she says has everyone moving. Their picnic table is empty by the time Gus and I join the end of the line. They're gone before anyone else arrives, peeling out in three luxury cars.

I'm not sure why Wren ignoring me feels worse than anything else she might have done, but it does.

CHAPTER 22

Sawyer

"**W**hy are we stopping here?" Gus asks as Wade takes a left toward the country club.

"I told Ricky we'd pick him up," Wade replies.

"We wouldn't have to make an extra stop if he'd stayed at the marina," I comment.

Dusty wouldn't have needed to hire new guys either.

"C'mon, Cap," Wade says. "He makes better tips caddying."

I grunt.

"What the hell is going on?" Wade adds as he circles the lot. "Every spot is full."

"There's a tennis tournament," I tell him, noticing the large sign advertising it ahead.

"Great," Wade comments sarcastically. "Can someone call Ricky? Ask him to meet us out here?"

"Can you pull up front?" Gus asks, pointing ahead. "I need to piss."

I listen to a series of rings as Wade brakes by the main building.

"No answer," I announce, popping my door open. "I'll find him."

"Cool. I'll circle," Wade says, then drives off.

"Meet you back here?" Gus asks.

I nod. Gus heads for the entrance to the country club. I try to call Ricky again. It goes straight to voicemail this time, so I release a frustrated exhale and follow Gus inside.

Damn, this place is fancy. I've driven by Atlantic Crest hundreds of times since it's right by the marina, but never actually been inside the building. Normally, you have to be a member or accompanied by one to be on the property. They must have relaxed the rules a little because of the tournament since no one stops me or asks for identification.

I wander through the wood-paneled lobby, past a dining area, and out onto a stone patio. People are milling around out here, sipping drinks and snacking off silver trays being whisked around by servers. Past it, the brilliant green of the golf course stretches to the edge of the water. Before it are the tennis courts, the stands surrounding them full of spectators.

I turn back toward the building, pulling my phone out to try Ricky once more. It'll be impossible to find him in this crowd.

"Are you lost?"

I hesitate before glancing toward the voice. Not least to get the sudden spike in my heart rate under control. Also, whipping my head in her direction would look overeager.

Wren's dressed for tennis—short white dress, high ponytail, and a pink racquet bag slung over one shoulder. She looks good—she always looks good—but it's the sly smirk that captures my attention most completely. Ignoring her was supposed to tamp down this ridiculous draw. Instead, her smile makes me feel like a starving sailor glimpsing land.

"You look lost," she adds when I continue to stare at her silently, like an idiot.

"I've never been here before."

She nods, adjusting the bag on her shoulder. "Doesn't really seem like your scene."

I don't know if that's a dig or a compliment. I'm not sure if I'm supposed to act like us talking is normal or not.

I nod toward the courts. "You played in the tournament?"

"Yeah, the singles competition just wrapped up. They're starting doubles now."

"It wasn't, like, way too easy for you?"

Wren described herself as being "pretty good" at tennis in one of her letters to me. Meaning she could probably win Wimbledon.

She studies me. I guess I broke our unspoken rule: don't discuss our past. We're distant coworkers, at best, these days.

"Your compliments still need work," she finally says.

I fight a smile. "Well, I've never actually—"

"Cap! You came!"

Macie appears out of nowhere, flinging her arms around me enthusiastically. I hug her back automatically, glancing at Wren as I do. She's still smiling, but it appears thinner. Maybe that's just wishful thinking on my part.

"I didn't think you'd make it," Macie continues.

I feel guilty, letting Macie think I came here to see her play, but mentioning I totally forgot she'd told me about being in the tournament seems way worse.

I settle for hedging some. "I, uh … we stopped by to pick up Ricky. Thought I'd check it out while I was here."

Macie nods, then glances at Wren. "Hey!" She hugs Wren next, pulling back to beam at her. "Congrats, champ! I tried to come over after you won, but you were totally mobbed."

Well, I was right about it being too easy. She *won*.

When Wren commits to something, she goes all in. I feel a little sick with the realization that maybe that's what she tried to do with us. Writing to Wren was separate from the rest of my subpar life, and I freaked out at the first unexpected collision.

My phone buzzes; Ricky is calling. I answer, and neither Wren nor Macie notices. They're busy chatting with each other.

"Where are you, Cap?" Ricky asks. "We're all at the car, waiting for ya."

"Yeah. Uh, I'll be—I'll be there in a minute."

"Hurry!" he says, then hangs up.

Macie watches me slip my phone back in my pocket. "You've got to go?" she guesses.

"Sort of," I say awkwardly. "Gus tracked down Ricky, and there aren't any parking spots in the lot with the tournament …"

"It's fine," Macie says. "I haven't played since middle school, so this probably wasn't my best shot at impressing you anyway." She winks, and I tell my facial muscles to smile back. "I'll text you later, let you know how it went."

"Sounds good. Good luck."

"Thank—oh, there's Abby! Gotta go!" Macie jogs toward the bleachers.

I watch her braid swing back and forth until she disappears into the milling crowd, delaying looking at Wren. I'm surprised she's still standing here. No doubt she has much more exciting things to do.

"You won the whole damn thing?" I confirm once we're alone again.

"The singles tournament. Doubles has never been my thing."

"Congratulations, Wren," a woman says, passing by. "Give my best to your family."

"Thanks. Will do," she calls back. To me, lower, she says, "I know a shortcut to the parking lot."

"Lead the way," I say. My phone is buzzing in my pocket again.

"Great job, Wren," an older man calls as we approach the patio. "Let Hanson and Josephine know how much we're looking forward to the party on Friday."

"I will," Wren replies, cutting left.

The crowd is less congested farther from the tennis courts. We skirt the edge of the pool fence and walk along a line of parked golf carts.

"Watch your step," she tells me as the trimmed grass transitions to mulch. "It's just past—shit."

I don't have to ask her what's wrong. I'm hit directly in the face by the spray of a sprinkler that suddenly popped up from the ground. Another is aimed at my thigh, soaking half of my shorts. The flower bed seems to wrap around the entire periphery of the main building, meaning there's another hundred feet of sprinklers to navigate.

Wren's laughing as she darts ahead, and there's a reluctant grin on my face as I sprint after her, raising one arm in a pointless attempt to block the water.

I'm panting by the time we reach grass again. Wren looks barely exerted, despite playing tennis all morning, which is irritating and impressive.

"That"—I swipe an arm across my forehead like a windshield wiper, and water drips into my eyes—"was the worst fucking shortcut."

"Sorry." Wren doesn't sound the least bit apologetic. Mostly amused.

I shake my head like a dog, sending some stray droplets her way. Wren doesn't flinch or jump away, which is when I realize she's as soaked as I am. Which is *also* when I notice the shorts and bra she's wearing under her dress are entirely visible beneath the wet white fabric.

I do a shitty job of not staring.

"Nothing you haven't seen before, Captain."

I jerk my chin up, meeting her knowing gaze. Yeah, I have seen Wren naked before. But it's not really a sight you get sick of.

I'm shrugging out of my gray T-shirt before I can analyze if it's a good idea, tossing it to her.

Wren catches it, which I'm especially impressed by since her eyes are locked on my abs, not my throw.

"Nothing you haven't seen before," I remind her.

She doesn't startle at being called out. Her gaze sweeps back up my chest, slowly, lingering like a physical touch.

I have to repeatedly remind my dick that nothing is going to happen. Not with Wren. Not now, not ever again.

"What am I supposed to do with this?" She lifts the damp, limp shirt.

"Wear it. It's not see-through."

Wren shrugs, then tugs my shirt on.

I swallow, hard, as the fabric falls around her thighs. A thin strip of her dress is still visible beneath the hem, but it mostly looks like she's wearing my shirt with nothing under it, which is not a visual I needed.

We stare at each other, and suddenly, every second I spend around Wren Kensington seems like an increasingly dangerous idea.

"I've gotta go." My phone is periodically buzzing again. At least it's still functioning post-sprinklers.

"Okay."

"Okay," I echo, then turn and jog toward the parking lot.

Wade's sedan is easy to locate; it's loitering in the same spot as where he dropped us off. I can see the back of Gus's and Ricky's heads in the rear seat, so I open the passenger door and climb in.

Wade glances over, eyebrows raised as high as possible as he takes in my wet hair and bare torso. "What the hell happened to you?"

"Long story," I mutter.

It's short though. I got lost—in Wren.

CHAPTER 23

Wren

This year's Red, White, and Blue party feels different from last year's. I'm eighteen. Considered an adult and mostly treated like one. I'm expected to mingle and make small talk with my parents' and the Ellsworths' friends, not just peers my own age. There's no tent and bar set up on the beach. My cousin Kit was in charge of organizing that, and he's busy being a parent this summer. His girlfriend, Collins, gave birth to their son a couple of months ago.

The youngest Kensington—Dylan—is cute, but "could put sirens to shame," according to Bash.

Formerly holding that title always came with a certain degree of freedom. I watched my sister and my cousins head to college and choose careers, knowing my turn was coming but also appreciating how distant it felt. Suddenly, seeing Lili in a serious relationship, watching Kit cradle a baby, and listening to Rory talk about starting law school, it doesn't feel so far away. Bash has plans too—business school and then starting at Kensington Consolidated.

Then there's me. A little adrift. I chose a college, but nothing else seems solid.

"Good afternoon, Wren." My grandfather appears, setting his drink down on the linen cloth covering the high-top table I'm standing next to.

I glance toward Tanner Whitney, sighing when I see him stopped, talking to Thad Lange. Tanner left to grab me a drink from the bar a couple of minutes ago.

"Hi, Grandpa," I reply carefully, my spine straightening automatically as I meet his steely gaze.

My mom's parents are warm and welcoming. They spoil Rory and me—along with their other grandchildren—whenever we visit them in Los Angeles or they travel to New York.

My dad's parents? Very different. Dad's mother, Elizabeth, died a long time ago. Lili was named after her. And his father? Well, no one would describe Arthur Kensington as warm or welcoming. He's shrewd. Intimidating.

"This is quite a party," I add when Grandpa continues a one-sided inspection.

He nods in agreement, taking a sip from a tumbler. It's filled with amber liquid. Bourbon or scotch probably. Grandpa constantly has a glass in hand at any event I see him at, but I've never once seen him drunk. He's always in control. The type of person you call in a crisis. Someone most avoid challenging.

"Hanson has always had a flair for the frivolous," he comments.

"Have you been to this party before?" I ask.

"A long time ago. Hanson and I had overlapping business interests." Grandpa glances to where Aunt Scarlett and Uncle Crew are standing. "Which worked out nicely."

I steal another glance at Tanner. He's started this way, two glasses in hand, then spots who I'm talking to and veers an abrupt left.

I sigh. Hopefully, a member of my family will come over and rescue me soon, but I'm stuck until that happens. Everyone here knows you don't interrupt Arthur Kensington. And I know you don't end a conversation with Grandpa; he dismisses you.

"Was that the Worthington boy?" Grandpa asks, noticing my drifting attention.

"Whitney."

"Are you keeping company with him?"

I'm not sure what "keeping company" entails, but today is the first time I've talked to Tanner since Leah's pool party. I've mostly flirted with him in the hopes that he'd offer to get me a drink, which he did. Sort of. The delivery was lacking.

"He's not courting me or anything," I answer, toeing the line of impudence, but not bold enough to cross over.

Grandpa studies me, the weight of his scrutiny stifling. "Good," he declares. "No Whitney is worthy of a Kensington."

"Tanner is nice," I say defensively. And mostly to be contrarian.

"Stuart Whitney is sitting on a pile of debts and no capital. I'm sure he's urged his son to take advantage of any association with you."

I want to say Grandpa is being paranoid, but who knows? It's not like plenty of people haven't tried to use me in some way.

"There aren't many guys I can date with more money," I tell Grandpa. "It's not like Lili or Kit wound up with billionaires."

Lili's boyfriend, Charlie, is British. He comes from an important family, but no fortune. Collins, Kit's girlfriend, was roommates with Lili in college, which is how she and Kit met. She later wound up working for Kit. For the salary, not for my cousin's company, as she'd be the first to tell you.

"They didn't," Grandpa agrees. "But Charles attended Oxford, and Collins went to Yale."

Of course. I should have anticipated exactly where this was headed from the moment Grandpa appeared.

"Good for them."

"It is not too late to change your plans, Wren."

"It's way too late," I counter. "Orientation is next month."

Grandpa makes a dismissive gesture with his hand. "I could get you enrolled at any university in the world by tomorrow. The East Coast has plenty of exceptional schools. Oxford is an excellent institution. So is Cambridge. My uncle went there."

"I don't want special treatment."

"Want or not, you will receive it. You are a Kensington, and you are limiting yourself with this absurd choice."

"UCLA is an excellent college," I state stubbornly.

Grandpa lifts his glass, swirling the contents around. I watch the amber liquid splash up the sides and drip down, wishing he'd hurry up and make his point so I can go grab a lobster roll.

"Twelve generations ago, one of your ancestors was part of Harvard's first-ever commencement. Since then, every Kensington, including your father and sister, have attended the oldest, most prestigious academic institutions. The California universities might be 'excellent,' but they do not boast that type of legacy."

"Mom went to good schools too," I state.

"Your mother is a Kensington by marriage, not by blood. It is different for you, Wren."

I stop arguing, deciding that might be the best strategy to end this conversation soonest.

"It is your decision, of course," Grandpa continues. "Just make certain it's the correct one."

I nod as he *finally* walks off to speak to someone else.

Then I immediately start glancing around, trying to locate Tanner because I could really use that drink right about now.

"Shortcake?"

I glance at Bash, who's holding two plates of dessert. One is extended toward me.

"Thanks," I say, taking a plate.

I pick up a strawberry, swiping it through the pile of whipped cream before popping it in my mouth. The fruit is perfect—sweet and juicy.

"Man, I hate these things," Bash comments, taking the chair beside me and glancing around.

It's nearing sunset, golden light bathing the crowd sprawled across the patio and yard as the sky becomes a kaleidoscope of colors.

"They're your grandparents," I remind him, taking a bite of biscuit next.

"This used to be fun," Bash continues, glancing toward the beach. "Kit was up for whatever. Lili was … Lili. And now, we're not kids anymore."

"Trust me, I'm aware. I got a lecture from Grandpa earlier."

"About what?"

"About attending a *state* school." I glance at Bash. "You didn't help, going to Dartmouth."

He shrugs. "I look good in green."

I roll my eyes. "Is it bad that I want to do my own thing?"

"No. But do you want to do your own thing? Or are you trying to do something different just to prove you can?"

I don't have an answer to that, so I take another bite of strawberry shortcake instead.

"Grandpa wants the best for you, Wren. He has weird ways of showing it, I know, but that's the goal."

"You sound sage," I comment.

Bash grins. "Probably all the drinks I've had, dodging questions about whether I'll challenge Kit for CEO."

"You don't even work for Kensington Consolidated yet."

"I made that point a few times. No one cared."

"Typical." I take another bite. "This shortcake is really good."

"Gigi orders it every year."

"I missed it last July."

I was too preoccupied acting busy on the beach, avoiding the boy who was waiting on the dunes. I've been avoiding Sawyer again, for weeks, pretending to be oblivious when, sometimes, he's all I can see. When all I really want is for him to ask if I'm free again.

"Incoming," Bash mutters. He grabs his plate, standing.

I glance at Tanner walking this way, then at my cousin. "You can stay."

"Nah. I need some coffee if I'm going to make it until the fireworks." Bash yawns. "My nephew has set me back, like, twenty years on ever considering having kids. See ya later."

He nods at Tanner as he passes him, and Tanner nods back.

"Sorry about earlier," Tanner says sheepishly, tucking his hands into his tux pants pockets.

I polish off the last bite of my dessert. Hand the empty plate off to a passing waiter, then stand.

"Don't worry about it," I say, meaning it. "See you next summer."

"Wait," Tanner calls as I start to walk away. "A bunch of us are headed down to the water to watch the fireworks. Come with? I'll even play that silly game you made up."

The silly game in question—SocVolley, a mix of volleyball and soccer, invented by my West Coast cousins—is the only sport, aside from tennis, that I excel at. If anyone else were suggesting it, I'd enthusiastically agree. But my primary motivation for "keeping company" with Tanner would be to annoy my grandfather, and I decide Bash is right; I should focus on what I want to do, not proving what I can do.

So, I shake my head. "Maybe next year."

Then I continue toward what I want to do.

CHAPTER 24

Sawyer

I swear under my breath, seeing the parked convertible. Fiddle with the keys, like I'm actually considering driving away.

I'm not considering driving away. I'm trying to distract myself from the thrill spreading through my chest. I confused it for adrenaline, standing on that cliff last summer. But it's relentlessly appeared since, in a pattern that makes it impossible not to associate it with Wren Kensington.

I drop my keys in the cupholder, grab a hoodie off the seat, and climb out of the cab.

She's sitting near where she was on her prom night, in yet another fancy dress.

I walk that way, tossing the hoodie down and taking a seat next to her. Mirroring the same pose, reclined on my palms.

"Can you not wear the same color two years in a row?"

Her dress is blue this summer.

Without looking over, she replies, "Does that mean you remember what color last year's dress was?"

"White, right?"

She huffs a low laugh. "You had a fifty-fifty shot."

I don't just remember that her dress the last Fourth was red. I remember it was strapless. Didn't have much else to do while I waited for her to talk to me, aside from memorize her outfit.

"I thought you'd be at the pier," she adds.

"I thought you'd be at the fancy party."

"Left early," she says, tucking a stray strand of hair behind one ear. "Kit was the one who always organized the fun part, and he was busy being a dad this year."

"Really?" I ask, surprised.

I don't remember exact ages, but Wren didn't make her cousins sound that much older than us. Seems young to have a kid, although my mom had me at twenty-three. That sounded ancient when I was younger, but it's suddenly not far away.

"Yeah. I'm happy for Kit, but it's a little weird. Makes me feel old."

I scoff. "You're not old."

"Older than …" She glances over. "When is your birthday?"

"January 10."

"Okay, technically, you're older than me. But maturity-wise, I probably have a decade on you."

I laugh. "We met because I had to oversee you jumping off a cliff. But, yeah, you're the mature one."

"One, you did not *have* to do anything. I was fine, going bluffing, which I totally proved. Two, you had *already* jumped off that same cliff, remember?"

"Yeah, but I did it in a mature way. Not alone and having done it a ton of times before."

"There had to have been a time you'd never done it before."

"Yep," I agree. "First time for everything."

Wren clears her throat, and I'm pretty sure we're thinking about the same thing.

I'm less sure when she says, "Thank you."

I glance over. Her eyes are on the darkening horizon.

"For what?" I question.

"For showing up a year ago. I know I made that conversation … difficult. I was trying to give you an easy out. I didn't think you'd wait for more than twenty minutes. But it meant a lot that you stayed, that you checked on me at all. And I realized I never told you that. So … thanks."

"I have brief bouts of not being an asshole."

"How concerning. Have you seen a doctor about that?"

I smile, letting one arm support my weight and scooping up a handful of sand with my other hand. "I'd always wanted to see how the other half lived anyway."

"Bullshit. You think my world is ostentatious and ridiculous, and … you're not wrong." There's a sad, hollow echo to her last three words.

"What does ostentatious mean?" I ask, hoping it'll annoy or amuse her.

She glances over. "I know you too well to buy that."

"Too well, huh?"

It's hard to tell in the limited light, but Wren might be blushing a little. "Well enough, I mean."

"Mmhmm." I lie down flat since my arm is going numb, supporting my weight. "When's your birthday?"

"Why?"

I roll my eyes, staring at the constellations overhead. "Because I told you mine."

She lies down, too, tucking one arm behind her head. The fireworks should be starting at any second. I'm dreading the disruption all of a sudden, wishing it were possible to linger in this stillness for longer.

"March 11," Wren finally answers.

Something about that date tickles the back of my brain, but I can't come up with any concrete reason why.

Wren reaches out, picking up my right hand and holding it aloft in the moonlight. My heart stutters, then starts again at a more rapid pace as her fingers graze the stain on my palm.

"What's with the paint?" she asks, letting my arm drop back to the sand.

"My mom has been doing some redecorating. House needed a makeover."

"I thought it was nice."

I snort. "You weren't missing the view of Central Park?"

A pause.

"Lucky guess, or you looked it up?"

"I had your address. Took two seconds."

"Have you been?"

"To Central Park?"

"Yeah. Or to New York."

"Never. Too far away."

"Seriously?"

"No. Not seriously, Wren. Yes, of course I've been to New York City."

She huffs. "I can't see your expression. I have a hard enough time reading you when I can."

"Mostly school trips," I say. "But my mom took me and—and I've gone a couple of times with family and friends too."

"What did you think?"

"It was loud."

"You only like quiet places?"

"I prefer quiet places."

"You can find quiet in the city. I go up to the rooftop of the Met to sketch sometimes. If you time it right, it's peaceful up there."

"Is that the only place you sketch?"

"No. But it's the only place I go *to* sketch."

"How come?"

"You're asking a lot of questions for someone who doesn't like answering them."

"I told you my birthday," I remind her.

"Did I forget to thank you for that highly revealing bit of information? Don't worry; I won't tell anyone that you're a Capricorn."

I scoff. "What else do you want to know?"

She's silent, thinking, and I internally panic. If she asks something about us, I don't know what I'll say. I already lied about not remembering her dress color. I'm more inclined toward honesty, lying on cool sand with her, and that's unlikely to end well.

"How'd you get the scar on your chin?"

"Decided to walk on top of the monkey bars rather than swing across in third grade. Slipped and clipped my chin. Three stitches. Took out a couple of teeth too."

"Ouch."

"It wasn't that bad. I don't really remember it. I did plenty of reckless shit like that as a kid."

"Only as a kid?" I can hear the smile in her voice.

"Mostly as a kid."

I wasn't half the daredevil Skylar was. She was always striving toward the next challenge. Organizing a push-up contest. Practicing gymnastics. Swimming farther offshore than anyone else.

"I only have one scar," Wren says, pulling me back to the present.

"How fasci—"

"Here." She lifts one leg and twists her foot, flashing me the underside.

And the rest of what I was planning to drawl gets stuck somewhere in my throat as I recall the night Wren cut her foot. Wondering why she's bringing it up.

The first firework explodes overhead, and I'm saved from having to make any response by the colorful commotion.

Wren sits up to watch the display, but I don't move. From this position, I can watch her and the sky.

We're silent through the thirty-minute show. I toss Wren my sweatshirt when she starts shivering halfway through, and she yanks it on without saying a word.

I came here to be alone, and it seems like she did too. But no part of me was disappointed to find her here. Wren easily could have made up an excuse to leave if she wanted to. Yet she stayed.

Later, alone in my truck, I pull out my phone and scroll through photos. We got an unexpected snowfall mid-March. I took a photo to send to Mom after waking up repeatedly during the night, unable to sleep after Wren's call.

I find the photo a minute later and click on the details to check the date.

March 11.

CHAPTER 25

Wren

He arrives at eleven thirty, almost a full half hour after Gus and his other friends showed up. And he's not alone. Macie is beaming up at Sawyer like he just told the world's funniest joke. Highly unlikely since any sense of humor is buried under a whole lot of brooding.

I turn away, refocusing on Aaron. "Wanna go upstairs?"

"Yeah." He downs the rest of his beer in one hasty gulp. "Upstairs. For sure."

I grab his hand and pull him toward the staircase. We pass Abby, who winks at me. And Gus, whose expression is impassive. I avoid eye contact with Sawyer's best friend, even though I'm doing absolutely nothing wrong. It's just that Gus was the only person who ever seemed supportive of me and Sawyer being ... anything, so it feels strange to flaunt how, now, we're ... nothing.

I've never been to this house before, but there's a guest room off the landing that's easy to navigate to. I pull Aaron inside, shut the door, and

press back against it, my spine flush with the firm wood. The bed would be much more comfortable, but I haven't decided how far I want this to go. Plus, I don't know Aaron that well. Easy exit.

Aaron's chest rises with a deep breath before he steps closer and kisses me.

It's brief. More of a brush than a kiss. I've barely registered the contact before it's gone.

Aaron is studying me, his head tilted a little to the left. "Huh," he says, making the word sound like a discovery.

"Huh?" I repeat, sounding … confused.

Effusive praise isn't necessary, but I'm accustomed to more of a reaction than just a solitary syllable.

Aaron takes a step back, shoving his hands in the pockets of his jeans. "Yeah, I—" He exhales for so long that I'm not sure the sigh will ever stop. "Can I tell you something? Something I've never told anyone?"

I say, "Sure," even though I'm apprehensive.

If he confesses to a murder or something, am I legally obligated to report the crime anyway? I'll have to ask Rory. As a hypothetical, of course.

"So, I think I might be … gay."

"Oh," I reply, relieved. Then I register his nervous expression and immediately add, "That's cool."

Aaron wanders away, taking a seat on the end of the bed. "I wasn't sure … I mean, I thought maybe there was a chance that I—but if kissing *you* wasn't … I think I am."

I sit down beside him. Not speaking, just listening.

"I also, uh … you know Cap? He works at the marina. I don't actually"—he chuckles awkwardly—"even know his real name. But he's … fuck, he makes me nervous. He must think I'm a complete idiot because I can't focus on anything around him."

"He is distractingly hot," I say.

Aaron chuckles. "Yeah, he is."

"But who cares what he thinks?" I ask, a motto I'm personally striving hard to internalize. I nudge my shoulder against Aaron's. "How come you've never told anyone? If you don't mind me asking, that is. We don't have to talk—"

"No, it's fine. I just—I wasn't sure, and there was no one I felt like I could …" He glances at me suddenly. "Don't—you won't tell anyone, right? I'm not sure I'm ready for …"

"I won't tell anyone," I assure him quickly. "I swear."

He relaxes. "Thank you."

I hold out a hand. "Give me your phone."

"My … why?" He's already pulled it out.

"Unlock it. I'll give you my number, in case you ever want to talk."

Aaron hands me his phone, opened to a new contact. I type in my number, then pass it back to him.

"I've wanted to ask for your number for weeks." He smiles ruefully, staring at the screen.

"Congratulations. You got it."

"Thanks, Wren. Really."

"Of course." I nudge his shoulder again. "I mean it. Use it whenever."

"I will."

I stand, sensing he might want a minute alone. "See you downstairs?"

"Yeah." He nods. "See you downstairs."

I leave, getting pulled into a conversation with a couple of the other waitresses as soon as I reenter the kitchen. I procrastinate until the last possible second, but finally announce that I have to go, shooting Aaron a flirty wink as I pass him by on my way to the front door. The guys surrounding him hoot and holler, and I doubt a single one would guess what really happened upstairs.

Outside, I suck in a deep breath of cool, salt-scented air. For someone who grew up in hectic New York and chose a smoggy city for college, I'm coming to love the uninhabited presence of having the ocean nearby. Of no sound, except for waves pounding sand or seagulls shouting commentary, and the space it allows you to think.

Not that my thoughts have been an amiable companion lately. And they become even more volatile when I reach the street and spot a tall figure leaning against the side of my convertible. I panic, register who it is, and freak out for an entirely different reason.

His arms are flexed, gripping the doorframe since I left the window and roof down, his posture casual. Yet my heart riots in my chest like he's a predator, poised to strike. Because I've never told him—and I've done my damnedest to pretend otherwise—that he's one of very few people with the power to hurt me. I know—because he *has* hurt me.

I suck in a deep, bracing breath as I reach my car.

Sawyer doesn't look mad—doesn't look anything—but I instinctively know this will be a battle. All of our recent conversations have been battles, with no clear winner or loser. With no clear purpose at all, which are the most dangerous conflicts.

"You leaving?" he asks without really looking at me. He's staring in what I think is the direction of the ocean, jaw working a couple of times as a muscle there clenches, then relaxes.

"Yeah. Curfew."

"Lame."

"Says the guy who left the party to … lean against my car?"

Sawyer says nothing in response.

"Don't fuck up the paint job," I add snidely to emphasize I noticed he was out here waiting for me and for him to explain why.

He shoves away from the side of the car without sharing any reasoning. "Have fun?"

There's a low, dangerous undercurrent to his question. One that suggests *yes* is the wrong answer.

"Yes."

"Great," he says, tone implying the opposite.

"I can do whatever I want, Cap."

"You can," he agrees, stepping closer.

Emboldened, I add, "It's none of your business what I—"

Sawyer takes another step, and I fight the urge to backtrack and retain the same amount of distance between us.

Especially once he touches me, tilting my chin up and tracing my jawline with his thumb. I hold his gaze, defiant, and a grin ghosts across his face.

The many times I told myself I was over him? They're such blatant lies all of a sudden. Aaron said Cap makes him nervous. Sawyer Bennett makes me forget there are other people on this planet.

"Just like being the first guy to fuck you was none of my business?"

My annoyance is increasingly slippery to hold on to. Truthfully, I'm thrilled he's out here with me instead of inside with anyone else, acting jealous and territorial.

"That's ancient histo—"

He kisses me, swallowing the rest of my rant into his mouth as he sucks on my tongue.

Some people are puzzle pieces. Being around them is effortless, like two pieces fitting together. It doesn't mean it's right; it doesn't mean it's reliable.

But that's how I always feel around Sawyer—like I found my other half.

I don't believe there's some mysterious alchemy to kissing—it's like holding hands, except mouths touching—but there's some special sensation every time I kiss Sawyer, no matter where we are or how long we've known each other.

It accelerates instantly, like a match tossed on a steady stream of gasoline. His hands are on my face, then roaming lower. I slide my hands into his hair because I think about doing so every time I see him do it, but have always had to suppress the urge to. As soon as I do, he kisses me harder. His tongue traces my lip, and I start to feel unsteady. My arms fold around his neck, using the solid stretch of his shoulders for support. Did he get *more* muscular since last summer or—

I'm kissing him back, I suddenly realize. Rather enthusiastically because I want to kiss him, but I did not want Sawyer to know that.

I withdraw my hands and yank my head away, separating our mouths. Only by a couple of inches since Sawyer's still holding me so I can't pull very far away. We're too close for me to disguise how fast my breathing is, but I attempt to hide that I'm practically panting.

"*Why* did you do that?" I ask, hoping he catches the extra emphasis on the first word.

"I wanted to," he replies, dropping his arms.

It's not that chilly out, but I feel colder.

"Why?" I press.

He huffs. "You kissed me randomly, repeatedly, last summer. I can't kiss you once?"

"No," I snap. "You can't. Because I did it before …"

"Before what?"

I cross my arms. "Do you really want to do this?"

"Do what?"

I can't tell if he's being deliberately obtuse or if he's truly clueless.

Neither is ideal. Both feed my irritation.

"Why do you think I came to see you on New Year's?" I demand.

He shifts his weight between his feet, finally seeming to grow uncomfortable with the topic at hand. "Sex?" he suggests.

I scoff. "I can get that anywhere. I *do* get that anywhere."

His jaw clenches. "I know what you look like after you've come, Wren. Whoever you went upstairs with either couldn't get you off or nothing happened. My money's on the latter."

I hate that he's using how I react to him against me. I hate even more that he's right.

"What money?" I snap.

A dig I should feel bad about, probably, but that's one thing I love about Sawyer: he gives it right back to me. If I'd said that to any other guy—and I do mean *any* other guy because I'm richer than all of them— they would have gotten defensive.

One thing I *used* to love about Sawyer, rather, because starting now, I've resolved to focus only on his flaws.

Sure enough, he smiles. "It's an idiom, Wren. You might've learned about them … in English class."

I want to shout, *You wrote me back!*

Instead, I dig in my heels. "It was the hardest I'd ever come."

A cruel smile touches the corners of Sawyer's lips. "You probably pretended it was me."

I can't come up with a cutting enough response. I'm too aware of the heat spreading through me, terrified of the way he's invaded my inner thoughts. He's not just tattooed on my skin. He's deeper. Cells in my blood. Marrow in my bones. So entangled that I can't remove him without cutting myself up.

I allow some honesty out. Maybe that's the only way to excise him.

"I wanted more, okay? I thought we *were* more. That's why I showed up on New Year's. You obviously felt differently, so—"

"I never said that," he interrupts.

"Right. You said, 'Why?' when you fucking knew why I was really there. That wasn't humiliating enough? You need me to spell it out for you seven months later?" I shake my head, then move toward the car door.

Sawyer steps left, blocking me. "I'm sorry, Wren," he says quietly.

"I don't need an apology from you. I don't need *anything* from you. I wanted things from you. I've moved on. You can't decide you want me now because I did."

"You think that's why I'm out here?"

"*I don't know* why you're out here, Sawyer."

He exhales. "I'm fucked up, Wren. I fuck up. You have no clue what you're getting into with me, and I have no idea why you'd even want to."

"Want*ed* to." I emphasize the past tense.

One corner of his mouth curves up. "You kissed me back."

"It was a reflex."

"What about stroking my hair?"

"I wasn't *stroking*."

He hums, not really agreeing or disagreeing, and then his expression turns serious again. Tense too. "I really came out here to check ... you're okay?"

"Okay?" I echo. "Like, sober?"

"Yeah, that. And ... the guy upstairs ... he didn't do anything ..." He clears his throat. "Nothing, uh, happened that you didn't want to happen?"

The only other time I've seen Sawyer so uncomfortable was when he showed up at the Red, White, and Blue party. And I'm experiencing the same overwhelming, conflicting mixture of emotions now that I did then. Because it's confusing. Because I can't tell if he truly cares or if he's as indifferent as he mostly acts. If this is the bout of not being an asshole he referred to or if this is a glimpse of him not hiding how he honestly feels.

I shake my head. "Thank you for … checking," I say awkwardly.

He nods, stepping aside so I can reach my car.

I should leave. Probably. Definitely. But instead of grabbing the handle, I wind up mirroring Sawyer's step so we're still facing each other. And then rising on my tiptoes and wrapping my arms around him.

I've never hugged a guy who wasn't related to me before. I sort of expect Sawyer to stiffen or to pull away, but he does neither. He rests his chin on the top of my head and folds his arms around my back. Then releases a breath that sounds like it's been held for a while.

I don't want to move. I want to move less and less with each passing second. He's solid and warm, and he smells like Sawyer. I feel content and also exhilarated, like being held by him is the securest form of a thrill-seeking activity. Skydiving into a safety net.

He says nothing. Neither do I. Yet it feels like handing him another slice of my heart.

I have no sense of how long we've been standing here, but I eventually loosen my grip. His hands drop too. I dart my eyes around the street, wondering if anyone saw us and also looking anywhere except directly at him. "I, uh, I'll see you?"

"Yeah," he says, his voice still that soft tone that I realize I've only heard him use with me.

" 'Kay." I finally climb into my convertible, wincing when I register the time on the dash. Even so, I'm tempted to linger longer.

I turn on the car, glancing in the mirror before I start driving to ensure there's no oncoming traffic. And then again once I'm partway down the road to check if he's still standing in the same spot.

He is.

I'm scared if I wait, it will never be me. If I move on, it will never be him.

CHAPTER 26

Sawyer

"**W**hat about you, Cap?"

I lift my gaze from the napkin I was slowly shredding. "What?"

Macie's smile tightens before she shakes her head. "Nothing. Never mind."

I glance down at my water glass, wishing I'd ordered something stronger.

Brett Nichols passes our table, aiming his typical smarmy smirk my way en route to the bar. He was already here when we arrived and made a few of his typical comments then, but has kept his distance since. He's getting a refill now, I'm guessing—since I doubt he's leaving this early.

One can hope.

Across the table, Wade scoffs. "Typical Nichols, going after the hottest girl."

Macie, nearest, overhears. She balls up a napkin and tosses it at him. "Thanks a lot, jerk."

"That's not—" Wade looks to me for help, and I shrug a shoulder. He's going to have to dig out of this hole solo. "You're hot too," Wade says. "Wren's just …"

My head whips left, and I scan the area by the bar. Wren was back by the pool table, talking to Aaron and some of the other guys, last I checked. Now, she's standing by the bar, watching Brett fucking Nichols do his damnedest to impress her.

Water sloshes over the rim of my glass, running over my knuckles. I relax my grip on the plastic, but the clear material remains crinkled and cracked. Irrevocably damaged, like me.

Gus leans over to toss a stack of napkins on the spilled liquid. "She can handle herself, man," he says, low enough for only me to hear, although I barely do over the blood rushing in my ears.

Every muscle in my body is tense, stiff with the effort of staying in place.

I glance over again.

Wren is leaning against one end of the bar, presumably waiting for a drink. Owen is at the other end, serving someone else. And Brett is all over her.

Wren says something, and his smile falters. But Brett recovers quickly, pulling out his wallet. Offering to buy her drink, I'd bet.

She shakes her head. He steps closer, crowding her space.

The roaring grows louder. I'm not even pretending to pay attention to what's happening at my table anymore.

Wren will hate if I intervene. Nichols will love it, especially if he realizes what Wren means to me. If he does, he'll be even less likely to leave her alone.

She's fine, I tell myself. *She's fine, and she doesn't want or need your help.*

Then her head turns.

Wren doesn't look for the bartender. She doesn't look at Aaron. Her gaze doesn't wander. It lands straight on me, and it stays there. I wasn't sure she'd even noticed I was here tonight.

I'm already off my stool, pushing through the crowd. Ignoring the protests as I literally shove my way through or the shouts of, "Cap!" behind me.

I don't stop walking until I'm close enough to step between them, forcing Nichols to move back.

He grins at me, expression lazy and superior. "I saw her first, Bennett."

"Walk away," I say, startled by the steel in my own tone. I sound … dangerous.

Brett blinks rapidly a few times, taken aback by it too. He's not accustomed to me engaging in our conflicts, let alone escalating them. But he regains his arrogance quickly. "It's a free country. I'll hook up with whoever I want."

"I said, *walk away*, Nichols."

He laughs before shaking his head and shifting closer to Wren. She hasn't said anything, but I can feel her hovering beside me. "I don't take orders from you, Bennett. We both know you won't—"

I make sure Wren's out of the way, then swing. And it's supremely satisfying, seeing my fist connect with his shocked face. I also enjoy watching Brett stumble back, trying to regain his balance, taking the stool he grabbed down with him.

And then the high fades, and reality rushes in. The stares, the pointing, the wide eyes.

"Out, Bennett!" Owen yells, which is no surprise.

No fighting is pretty much the only rule Lucky's enforces.

Brett is getting to his feet. There's a crimson mark on his left cheek. His right is red too, probably from embarrassment. I knocked him down with one hit.

"You're going to fucking pay for that," he snarls.

"Work on your listening skills," I retort, knowing I'm likely making things worse.

It's freeing though. I've spent so long stifling strong emotions and hiding any characteristics that are similar to my father. I lost parts of myself in the process, and rediscovering them is bittersweet.

"*Out*, Bennett!" Owen repeats.

I shove past Brett, pausing next to Gus. He, like everyone else, rushed over to the action.

"Make sure he stays away from her," I mutter, then continue outside.

I head for my truck, raking my hands through my hair as the full force of possible repercussions hits me. *Fuck.* Nichols will try to make me pay, and he has a case. I let him get to me. Gave him exactly what he'd wanted, what he'd tried to goad me into for years, because I couldn't think straight around Wren. I should regret it, but I really don't.

I grip the tailgate, hanging my head and breathing heavily. My body is still swimming with adrenaline, and my right knuckles sting. They're bruised, maybe split. I kick a back tire once, attempting to expel some frustration.

"Here."

I spin around, staring at Wren. She's standing a few feet away, holding a plastic bag full of ice toward me.

"Thanks," I say, taking the bag and pressing the cold cubes against the back of my hand.

She crosses her arms once I do, studying me. I scan her expression, looking for anger—or worse, fear. She appears totally impassive.

"I'm sorry." I sigh. "I shouldn't—I shouldn't have gotten involved. I wasn't—Nichols and I have history. We always get into it."

I brace for her ire. For her to tell me to fuck off.

Wren reaches out, lifting the ice bag and glancing at my pink knuckles. "So, it had nothing to do with me?"

She doesn't know that I've never hit Brett before. I could blame all of this on the past, let her think I was settling some old score. But I'm sick of lying about how I really feel. I think I'm doing a shitty job of it anyway.

I clear my throat, but the words still come out husky. "It had a lot to do with you."

"Can you give me a ride home?"

"I, uh, yeah. Sure." I stumble through the simple answer, taken aback by the request.

She's already walking to the passenger side. Climbing inside my truck.

My phone buzzes in my pocket.

> **Gus:** She left.
> **Gus:** Nichols is still here, whining about his face.
> **Gus:** Nice right hook.

I smile, shoving my phone back in my jeans and heading for the driver's side.

Wren has gotten comfortable, slipping off her shoes and reclining against the seat, cross-legged. I wonder if she really does like my truck or if she was just bullshitting me last summer.

I start the engine without asking. Brett will leave at some point, and it's better for all of us if I'm gone by then. I'm not sure if he'll actually go to the cops, but he might.

Wren flips on the radio as I drive, but doesn't say anything, aside from sharing directions. The house her family is renting isn't far from the Ellsworth compound, on the ocean, in an exclusive neighborhood.

"Want me to pull in?" I ask, braking when we reach the hedge that borders the end of the driveway.

She nods. "My parents are gone for the weekend. They went to some charity gala in the city."

I flip on my blinker, even though the street is empty, then roll up the clamshell drive. The house—mansion—appears around the bend, pretty much exactly what I expected. Wren's convertible is parked in the circular drive that ends in front of a four-car garage. I park by the water fountain set in front of the gray-shingled house. Six white columns support the front porch that stretches the entire length of the house, gable peaks above it.

I knew her family was rich, but … damn. Seeing this is something else.

"Want to come in?"

My gaze snaps to Wren, who's watching me expectantly, hand poised on the door handle.

"Now?" I ask, like an idiot.

"Yeah."

I turn the key and pocket it, climbing out of the cab. Follow Wren along the pavers that lead to the porch and up to the front door. She unlocks it, then immediately types a code into an electronic panel to the left.

I close the door slowly, looking around. There's a pool I can see through the French doors straight ahead. And a sweeping staircase to the right of the entryway, which Wren heads for after slipping her shoes off. I step out of my sneakers, glancing left into a living room with one, two, three, *four* couches before starting upstairs.

"My room's this way," Wren says, turning left at the top.

I continue down the hallway after her, past artwork that looks awfully expensive, and into a room decorated in shades of blue.

I recognize too much. The bag she packed for her prom. The sunglasses she was wearing when she got to work yesterday. The pink tennis racquet leaning against her desk.

She has her own private bathroom and balcony. The suite is roughly the same size as my entire house. I don't resent Wren for it, but it does make me question what the hell I'm doing here.

Then Wren pulls her shirt over her head, flinging it toward the hamper (and missing) and I forget what a question is.

"You're wearing too many clothes," she says without glancing over to check my state of undress.

I shrug my T-shirt off, snagging the condom out of my pocket before dropping my jeans. Wren is on the bed, in nothing except a matching set of lacy underwear. Her eyes are on my dick as I approach, and it hardens even more under her gaze. It's been … fuck, it's been so long.

Parts of this should feel rote. We've had sex three times before. But despite the flood of lust that's fueling impatience, there's a fluttering of nerves and uncertainty as I reach the edge of the mattress.

Wren rises up onto her knees, trailing her fingers down the center of my chest. They linger in the strip of hair below my navel, and it feels like all the blood in my body is rushing to that spot.

"Are you going to last more than five minutes this time?"

"Probably not," I admit, tangling one hand in her hair.

She giggles.

I wonder what she'd say if I explained why I came so fast with her. Before I can give it any more thought, Wren starts stroking my erection. Slowly, but speed barely matters at this point.

I rip the condom wrapper open with my teeth so I don't have to stop touching her.

"Let me do it," Wren says, taking it from me.

I hand it to her, fighting the urge to thrust as she rolls it on me. As soon as it's in place, I crawl over her. Kiss her, gently at first, then rougher. I'm still on edge from earlier. Still … jealous.

I know I am, and it's not the first time it's happened. I was jealous when she called me to brag about her boyfriend. I was jealous when she went upstairs at the party last weekend. And I was jealous when Brett Nichols was talking to her. If he'd simply said hello to her, then kept walking, I would have been jealous.

And that's a massive fucking problem because Wren Kensington isn't mine. She'll never be mine. She'll wind up with a guy with a trust fund and a future that isn't a dead end, who drives a car manufactured in this century.

"I need you," she whispers, wrapping her legs around my waist. Squirming and shifting under me, trying to take my dick.

I roll us both on our sides, lift her leg, tug her thong to one side, and thrust. She gasps, spine arching as she adjusts to the invasion. I don't give her much time to, sliding out and then filling her again. Getting off on her needy whimpers as much as the tight clasp of her cunt. She called me while out with her ex-boyfriend. Kissed me back after going into that bedroom. Possessiveness streaks through me. I don't think she'll call or kiss another guy after this. I think that means I have her in a way neither of them did, and that's enough. That will have to be enough.

I don't think I last five minutes, but Wren comes first. Comes loudly, so it's good her family is out of town.

I flop on my back, breathing heavily as my body tingles with the aftermath of the best release I've experienced since December. Roll off the mattress once I catch my breath, walking into the bathroom. I'm blinded by marble as I flip on a light. There's a huge bathtub, a glass shower, and two sinks. I shake my head, grabbing a tissue to take care of the condom, and then wash my hands. The soap smells good.

Wren walks in as I'm drying my hands on a fluffy towel. I was too impatient to take off her bra before sex, but she's naked now. She walks to the toilet, pees, flushes, and then uses the sink next to me. I alternate between glancing at the curve of her ass and her boobs. It's all right there, and I've never had the time or space to explore her body the way I want to.

I know I'm getting hard again, even before Wren glances down. Rather than impressed, she appears smug. She should, I guess. I'm reacting to her.

"Want to take a shower?" she asks.

I swallow, physically pained by the next words that have to come out. "We can't. I don't have another condom."

"I have some."

Wren pulls a drawer open, revealing a familiar box. It's the same brand I always buy, which is convenient. The box is open, but there aren't many missing. She grabs one, hands it to me, and then walks over to the shower and turns the spray on. The water heats up instantly, steam collecting on the glass. She steps inside the stall, leaving the door open an inch.

I follow a few seconds later, condom curled in my fist. I'm glad she had some, and I also sort of hate it.

I pin her against the white tiles, kissing her again. Biting her bottom lip, then soothing the sting with my tongue. The shower is full of steam by now, coating our bodies with a warm sheen. My dick is poking her stomach, throbbing and insistent.

I suck in a ragged breath, then open my mouth to make sure she's ready for another round.

Before I can say a word, Wren reaches for my right hand, lifting it. I don't realize why until she peers at my knuckles. One did split, and she kisses it so lightly that I barely feel the brush of her lips.

"Did I scare you?" I ask.

She straightens, expression confused as her eyes meet mine. "What?"

"Earlier." I swallow. "When I hit him. Did that ... scare you?"

"No," she says swiftly. "Of course not."

"I know I shouldn't have. And I'd never—I'd *never* lose control like that with you. I need you to know that."

"I know that, Sawyer."

There's nothing except sincerity and a little surprise on her face.

I nod, relieved by her reaction. "Okay. Good."

"You're the only person I—" She clears her throat. "I've never told anyone else what happened with Third. I-I trust you."

I exhale, bracing a hand against the tiles beside her head. "My dad embezzled money from the force. That's what he went to prison for. Nichols's dad was chief when it happened. My dad made his look like a fool, got him fired. That's why—part of why—he hates me so much."

"Why else?" she asks quietly.

I half smile. "I beat him out for the starting pitcher spot."

"I didn't know you play baseball."

"Used to. I don't anymore."

She bites her bottom lip. "I didn't flirt back. If I had ... it would have only been because you were there with Macie."

"I wasn't there *with* Macie."

"So, you're not ..."

"I've never touched her, Wren."

I slide my palm down her ribs, over the curve of her hip, and then between her thighs, fingering her slick, swollen pussy. She moans softly, head tilting back against the tiles.

The tip of my cock is leaking; I'm so hard. But I don't open the condom. Don't end the torture. I rub her clit and then fuck her with my fingers, smiling when her moans come louder and closer together. It's fast and messy, my hand picking up pace as she grinds against my palm. But there's something soft about it too—maybe because I know I just let her in a little more despite my resolve that I wouldn't.

It's only July. What will my willpower look like by late August? I'm the one who will get left behind when Wren goes to California.

She comes hard, again, squeezing the shit out of my fingers. Blinking at me with a dazed, sated expression.

I smirk, tipping her chin up with my left hand. "Not used to coming twice?"

Wren glares, batting my hand away. "You're an asshole."

"I know." I press closer, letting her feel how hard I am. "And so do you."

Her hands brush the damp hair off my forehead. Her fingers trail down the side of my face, thumb stroking the scar that splits my chin. Her lips part, like she's going to say something, but then her other hand grabs the chain around my neck, using it to jerk my head down. She rises up on her tiptoes, kissing me again.

This—we—won't last.

And I'm terrified by the sudden realization of how much I'd like it to.

CHAPTER 27

Sawyer

I'm more comfortable in a police station than the average person. But it's still daunting, sitting in an interrogation room, waiting to be questioned. My knee bounces nervously beneath the table, and I hope the cameras in here can't pick that angle up. It'd probably be interpreted as an admission of guilt. And I *am* guilty, technically, but I only hit him once. Didn't break his nose. Nichols was back on his feet a few seconds later, spewing threats. Despite what my dad did, I'm more popular around here than Brett or the former chief is. But my father sure didn't do himself any favors with the local police force.

The door opens.

I glance up, knee stilling.

"You grew up, kid."

I exhale, recognizing the officer. Mason Howard is who I would have requested, if I'd been given a choice of interrogator. He'd always hand me lollipops when I visited my dad at work. More importantly, he's

a decent guy. Fair. The type of cop I thought my father was.

"Yeah," I say, forcing a smile. "Good to see you."

"You too. Wish it were at a game."

I nod once. Mason has a kid a couple of years younger than me. We played together on a few teams over the years. I think Max Howard used to look up to me the same way Mason Howard used to look up to my dad.

I wonder if Mason knows I quit baseball. Probably.

"All right," Mason says, settling across from me and flipping open a folder. "You know why you're here?"

"I think so," I reply, unsure if that's the proper response. Wondering if I should request a lawyer. I've never been to a police station for any reason unrelated to my father's job. I've been disciplined at school for skipping or for not turning in assignments on time. My dad doled out his version of punishments at home. But I've never actually been arrested or had any interaction with a cop who wasn't a coworker of my dad's.

"A Mr. Brett Nichols alleges an altercation took place between you and him on July 19, around 11 p.m., at Lucky's Bar. Were you there that evening?"

"Yes."

"Were you drinking?"

"No."

Mason nods. "The bartender, Owen Powell, confirmed you weren't served." He flips to a new page. "Was Mr. Nichols drinking?"

"I think so. I'm not certain. He walked by our table after we arrived, and he was holding a beer then. I never actually saw him drinking."

Another nod. "Now, for the altercation itself. Mr. Nichols alleges you approached him?"

I swallow. "That's true."

"Why did you approach him?"

"It looked like—he seemed to be bothering a friend of mine."

"And that friend is?"

"I'd rather not say."

Mason flips through more papers. "According to witness reports, it was Wren Kensington."

I nod once.

"I need a verbal confirmation for the record, Sawyer."

"That's correct."

"All right. So, you believed Mr. Nichols was harassing Ms. Kensington. Then what happened?"

"I went over there to tell him to leave her alone."

"Did Ms. Kensington ask for your assistance?"

"I could tell he was making her uncomfortable. But, no, she didn't explicitly ask me to get involved. We were across the room from each other."

"What happened once you went over there?"

"I asked him to move away. Brett wasn't listening. He got aggressive, was in my face. So … I hit him." I shift in my chair, quickly adding, "Only once."

"Reports stated Mr. Nichols fell to the floor. You only hit him once?"

I'm probably imagining it, but there's a glimmer of what looks like amusement, maybe even pride, in his eyes. I wonder what my dad would think if he still worked here and quickly banish the thought.

"Correct." I clear my throat. "I wasn't trying to injure him. Just get through to him that I wasn't fuc—I mean, kidding around."

Mason closes the folder. "Thanks for coming down, Sawyer."

I glance around the bare room. "That's … it?"

"That's it. Your statement was corroborated by other witness statements. Mr. Nichols was described as aggressive and volatile by multiple patrons. They also saw him drinking. That does not mean your response was warranted, but it doesn't make him a credible witness either. After he was informed of that, Mr. Nichols opted to drop all charges. Lucky's Bar also chose not to pursue the matter. I just needed to take your statement as part of the procedure before we officially closed the matter."

Mason stands, holding a hand out to me. I stand, too, shaking it.

He doesn't let go right away. "Off the record, you got lucky, Sawyer. If fewer people had seen him drinking or if you'd broken his nose … we'd be having a very different conversation. I know you've had a rough go of it lately, but that's no excuse to be getting in bar fights."

"I understand. It won't happen again."

"Good. Also, your father was wrong about a lot of things. But he was right about one: plenty of people in this town play by their own rules. Powerful friends can become enemies. Be careful."

I frown. "I don't know what you're talking about."

Mason sighs. "Someone hired a real pit bull of a lawyer on your behalf. She had a case prepped against Lucky's for serving minors and dug up a lot on Mr. Nichols that discredited him even more than being intoxicated at the time of the incident. Someone was looking out for you because I know you didn't hire her yourself. Those types of people work for who is paying them. They can make problems disappear … or appear. It worked out for you, this time, but don't assume it always will."

I nod as our hands drop. "Thanks."

Mason ushers me out of the room and past the reception desk. "I'm rooting for you, Sawyer," he says, shaking my hand one final time before heading toward the bullpen.

I call a, "Thanks," after him, then head outside and climb into my truck.

I told Dusty I had a doctor's appointment this morning to explain my tardy arrival at work.

He's standing in the lot when I arrive, talking to one of the valets, giving me a scrutinizing look as I approach. "Everything okay, Bennett?"

"Great," I say, not lying this time.

I had no real idea how that meeting was going to play out, and it couldn't have gone much better. I'm still bothered by Mason's warning and the niggling realization that I only know one person who would have hired a fancy lawyer on my behalf.

I pay attention as Dusty gives me a list of tasks to prioritize, then step over the rope fence and head for the yacht club's main building as soon as Dusty heads to his office. Technically, we're allowed to stop in the kitchen to grab water, coffee, whatever.

I do grab some coffee, and then I go looking for Wren.

She's out on the patio, cleaning menus with a couple of the other waitresses. It's too early for lunch, so the tables are all deserted.

I nod greetings to Macie and Abby, then focus on Wren. "Can I talk to you for a minute?"

"Mmhmm." She tosses the wipe aside and stands, walking over to me.

The sun is bright and brilliant today, turning her hair golden. She's wearing the standard uniform, but I scan it like I've never seen the polo and skirt before. I focus on her mouth last, watching it curve up as she notices me look at her.

Some of my annoyance fades. We haven't really spoken since Saturday night, and I missed her. When I'm around Wren, it's too easy to forget about other important things, which is how I ended up at the police station this morning.

The reminder counteracts a little of the lust heating my bloodstream.

That's another problem of mine—no matter how many times we have sex, I still wind up wanting more.

"This way," I say, walking down the ramp to one of the private docks.

The restaurant isn't open yet, but the marina is. I don't want anyone overhearing us.

"Did you hire me a lawyer?" I ask, turning to face Wren as soon as we've reached an empty slip with no one nearby.

"No."

I cross my arms. "Someone hired a fancy lawyer who dug up dirt on Nichols and helped get the charges dropped. That wasn't you?"

"They dropped the charges?" Wren asks, her attempt at sounding surprised pretty underwhelming.

"Don't lie to me, Wren. You're the only person who knew what happened with the money to hire someone like that. Admit it."

"*I* didn't hire anyone." This time, she emphasizes the pronoun.

I scowl, unamused by the technicalities. "Who did, then?"

"I asked my sister for a favor. She's starting at Harvard Law in the fall, and she spent all of college doing internships at top firms. I explained the basics. Rory knew who to call."

One phone call. That's all it takes to fix a mistake in Wren's world.

"I didn't ask for your help."

She scoffs. "Yeah. *You're welcome.*"

"They were going to drop the charges anyway!"

"That wasn't a guarantee."

"It was my mess to handle, Wren."

"No." She shakes her head. "You hit him because of me."

I sigh. "I told you, there's bad blood there. And I'm the one who chose to swing. None of it was your fault."

She holds my gaze. "Then why is everyone talking about how shocking it was? How that guy goads you every chance he gets, and you never ever take the bait?"

"They're exaggerating," I say, although … not really. "You know how gossip is."

Wren looks down. Low enough that her ponytail spills over one shoulder, helping to hide her expression. "You knew him crowding me like that and not listening would remind me of what had happened with Third. And you only knew that because I had told you what happened with him. So, it *was* my fault, and I—"

"You're wrong." I touch her chin, lifting it until her face is visible. "I meant what I said—that punch had been a long time coming between us. Yeah, I got mad he was all over you. But I would have been pissed about it, no matter what you'd shared—or not shared—with me before. For the record, I'm glad you told me. I was the one who hit him, and I was the one who should have handled the consequences. I'll pay you back the legal fees."

Wren shakes her head. "I'm not taking your money."

"I'm not taking your charity. I wasn't asking, Wren. Like you didn't ask before getting involved."

We stare at each other, both too stubborn to back down.

Until she asks abruptly, "What are we?"

Probably the one question that could catch me off guard right now. Because there's never been an obvious answer to it, not since the night we met and I jumped off that cliff after her for some idiotic reason, and it's only grown more complicated over time. It feels especially complex right now because everyone is right—I don't get in fights. It's always been a hard limit for me, ever since the truth about my dad came out. We look alike. I spent most of my childhood trying to impress and please him. The comparisons were there, but one thing I could control was my temper.

Until Wren was involved.

We haven't felt like strangers since the first time we had sex. We rarely seem like friends—the footing between us is too rocky compared to the smooth ease of spending time with Gus or Wade or anyone else I place in that category. Our chemistry is flammable—and not only in person. She's the only person I can picture to get off solo anymore.

The scene with Brett took place because I was trying to protect her. And this is another attempt—to protect her from me. Because I'll let her down, over and over again, and she should have learned that lesson by now.

I open my mouth.

Close it.

The silence drags on until she takes a step back, putting more distance between us. "Yeah. That's what I thought. Good talk, Cap."

I swear under my breath as she spins and walks away, blonde ponytail swishing as she heads for the ramp.

"How much was the lawyer?" I call after her.

"Nineteen dollars and ninety-nine cents," she says, passing a sign that advertises the lunch special as … nineteen dollars and ninety-nine cents.

I groan, drag my palms down my face, and then head over to the marina to do something productive.

CHAPTER 28

Sawyer

"**H**ey, Wren! Wanna come bluffing?"

I glower at Gus, then quickly glance at Wren. She's about fifteen feet away, unlocking her convertible. Not meeting my gaze.

We've avoided each other since our argument on the docks. I've lain in bed for the past ten nights, tossing a baseball at the ceiling, listening to, "What are we?" echoing in my head.

"Yeah, sure," she calls back. "I just have to swing by my house. Grab a suit."

"What about skinny-dipping?" Aaron calls, and a muscle in my jaw jumps.

I see them talking a lot, but I don't think he and Wren have hooked up. I don't know for sure though. Maybe there are other guys besides Aaron. Maybe Wren isn't as confused about us as I am.

I stride toward my truck, not waiting for Gus.

He checks with Wren, making sure she remembers where to go, then

jogs over to climb into the passenger seat.

"Why'd you do that?" I ask Gus as soon as the door is shut.

"Do what?"

I reverse out of the spot, sending a spray of gravel flying as I accelerate toward the street. "Invite her," I grit out.

"Cammie? Abby? Macie—"

"You know who."

"Wren?"

I nod.

"Because you're in love with her and you're doing nothing about it."

I nearly drive off the road, swerving the tires straight just before they cross the white line.

"Jesus!" Gus yelps.

I care about Wren a lot. I can admit that much to myself. She's like no one else I've ever met, and there's an intrigue to that. We have chemistry.

But I am absolutely, definitely, definitively *not* in love with her.

Right?

"I'm not," I tell Gus.

He snorts, then says, "Okay," in that obnoxious tone people use when they don't believe you, but don't bother saying so.

"I'm *not.*"

"You punched Nichols."

"He deserved it."

"He always deserves it," Gus agrees. "But you don't always show off your right hook. You haven't hit anyone in years ... until Wren was involved."

I unclench my jaw to say, "I lost my temper. It happens."

"Fine. Then why did you get wasted on New Year's Eve after she left?

Why did she spend the night at your house back in May? You never bring girls home. I saw the look on your face when people were talking about her going upstairs with Aaron. You've barely said a word to the poor kid since then, and you treat all the other guys the same."

"Poor kid? He's nineteen. And he forgot to charge a customer for gas yesterday."

"I'm not saying you want to be in love with her, okay? Maybe you're so deep in denial that you actually believe you aren't. But I'm telling you, as your best friend and as someone who's spent time around you two, you are. And you're going to lose her if you don't accept it soon. We both know she's got plenty of other options. She won't wait forever."

I scoff. "She's not waiting now."

"She went upstairs with him *after* you showed up with Macie, Cap."

"Whose fault was that? You called and asked me to drive Macie—"

"Yours," Gus interrupts. "If you'd told Wren how you felt before then, it wouldn't have mattered who you showed up with."

When I say nothing, he continues, "I haven't seen her with any other guys since then. I think you've got a shot."

"I don't *want* a shot," I snap.

"Sure," Gus sings in that maddening tone again.

I shake my head, turn up the radio's volume, and roll my window all the way down. Rest one elbow on the door, keeping my gaze on the road ahead. Between the wind and the blaring music, I won't hear anything else Gus says.

But it doesn't matter. His words are already burrowing into my brain.

Fuck. Am I in love with her? How am I supposed to know, to tell? I've tried to downplay any reaction around her, and Gus still thinks I am. If I'd done what I really wanted to—chase after her on New Year's Eve, fuck her in my bed on her prom night, punch Aaron for touching her at that party, tell Nichols, "She's mine," when he commented that he'd seen her first—what the hell would he have thought then? Not that he was wrong about my feelings—that's for damn sure.

Arriving at the cliff is a relief. Gus won't say anything about Wren in front of everyone. He's loyal. Always has my back.

Which makes his observations harder to dismiss. He *does* know me, has seen me with a lot of girls. I know his comments aren't baseless. I just need them to be a little rickety. Wren hasn't said a word to me in over a week. I already lost her, probably. I lost her in that damn storage closet, most likely.

And what would a relationship between us even look like? She's moving to California next month. And I'm … well, past the marina closing, I have no clue what I'll be doing. Most of the jobs around here are seasonal. Lucky's might hire me around the holidays—they're always short-staffed that time of year, and I think Owen likes me enough to look past the Brett incident. I have enough savings to make it to next summer. Longer if I keep living at home. But I don't know what I'll *do* if I stay right where I am.

Sadness about Skylar and anger at my dad turned my future into a dead end. Crappy grades and no baseball mean I couldn't even get into the community college Gus is going to.

Wren might have chosen UCLA, but she could have gone anywhere.

Her opportunities are endless. Mine are practically nonexistent. That's partly my fault, which makes it even worse. I want to be someone who triumphs over adversity rather than allows it to sink them, but I barely know where to begin that battle.

"Let's go," Cammie announces once everyone has climbed out of cars.

I scan the line of parked vehicles. No convertible.

"Wren isn't here yet," I say, avoiding looking toward where Gus is standing.

Cammie rolls her eyes. "She knows the way."

I shrug a shoulder, then lean a foot back against my truck.

"It'll be dark soon," Cammie adds.

I glance up at the sky. It's barely six. "Sun won't set for a couple of hours."

"We should wait for everyone," Aaron says, glancing at me like I'll be impressed by him agreeing.

The only reason I fight the scowl that wants to appear in response is Gus's lecture. He's right; I don't have to be best friends with the guy, but it's unprofessional and unfair—and obvious, apparently—to treat him differently simply because of whatever has or is happening between him and Wren.

Cammie sighs, but quits arguing after Aaron chimes in.

Wren's convertible arrives a few minutes later. She parks at the end of the row of cars, climbing out, and Aaron jogs over to her like an eager puppy.

I tug on the brim of my ball cap as I straighten and start walking toward the path, tracking Wren's progress out of the corner of my eye. She's smiling in response to whatever Aaron said to her, tucking her hands into the front pocket of her hoodie. I do a double take, gaze lingering in that direction.

She's wearing my sweatshirt. The one I gave her on the beach, on the Fourth, while we watched the fireworks. I'm just realizing she never returned it.

I don't know what her wearing it means. If she just happened to grab it or happened to have it in her car.

But I do like seeing her in my clothes, and if I asked Gus, I'm pretty sure he would say that's another tally in the *Love* column.

No one else is in the clearing. We're too large of a group to all approach the cliff ledge at once—I'm not even sure if everyone who came is planning on jumping, but I am. So, I walk ahead as part of the first group. So does Wren.

"Want to go first?" Aaron asks her as she pulls off my sweatshirt.

"Sure," she answers, tossing the hoodie on the ground and walking closer to the edge.

Wren doesn't hesitate this time. Nor does she kiss Aaron, in case she's about to die, which is a relief. She runs and leaps, allowing plenty of clearance from the rocks clustered against the cliff's face.

Aaron steps ahead to jump next. No doubt hoping for a romantic moment in the water before the rest of us join them.

Gus holds a hand out, blocking him. "Wait for her to come up first."

I frown, taking a step forward so I can peer over the edge. All I see are blue waves topped with whitecaps. No blonde hair. It's choppy, but not dangerously rough. Especially for a strong swimmer.

More seconds tick past. I'm too panicked to count them precisely, but the number I do is too high. She should have surfaced by now. Icy terror floods my veins, freezing my heart and stalling my breathing.

Gus glances nervously at me. "She cleared the rocks fine, so—*Cap!*"

I barely hear his shout over the wind whistling in my ears. Salty water closes over my head a few seconds later. I kick my feet viciously, realizing I didn't take my T-shirt off. Saturated cotton sticks to my arms, billowing around my chest and hindering my progress. Still, when my head breaks through the waves, it looks like I'm the only one in the ocean.

"Wren!" I yell, treading water and rotating in circles as I desperately search the surf for another head.

It gets deep here, fast, which is why it was selected as a jump spot. But she could have gotten slammed by a piece of driftwood, or there could be a shark or a jellyfish, or—

"Hi!" She pops up like a buoy right in front of me, slicking blonde hair out of her face and smiling hugely as she sucks in a deep breath. "I've been practicing in the pool. I can do three laps now without—"

I nearly sink; I'm so weak with relief. And then? Then I'm fucking furious. So mad that I can't say a word. I start swimming toward the shore, my waterlogged shirt barely slowing my angry strokes.

"Sawyer!" Wren calls, but I can't stop. Can't talk.

I reach the sandy section of the shore in record time, yanking my shirt off as soon as I can stand. It rips, and I couldn't give a single shit.

"Sawyer!" She's still following. Still shouting my name.

I'm out of the water, striding toward the path that leads back up to the top. Except I'm not headed there. I need to be somewhere— anywhere—else. Gus can catch a ride home with someone else. All our friends are here.

"Hey!" Wren sounds angry now too.

And she's catching up. I can hear the splashing as she reaches the shallows. Hear her rapid breathing as she runs after me, grabbing my arm and yanking me to face her.

"What the—"

"Did you think that was *funny*?" I barely recognize the sound of my own voice. Each syllable seethes with fury.

Her annoyed expression wavers. "I mean, I was just holding my—"

"My sister fucking drowned, Wren. Skylar got caught in a rip current, and they couldn't save her in time."

Wren's grip on my arm goes slack. I literally see the blood drain from her cheeks, turning her flushed face pale.

"I-I had no idea."

I close my eyes. "I know."

Another thing I've fucked up. Because I didn't know how to tell her. Because I'd never had to tell someone before. This was the worst possible way to go about it—blaming her for trauma she hadn't even known existed.

"I'm *so* sorry about your sister, Sawyer. I-I didn't mean to … I wasn't—I didn't think I was under for that long."

I have no idea how long Wren was under for. Each second felt like hours dragging by since I freaked out as soon as she didn't come up right away. Not only because it was a reminder of what had happened to Skylar, but because it was Wren who might have been in trouble.

Gus was right.

I love her.

I wouldn't have freaked out that way if it had been anyone else slow to surface. I would have been concerned, but I would have been coherent.

"It's fine," I say stiffly. "I overreacted."

"No, you didn't. I swear, if I'd known, I never would have—"

"I have to go," I say, turning and walking away.

She calls my name again, but I don't stop. And I sure as hell don't look back.

CHAPTER 29

Wren

Nerves wriggle in my stomach as I knock on the wooden frame of the screen door. I run my tongue along the backs of my teeth, ears straining for any sound inside the house.

"One sec!" he calls.

I tuck a piece of hair behind my ear, then dry my damp palms on my jean shorts. It's ridiculous that I'm this anxious to talk to him. That I'm this worried he'll say no or not want to see me.

"He just needs some time," was what Gus told me last night.

Cammie commented how important water safety was, as if I hadn't already felt terrible enough about testing how long I could hold my breath. Aaron said he would have jumped in to rescue me if Cap hadn't. Everyone else was just confused by Sawyer's sudden disappearance.

A large shadow looms on the other side of the screen, and then the door swings open with a creak of protest. Sawyer is in the middle of pulling on a shirt, head through the hole but torso still bare. I'm treated to a tantalizing glimpse of his abs and the band of his boxer briefs before

the white fabric falls. He's propped the door open with his foot, and I wait for it to withdraw as soon as he registers it's me. He made it pretty clear he didn't want to talk to me last night, and Gus probably meant more than twelve hours when he said that Sawyer needed time.

The door remains open.

"Hey," he says carefully, resting a shoulder against the doorway. His expression isn't unfriendly, but he's not inviting me inside either.

"Hey," I reply. "Bad time? Are you busy?"

He shakes his head. "I have the day off."

I nod. "I know. I swapped shifts with Abby, and I was wondering …" Deep breath. "Do you want to go sailing?"

His eyebrows inch up his forehead. He's surprised, but I can't gauge anything else. "Sailing?"

"Yeah. I rented a boat."

"You rented a boat."

"You can stop repeating everything I say."

He crosses his arms, one corner of his mouth kicking up. "Do you know how to sail?"

"Nope."

"So, you want me to sail you around … for free?"

I roll my eyes. "I brought lunch. I checked with my cousin who sails, and Kit assured me it's a really nice boat. And I'll give you a blow job in the below-deck-cabin thingy, if you want."

He coughs, quickly glancing over his shoulder.

A pit appears in my stomach. Does he have a girl over?

"No worries. Never mind." I'm doing an awful job of hiding my disappointment, so I offer a small wave, then spin and start walking away, silently cursing my own idiocy.

"Wren, wait."

"It's fine," I call without turning back around.

The screen door slams, and then he calls my name again. Closer this time. He also grabs my arm, halting me in place before stepping in front of me. "My mom is still on a decorating kick. She wants to repaint the kitchen today. I promised her I'd help."

"Oh," I say.

"Otherwise, I would, okay?"

"Okay. I would have, uh, texted to see if you were free, but I don't have your number."

No way was I calling his house again.

A rare full grin appears. "If you want my number, Wren, ask for it."

I roll my eyes again, secretly giddy. He's flirting with me, I think. "I'm not asking for it. I was just explaining why—"

"Sawyer?" A woman steps out of the front door, glancing around the yard. Surprise spreads on her face when she spots me.

I'm assuming she must be his mom, but she's younger than I would have expected. Wearing no makeup and a paint-splattered shirt, she could pass for being in her late twenties.

"Hello," she says pleasantly, walking over.

Sawyer clears his throat. "Mom, this is Wren. Wren, this is my mom."

"Addison," his mom says, smiling as she extends a hand to me. "I know they don't look it, but they're clean."

"Hi," I reply, smiling back as I shake her yellow-streaked palm. "It's nice to meet you, Addison."

"Very nice to meet you too, Wren." She sounds like she means it, not only like it's a common pleasantry.

His mom seems really great, and there's a pinch in my chest as I think about what Sawyer has shared about his family, especially last night's revelation. His dad's destructiveness … his sister's death. A betrayal by her husband and the loss of a child. I've been called fortunate and privileged and lucky my entire life, but I've never felt more so than I do right now, knowing I've never endured that sort of tragedy.

I hope my first impression didn't involve Addison hearing me joke about blow jobs. I'm realizing that's probably why Sawyer looked so uncomfortable when I did.

"Would you like to come inside?" Addison asks kindly.

"No, thanks. I was just leaving," I respond, not wanting to trap Sawyer into having his mom host me or ruin their day together. "Sorry to come by so early. I work at the yacht club, so I knew Sawyer had the day off, and I was … he said you're painting today. So, I was just leaving."

You already said that.

"We can paint another day," Addison comments, glancing at her son.

"It's really fine," I say quickly before Sawyer can utter a word.

"I haven't even settled on a color," she tells me. "And it's a beautiful day. You kids go have some fun."

"I'm eighteen, Mom," Sawyer says dryly.

"Don't remind me," Addison replies, smiling at me again before she turns back toward the house. "I hope to see you again, Wren."

"You too!" I call after her, then glance at Sawyer. He's already looking at me. "I like your mom."

"Me too."

"You don't have to change your plans."

He shakes his head once, impatiently. "Do you want me to drive?"

"No. I'll drive. I know where we're going, and you don't."

A faint smile crosses his face.

I head for the driver's seat. As soon as he can't see my expression, I allow the giddy smile to spread across my face.

It sort of feels like Sawyer Bennett just agreed to go on a date with me.

"Just let me do it," Sawyer insists.

"No. I want to learn how."

"There's nothing to learn, Wren. You're just going to get a blister."

I keep a stubborn hold on the oars, and Sawyer sighs before leaning back and throwing his hands up in a *whatever* gesture.

"Okay. Fine. We'll get there by sunset, probably. Perfect timing to turn back around."

If I wasn't concerned about losing a paddle, I'd drop one and flip him off.

We're in a small rowboat, about ten feet from the dock. There are only two seats, and Sawyer tried to take the center one. But I wasn't downplaying my nautical abilities. Once we get on board the sailboat, I won't know what to do with any of the ropes or with … anything. Won't be able to contribute.

I doubt the guy would have agreed to let me take the rental out actually if Sawyer hadn't been with me to impress the marina crew. We're about an hour from Atlantic Yacht Club because an outing at work didn't sound all that special. But we could be at that marina because this one looks exactly the same. Especially from this vantage point in the water.

Rowing sounded noncomplicated. It's not complicated, but it's not easy either. I lean back, pulling the oar handles to my chest.

"Let me know if I'm about to hit anything," I tell him since I'm sitting backward.

"They'll have pulled the other boats out for the winter before we reach them."

I glare at him. "I play tennis, and I ride horses, okay? I can be athletic."

"How is Apollo?" he asks casually.

"She's, uh … she's good," I respond, momentarily startled by the question. I don't think I've mentioned my mare's name around him this summer. Meaning he remembered it from one of my letters this past fall.

It's disconcerting, flipping from acknowledging all we know about each other and all we're pretending not to. Especially since learning last night that there are major things I don't know about him. I told him I trust him, and I meant it. But I'm not sure he trusts me, and that bothers me—a lot.

"She's here," I add. "I had her trailered from Connecticut so I could ride her more this summer."

"So, your horse has a summer place too?"

"Yep."

I fight a wince as the wooden handle rubs the heel of my hand. Sawyer might have been right about the blisters.

"Willowbrook?"

"Yeah," I say, surprised he knows the name of the stable.

Sawyer nods once. "Skylar took lessons there for a bit."

"Oh."

I wasn't sure we'd discuss his sister today. Now that he's brought her up, I don't know if I should ask more questions or not.

Before I can decide, Sawyer continues, "She loved clothes and fashion too. She used to paint her nails a different color every day of the week. Made the whole house stink constantly."

"Sounds like a kindred spirit. Rory hid all my nail polish once; she was so sick of the smell."

"Yeah." He glances left, at the row of boats we're slowly moving past. "Yeah. She would have lo—been obsessed with you."

I'm glad he isn't looking at me. Because this is worse than him shutting me out entirely. It's a different yearning from the glimpse of him shirtless earlier. It's a tease of more. A taunt of what it could be like—of what we could be like—if we escaped from this state of … something. Not nothing, not everything.

I asked him what we were, and he stayed silent, which felt like the worst reaction at the time. But there's space in uncertainty.

Or maybe that's just hopeful thinking.

"Move right," Sawyer says suddenly. He's refocused this way, looking behind me, not at me.

"What? Why?" I twist my head, trying to spot whatever he's seeing. Slowing our progress down to nonexistent and making the entire dory rock.

Sawyer says my name like a swear, grabbing both sides of the small boat to steady us. "There's another boat coming in. It's fine; they see us. Just move right."

"My right or your …"

"*My* right." He leans forward, adjusting my grip on one oar. "Exert more pressure on this side."

"You should take over," I blurt.

I wanted to contribute, but I'm not trying to capsize us either.

"Nah, you've got it." He slumps back, arms propped on either side, like he's reclined in an armchair.

"You've been asking to take over since we left the dock," I remind him. "Now, you're happy watching?"

"You're doing fine," he tells me.

"Fine, huh? Your compliments still suck." He opens his mouth to reply, but I forge ahead first. "Also, you're the one who *likes boats*. Presumably, that means you know how to steer them, so you should really take over."

Sawyer smiles. "You have this, Wren."

Which would be sort of sweet, if he didn't follow it up with, "Told you so," once we finally do reach the sailboat.

CHAPTER 30

Sawyer

"What are you doing down here?"

"What are *you* doing down here?" Wren counters.

"Who's steering the boat?"

I grin. "Worried we'll hit something?"

"We could. A whale or—"

"We're not gonna hit a whale."

"What, because there aren't any whales in the ocean?"

"Because we're moving slower than any whale swims. They'd have plenty of time to get out of the way." I walk down the rest of the stairs, ducking my head to avoid hitting the cabin ceiling. "Let me see."

"See what?"

I glance pointedly at the notebook she flipped over as soon as I appeared in the doorway.

"It's nothing."

"So, show me."

Wren sighs, then reaches out and turns it over. It's a simple pencil sketch, but impressively detailed. There's texture to the water visible behind me and to the rope of the rigging. There's definition to my forearms, too, as I secure the sheets, my hair ruffled by the wind. I'm smiling, expression relaxed and focused.

It's flattering—to think this is how she views me. And that she bothered to draw me at all.

"You've improved," I say.

Wren scowls. "I don't usually draw—"

"Which I didn't think was possible," I finish.

She picks the pencil up off the table, spinning it around one finger. Her cheeks are a little pink, I notice.

"You didn't answer me. What are you doing down here?"

"Down here, in the below-deck-cabin thingy? I heard blow jobs were being offered."

She grimaces. "Do you, uh, do you think that your mom heard that?"

"I'm not sure," I answer honestly. "She won't care though. I'm eighteen. I think she's assumed I've moved past passing girls *I like you* notes."

Wren smiles. "You did that?"

"Once, in middle school. Cammie dared me to."

"Was the girl her?"

"No." But in retrospect, I wonder if that was a test. One I failed.

"You and she never …"

"We hooked up. Once. The summer after my sophomore year, right after Skylar died. I was—I was in a bad place. Looking for any distraction. Sex, drinking, even some drugs. It didn't mean anything to me. I never … felt that way about her. And I didn't realize she felt that way about me until … too late."

"Is that why she hates me?"

"It probably didn't help. But I think her issue is more with how your life looks. Cammie grew up with a single mom, who she's mostly supported since high school. From the outside, you—and anyone with money—has security she's had to work really hard for. Has family who takes care of them versus the other way around. It's not personal to you. Most of the summer people don't spend any time around locals, so you're the only one she can take any frustration out on."

"Is that how you see me? Spoiled?"

I shake my head. "No, of course not. It's not like you had any say in who your family was."

"Neither did you."

I've never told Wren how much the comparisons to my father unnerve me, yet she seems to have realized it anyhow.

I nod, then jerk my chin toward the door. "I should go check for whales."

She stands from her spot in the eating nook. "Before you get what you came for?"

"I was kidding, Wren."

She walks closer, running her tongue along her lower lip in what I think is a purposeful move to draw my attention to her mouth. It works.

"Well, I wasn't. I've never given you one before."

I'm amused by the way she says it, like I'm possibly unaware.

"I know."

"I was going to … that night in my room. I was going to blow you and then put the condom on, but I got … it'd been a while since we'd—I got nervous, I guess. And I'd thought about doing it in your truck, in the driveway, but the angle was … I wasn't sure how to—" She stops talking, meeting my gaze and noticing the smile on my face. "What?"

"Nothing."

"*What?*"

"Seriously, nothing. Keep describing all the times you've thought about blowing me."

"That would take too long."

My eyebrows rise. Not the answer I was anticipating. Just knowing that Wren has thought about sucking me in her mouth has me getting hard. Knowing it's happened often? It's not just a physical response.

"Sit," she says, shoving my chest, pushing me toward the beige couch.

It's barely a couch, really more of an oversize armchair. Not that comfortable, but I'm not focused on the flat cushions right now. My full attention is on Wren, sinking to her knees between my spread thighs.

"Have you hooked up on a boat before?" she asks conversationally, playing with the strings on my shorts. "Lie if you have."

"I haven't. Truth."

She tugs down my shorts, thumb circling the flared head of my cock, smearing around the liquid already leaking from the red tip.

"I've barely touched you," she comments, sounding amused. Wren blows on the wetness, and my hips jerk forward of their own accord. "*Barely.*"

"Are you gonna talk or suck?" I grit out, feeling like I might die if the second doesn't happen soon.

Her eyelashes flutter as she looks up from under them. "Do you have a preference?"

I drag a palm down my face, then form a fist, tempted to shove a hand into her hair and guide her mouth where I want it. I don't. Wren might be the one on her knees, but we both know she's holding all the power right now.

"*Suck*, Wren."

She does, and fuck if it isn't even hotter than I imagined it being.

"You look good with my cock in your mouth."

Her right hand moves from playing with my balls to flip me off.

I laugh, a fresh flood of arousal building at the base of my spine.

If I believed in soulmates, I'd accept Wren Kensington was meant for me. If I thought she'd ever be happy with the nothing I had to offer her, I would admit I was in love with her.

"I'm close," I grunt in warning after an embarrassingly short amount of time has passed.

She hums, the vibration sending me straight over the edge. I come hard and fast, filling her mouth with so much cum that it spills out, dripping down her chin. Feeling her swallow is its own nirvana, and then I'm hauling her onto my lap, unbuttoning her shorts and slipping a hand inside, finding the wet spot in her underwear. Circling her clit and having her ride my hand until she comes with a moan she muffles against my shoulder.

"You know no one can hear us out here, yeah?"

Wren lifts her head. "You know where here is, yeah?"

"Approximately. I haven't been up on deck for a while, so …"

"Hey, all you had to say was that you didn't want me to suck your dick."

"Wren," I say very seriously, "that is a sentence that will never ever leave my mouth."

She smiles, then rolls off my lap and walks into the bathroom. I grab a water out of the fridge and then head back up to the deck, easing the sails a little and adjusting our course before taking a seat on the bench along the back of the stern.

Wren reappears a few minutes later, focusing on me before she glances at the sea surrounding us. She pads across the pristine deck, sitting beside me and tucking her legs under her. She holds her phone up, snapping a few photos of the boat and the water, then leans toward me, passing me her phone. "Your arm is longer."

"You want one of us?"

She nods, so I flip the perspective and take one. It's the only picture we've ever taken together, and it's a good one. We're both smiling. The wind is blowing her hair behind us. We look happy, and it scares me.

I'm too jaded to trust happiness will last. And I love Wren enough to push her far away from my problems. She'd probably try to fix them for me, like she did with that fancy lawyer.

"If I had your number, I'd send it to you," Wren comments, glancing at the photo before dropping her phone on the bench.

Her tone is casual, nearly breezy. I've realized—maybe too late— that's a signal she's saying something important.

I play along, answering the same way I did earlier. "If you want my number, Wren, just ask."

She doesn't.

She trails her fingers up my arm, lingering just below my left elbow. "Which tattoo was your first one?"

"That one," I say, twisting my arm so she can see. It's a black outline of a baseball's stitches. Small, only a couple of inches long because I didn't want my mom to spot it.

Wren traces it lightly. "Why did you stop playing?"

"It was my thing with my dad. I didn't like being reminded of him."

She nods, touching the anchor next. "I like this one." She weaves her fingers through my other hand, lifting and inspecting that arm too. "The vines are cool too."

"Thanks."

"I'm glad you don't have a skull or something fake macho."

I laugh.

"You don't, right?" She glances me over again, like she's worried she accidentally missed it.

"You know I don't. You've seen me naked."

"Yeah, but when you're naked, I'm not looking at your tattoos."

I laugh again, my fingers tangling in her hair as the wind continues to play with it.

Her hand moves to my wrist, flipping it and brushing against the name there. I tense, but don't pull away.

"How old was she?"

"Thirteen."

"Was your dad already in prison when it happened?"

"No. He was stealing from the station, had been for years, but he hadn't gotten caught yet. He got sloppy after Skylar died. She was the center of his world. He loved me when I pitched a no-hitter or did something else he considered impressive. But Skylar couldn't do anything wrong. He adored her, and she adored him. At least"—my voice catches—"she never found out about … everything."

I still haven't told Wren the full truth about my father. Why his sins are so unforgivable. I'm not sure it's something I want her to know about me. And right now, this perfect afternoon, doesn't feel like the right time to bring any of the ugliness up.

"Are you excited about UCLA?" I ask, changing the subject.

Wren turns her head, meeting my gaze. "How'd you know that's where I picked?"

I debate lying, then decide the truth is pretty harmless. "If you don't want strangers looking at your social media, you should make your accounts private."

She smiles. "You looked me up?"

"It took, like, two seconds. Wren Kensington isn't a common name."

"A whole two seconds, huh?" She snuggles a little closer, her head fitting perfectly under my chin. I can't see her expression anymore, and

I'm not sure if that's better or worse. "No."

"No what?"

"No, I'm not excited. I don't know if I want to go to college."

Surprise trickles through me. "What? Why not?"

"I never have. The thought of being stuck in one place, with the same people? With a set schedule that looks the same every week? I don't know what I'd major in. I'd rather go to Greece than take a Greek mythology class. Or intern at a company rather than take a business course. I'm a kinesthetic learner, according to my guidance counselor. Sitting and listening, taking notes? Bores me to death. And that's what most of college is."

"Then why are you going?"

She sighs. "It's important to my parents. *Very* important to my grandfather. He's already disappointed I'm not going to an Ivy. There are certain expectations that are part of my family, and I laugh at or ignore some of them, but others? Pretty nonnegotiable. College is what all my friends are doing, what my sister did, what all my cousins did. Everyone says I'll love it once I'm there. I have no idea what I'll do after, once I have a degree, but that's a later problem. I'm sure all of that sounds stupid to you, but it's … it's my life."

"I don't think it sounds stupid," I tell her. "My parents both went to college. It's not like I'm unfamiliar with the concept."

"Why aren't you going?"

"Isn't an option," I say, hoping that'll be the end of it.

But Wren scoffs rather than agrees. "I saw the letters."

"What?"

"Technically, yes, I was snooping, but the drawer was open a little bit. There were at least a dozen schools, all recruiting you."

I relax some. She doesn't mean her letters. She doesn't know I kept them all.

"That was before. Before I quit baseball, before I stopped taking grades seriously."

"You could still go, if you wanted to. You didn't even apply anywhere, right?"

I stay silent.

No, I didn't. Because I knew what the reply would be and because no one, with the exception of my mom maybe, expected anything different.

"I don't want to talk about it."

"You can't just avoid—"

"I said, *I don't want to talk about it*, Wren. It's *my* life. Doesn't have a damn thing to do with you."

"Right. Of course."

The words themselves aren't bad, but her tone tells me, she's pissed. Hurt too, probably. My fault again.

"I just meant—"

"You're the one talking about it now," she tells me, reaching into her bag and pulling out a tube of sunscreen.

I sigh, then stand. "I should check ..."

"You should," she agrees, not even letting me finish the sentence.

I walk toward the bow. I could check over this entire damn boat and still not know how to explain to Wren that going after things I want— college, her—means risking losing them.

I don't tell her that.

But I do end up asking her to text me the photo of us. Because I want a copy. And because I want her to be able to reach me by other means than a letter or landline, if she ever wanted to.

CHAPTER 31

Wren

"**S**ome hot older guy requested your section, Wren," Abby tells me as soon as I return from my break.

I glance toward the windows, making a face when I realize who she's referring to. "Gross. That is my dad, Abby."

And Dad has spotted me, lifting one hand in a small wave. I grab a menu and head that way.

"What are you doing here?" I ask once I reach his table.

Dad smiles, reclining in his chair. "I missed you too, honey."

He's been in Europe for the past week, meeting with executives from some corporation Kensington Consolidated is considering partnering with. Honestly, I lose track of my dad's frequent meetings and regular trips. He wasn't gone for as long or as often when Rory and I were younger, but that's starting to change now that we're adults.

"Of course I missed you," I say. "But I wasn't expecting to see you until tonight. And at home. Not at my job."

"I wanted to see where you work," Dad tells me.

I arch an eyebrow. "It's members only. You didn't …"

Buying a membership just to visit me at work is something my dad would do. I already feel strange about the fact that everyone knows I'm not waitressing because I need the money. I don't know exactly how much the memberships here cost, but my guess is, the average person would consider it expensive.

"I didn't become a member," Dad assures me. "I'm here as a guest of Hanson's."

I nod, relieved.

"Now"—Dad flips open the menu—"what's good here?"

"The burger is popular," I reply, tapping it with my pen. "So is the lobster roll."

"We're having lobsters tonight. I'll have the burger."

My pen stills. "We are?"

"Yes. Rory and Carson are visiting this weekend."

I grimace as I scribble *burger* on the order pad.

"Wren."

"I'll be nice," I mutter.

"Is there anyone you'd like to invite?"

My head snaps up, and I meet Dad's gaze. I haven't introduced them to a guy since I dated Third, and I think my parents are torn between concern that I'm scarred from how that ended and relief that they haven't had to worry about any guy I'm dating.

"No," I reply, shoving thoughts of Sawyer far away. "No one."

I can't picture him sitting down to eat with my family. Or having anything in common with Carson, who has a trust fund and I've never seen *not* wear a suit. I only met Sawyer's mom by accident, and him meeting my family sounds very boyfriendy. He never answered my question—asking what we were—which is a reply in itself, and I'm too proud to ask again.

I underline _burger_, then glance up. "Medium rare?"

Dad nods.

"Fries or salad on the side?"

"Fries."

"Anything to drink?"

"I'm good with water."

There's already a glass on the table, which Abby must have delivered after seating him.

"Okay." I tuck the order pad back in my apron. "It'll be right out."

"This place is nice," Dad says, leaning back in his chair and glancing around. "Maybe we should become members."

"Isn't Mom's project wrapping up this summer?" I ask. "When would you ever use it?"

"We've talked about buying a place here. It's nice to get away from the crazy pace of the city, especially now that you and your sister are older. More quality time. Fewer places for you to sneak off to, although you've obviously managed to find some."

I roll my eyes. "I haven't snuck out this summer."

Dad tips his water glass to me. "You've earned a lot of responsibility points with this job too. I knew, Wren, from the second the nurse handed you to me, what a fighter you were. Don't let anyone—me or your mom included—tell you what you can or can't do. Within reason, of course," he adds hastily. "You still have a curfew, and I still pay your car insurance, so I can take the keys away whenever I want."

"I could pay it myself now," I tease.

He sips some water. "Great. Write me a check."

"I said I _could_, not that I will."

Dad shakes his head, but he's smiling.

"And thanks, Dad. I know waitressing isn't interning at a courthouse, but—"

Dad sets his glass down decisively. "Wren, what your sister does with her life is her decision. Whatever you decide to do with yours, your mother and I will be proud of you and support you. Do you hear me?"

"I hear you." I fiddle with the pen, rolling it between my fingers before admitting, "I'm still not sure about college."

A crease of concern appears on Dad's forehead. "About UCLA?"

"About … anywhere."

"It's a big change, Wren. It's normal to feel nervous about it."

I sigh. "Grandpa is mad I'm going to UCLA. He told me over the Fourth."

Dad sighs too. His is heavier than mine. "I spent a long time trying to not disappoint your grandfather. Trust me, it's impossible. He wants the very best for you. In his mind, that's tradition. Reputation and prestige. He had very specific expectations for me and your uncle. Some benefited us; others didn't. You picked UCLA. Unless *you* have changed your mind, then that's where you should go."

I smile. "I love you, Dad."

I feel lucky to be a Kensington. I feel *really* lucky to be Oliver Kensington's daughter.

He smiles back. "Love you too, Birdie."

Dad hasn't called me that in a while. I started telling him not to; I suddenly wish I could go back in time and not. One apprehension I didn't mention to Sawyer when he asked why I wasn't excited: I'm anxious about leaving my parents.

I value my independence. I've gone away to summer camps and visited Europe with friends, been away from them for longer stretches of time. But I've never left home so far, for so long before. Even being in a familiar city, close to my grandparents, doesn't make it sound less daunting.

California is far from *here* too. And I'm not frivolous enough to build my future around a boy—let alone one who has repeatedly knocked down any attempt to—but I've never been that far from Sawyer since I met him. We've always lived in the same state.

"I'll be back with your food," I tell Dad, stopping at another one of my tables to see if they need anything and then continuing toward the kitchen to put in Dad's order. I drop off the slip of paper, attempting to ignore the fact that a few of the guys from the marina—including Sawyer—are grabbing their lunches.

"Abby said your dad is here?" Macie asks, appearing next to me.

"Yeah," I confirm.

She giggles. "She also said he's hot."

"And married. To my mom."

Macie laughs. "Hey, I didn't say it. Older men don't do it for me." She glances toward the guys. Toward Sawyer, who's laughing at something Gus said.

Sawyer said he hasn't touched her, and I believe him. I don't know why he hasn't though. Macie is smart and funny and pretty, a year older than us, so she's already in college. She goes to a small one, up in Maine, then spends the summers here with her grandparents. She could easily visit on the weekends. She comes from a normal, nondescript family.

"Wren!"

I jerk my attention back to Macie. "Sorry. What?"

"I said, I'm having a party tonight. You free?"

"Oh. I'm not sure. I have a family-dinner thing tonight. So, probably not."

Macie pouts. "I'll text you my address, in case you can make it."

She skips away, probably to invite the guys. The kitchen bell dings, indicating an order is up. I walk over to the counter, picking up the fish and chips for table five.

My phone buzzes in my back pocket. I pull it out, assuming it'll be Macie sending me her address.

It's not.

Sawyer: You should come.

CHAPTER 32

Sawyer

My phone lights up with a new text as I park in Macie's driveway.

"Nice background." I can hear the smile in Gus's voice.

I roll my eyes, pull the key out of the ignition, then grab my phone off the seat. Look at the photo first before checking to see who messaged me. I'd had the same background forever—a slightly blurry shot from the marina dock I had taken the first summer I started working there—and felt like changing it. I didn't intend to swap it for the photo Wren had taken of us sailing, and I *did* intend to change it to something else after a few hours, but I never did.

"That's more serious than asking a chick to prom," Gus adds.

I roll my eyes, typing a quick response to my mom, letting her know I won't be home until late. "Focus on your own love life."

"Nothing to focus on, Cap." He says it sarcastically, but there's an undercurrent of something else, bitter enough that I glance up.

Gus notices my surprised expression. "C'mon, man. We both know girls talk to me to get to you. It's always been like that. Maybe now that you're taken, someone will settle for me."

"Hey. That's not true."

"This isn't a pity party, Cap. I'm just telling it how it is."

"You're the most loyal, trustworthy, supportive person I've ever met, Gus. Anyone who doesn't see that—who doesn't appreciate it—doesn't deserve you. I sure as hell don't, but I'm so fucking glad you've stuck around and are still my best friend."

Gus grins. "You forgot to mention how sexy and charming and—"

"Yeah, your ego is fine," I say, popping my door open and climbing out of the cab.

Gus laughs, jumping out too.

The house is packed when we enter it. It's nice, bigger than mine, but nothing too fancy. I recognize most of the people here, but not all of them. Macie has been coming here in the summers since high school and has worked at several local businesses, crossing paths with other summer residents in addition to locals.

I grab a beer and start talking to Axel Rogers, a former baseball teammate who's a junior at Penn State now. I haven't seen him since he graduated, and he's telling me about his college team when he suddenly breaks off mid-sentence, gaze focusing behind me.

"Goddamn. Who's that?"

I wish I didn't know just from the look on his face that Wren has arrived. I wasn't sure if she'd show up tonight since she never replied to my text. Maybe I should have slipped her a note instead, defaulting to our former means of communication.

"She's taken," I say.

I'm hoping Wren isn't within earshot because she'd probably have a lot to say about me making decisions for her. We're not together; she has every right to do whatever she wants. But I'm not going to stand off to the side and watch this time. I glance around, confirming every guy in the immediate vicinity is looking where Axel is. One fewer admirer is still a lot of guys, but less.

Except Axel is still staring. "You sure?"

"I'm *sure*." I add a little more bite this time, and it's enough to make him glance my way. Realize why I'm sure.

His eyes widen. "Oh. Shit. Your girl?"

"Yeah," I say, resenting how right the confirmation sounds.

"Lucky bastard," he mutters, sucking down the rest of his beer. "I'm gonna grab another."

"Sounds good," I say, turning to survey the rest of the first floor.

The plan is open concept, convenient for entertaining, although I doubt Macie's grandparents had this sort of party in mind when they purchased the place.

Wren is holding court in the kitchen, leaning a hip against the island as she talks to the four guys gathered around her.

I head that way, ignoring Gus's shit-eating grin as I pass him, talking to Wade and Cammie. Cammie rolls her eyes; Wade flashes me a thumbs-up.

I shove right through the group of guys, jaw clenching when I get a good look at her outfit. Wren seems to own an endless supply of short dresses.

I unclench my jaw when one of the guys greets me by name, looking over to figure out his identity. "Hey, Schultz. Back up, yeah?" I glance around, including the other guys in the directive.

They all scatter, and then my eyes return to Wren.

She crosses her arms, pushing her boobs up. I stare, and she smirks.

"That was rude, Cap."

I take a step closer so she has to tilt her head back to hold my gaze. "Can I talk to you?"

"We're talking right now."

"Outside."

Everyone in the kitchen is attempting to eavesdrop on our conversation. And not very subtly.

"I was about to dance actually."

I glance toward the living room, tempted to grimace. I hate dancing. Something Wren has probably guessed, and that's why she's mentioning it.

"Okay. Wanna dance with me?"

Surprise flashes across Wren's face before she schools it. "Can you dance?"

I look toward the far corner of the living room again, where the speaker is set up and the dancing is taking place. The "dancing" in question is mostly a guy rocking in place while a girl grinds her ass against him.

"I think I can figure it out."

She scoffs, then strides away, toward the music.

It's not exactly an invitation or an acceptance of my invitation, but I follow her anyway.

Wren stops at the guy who's got an amateur DJ setup, leaning down and whispering something that has him nodding and smiling up at her. She straightens, missing the way he checks out her ass, glancing at me expectantly.

She's waiting for me to lead, I guess, and this is the one activity I'm really not comfortable doing so. I can show off pitching or sailing, but dancing? *Way* outside my comfort zone. I danced as a kid, putting on fake concerts with friends, but I've never attempted it as an adult. I skipped every school-sanctioned event that wasn't mandatory—and some that were after Skylar died—never attending homecoming or prom.

But I swallow my uneasiness and hold a hand out to Wren. She takes it, a quick smile appearing when I use our hands to pull her into my chest. We collide, and I let her hand go to wrap my arms around her lower back. She rests her wrists on my shoulders, head tilted back to maintain eye contact.

We sway like that, and I decide I don't hate dancing. Not with Wren at least.

I bend my head, brushing my mouth right next to her ear. "I'm sorry for how I acted when you asked about college. I was only … it's different for me than it is for you."

Her fingers graze the short hairs on the back of my neck. "Just because it's easier for me doesn't mean it's impossible for you."

"It feels impossible."

I'm still at war with my father's expectations. I graduated high school with a 2.5 GPA. I looked up what UCLA's out-of-state tuition is—my savings would cover about an eighth of it. Other schools that previously expressed interest in me are equally expensive. I'm sure as hell not going to qualify for an academic scholarship, and quitting baseball means no athletic eligibility either. I basically trashed my future, and I made my peace with that. Assumed I'd scrape by, working at the marina or other local jobs. Get a place of my own eventually. Buy my own sailboat one day, if things went really well.

And then Wren Kensington had to come along and make me question if that was enough.

The song changes, slow, sultry music switching to an increasingly upbeat tempo that I immediately recognize.

Wren smirks as my favorite song continues to play. I know without asking what she said to the DJ.

I love her. I really, really love her. And I'm increasingly concerned it's not a feeling that's going to fade away. I saw her leaving for college as the natural end to us, and it's occurring to me that I based that on nothing at all. I'm still grieving Skylar two years after she died, and grief is essentially mourning the loss of love.

What if I still love Wren Kensington in two years? What if my pathetic future includes pining away for a girl who's out of my league in every possible way? I don't have one single thing to offer her—not even myself. I'm too damaged. Too unpredictable. The antithesis of everything I praised Gus for being earlier. Wren made a massive mistake, going into Wade's bedroom with me instead of Gus or one of the other guys at that party. Anyone else would have been a better choice than me.

"You don't give yourself enough credit," Wren tells me.

At first, I fear she read my mind. Or that I accidentally said some of that aloud. Then I realize she's just replying to my mention of impossible.

I hate that she has faith in me. Mostly, all I've done is let her down or push her away.

Wren rises up on her tiptoes, tightening her grip on my neck. Pressing her mouth against mine so lightly that it barely qualifies as a kiss.

My hands slide lower, covering her ass, and I feel her lips curve up against mine.

"Pretty sure all the guys here already got the message."

"I'm not doing it for their benefit," I say, then kiss her harder.

She moans. I can't hear it, but I feel the vibration against my tongue as it slips inside her mouth.

We're causing a scene, probably, and I couldn't care less. Kissing Wren doesn't fix my future, but it's absolutely improved my night.

I'm close to suggesting we head somewhere more private when I hear commotion. Raised voices. A clatter. The music cuts out a few seconds later.

My head turns. Sure enough, lots of people were looking this way. But they're starting to focus on the front door, where Brett Nichols is standing with one of the same guys he was at Lucky's with in November. Brett glances this way, grinning when he sees me. Grinning wider when he sees Wren.

I scowl back.

Wren fists the front of my T-shirt urgently. "Do *not* hit him," she whispers to me. "No matter what he says."

I keep my gaze locked on Nichols, but I nod, confirming I heard her, before walking that way.

Gus and Wade have already confronted him.

"You weren't invited," Wade says.

"Yeah, I was," Brett retorts.

"Well, we're uninviting you," Gus says, glancing at Macie, who nods.

This is a private residence, not a bar. He's trespassing technically, if Macie doesn't want him here. I'd rather not involve the cops, but I'll call them if I have to.

"I came to talk to Bennett," Brett says.

"I've got nothing to say to you," I reply, pausing my approach a few feet away. Pull my phone out and add, "I'll call the cops myself if you don't get out of here."

Brett sneers, "Go ahead. Like they'd side with a *Bennett*."

With the music gone, the room is quiet enough that I can hear the mutters. Everyone knows that my dad was a dirty cop. But not many people are brave enough to mention it to my face. Not that Brett's brave. More bitter.

"Wanna find out?"

They might resent my dad, but there are officers—like Mason—who don't blame me for his bad decisions. Who are fair and by the book and would take my claims seriously.

Brett's arrogance falters a little. He doesn't want to find out, I'm guessing. He might get me in trouble, but he'll wind up in some too.

He focuses his attention behind me. "That's why you lost it at Lucky's, huh? You got yourself a rich girl? She doesn't care your dad is a thief? And a wife beater?"

There's a collective inhale around me. Not many people talk about the crimes my father was convicted of. No one has ever mentioned the ones he got away with to my face.

"Get the fuck out of here, Nichols," Gus snaps.

It's the angriest I've ever heard him. Beneath the fury—the shame—I experience a flash of appreciation. I meant everything I said earlier—I'm damn fortunate to call him my best friend.

"This party sucks anyway," Brett comments, finally turning to leave. His buddy follows.

A smaller hand slips into mine, another curving around my forearm. I glance at Wren beside me, searching her face for some reaction to the revelation about my dad's domestic abuse.

She squeezes my palm once. "Normally, I'm a pacifist, but he *really* deserved that punch."

I crack a small, grateful smile, squeezing her hand back before tugging her left. I've never been here before, but there must be a back door somewhere. I don't want to risk running into Brett out front. He's probably lingering, pissed he didn't get his way.

I find a sliding door that connects to a small patio and lead Wren outside. There's a firepit in the backyard that a few guys are sitting around, smoking weed, but no one else in sight.

I rub my face with the palm of my free hand. Exhale. "I should have told you myself. I—fuck, I hate talking about it. More than anything else."

Skylar's death was a tragic accident. My dad embezzling money? Awful, but most of it was "donations"—bribes that wealthy residents paid to erase incidents. Him dipping into those funds wasn't hurting anyone directly.

Finding out that my hero hurt my mom? That he had been hurting her for years? I'm so furious and sad every time I think about it that it feels like the mixture of emotions stifles me. That I'll never escape their weight.

"I didn't *want* you to know," I admit. "Didn't want you to look at me differently."

"Did he ever hurt you?"

"No. I knew he had a temper; he'd always had a temper. It was mostly yelling. Breaking dishes sometimes. But he never hit me."

"I'm so sorry, Sawyer."

"Yeah. Me too." I glance down, scuffing my sneaker against the pavers. "It was happening in the same house for years, and I had no fucking clue. That part kills me. That I could have stopped it, somehow, if I'd—"

"Hey." I watch Wren's feet step closer. "Look at me."

I blow out a shaky breath, then lift my chin to meet her gaze.

"Remember when you told me it wasn't my fault, what Third did? Nothing your dad did was anything you had control of. No kid assumes anyone is capable of that, especially their parent. We never have to talk about it again, but don't ever blame yourself for not knowing." Wren rises on her tiptoes, wrapping her arms around me, whispering, "You're not an asshole, Sawyer Bennett. Not even kind of."

I could say it now. It would be so easy to let those three short words slip out. But I don't want my dad to play any part in that important moment.

So, I just tighten my hold on her, trying to wordlessly convey how I'm feeling.

When we separate, she asks, "What time is it?"

I pull my phone out to check. "Twelve forty-five."

She says nothing, just stares at the screen. And it takes me a beat to realize why.

I clear my throat awkwardly, like a middle schooler with a crush, not sure what to say.

Finally, Wren speaks. "It's mine too."

CHAPTER 33
Wren

Someone shouts my name. I spin to glance at the black Range Rover that just parked in the lot. Flynn Parks is climbing out of the driver's seat, a wide smile stretched across his face.

"Hey!" I call back, walking toward him. "What are you doing here?"

"Enjoying my final minutes of freedom," Flynn says somberly.

I raise my eyebrows. "Cops are after you?"

"Worse. My father." His tone is grim, so I can't really tell if he's kidding.

I've surmised, based on comments Kit has made and the number of holidays Flynn has spent with my family instead of his own, that he's not close with his parents. But I don't know any details.

"What's your dad doing?"

"He's making me go to law school."

"That's not that bad, is it?"

Flynn lowers his sunglasses to give me a serious look. "I looked up the textbook for one of my intro courses. Guess how many pages?"

"Uh, five hundred?"

"One thousand eight hundred twenty-four." He shoves his sunglasses back up the bridge of his nose. "I'm sure the others are equally bad, but I haven't mustered the courage to check yet."

I smile. "Well, you remembered exactly how many pages are in the book. Now, you just have to memorize everything in it, right?"

He chuckles. "Yeah, that's encouraging. Thanks."

"Anytime." I tilt my head. "Where are you going? For law school?"

Flynn tilts his head. "C'mon, Wren. You know there's only one option."

"Rory's going there in the fall too."

"Oh, I know. I think it's the only thing I've ever heard her talk about. *Harvard Law* this. *Harvard Law* that."

"Hey." I give his chest a light shove. "Yes, Rory can be annoyingly academic. But she's still my sister. If you were nicer to her, she'd help you study that obscenely thick book."

"You think so, huh?" Flynn asks dryly.

I don't actually. Flynn Parks is the only person I've seen my sister act even remotely rude toward. He and I have similar personalities, but Rory has no biological obligation toward him.

"So, that's Marina Guy?"

I glance over my shoulder, following Flynn's gaze. Sawyer is standing by the dumpsters behind the yacht club, but he's not alone. Several other guys, including Wade and Gus, are with him.

"How'd you know?" I ask, refocusing on Flynn.

He smirks. "Only one who looks murderous. You were right—he could take me. But I'd get my ass kicked for you if he's still pulling shit."

I smile. "He's not. But thank you. And for that night. I never ..."

Flynn waves my thanks away. "Getting drunk with two hot chicks was on my New Year's Eve bucket list."

"You think Rory is hot?" I tease.

He rolls his eyes. "That's not what I said."

"Uh, it sort of is."

"Is your scary boyfriend the one I should ask about taking my dad's boat out?" Flynn asks, swinging his keys around one finger.

Interestingly, he seems to want to change the topic. Normally, he'll discuss anything.

"No, you should ask Dusty. He's the manager." I point toward the marina office. "He'll assign someone to help you."

"Cool. You want to come out with me?"

"I can't," I say, gesturing to my outfit. "I'm working."

"Working where?"

"Working *here*. I'm waitressing at the yacht club this summer."

He looks confused. "Why?"

I roll my eyes. "Most eighteen-year-olds have summer jobs, Flynn."

"I didn't."

"That does not shock me."

Flynn smirks, unabashed. "So, this is like a riches-to-rags kind of thing? See how the other half lives?"

"I'm just trying something new. Like you, with law school."

"Law school is not me trying something new. It's my father's ultimatum—go or get cut off."

"Oh. Sorry."

He sighs. "I should have told him to fuck off … but I really love being rich."

I laugh, shaking my head.

"Was probably time to try something else," Flynn continues. "Kit has a career and a whole-ass kid already. I'm way behind."

"Measuring your life against someone else's means you're living theirs, not yours," I tell him.

Flynn gives me a faux-impressed look. "And everyone says you and Rory couldn't be more different."

"Since you hate my sister, I'm not sure that's a compliment."

"I don't hate her. *She* strongly dislikes *me*, and I gave up on changing her mind."

"Huh," I say.

Flynn waves at someone behind me. "There are Joe and Vance. See ya, Wren."

"Bye, Flynn," I reply, then continue toward the patio.

Aaron is exiting the kitchen entrance as I approach, a mug of steaming coffee in one hand. He smiles when he sees me, but it's a little uncertain.

"I'm sorry," I blurt when I reach him.

"You don't need to apologize. I was just ... surprised."

"We had a thing last summer, and I thought it was over. I never expected him to dance with me or kiss me in front of everyone."

"Wren, seriously. It's fine. You don't owe me any explanation. I'll just have to find a new crush now that I know Cap is super straight and super into you." Aaron blows on his coffee. "Also, I'm now realizing that flirting with you was the worst possible strategy to get Cap to like me."

I wince. "We're not actually dating or anything. I'm not sure he cares—"

"He cares enough to be walking over here, looking pissed," Aaron interrupts.

I glance over my shoulder. Sure enough, Sawyer is stalking this way. And he does appear irritated.

"Gibson," he barks. "Ken Thompson needs help launching from the ramp."

"Headed there now, Cap," Aaron says, then beelines toward the marina.

Sawyer continues toward me. I feel a little like prey, if prey is ever seized with the urge to kiss its predator. I understand now why Sawyer was worried how I'd react to him punching another guy. But I've never felt the least bit unsafe around him.

"Who was the guy?" he asks.

I raise my eyebrows. "Aaron Gibson. You've worked with him all summer."

He's in no mood for jokes, it seems. "Who was the *rich* guy, in the parking lot?"

"Flynn Parks. He's best friends with my cousin Kit."

"Are you sleeping with him?"

"Wh—" I'm too surprised to finish the question. "What? That's—"

"I swear to God, Wren, if you say it's none of my business—"

"I was going to say, that's ridiculous. He's twenty-four. He's way too old for me."

"Are you sleeping with anyone age-appropriate?"

"Are *you*?" I shoot back. "Or *older women*, your preference?"

"I asked you first."

I laugh. "Seriously? You want to have this conversation here, now, and you're calling dibs on the *other people* question?"

He holds my gaze. "Yep."

I stare back. "Fine. No. I'm not."

"Do you … want to?"

My heart rate quickens all of a sudden. Because there's only one reason I can conjure for why he'd be bringing this up, and I basically gave up on Sawyer ever participating in this conversation, let alone initiating it.

I shake my head. Then, in case he possibly misinterpreted the motion, I add, "No. I don't want to."

I've never wanted to.

He exhales a long breath that sounds … relieved.

"Do you?" I whisper.

"No." His answer is hasty. Decisive.

I bite my bottom lip, then state, "That sounds similar to a relationship."

He nods. "It does."

"Would you—"

The radio attached to Sawyer's belt crackles, followed by Gus's voice saying, "Hey, Cap. I've got a couple of renters here who aren't sure what they rented, and I'm not clear either. Can you come over to the office?"

Sawyer grabs the radio and hits a button. "Be right there, man." To me, he gives an apologetic smile. "This, uh, probably wasn't the best time to discuss …"

"Probably not," I agree, smothering my disappointment.

"Jerry King thinks his steering is stiff. Probably a rudder post issue or hydraulic problem. I can't tell dockside, so I told him I'd take it out for a sail test after my shift to see how *Odyssey* acts under load."

"I understood about a third of those words."

He grins. "I have to work late, but I should wrap up by six. Wanna meet me here then, and we can talk more? Grab dinner? My mom is visiting her brother this week, so I have the house to myself."

"I'll check my schedule. See if I can fit you in."

"Yeah, you do that." Sawyer steps forward, spinning his hat around and pressing a quick kiss to my lips. He grins at my shocked expression, taking a couple of steps backward before turning and jogging toward the marina office.

And I allow myself to hope, just a little bit, that he might actually love me back.

CHAPTER 34

Sawyer

"It's getting worse, Cap."

"I know," I say grimly, watching another wave sweep across the hull. Locking my knees as we rock with the motion. Wade checks his phone. "Still no service."

"You won't get any out this far."

It was stupid to sail past the lighthouse. Wade wanted to, and we were flying so fast that I didn't think going out farther would add that much time. Until the winds shifted, and the water got rough, and I recalled the many times Jerry King had boasted about how his father had this vessel custom built. He's meticulous about maintaining it, but not modernizing it. Meaning there's no digital navigation, let alone the smart sensors or infotainment system or security cameras that are practically standard these days. Distractions, I thought privately in the past, but some of that tech would be helpful now.

What's *really* not helpful? That I didn't bother to do a full safety check before we left the harbor on what was meant to be a quick trip,

and the VHF radio didn't turn on when I ducked into the cabin to grab Wade and me life jackets.

I sure as fuck didn't mention that to Wade, who was already looking pale as the boat continued to rock faster, and I didn't take the time to troubleshoot, but the possibility there's a bad connection or a dead battery is a heavy weight on the back of my mind. Because the lack of tech also means that radio is our one means of calling for help. If this storm picks up rather than settles and the sun fully sinks, we'll be in serious shit.

"Shouldn't we be heading closer toward the shore?" Wade calls.

I shake my head. "It's safer out here. Room to maneuver or run off."

Another wave hits, soaking Wade's shorts. "Sounds fucking counterintuitive."

"Well, one of us took sailing lessons, and it wasn't you."

"I didn't foresee being stuck out in a damn hurricane and needing to know how to sail."

"It's not a hurricane."

I glance at the darkening horizon. I saw rain was predicted tonight, which is why I scrapped the plan to take Wren to the beach later.

Wren.

I have plenty of regrets. But the one that is suffocating me now?

I never told her.

If this boat never makes it back to shore, Wren will never know I love her. I'll never get to say the words to her.

I've never been especially careful with my life. Not careless, aside from that dark period right after Skylar was suddenly gone, but not careful either.

This wasn't careless. It was supposed to be a short trip. I didn't even mention it to Dusty because Jerry King offered to pay me five hundred dollars under the table for checking the steering, which I'm probably not supposed to accept as a marina employee.

The gray clouds overhead split open, dumping a deluge of water on me and on Wade and on the sea. Salty wind whips, and there's too much slack in the sail. The wind is shifting direction again.

"Cap." There's true panic in Wade's voice now.

He's one of my oldest friends, and he takes almost nothing seriously. He took a job at the marina because Gus and I did, and we do most things together, not because he had much of an interest in anything nautical. If we don't make it through this … it'll be entirely my fault.

"You should head in the cabin," I say. "Make sure everything's secured."

"There's a radio in there, right? I should call for help?"

I blow out a breath. "It wasn't working."

"*What*? What do you mean, it's not working?"

"I mean, I should have checked it before we left, but I didn't, and I tried to turn it on when I grabbed the life jackets. Let me know if you get it working. Channel 16 is for emergencies."

"So, this is an emergency now?"

Another huge wave hits. I need to heave to, or we're going to capsize.

"What do you think?" I shout, shoving my hair back so I can try to see the helm clearly.

"I think I should have switched to caddying like Ricky did," Wade calls. "No one ever dies golfing."

"We're not going to die," I yell back before he disappears below deck, relieved he said it aloud so I had a chance to deny it. "Probably," I add under my breath as I initiate a slow tack.

Once I've locked the tiller, I head into the cabin to check on Wade.

He's sitting on the bottom berth, tossing a deck of cards between his hands.

I glance at the radio. "No luck?"

"Nope."

"It's not getting any worse," I say. "We just need to sit tight for a little bit."

Wade nods, and I appreciate him at least acting like I know that for certain.

He holds up the deck. "Wanna play? I could use a distraction, and old man King doesn't stock this ship with any liquid courage. I already checked."

I exhale. "Yeah, sure."

I could use a distraction too.

CHAPTER 35

Wren

I knock hesitantly on the shut door.

"Come in."

I turn the handle carefully, checking my phone one final time before entering the small office. I've never been inside the marina building before.

Dusty, the manager, leans back in his swivel chair. It creaks, and that's the only sound until he says, "Hello. What can I help you with?"

"I'm Wren," I tell him. "One of the waitresses."

No recognition appears.

"I was, um, I was supposed to meet Sawyer a half hour ago. He's not back yet, and he's not answering his phone, and it looks like it's about to rain. I was wondering, is there some way you can call the boat? Check on him?"

Dusty isn't reclined anymore. He's sitting, then standing, a confused, concerned expression appearing on his face. "What are you talking about? Bennett has a boat out?"

"Yeah." *I think.* "Someone named King wanted him to check steering? He told me more, but I don't really know anything about boats and didn't understand all the details …"

Dusty isn't listening to me anymore. He's talking on the phone, tone low and serious as he speaks. I can only make out snippets of the conversation, not enough to tell me what's going on. But I hear enough to tell me Dusty is distressed, and that freaks me out.

I wish I had Gus's number. Or Wade's.

Dusty hangs up.

"Are you calling the boat?" I ask.

"We'll try."

"*Try?*" I repeat incredulously. "Can't you take another boat out? Go find them?"

He shakes his head. "Not in these conditions. That was the harbormaster. The storm is expected to worsen in the next couple of hours."

"So, we should go *now*, before it gets worse."

Dusty is already shaking his head. "Too dangerous. We don't know where they are. No distress signal or coordinates have come through."

"Something is definitely wrong, then."

"I appreciate you bringing this to my attention. We'll do everything we can."

That sounds like something doctors say before, *There was nothing we could have done.*

"What about the National Guard?" I ask urgently. "Or the Coast Guard? His mom is in the Coast Guard. Maybe she knows someone? There must be someone you can call. Something that someone can do!"

I'm near hysteria, in this stranger's office, and there's no thought that reins my spiraling emotions under control. This isn't a problem that can be solved with money. I feel completely helpless, and I hate it.

"We will do everything we can," Dusty repeats calmly. "I need to make some more phone calls, so if you don't mind waiting outside …"

Numbly, I leave his office. Outside the building, it takes me several sodden steps to realize it's started pouring.

I walk over to the edge of the lot, staring at the harbor. I can't see much, between the lashing rain and the waning light, but I can see the boats, safely in their slips, are rocking. How much worse it must be out in the open water.

I glance left, at the picnic table Sawyer always chooses to sit at. It's the only table with a clear shot of the lighthouse, which is why he likes it, I'm assuming. I figured out which spot in the lot has an unobstructed view. It's where I park every morning so I can watch him sip his coffee and stare at the boats. It feels like a metal band is contracting around my chest when I realize I might never see that again.

"Wren!"

I turn to watch Gus jog toward me. He has a raincoat on with the hood pulled up, but it's not doing much. His bangs are dripping.

"Have you heard from Sawyer?" I ask immediately.

Gus shakes his head. "Not since the end of our shift. He and Wade were taking the *Odyssey* out for a quick trip. Wade let me drive his sedan home. Cap was supposed to drop him off at my place to grab the keys. He still hasn't shown up, and I thought they might need help coming in with this wind. And rain." He glances toward where I was just looking, scanning the horizon. "They're not back yet?"

"No. I told Dusty. He seems concerned, but he's doing nothing. He said it was too dangerous to go after them."

Gus nods. "It is."

"Why aren't they back yet?"

"It can be safer to stay offshore and head for open water. Nothing to crash into out there."

"Whales," I mutter.

"What?"

"Nothing. You really think they're fine?"

"I think that if I had to be stuck on a sailboat in a storm with anyone, I'd pick Cap. He knows what he's doing, and he's good under pressure. And Wade is … well, he's probably not being helpful, but at least Cap has a second set of hands and someone to talk to. They'll be fine."

I nod, more reassured than I was talking to Dusty. We're talking about Gus's two best friends. If he's calm, I must be overreacting.

But then two things happen. One, thunder rumbles in the distance, menacing and ominous. Two, the marina's exterior lights turn on, determining it's darkened enough for them to be necessary, and I see that Gus is white-knuckling the railing.

"I should go talk to Dusty," he tells me, turning and heading toward the building behind us.

I slide my phone out with clammy fingers. It's seven thirty, almost two hours after Sawyer said he'd be back. Will they stay out there all night, waiting the storm out?

The screen is slick, even though it was in my pocket. My clothes are nearly soaked through.

Still no reply from Sawyer, although I've stopped expecting his name will show up. He doesn't have service, or his phone is dead, or both.

I call my dad, and he doesn't answer. He's away on another business trip—I forget where—and apparently unreachable.

So, I call the one other person who might be able to help. My last name means I have more than money at my disposal.

He answers on the second ring. "Arthur Kensington."

I suck in a deep breath. "Hi, Grandpa. It's Wren."

A stunned pause follows. At least, I'm assuming surprise is the reason for his hesitation. I don't think I've ever called my grandfather directly before. Dad's the one who normally reaches out on Grandpa's birthday or holidays and then passes the phone around to the rest of us.

"Hello, Wren," he finally says. "How are you?"

"Right now, not so good."

"No?" His tone sharpens. "What's wrong?"

"I need a favor. I-I'm working at the Atlantic Yacht Club this summer."

"Yes. Hanson mentioned it." Grandpa's tone is dry, and I'm assuming his reaction was less supportive than Dad's.

"I've made some friends, working here, and a couple of them took a boat out earlier. There's a bad storm, and I was just wondering if you … knew anyone who might be able to help. No one here is doing much."

"For a few kids who neglected to check the weather report? I'm hardly surprised."

I swallow hard. "Please. I'm asking … as your granddaughter."

"Is one of these 'friends' a boy named Sawyer Bennett?"

It's a shock, hearing Grandpa say his name. My parents don't know it. Rory doesn't know it. And I'm a lot closer with my immediate family than my grandfather.

"Yes."

"The same Sawyer Bennett my personal attorney was tasked with defending in an assault case?"

Shit. I didn't ask Rory any questions about who she was calling, figuring she would know best, and it never occurred to me the lawyer might have some connection to my grandfather.

"He wasn't charged."

"He wasn't innocent either. I reviewed the file myself. An underage bar fight, captured on security footage, with plenty of eyewitnesses, I believe."

"So, he deserves to drown because he punched someone once?" I snap.

This was a mistake. A huge, huge mistake. I had known it would be before I called. My grandfather might love his family, in his own twisted way, but he earned the ruthless reputation that still follows him around. You don't become as feared as he is by playing nice.

"I had a background check run. Father in prison, mother investigated for neglect, domestic abuse allegations, atrocious grades—"

"Goodbye, Grandpa."

He speaks before I can actually hang up. "This boy must matter a great deal to you, if you're asking me for help."

I say nothing because he already knows the answer.

And because *duh* is unlikely to make him more sympathetic.

"I don't do favors, Wren. They're messy and uneven, especially within families. But I will make a deal with you. I will hang up with you and call a dozen people who could help in this situation and ensure that every single one of them prioritizes this. In exchange, you will do two things for me. One, you will stay away from this boy in the future. Two, you will select a different university—one worthy of you."

I huff a disbelieving laugh, but he's serious. I know he is. Grandpa doesn't know what a joke is.

Fear battles logic. I don't believe Dusty will abandon Sawyer and Wade. But I do know he doesn't have the influence my grandfather does. What if the longer time it takes him to mobilize anyone matters? What if they can't do anything and I could have done something?

I don't want to go to UCLA, not really. Does it matter where I go to college instead? And how long would Sawyer and I last once I leave anyway? However I can protect him—from this storm, from my grandfather interfering with his life—I will.

I need Sawyer Bennett to exist. I don't need him to love me. I don't need to see him every day. But his existence is nonnegotiable. It's necessary that he be alive, even if he's distant or distanced.

"Okay," I whisper. "Deal."

"I'll update you soon," Grandpa says, hanging up immediately.

Some part of me appreciates the efficiency. The lack of smugness for getting his way. The rest of me is preoccupied with, *What the hell did I just do*?

I stare at the background of my phone. We look so happy. So unburdened. What I wouldn't give to be back there now.

Sawyer did everything that day. Knew what to do with everything that day. I have to believe Gus is right—that he'll know what to do until help arrives.

"Dusty's calling everyone he can," Gus announces, returning to the same spot beside me a few minutes later. "But he's having trouble getting through to the nearest Coast Guard station. They must be getting a lot of calls tonight. People often panic when storms turn worse than predicted. They issued a wind warning, but a little late." He glances at the flagpole next to the yacht club, where the red, white, and blue is basically a blur of color. "Cap's mom is in New Hampshire, but he's trying to reach her too."

I nod.

My phone lights up with a text. I peer at it hopefully, thinking it might be my grandfather—although I'm not even sure he knows how to text—but it's Gia, asking if I'll come back to the city next weekend to go to a concert with her.

"He made his background the same photo, you know," Gus comments.

I manage a small smile. "I know. I mean, I saw."

"I'm glad for you guys. You … work."

My smile slips. "Not all stories have happy endings, Gus."

My phone buzzes again, this time with a call from my grandfather.

I answer immediately. "Yes?"

"They've sent out two response boats and a cutter. Air assets should be off the ground shortly."

"Air assets? Like a helicopter? They sent a helicopter out in *this*?"

"They're unable to reach the vessel by radio. Based on the size and origin, they established a search area for where the boat is most likely to be. They'll sweep that first, then fan out if necessary. I'll let you know when the boat has been located."

Again, Grandpa hangs up without saying goodbye.

Gus is staring at me. "Uh, why are you getting phone calls about helicopters?"

I exhale. "Remember the night we met? On the cliffs?"

He nods.

"You were concerned about me jumping. Cammie said since I was a rich brat, my family would send the Coast Guard out for me."

Gus frowns. "Okay. What does that—"

"She was right. And I'd do the same for him."

CHAPTER 36

Sawyer

"Y**ou've reached 332-52—"

"Dammit," I growl, tossing my phone on the seat and refocusing on the road ahead.

I called Wren on the way to the hospital to get checked out last night. On my way home from the hospital, with Gus casting concerned side-glances so often that I worried he was going to total my truck. After a panicked phone call with my mom, who was suggesting she drive back from New Hampshire in the middle of the night. As soon as I woke up this morning.

She hasn't answered a single call or text. Not since the string of undelivered texts and missed calls from her finally came through when we made it back to land last night. I've listened to her automated voicemail so many times that I could recite it from memory.

I'm working today, even though Dusty strongly encouraged me to take the day off, and I left home a half hour early so I had time to swing

by Wren's mansion on the way to the marina.

I could have died. I didn't, obviously, but I was expecting a *glad you're okay* text from her, at minimum.

Weirder still, Gus said Wren was worried. That she was at the marina. That she was the one who got the Coast Guard to send five times the resources they normally would for a small rescue. And then she disappeared, allegedly, shortly before we returned to shore.

None of it makes any sense. Obviously, I didn't intend to stand her up last night. And even if she knew I was okay from updates at the marina, her lack of checking doesn't explain avoiding my attempts to talk to her.

The strangest, worst part?

Wren is carrying a suitcase out to her convertible when I pull in her driveway. I debated parking on the street because I wasn't sure what, if anything, she'd told her parents about me—about us—but apparently, time is of the essence.

Because Wren appears to be leaving. And not on a short trip either. There are already several suitcases piled in her car.

I shut off the engine and jump out of my truck. She barely reacts as I slam the door shut, simply tossing the latest bag on top of the rest before adjusting her sunglasses.

"What the hell is going on?" I call out, striding over to her. "Why aren't you answering my calls? Why are you ... packing?"

I glance at the stack of bags. She's pack*ed*.

"I'm leaving," Wren replies.

Simple. Straightforward. Succinct.

I stare at her. Am I awake right now? Did I die last night after all? Am I about to hear my alarm and be in my bed?

But I blink rapidly, and nothing about the scene in front of me changes. Blue sky. Blue hydrangeas. Blasé blonde.

"You don't have to leave until the twenty-ninth."

There's a spasm of some emotion on her face, but it disappears before I could assess what it was or determine if I imagined it entirely.

"I'm leaving early. I'm bored."

"Bored," I repeat.

"Yes." She waves a dismissive hand around. "I tried the whole quiet, normal, small-town summer thing, and I'm over it. Gia got tickets to see our favorite band next weekend, and I haven't been to Europe in months. The South of France is *gorgeous* this time of year. Have you ever been?"

"To Southern France? No."

"You should go. It's—"

"Gorgeous. Yeah. You said." I feel like I was just spun around in circles, then instructed to stay standing.

"Well, I've got a couple more bags to grab," she says brightly, spinning toward the porch. "Don't you have wor—"

"*Wren.*" I grab her hand before she can walk away. "What the actual fuck is going on? You're—you're acting like a different person."

"No." She shakes her head, yanking out of my grasp. "I was pretending to be a different person. *This* is who I am, Sawyer. I get bored. I don't waitress. I don't do … exclusive."

"Is that what this is really about? Because I asked you about other guys? You're scared because this thing got real between us?"

"If you'll recall," she says icily, "*I* was the one who tried to make this real between us a long time ago. You're the one who's been scared."

"I said I was sorry about that. And I'm not scared now. I'm in this, Wren."

"Yeah? How often are you planning to fly to California to visit me?"

"I—"

"Or drive into the city to visit me? How exactly did you think this 'thing' "—she uses air quotes, which strikes me as unnecessary—"was going to work between us? Or were you expecting me to continue being the one who always comes to see you?"

I don't have answers, let alone whatever ones she's looking for. I *just* accepted that I am, in fact, in love with her, that she isn't a passing attraction I can successfully ignore.

"Why are you leaving?"

She scoffs. "I just explained—"

"At all," I clarify. "Why are you leaving at all? You said when we were sailing that you don't even want to go to college. So, don't. Stay here. You have money from waitressing. A trust fund. You have options, Wren, a hell of a lot more than most people do. You're going to California to, what? Make your family happy? You're fearless, Wren. You jump off cliffs, and you give me shit. You don't commit four years of your life to getting a degree you don't really want, just because it's what you're expected to do."

"You don't get it," she says.

"You're right; I don't. Stay, Wren."

"I. Can't. I-I changed my mind, okay? I'm allowed to do that."

"Changed your mind about college? Or about me?"

Wren exhales. There's another spasm of ... something on her face, so I push harder.

"Because you seemed sure about not wanting to go to college when we went sailing. And you seemed sure about us when you told me you didn't want anyone else yesterday. What the fuck changed between then and now?"

She hesitates, and I think something I said finally got through to her.

But then she holds a hand out to me. "Goodbye, Cap."

I stare at her, not reaching for her offered palm. I shove my hands in my pockets instead. Fuck ending this like a business meeting.

"There were a few moments last night when I thought that … when I thought that we might not make it back to shore. And all I could think about was how much I wanted to have one more conversation with you. What a fucking waste of last words that would have been, huh?"

Then I turn around and walk away.

She says nothing. Does nothing to stop me.

And I'm awfully devastated by it, for someone who was supposedly convinced we'd never work out.

CHAPTER 37

Wren

"Tell me that's not what I think it is."

I glance at my sister. Rory is blinking at my left hand, eyes sleepy yet expression scolding.

"It's not what you think it is," I parrot.

Rory's lips purse. She frowns, looking tenser, not relieved. "It looks like an engagement ring, Wren."

"It's not an engagement ring."

Rory exhales, but twin lines linger between her eyebrows. "Then why—"

"I mean, technically, it is an engagement ring," I say. "Pierre proposed—"

"What?" Rory yelps.

Our driver flinches, but the tires don't deviate from the road. Miles

has worked for our family for as long as I can remember. He's witnessed plenty of drama in that time, but I'm normally the one overreacting, not Rory.

And she is overreacting.

"I'm not engaged. Just … thinking."

"Thinking while wearing a diamond ring?"

I snap my fingers. "Exactly."

"So, you're actually considering it."

I sigh. "No. I'm not. I'm just … waiting."

Pierre proposed my last night in London. During a dinner I'd planned to break up with him. I'm not sure how we managed to be on such wildly different pages regarding our relationship status, and I don't actually think we were. We just came up with opposite solutions. I thought a summer home, followed by a year abroad in Italy, was a logical time to take a break. Pierre saw that same separation as a sign we should commit the remainder of our lives, inclusive of the approaching fifteen months in different cities, to each other.

Even I, who has been accused of being emotionally unavailable more times than I can count, am not cruel enough to reply to a proposal with, *Actually, I was thinking we should break up.* So, when Pierre correctly interpreted my shocked expression as a sign I wasn't about to enthusiastically accept, he launched into a spiel about how he understood I was surprised and begged me to think about it for a few days. And then what really silenced me was the velvet box he handed me. The proof it hadn't been an impulsive suggestion in response to me withdrawing, that he'd planned it through to the point of purchasing a several-carat diamond.

"Waiting for what?" Rory questions.

"Nothing really." I glance out the window, stomach writhing with the realization I'm recognizing the scenery.

I twist the ring around my finger, working it off and wishing I'd never slipped it on while Rory was napping.

I thought it'd be harmless. A tiny glimpse into a future I could choose, but won't.

I don't want to be engaged. And I don't want to marry Pierre.

Two truths I was already certain of, but the ocean flashing by hardens my resolve. Sunlight reflects off the sea's surface, blinding me. I pull a pair of sunglasses out of my bag, slipping them on to hide my eyes as much as to protect them from the glare.

He's not here.

But I'm haunted by ghosts of the past anyway, slipping off the ring and hiding it back inside the little black box it came in. I can feel Rory's curious gaze on me, but I don't glance over.

I put the Atlantic between us for two years, and it wasn't enough. I wouldn't have left Manhattan if not for Lili's engagement party. She and Charlie met in the Hamptons, and celebrating the next step in their relationship here makes romantic, nostalgic sense. I just really wish it hadn't. That they'd chosen to celebrate *anywhere* else.

We arrive at the house ten minutes later. My parents wound up purchasing the previous rental, but I haven't been here since they bought it. They attended the Red, White, and Blue party last year, and Mom said she was inundated with requests for projects here. This has become their main residence in the summer, so I've cycled through every possible excuse to avoid visiting. Until now.

So, yeah, I'm stuck spending this weekend at the location of my most painful memory. And the location of some very pleasant memories, like the night Sawyer drove me home after punching the guy at Lucky's.

Rory has spent hardly any time here. She steps out of the SUV, smiling at the blooming blue hydrangeas and even bluer sky like this is a charming vacation spot.

I open my door, slipping off the cool leather seat into the hot sun. Squinting despite my sunglasses, partially to hide my growing scowl, I survey the house.

I don't want to be here. And I'm mad about that because I've never avoided anywhere before. I didn't miss a day of school after what happened with Third. I avoided being alone in the locker room after that awful afternoon, but that was the only way in which my behavior changed.

Mom and Dad are approaching, and I force a smile on my face. I don't want them to worry or to think I didn't miss them. I've adjusted to almost everything about Cambridge, and they've commented—with obvious relief—on how happy I seem when they've visited me there.

I've grown up some, I guess, because being viewed as steady and settled no longer makes me want to make the next possible impulsive decision.

I hug Dad first, then Mom, my smile easier to hold as they exclaim over me and Rory, showing us around the changes they've made to the first floor. My expression doesn't droop until I'm upstairs, alone in my bedroom, wishing it didn't look identical to the last time I was here.

I drop my purse on the desk, walk over to the bed, and crouch down to lift the comforter's corner. Tug the fitted sheet free and retuck it the way I like, repeating the process on the opposite corner.

There are still two hours until Mom said we needed to leave for Atlantic Crest Country Club, where Lili's engagement party is being held. I use every minute, taking a lengthy shower, shaving, moisturizing, straightening my hair and then curling it. I try on every single dress I packed, settling on the same one I originally planned to wear.

I don't even know why I'm so jittery. The party tonight will be attended by a bunch of people I've met many times before. None of them know anything about my new life outside London. Pierre didn't make an announcement about his proposal. He and I and Rory are the only ones who know. My sister won't say anything, and I'm certainly not planning to share the news.

It's being back here, not the party tonight or the unpleasant conversation I'll need to have with Pierre soon, that I'm uneasy about.

"Where's Dad?" I ask when I arrive downstairs and only Mom and Rory are waiting in the foyer.

"He went to pick up Arthur," Mom replies.

I nod. I knew Grandpa would be attending tonight—Lili is his favorite, and I don't think he'd miss an engagement party for any of his grandchildren. Assuming he approved of the match, of course.

Mom and Rory talk excitedly on the drive to Atlantic Crest. I chime in occasionally so they're not suspicious of my silence, but I already confessed I was out late last night with Gia and other friends, so they know I'm sleep-deprived and likely hungover. I'm not though. Well, I am tired, but that's mostly because I lay awake last night, dreading today's destination. But it's hard to be hungover without drinking a single drop of alcohol, which is what happened last night.

The driver drops us off right in front of the main entrance, waving away the waiting valet. I climb out first, striding toward the heavy oak doors. Trying to set the tone for tonight, to be the confident, carefree Wren Kensington that everyone expects.

"This is so exciting," I hear Mom tell Rory behind me. "I can't believe it'll be you girls getting married next!"

I don't look back to confirm, but I can feel my sister's eyes boring into my back. I'm going to have to have another conversation with Rory about Pierre, and I'm dreading it almost as much as the conversation with Pierre himself. It's another misstep I've made, somehow fooling a guy into thinking I'm ready to commit when the truth is laughable.

"If you meet the right person and want to get married, of course," Mom adds, misreading Rory's silence.

Or maybe she's talking to me, not Rory. I'm the unconventional one. Or I was.

The imposing oak door opens right as I reach for the handle, a tattooed arm appearing, pushing it open.

I freeze. Blink. Blink again, still not comprehending the shape I'm staring at.

I know that sailboat. I drew that sailboat. And I recognize the anchor inked below it and the script on the wrist. My gaze skates in the opposite direction, up over a muscular bicep and along a broad shoulder, finally landing on his face.

Suddenly, I'm numb. My thoughts are spinning too fast, yet they've also screeched to a shocked standstill. I'm oblivious to everything that was paramount before—the pinch of my heels, or the silk fluttering around my calves, or my posture.

It's not until Rory catches up with me and bends down that I realize my fingers went slack. My clutch has fallen, the contents spilling across the carpeted stair. A valet hurries over, assisting my sister with picking up my phone and lipstick and … the diamond ring that's fallen out of the box I apparently didn't close very well after trying it on earlier.

Mom gasps audibly, staring at it.

Rory straightens, handing me my clutch.

I'm most concerned with Sawyer's reaction. He glanced at the ring, but his expression doesn't flicker or shift. And now, he's stepping around us, headed toward the parking lot, the guy he's with following. Not saying a single fucking word.

I deserve the silent treatment. Probably. Definitely, considering the way our last conversation ended and that I haven't reached out once in two years.

"Wren, what—" Mom starts.

The valet is holding the door open, waiting for us to enter. I can feel the air-conditioning seeping out of the building, the cold rush doing nothing to cool my overheated skin.

He's here.

"One minute, Mom." I spin, hustling down the steps and striding after him at the fastest pace my stilettos allow. "Sawyer!"

He doesn't stop. But he slows, already halfway across the lot, head swiveling to say something to the guy next to him. The guy nods, aiming a curious look at me over his shoulder, then continues walking away.

Sawyer turns, shoving his hands into his pockets to watch me approach. His stance is eerily similar to the last time I saw him, standing in my parents' driveway.

I slow to a fast walk instead of the hobbling jog from before. Not only because my feet are hurting and I have a full night ahead in these heels, but because I haven't decided what to say.

I settle on, "What are you doing here?"

He smiles. But it's not the one I remember. It's mocking. "I live here."

"I thought the season ran until September?"

I get my first glimpse of real emotion. Irritation breaks through his mask. He doesn't like that I looked him up, I guess.

A muscle in his jaw jumps. "I got injured."

I look him over, eyes lingering on his left forearm. It's turned, so I can't see the sailboat anymore, but I know it's there. I wouldn't have imagined a detail that specific.

"What happened?"

He releases a long, frustrated exhale. "Look, we don't need to do this."

"Do what?"

"Catch up. Pretend to give a fuck."

I scoff. I forgot how … blunt he can be. "I'm not pretending."

"I've gotta go," he says, nodding toward his waiting buddy. "You have a party to get back to. And a fiancé."

Sawyer turns, jogging the remaining distance to his truck like he can't get away fast enough. Can't be bothered to spend another second swapping words with me.

Confirmed: he saw the ring.

Also confirmed: he doesn't seem to care.

One of those bothers me a lot more than the other does.

CHAPTER 38

Sawyer

Gus has already heard. I know the second he steps into my office, feigning casual as he goes on about how disappointing the stale bagel he had for breakfast was, then about the weird noise his sedan is making, finally asking where I think he should take Lissa, the waitress he's interested in, on what will technically be their first date.

When he brings up the weather—"Nice day, right? Warmer than yesterday."—I lose patience.

"I know she's here, okay?"

Gus shifts in the chair he's commandeered. "Oh. Wren is in town?" He sips some coffee. "I hadn't heard—"

I sigh, tossing the pen down and reclining in the chair. I requested a new one after inheriting the manager title from Dusty, along with his office, and this one isn't much more comfortable than the last. "You're a terrible liar. Also, I never specified who I was talking about."

"Okay, yeah. I heard." Gus leans forward, eyes alight with curiosity.

"Have you … seen her?"

"Accidentally."

If I'd known the Kensington event at the country club was taking place last night, I wouldn't have been within ten miles of the place.

Gus studies me. "Did you talk to her?"

"A little."

I made it pretty clear that Wren wasn't a topic I was willing to discuss after her sudden departure two years ago. Everyone—including Gus—respected it then. But either Wren's return has overridden it or he's assumed enough time has passed that discussing her is no longer off-limits because Gus presses me.

"And?"

"And nothing. She's engaged."

Gus sighs, slumping in his chair. "Shit. I'm sorry, man."

I shrug. "It's for the best."

Based on the size of the diamond, the guy she is with has money. He's probably been to the South of France dozens of times.

"If you say so." Gus's tone makes it obvious he disagrees, but there's no way I'm engaging in that conversation.

I'm not surprised she's with someone. I am shocked she's engaged. Unlike me, Wren has two happily married parents. She's repeatedly witnessed an example of what a healthy relationship is supposed to look like. She must really love this guy to commit so entirely at twenty.

The thought doesn't cheer me up at all, which only darkens my mood more. I should want that—happiness—for Wren. Part of me does. A larger part of me just wanted that happiness to be conditional on me. For her to have spent the past two years with a hole in her life, mirroring her absence in mine.

"How'd you find out she was here?"

"Ricky. He still has friends at the club."

"Right. So, everyone knows?"

Gus scratches his jaw. "Pretty much. How long is she here for?"

"No clue. We didn't discuss … it wasn't a long conversation."

Because I ran away—literally. Because I was so unsettled from seeing her, from the realization she'd seen the tattoo, from the ring, from her chasing after me rather than ignoring me, from learning she knew part of how I'd spent the past two years, from the surrealness of her suddenly being right in front of me that leaving felt like the only option.

I sort of regret it now. Last night was probably the last time I'd ever see Wren Kensington. I wish I'd stared at her a little longer.

"You sure you're okay?"

"Yeah. I am."

I'm okay; I'm not great.

Gus has been there through everything. He played catcher for hours when I decided to give baseball another shot. Road-tripped with me to try out for a Frontier League team. Celebrated when I signed with them and commiserated when I partially tore my UCL, ending any career I could have had. The team wasn't going to wait for my recovery, and I didn't want to pay for surgery. Then he hung out while I actually studied for the SAT, determined to score high enough on the exam for a decent school to overlook my mostly abysmal academic record.

He'd happily listen, but I don't want to burden my best friend with more of my problems. Wren will leave again soon. Maybe she already has. Not to mention, she's obviously moved on.

"Well"—Gus stretches—"I should probably get back to work."

"Great idea," I say dryly.

He salutes me, grinning. "See you at lunch, boss."

"Get out of here," I grumble, reaching for the stack of paperwork I have to approve before then.

I only took this position when Dusty offered it because it came with a pay increase and I needed the extra money. Truthfully, I'd rather be headed down the docks with Gus.

But we don't always get what we want.

CHAPTER 39

Wren

Two days (and one phone call with Pierre) after Lili's engagement party, I drive to his house. I was supposed to head back to Manhattan yesterday, but Rory returned alone to resume her internship. My parents were thrilled for me to extend my time here until my trip to visit my grandparents. Especially thrilled after a lengthy conversation explaining the diamond ring I've since shipped back to England. My parents liked Pierre on the few occasions they met him, but were obviously relieved when I said I wasn't ready for that sort of commitment. As many times as they've encouraged me to grow up, I'm not sure either of them—especially my dad—is prepared for that to truly take place.

Church Street looks the same as it did two summers ago. So does number twenty-three.

I park alongside the curb, leaning over the center console to study the exterior now that I'm not distracted by driving. Interior lights are on,

and his truck is in the driveway. He's home, it seems, but that doesn't mean he's home alone.

I'm filled with grim determination as I climb out of my convertible and start up the walk. If he's not alone, that might be better. Will mean we can't "catch up" and "pretend to give a fuck." Will mean he's moved on, the same way I tried to, and hopefully ensure I can leave this town with some shred of closure.

He opens the door alone. And shirtless, which is almost worse.

As long as I've known Sawyer Bennett, I've been attracted to him. Seeing him this time, the awareness is so sharp that it's painful. At Atlantic Crest, he was detached and distant. This—him leaning a shoulder against the doorframe, wearing nothing except a pair of mesh shorts slung so low on his hips that I doubt he's wearing anything underneath them—is too familiar. Too exactly what I've spent the past twenty-three months desperately missing.

He says nothing, which I'm not entirely surprised by. It tracks with his dismissiveness at the club. And with the fact that I've shown up at his home, seeking him out. Forcing this conversation.

All he does is shove the screen open wider when I reach the doorway. Which is, I guess, better than slamming the storm door in my face.

I slip through the opening, barely aware of the *clap* as it swings shut. Still, he's silent.

I reach out, grabbing his wrist and rotating it so the inside of his forearm is exposed. So I can stare at the sailboat there.

It's not an *I missed you* or a love declaration. But it is something. Some evidence that I crossed his mind once in the past two years. That he liked something I'd created enough to permanently ink it on his person. That he wasn't entirely averse to a reminder of me, although that could also mean it didn't bother him to have one.

He doesn't pull away. His arm looks fine, uninjured, so I'm no clearer on what happened with baseball.

I drop one wrist and lift his other. No new tattoos. And no visible damage. My thumb settles against the divot above his palm, feeling the steady pound of his pulse. It feels fast—affected—but that's likely wishful thinking, plus my nonexistent medical training.

Still, he says—does—nothing. Doesn't ask why I'm here. Doesn't ask what I'm doing. Appears unconcerned about my "fiancé" as I fondle his wrist.

So, I step closer, rise on my tiptoes, and kiss him. Kiss him for real, with my tongue in his mouth and with my hands in his hair, the way I know he likes. He doesn't groan like he used to. But I can feel the chemistry crackling between us, the leashed power as his muscles tense to stave off any reaction.

I suck his lower lip between mine, biting gently, then slide my right hand out of his hair and down the center of his chest.

Finally, Sawyer reacts. But not in the way I'm increasingly needy for. He stops my hand before I can discover if he's boxer-less, spinning us so I'm the one against the wall and pinning my hands overhead.

I try to pull my hands free, and his hold on them only tightens. My heartbeat turns frantic, a wild rhythm banging against my rib cage so loudly that I'm worried he can hear it.

Because I like it, not because I don't.

Because I know Sawyer would never hurt me—not physically at least—and that certainty means him holding me hostage is thrilling, not threatening.

I missed this. Him. Sex. Being treated like I'm durable, not dainty.

"Wren." My name comes out like a curse, his tone low and dark and aggravated. "Get out."

Disappointment free-falls through my chest, originating awfully close to the organ that was formerly thrashing.

"Or get naked."

My gaze snaps up, meeting the challenge in his. "Those are my only two choices?"

"Yes."

"I can't do either while you're holding my hands."

He releases them, the rush of blood as my arms fall hot and hurting.

My decision isn't much of one. It was made when I came here. Made when I followed him to the parking lot. Made when I followed him into Wade's bedroom. If I *had* to trace it to a singular moment, I think it was when I kissed him before jumping. Some part of me has known since the second I saw him, if there was a choice between Sawyer Bennett and anything else, I would choose Sawyer Bennett.

He doesn't think I did two summers ago, but I did. I chose to save him at the expense of us.

Tonight, those aren't my options. So, I choose him over and over and over again, until we collapse in his bed an hour later, both sweaty and breathless.

I keep waiting for him to tell me to leave, but he doesn't. Not before I get up to use the bathroom and not when I return to his bedroom. He just shuts off the lamp and rolls over on one side, punching his pillow once.

So, I take the other side, the same half of the bed I slept on the last time we spent a night together. Stare up at the ceiling, split between happiness and despair. I can't separate sex and love, but I know Sawyer has. Does. I've seen him switch it off—go from fucking me one minute to asking, "Why?" the next. The sooner I fall asleep, the sooner I'll wake up to that indifference. I'm tempted to leave tonight anyway, just to avoid it.

His voice startles me. I thought he was already asleep. "Does he make you happy?"

I open my mouth to reply. Close it again. Silently debate how many details to share. All but once, he ran when things got serious between us. And the time he didn't run, he never chased after me. It's better for both of us, probably, that he thinks I'm not still devastatingly in love with him. That I came here, seeking nothing except pleasurable nostalgia.

"He doesn't make me sad."

Sawyer doesn't reply.

Maybe he did fall asleep in the time it took me to come up with that response.

I sense him start to shift in bed beside me, preparing to get up. Surprising since I'm a deep sleeper, but I'm not accustomed to having someone else in bed with me.

I roll over, trapping his arm under me. "Stay."

"I know steady employment is a foreign concept to you, but I have to go to work."

I try to scowl, but it's hard to do with a wide smile on my face. I'm happy. I'm really, really happy right now.

And there's a softness to Sawyer's expression as he turns his head to study me that makes me think I'm not the only one appreciating this start to the day.

"You can be a little late." I sit up, then twist so I'm straddling his stomach. Keep a smile fixed on my face, not saying what I'm really thinking.

This could be it.

Every time I have sex with Sawyer, it feels like a first and last time. Maybe that's the root of my obsession with him, why I can't seem to flush this craving out of my system. We're a thrill. Remnants of a teenage crush, the sort of obsession and adoration and giddiness that borders on addiction.

If we started that way, it shifted a long time ago. For me at least. What I want, more than anything, is assurance we're not finite. I can handle everything else in the world changing, even embrace the constant newness of it, but I want us to stay the same. Stay like this.

I move down the bed, pulling the covers with me. Slowly kiss my way down his chest and over his abs, lingering at the start of his happy trail. Glance up, meeting his heated gaze. "Too bad you have to go …"

"I have some time," Sawyer says quickly, not even looking at a clock.

"It won't take more than five minutes," I say.

He glares.

I laugh, then suck him into my mouth.

He swears loudly, hips jerking as the head hits the back of my throat. I slow my speed, lifting my head until only the wet tip remains in my mouth. Let that slip out too, meeting his gaze again.

Sawyer says nothing, tucking one arm behind his head in a casual pose. But his expression is ablaze with emotion. Lust and arousal, yeah, but maybe some awe. Heated possessiveness. I feel worshipped, even though I'm technically the one pleasuring him.

It's one of the most intimate moments we've ever shared, and my battered heart beats faster.

Why does something that feels so inevitable never come to the right conclusion?

Would he ever love me the way I've loved him?

Will I ever be brave enough to tell him everything?

I resume blowing him. This is one thing I can control. And I missed this part too—the physical feel of him in my mouth and the power of knowing I'm controlling his pleasure. The private familiarity of knowing exactly what he likes.

I moan and slurp and lick and tease until he chokes out, "Wren, I'm gonna …"

I don't pull away. I suction harder, satisfaction flowing through me as he swells in my mouth, flooding it with warm liquid. Swallow quickly because him warning me, him not expecting me to, makes me want to even more. Keep sucking once his cock is clean, until he starts to harden again.

Sawyer sits up, reaching for me and pulling me onto his lap. He kisses me hard, urgently, sliding a hand in my hair and tugging the strands. His grip is demanding, and so is his tongue. He's a current I allow myself to get swept away in, even knowing it's dangerous.

I swivel my hips, begging for more against his mouth. He came, but I haven't, and I woke up wet, as soon as I realized I was in bed with him.

His hands slide from my hair down my back, finding my hips and adjusting me. And then I feel him there, and it feels so good that I can hardly stand it. I wrap my arms around his shoulders, breathing heavily as that delicious stretch starts.

Suddenly, Sawyer freezes. "I'm not—I need a condom."

I still too, stunned that it never occurred to me. "Right," I say quickly, lifting my pelvis so he slips out. Move away a few inches as Sawyer reaches for the drawer next to his bed. Stare at the comforter as I hear the crinkle of a wrapper.

"You're, uh, you're on birth control, right?"

I glance up, flipping the strands of hair that fell in my face over my shoulder. "Of course."

Relief spreads across his face. "Okay. Good."

He reaches for me again, and I go willingly, letting pleasure wash away the bitterness of my lie.

But a little lingers as I slump on the sheets after. As Sawyer kisses me a final time, then leaves for work.

If I told him the truth, he might have asked, *Why?*

And I don't think that's a question he wants the answer to.

CHAPTER 40

Wren

"Can you get pregnant from just the tip?"

Gia lowers her mimosa and starts coughing.

Nope, I realize a few seconds later. She's not coughing; she's laughing.

"God, I missed you, Wren," Gia tells me, literally wiping tears from her eyes. "Life when you're in England is so boring."

I roll my eyes, reaching for my own flute of orange juice–flavored champagne.

"Can you drink in your condition?" Gia mock whispers.

I glare at her, downing most of the glass just to prove a point. We're tucked away in a private corner of the patio, so close to the water that the briny breeze keeps attempting to steal our linen napkins, but we're not the only ones sitting out here.

"Mrs. Danvers would be so disappointed," my friend continues, referring to our former health teacher. "The tip is the only part that can get you pregnant."

My stomach does an uncomfortable shimmy. A side effect of the bubbles probably. The odds that I got knocked up this morning are extremely low. I just became accustomed to no odds—the sole upside of celibacy. And I figured Gia would laugh off the possibility, not reference an anatomy lesson.

"Pierre was too impatient to wrap it, huh?" Gia smirks, taking another sip of her drink. "That's hard to picture."

Gia only met Pierre once. She visited over New Year's, and we went clubbing. Danced while Pierre dutifully watched our drinks, even though I tried to pull him out with us. Gia's not wrong—that glimpse of his personality was pretty accurate.

"Pierre and I broke up."

She nods, not looking terribly surprised. "You broke it off because of Italy?"

"I was planning to. Then he proposed."

That sets off another round of hacking giggles. "Oh. My. God." Gia reaches for her glass, realizes it's empty, then motions to the waiter for a refill. "Ring, one knee, the whole shebang?"

"Yeah."

"Were you tempted?"

"To say yes?"

Gia bobs her head, thanking the waiter who's refilling her glass.

I glance away, toward the ocean. Today's a perfect day, clear and sunny, the sea and the sky contrasting shades of blue. So tame. So different from my last trip here. "No. I was … shocked. I mean, we weren't that serious."

"He was serious about you."

I adjust my sunglasses, then glance at Gia. "Well, I know that *now*."

"He saw his one shot, and he took it. Honestly, I respect it."

"He saw dollar—pound—signs."

Pierre didn't really need my money. He asked me out without knowing my last name. But his dad had died when he was young, and he's taken care of his mother—and her expensive tastes—ever since. He was part of a crowd at Cambridge, made up of descendants of nobility and royalty and prime ministers. Families like the Marlboroughs, who Lili is marrying into. Pierre wouldn't have married me for my money, and I'm sure he would have been a model husband in every way, but he certainly viewed my wealth as an asset.

"Would you tell him?"

It takes me a few seconds—and a meaningful look at my stomach—for me to comprehend what Gia is asking.

"There wouldn't be anything to tell Pierre."

Gia winks. "Ooh! I love a summer fling."

She doesn't judge me for moving on so quickly, which is one of the reasons we're such good friends. We're entertained by each other's questionable decisions, not scolding.

Besides, I didn't move on. Pierre was an attempt at moving on. But in the end, all it did was show me I'm still stuck in the same place I've been since I was seventeen.

Gia gets up to use the restroom a few minutes later. I relax into the wicker chair, scanning the patio of the hotel restaurant. I've only been here a handful of times before, and I've never spent the night at the hotel. I've always stayed at my aunt and uncle's place or my parents' house now. Gia's family has a place on the Cape, so they stay here when they're in the Hamptons.

I finish my mimosa, waving the waiter off when he moves to refill it. Unlike Gia, I have to drive home.

After Sawyer left, I snuck back to my parents' early, showering and making a production of getting ready for brunch while Mom answered work emails in her office down the hall. I'm ninety percent sure she has no idea I was out all night.

I sort of wish Mom had caught me. Wish I had to tell someone what happened between me and Sawyer because I have no idea what the next move is with Mr. Get Out or Get Naked. I don't know how he got injured or if he's finished with baseball for good. Don't know if he's back here for good or only for the summer. Don't know anything really about his past two years or his plans for the remainder of his life.

Last night, he just wanted to get laid. But this morning? This morning felt different. Felt like before, and I'm simultaneously relieved and scared that sensation can still exist between us.

A woman walks out onto the patio and over to the small building that serves as the outdoor bar, saying something to one of the men working there.

I stand and walk that way. The woman turns, pausing when she sees me, surprise blanching across her face.

"Hi, Cammie." I smile, shoving my sunglasses up to the top of my head. Bonus: they keep my unruly hair from sticking to my lips. "How are you?"

"Wren." She sort of sighs my name as she steps closer. "I'm fine. You?"

"I'm great!" I reply, keeping my tone cheerful. I know Cammie didn't like me before, but I never had a real issue with her. And I figured she'd be thrilled I'd removed myself from Sawyer's life. "I came for my cousin's engagement party."

"Oh. Yeah." Cammie crosses her arms. "I heard about that. Are you staying here?"

I shake my head. "Just grabbing brunch with a friend."

"How long are you staying for?"

I raise an eyebrow. "I haven't decided yet. Want to hang out before I leave?"

I'm teasing mostly because Cammie doesn't seem to like me any more than she used to. I'm not opposed to the idea though. I missed Gus and Sawyer's entire group of friends. With the exception of Gia, I've hardly kept in touch with anyone from high school. Everyone scattered to different schools. Plus, I've been in a different time zone. On a separate continent.

She ignores the question, asking one of her own instead. "You aren't going to the marina, right?"

"I wasn't planning on it. Why?"

I think I know why. But I'm curious what answer she'll give.

"I'm glad you're *great*, Wren, but I can't say I'm glad to see you. Not after the shit you pulled, just disappearing like that—"

"Aww. You missed me?"

A grimace twists Cammie's expression. How she normally looks at me. "Everything is a fucking joke to you, isn't it? Must be nice, never having any consequences. Doing whatever you want, whenever you want, never giving a shit who you hurt in the process."

Now I'm scowling too. "You don't know anything about my life."

"Of course I do, Wren. I watched you sail into this town like you owned the place. Was here when you left without a word too."

"We weren't friends, Cammie. You expected a goodbye?"

"I'm not talking about me!" She releases a long exhale. "Look, all I'm asking is, you stay away from the marina. Cap is doing really well. He's manager there now and starting college this fall—"

"What?" I whisper. "He is?"

Cammie's expression hardens into a mask of disapproval. "I never liked you because I knew exactly how you and Cap would end. And it was so much worse than I'd thought it would be. You fucked him up good. As someone who had to drive his truck home more than once because of the damage you had done, all I'm asking is, you avoid the places you know he'll be. If that's too much trouble, you're even more of a bitch than I thought you were."

I gape at her. "I'm great now, Cammie. I haven't been great the past two years. It hurt me, too, when we ended, and you don't know the half of what you're talking about."

"I don't? So, you didn't write him back … because, what, the letters got lost in the mail?"

"What letters?" I ask, bewildered. "From high school?"

"High school?" She shakes her head impatiently. "No. After you left."

"Are you ordering another round?" Gia appears next to me, glancing at the bar, then at Cammie.

Cammie shoots her a tight smile. "I work at reception, not in the restaurant. But Robbie or one of the other servers would be happy to take your order." She turns on her heel and heads back inside without another word to me.

Gia elbows me. "So? You ordering another drink?"

"Uh, no," I say as we head back to our table. "No, I'm all set."

My head is already spinning. But it has nothing to do with alcohol.

CHAPTER 41

Sawyer

"**W**hat about mini golf? Is that too high school?"

I'm trying to focus on Gus's problem—where to take Lissa for their second date; I really am. But I'm preoccupied by the emails piling up, detailing various members' problems. And even more distracted by thoughts of Wren.

Will I see her again? She didn't mention when she was leaving town. Will she tell her fiancé what happened? Does she *have* a fiancé? Will I be able to keep my hands to myself this time, if I do see her again?

I've never really known where Wren and I stand. Partly intentional. Partly my fault. But I'm absolutely older and theoretically wiser, and I resent that Wren showing up and kissing me is all it took to erode all my willpower.

"Cap!" A wad of paper hits the center of my chest.

I pick it off my lap and smooth it, holding the crumpled paper aloft. "This was an invoice for Mr. Worthington. Now it looks like I sat on it before mailing it to him."

Gus doesn't manage to hide his grin very well. "More like you slept on it actually."

I roll my eyes, then hit Print on a fresh copy.

"If you were listening to me, I wouldn't have to resort to such measures."

I sigh, relaxing in my chair. "You're asking the wrong person, man. I've never been on a fucking date."

"Ouch. I thought our picnic at sea was rather romantic, myself."

Gus whips around so fast that I swear I hear a crack. I glance at the doorway much more reluctantly.

Wren appears well rested, although I know for a fact that she didn't get much sleep last night. She's wearing a strapless blue-and-white striped dress. Half of her hair is pulled up, the rest falling over her shoulders. She's still not wearing the ring, and I hate that I checked.

"Wren. Hey." Gus has stood, hands shoved in his back pockets, glancing between us uncertainly. His gaze lingers on me mostly, waiting for some cue on how to act.

Wren realizes. She smiles. "You're a loyal friend, Gus. Can I get a hug even though you hate me?"

"I, uh, don't …" Gus shoots me a helpless look as Wren wraps her arms around his back. The sandals she's wearing have a heel, so she's only a few inches shorter than he is.

They separate, Wren still smiling.

"You're dating someone?"

"Uh, not really." He scratches the back of his head. "I mean, we went out once."

"Do I know her?"

"No." Gus swallows, casting me another quick look.

Wren hasn't glanced at me once, and I'm as annoyed about that as I am about her randomly showing up here.

"She just started working at the yacht club this summer."

Wren takes one of the open chairs across from me, making herself comfortable in my office. "Where'd you go on your first date?"

"We had dinner at Shells," Gus answers. "And it went great, but I wanted to plan something more … original for the next time. You guys, uh … you guys did a picnic? Anything else?"

Wren's smile wavers for the first time. "We were, like, kids. Not a ton of options." She tosses her hair over her shoulder. "What about the drive-in? That could be cute for a second date. Bring candy and a blanket. Or an outdoor concert—don't they have those in the park sometimes? Or …"

I lose the battle with listening to her other suggestions, too preoccupied with the realization that Wren planned our one and only outing that could be categorized as a date. We had sex, we went to parties, our paths crossed at Lucky's. That was it. I was a shitty … whoever I was to her.

I'm mad she left. Mad about how she left. And I'm equally frustrated with my own past decisions.

Gus seems to realize my attention is diverted, though I'm not sure he really knows why. I'm not sure I know. I thought about Wren when she wasn't here, and now I'm thinking about her while she is instead of assisting with my best friend's love life.

"I should get back to work," Gus says, inching toward the door like he's escaping a volatile situation. "It was, um, good to see you, Wren. And thank you for the ideas. Really. I appreciate it."

Wren nods. "If you need more advice, you know where to find me."

Gus smiles. Nods back. And then hurries out of my office, shutting the door behind him.

I reach forward, pulling some papers closer to the keyboard so I can at least pretend to be busy. "Does that mean you're staying a while?" I ask lazily, like I give zero shits about the answer.

She doesn't give me one. "You sent me letters?"

When I glance up, she's leaning forward, elbows on her knees.

"You started it," I reply, grabbing a pen out of the cup and spinning it around my finger. "It was *your* stupid senior-year assignment, remember?"

Wren shakes her head impatiently. "Not in high school. After. After I left for college."

I stiffen, not replying. But I don't really need to, I guess. My silence says enough.

"I didn't know, Sawyer. I didn't get them."

"There was more than one Wren Kensington at UCLA?" I ask dubiously.

Realizing, too late, that question confirmed something I never planned to share. I figured she was preserving my pride, not mentioning my phase of being a lovesick fool, but I should have known better. Wren and I have never tiptoed around the other's feelings.

"I never went to UCLA," she informs me. "I wound up at Cambridge. I've spent the past two years in England." She barely allows me a second to register that information before adding, "What did you write?"

"Fuck you mostly," I say evenly.

"Sounds like a waste of paper." Wren relaxes back into the chair, surveying me. "What did you write, Sawyer?"

This time, I say nothing.

She seems unbothered by my secrecy. She tries again. "Why did you write?"

Still, I stay silent.

"You're starting college in the fall?"

Where is she getting all this information? I know it's not from Gus—he's too honest to be a convincing actor, and just now was obviously the first time he'd seen Wren recently. My mom's deployed.

They're the only two people I can think of who would interfere, who ever believed Wren and I would do anything except wreak havoc together.

"I have work to do." I nod to the stack of papers on my desk.

She tilts her head. "Did you miss me?"

"No. Did you miss me?"

Wren smiles. "Coward."

"Liar," I retort.

"Hypocrite."

I sigh, running a hand through my hair roughly. "What the fuck does it matter, Wren? None of it matters."

"It mattered enough for you to mail them," she replies, undeterred. "How many letters did you send?"

"I shouldn't have sent *any*."

"So, more than one?"

I scowl. She's infuriating. And my dick—which should be satiated—is getting hard. For some fucked-up reason, arguing with Wren turns me on. I like her stubbornness, her strength, even though it rarely benefits me.

"I. Am. Working."

"Isn't part of your job listening to member complaints?"

"Yes. But you're not a member, so ..."

"I'll join now." She reaches into her fancy leather purse. "What's the initiation fee?"

I pinch the bridge of my nose. "There's a yearslong waiting list to join, as you know."

"Not for Kensingtons." She practically sings her last name. A checkbook appears, which Wren rests on her knee while looking at me expectantly. "Hanson Ellsworth will sponsor me."

I stare at her, jaw working, trying to gauge how serious she is. She's right; the board will make space for a Kensington. We both know it, and she knows I hate that's how this world works. Pushing this point—flaunting her wealth—makes me think she's more serious than I want her to be.

"You don't want to be a member of the yacht club, Wren."

Her chin juts stubbornly. "Yes, I do."

"You don't have a boat."

"Then I'll buy a boat too."

I scoff. "You're so fucking spoiled."

Wren smiles again, taking no offense. "You're so fucking secretive." She stands. "Think about it. Either tell me what the letters said or I'll show up here every day and sunbathe on my yacht. Is my own boat boy included? I'll need assistance in case I run out of champagne or need help applying sunscreen on my back. Does Wade still work here?"

Wiring my jaw shut wouldn't clench it tighter. If I open my mouth now, who knows what will come out?

Wren glances down, like she suspects I'm hiding an erection behind this desk.

I can control what I say around her, but I've never been able to control how I feel around her.

"Good luck with your *work*." Her emphasis makes it obvious she thinks I'm bullshitting, but I actually do have a lot to get done.

As soon as she leaves my office, I open a window. It lets out all the air-conditioning, raising the temperature in the room at least fifteen degrees, but somehow, it does nothing about the lingering scent of her floral perfume. Between shallow, irritated inhales, I wrap up as many tasks as possible—about half of what I normally accomplish—before bolting out of my office as soon as the clock hits five p.m.

Wade chases me down in the parking lot. "Boss!"

"Cut that shit out," I tell his grinning expression.

"Fine. If you agree to come to Lucky's later."

I sigh. "I can't tonight. I-I promised my mom I'd do some house stuff for her."

I don't like lying, but I can't tell Wade the real reason, and he won't know Mom isn't back until tomorrow.

Wren isn't patient. For all I know, she's already on the phone with the board, sweet-talking her way into receiving a nonexistent slip and researching yacht brokers. I have to decide fast—tonight—what I'm going to do about her ultimatum.

Wade nods. "I get it. Tomorrow?"

"Sounds good. Night." I open the truck's door.

"Hey. Was that Wren Kensington here earlier?"

I climb in my truck and pull the door shut, glancing at Wade out the open window as I turn the key in the ignition. "You know it was."

Wren isn't someone you confuse with anyone else.

He nods again, agreeing. "She want her old job back?" Curiosity drips from each word.

I laugh once. "No. She wanted to know more about becoming a member."

Wade's eyebrows lift. "So, she'll be around this summer?"

There's way too much interest in his voice.

"Ask her." I shift, reversing out of the spot and pretending not to hear his response as I drive off.

His, "She didn't come to see me," echoes in my ears anyway during the drive home, even though I crank the truck's radio as loud as it'll go.

When I turn on my street, I'm greeted with an immediate reminder of the woman who's already commandeered most of my waking thoughts today—Wren's convertible is parked in front of my house.

I pull in the driveway with a muttered curse, slamming the truck door so hard that the entire cab shakes.

Wren doesn't move from her spot on the front steps, a brown bag of groceries on either side of her.

I sigh, stopping a few feet away, spinning my keys around one finger. "I don't want to argue, Wren."

"Good." She uncrosses her ankles. "Because I came to cook."

I snort. "What?"

"You heard me, based on that rude sound." She yawns. "It took me, like, ten seconds to find your spare key, but I figured I'd wait out here to be polite."

"Before you *cook*," I drawl doubtfully. "You can't even brew coffee."

Wren smirks, reclining on the stairs. The hem of her dress inches higher, and my gaze snaps to the exposed thigh.

Attraction is a rush. It's fleeting, something your system processes until there's nothing left. Wren should be out of my system by now.

"I learned how to cook in England," she informs me.

I suppress another snort. "I doubt your British beau and I have the same taste in food."

Wren arches a brow. "You sound jealous."

"I'm not."

Not of the guy who gave her that gaudy ring at least. I knew the second she showed up last night that she didn't love him. I pity the poor guy, assuming he proposed because he loves her. Loving and losing Wren Kensington isn't an easy ordeal to endure. Whenever she goes back, if she ever starts wearing that huge diamond, she's already tipped her hand. She did when she took her clothes off for me again.

"Grab that, will you?" Wren stands, picking up one grocery bag and then continuing toward the front door. She reaches under the mailbox for the affixed key, unlocking the door and strolling inside without waiting for me.

I shove my keys in my pocket since, apparently, I will not be needing them and lift the second bag. By the time I arrive in the kitchen, Wren already has the first one unpacked on the counter. I scan the array of ingredients, reluctantly impressed by the variety. If she's lying about her cooking abilities, she's being convincing about it.

"I'm going to change," I mutter, heading down the hallway to my bedroom.

As I swap my polo and khaki shorts for a T-shirt and basketball shorts, I attempt to come up with a plan for tonight. I know Wren. She'll resume our earlier conversation at some point tonight, and I really need her to let it go. The first few months after she left were hard, and I'm haunted by the prospect of reliving any part of them. It's for the best she never received the letters, and it says a lot that she never bothered to tell me she was going to school in another country instead of California.

When I return to the kitchen, I linger in the doorway for a few seconds. Wren is chopping cilantro with an intense look of concentration on her face, the falls of her knife crisp and even. I guess she really wasn't lying about the cooking.

Before I can say a word, she glances up and catches me staring.

I clear my throat, taking a step closer. "Can I help with anything?"

Wren shakes her head. "I made the slaw, and the tortillas and fish are in the oven. Everything is almost ready. I meant to ask, are you allergic to anything?"

"Just cilantro."

Her face blanches. "Fuck. Really? I already added it to …" Her voice trails when she glimpses my grin, picking up a dish towel and flinging it my way. "Asshole," she mutters, resuming her chopping.

My smile fades as I walk over to the kitchen and pull out a soda. I offer one to Wren, and she shakes her head, leaving me to stand around, sipping, while she finishes dinner.

"This looks decent," I say as we sit down.

Wren settles a napkin on her lap. "Gee, thanks. High praise."

"I haven't tried it yet." I pick up a taco and take a large bite, making an exaggerated *mmm* sound.

I'm not even exaggerating that much. It's really good. The fish is salty and zested with lime. The tortillas are warm, and she drizzled some green sauce over the slaw. Depending on how the rest of the evening goes, I might ask her for the recipe.

Wren rolls her eyes, but she looks pleased too.

And because I like seeing that pride, I add, "Really, I'm impressed."

She reaches for her water glass, taking a sip. "Thanks. I'm spending my junior year abroad in Italy—fall in Florence and spring in Milan—so hopefully, I'll improve more."

I finish my taco in two more bites.

She goes to school in England. She's spending the next year in Italy. None of the details should matter to me—if she's not here, she's not here—but the realization that I know so little about her life is a bitter one. There was a time I would have bet I knew Wren Kensington better than anyone. Now, we're familiar strangers.

"Long distance doesn't bother the Brit? Or is he going with you?" I do an admirable job of keeping my tone neutral, I think, as I reach for my drink and take a swig.

I'm not sure Wren agrees. Because she pushes her untouched plate away, resting her elbows on the table and fixing me with a determined look. "We broke up."

My jaw flexes. "I'm aware."

"Not me and you. Me and the Brit. Although Pierre is French, not English, technically."

"Why?"

"Lots of reasons. I didn't want to marry him. I don't want to live in England for the rest of my life. I wasn't in—" She glances down at the table, squares her shoulders, then glances back up. "I didn't want to cheat."

My fingers flex on the can. "Not having sex with me was another way to avoid that."

"You weren't complaining last night. Or this morning."

"Why would I? I like getting laid."

"So, that's all it was to you? Just sex?"

"I …" I wasn't expecting that question.

Discussing the past with Wren is complicated. My current feelings? Even thornier. She was gone from my life for two years. She's been back for a matter of days. And I'm … I don't know what the hell I am. Her being here makes me mad and sad and happy and relieved.

Conflicted. I'm very conflicted.

Wren tosses her napkin on the table. "I guess that's my answer. Message received. I won't bother you anymore."

I listen to her steps down the hallway. To the screech of the spring I've been meaning to oil and the slap as the screen door meets the frame again. I think I'll be able to hear her car start, too, but her engine is too quiet.

The house is too.

I thought that's what I wanted. What I was accustomed to at least. But all of a sudden, I hate it.

CHAPTER 42

Sawyer

My phone buzzes as I stare up at the ceiling of my bedroom. I debate not checking, but boredom wins out. It's not like the white plaster is going anywhere.

The message is from Gus, which isn't surprising. We were texting for a while earlier, about his upcoming date and his plans to head to Lucky's with Wade and some other guys, me trying to make up for my lack of attention this afternoon. This message is about the one topic we didn't touch.

Gus: She's here.

No name. No context. I don't need either to figure out what he's saying.

Twenty minutes later, I enter Lucky's. The bar seems especially crowded tonight, but maybe that's just the contrast from my quiet house.

I spot Wren immediately. She's at a back booth, by the pool table, with a group of friends. The guys are sporting gaudy watches and preppy shirts; the girls are wearing makeup and heels. Since no one I grew up

with dresses that way, I think it's safe to assume they're all rich.

It's only been a few hours since she left my house, but Wren looks completely different. She's wearing jeans and a low-cut top, her hair pulled back in a tight ponytail that exposes the sharp angles of her cheekbones.

I watch her drain the glass she's holding. One of the guys she's with leans closer and says something. She nods, and he hurries toward the bar.

I turn away, heading for the table with my friends.

"Hell yeah, Cap!" Wade lifts his beer as I approach, drawing the attention of everyone in the immediate vicinity. "You made it!"

I don't check to see if Wren heard his shout or looked over. I'm here … I don't know why I'm here. I don't really want to be, but I don't *not* want to be either.

"Thought you'd show," Gus says quietly as I take the empty stool beside him.

I shrug. "Couldn't sleep."

"Sure." Gus's smile is easy. Unencumbered.

I'm envious of that ease, stuck in a state of permanent apprehension.

Gus met a girl he liked, asked her to dinner, and now he's happily planning their second date. I met a girl I liked, watched while a friend invited her to his party, then flirted with her, and I wound up fucking her in his room, entirely oblivious to the fact that it was her first time. I'm such an asshole. I don't get why Wren ever wanted a repeat.

"Hey, Cap." Cammie appears, her boyfriend, Luke, right behind her.

Luke gives me a wave, then starts talking to Wade while Cammie gives me a hug.

"How are you?" she asks, the concern obvious on her face.

"Me? Great. How about you? How's it going at the hotel?"

Cammie opens her mouth. Closes it. Sighs. "Wren was there for brunch this morning," she says finally. "I said a few things I probably … shouldn't have."

Well, that solves the mystery of where Wren got her information. Although I have no clue how Cammie knew I'd sent Wren letters. I must have left one out in my room or in my truck.

"I didn't say much," Cammie continues. "Just suggested she stay away from the marina."

On my other side, Gus grins.

Cammie glances between us. "She showed up there anyway, didn't she? Unbelievable."

"It's fine, Cammie."

"You always say it's fine, Cap. And that you're fine. Because you drank your way through the worst of it!"

My jaw works a couple of times. "That wasn't Wren's fault. I had other shit going on too. I mean it—I'm good now."

Cammie exhales. "If you say so. It's not like you ever listen to me anyway."

"Don't take it personally. I never listen to anyone."

She rolls her eyes, but she's smiling. It disappears slowly, as she stares at me. "I believe her. I don't think she got the letters."

"What letters?" Gus's nosy ass asks.

I ignore him. "How did you know about those?"

"I saw an envelope addressed to her on your desk one of the nights I drove you home. You had it with you when I ran into you at the post office just before Thanksgiving, remember?"

I don't remember, but saying so will prove Cammie's point. That fall is a bit of a black hole in my memory, as I floundered, figuring out what to do with the rest of my life, and mourned losing one of the few people who had any faith I would.

"It doesn't matter if she got them," I mutter, glancing toward the back.

A different guy is delivering a glass to Wren. She takes it, flashing a brilliant smile, then turns back to the dark-haired girl she was talking to. The guy turns away, a disappointed look on his face.

I fight a frown, asking Gus, "How long has she been here?"

He shrugs a shoulder. "I texted you when I arrived. She was already here."

"How was the date with Lissa?" Cammie asks Gus.

I listen to the recap I've heard three times today, battling the urge to check on Wren the entire time. She's not alone; she came with friends. She doesn't need—or want, I'm assuming after our conversation earlier—my concern.

It simmers anyway, like an itch I can't scratch or a leak I can't fix. My ears strain, trying to pick her voice out of the many overlapping sounds in here.

It wasn't just sex with Wren. It's never been just sex with her. And what would she say if I admitted that? *Ciao*? I put myself out there with her; I went over to her house, intending to tell her I *loved* her; and I got obliterated. What is any different now? She's headed to Europe instead of California? I have a destination, too, rather than flailing around here?

"Hey! Wren!" Wade, the unsubtle idiot, has apparently just realized who all is here.

I don't follow his gaze. I'm not sure if she'll come over here or ignore Wade's yell. I've rarely known what to expect with Wren, and my predictions right now are probably particularly inaccurate.

I sense her approach before I see her.

Know for certain she's headed this way when I hear a guy at the table one over from ours say, "Hey, gorgeous. Can I buy you a drink?"

"I have a drink," Wren's voice replies while I study the stack of napkins on the table to avoid making eye contact with anyone at my table.

I don't know if Wade thinks he's helping me, is thinking with his dick, or is simply stirring up shit for fun, but I'm going to make a list of the most unpleasant marina tasks first thing tomorrow and assign them all to him.

"Then what about your number?"

"Lame line," Ricky mutters.

"You want my number?" Wren asks.

"Oh, I definitely want your number," the guy replies.

"And what do I get?"

"Uh, my number," is the response, setting off laughter and jeers among his friends. "And a hundred bucks for your next round?"

"I'll think about it," Wren says.

I still don't glance up, but I hear chair legs screech before Wade says, "Been a while, Kensington. I wanted to say hi at the marina earlier, but didn't make it to the parking lot in time. Cap said you're becoming a member?"

"I changed my mind. I don't really like boats anyway."

When I look up, Wren is standing alongside our table. A drink is in her left hand, a hundred-dollar bill in her right.

"You were buying a boat this afternoon," I drawl. "You still split when shit gets real, huh?"

Wren takes her time looking over at me. "Did you really mean that insult, Cap? Or are you just *pretending to give a fuck?*"

I hold her gaze as everyone else shuffles awkwardly. Most of them have never witnessed us fight before.

"I'm not that good of an actor, Wren."

"I thought we weren't arguing. Or talking." Wren tosses the hundred on the table. "Good to see you guys. Enjoy a free round."

Total silence lurks in her wake, like a bubble has been dropped over our table while the rest of the bar continues with its usual commotion.

I rake a hand through my hair before sliding off my stool and striding after her. I pass the guy who asked for her number, who's gazing mournfully at the hundred she left behind, shooting him a sharp glance that quickly has him refocusing on his friends.

I catch up to Wren and grab her hand without saying a word, tugging her toward the alcove next to the side door.

"Let go of me," she hisses, and I do.

Wren doesn't stalk off the second I drop her hand, which is something at least.

"You're drunk," I state.

"Yep." She pops the *P* obnoxiously. "I started drinking more when you showed up."

I exhale. "I'll go. I just wanted to make sure you were—"

"You don't get it." A tear slips down her cheek. She swipes it away angrily.

I stare in shock. I've never ever seen Wren cry. And I sure as hell don't deserve her tears.

"I'm not mad you're here." She sniffs. "I'm mad *at* you. But I started drinking more when you arrived because I knew I could. Because I feel so safe around you, even when you're being an absolute asshole. *You* hurt me, but you'd never let anyone hurt me, so I can get wasted without worrying about anything except a hangover." Another sniff. "So, don't go, okay?"

"Okay," I say hoarsely.

Wren nods once, then turns and heads back toward her friends.

"Closing Time" starts playing at one a.m.

Gus glances over at me. He and I are the only two left at our table. Wade wandered over to a group of girls about an hour ago and never returned, and everyone else headed home a while ago. Like Gus and me, they all have work in the morning.

"What's your plan?"

"No clue," I reply.

He nods like me sitting here all night and coming up with no strategy makes total sense. Or maybe he's just accustomed to Wren's and my dysfunction.

"You should head out, man," I say. "You've got your big date tomorrow night."

"You sure? I don't mind staying."

"I'm sure."

Gus drains the rest of his water, stands, and claps me on the shoulder. "Good luck."

"Thanks."

"Night, Owen!" Gus calls, heading for the door.

"See ya, Gus!" the bartender calls back.

Wren glances at Gus's retreating back, then over at me. Walks this way, ignoring the nearby table of guys checking her out. One guy's hundred still sits on this table.

"Wanna take me home?" Wren asks when she reaches me.

"Sure," I reply.

She smiles a little. "I'm kidding. I've just always wanted to use that line during this song."

I stand. "Well, I was serious. You ready to go?"

"My friends called a car. Really, I'm good. Thank-thank you for staying."

"We need to talk, Wren."

"Now isn't a great time. I wouldn't be sure which one of you to talk to. Let's *catch up* next summer, 'kay?"

I exhale. "I didn't mean any of that. I was shocked to see you, and—"

"Are you the maybe baby daddy?"

I glance at the giggling woman who's just appeared next to Wren—the same dark-haired friend she was talking to throughout the night. Stammer a startled, "W-w-what?"

"*Never* become a spy, Gia," Wren says, then starts for the door.

"Have fun!" her friend calls, winking at me before I follow Wren.

She's moving fast, despite her tipsiness, but I'm sober with longer legs.

"You're pregnant?" I blurt as soon as we're outside and I'm reasonably certain no one else can overhear. The parking lot is mostly empty by this point in the night.

"*No,*" is Wren's emphatic reply.

I relax.

Then she adds, "I mean, I don't think I am."

My neck snaps her way. "What does that mean?"

"It means we forgot a condom this morning."

I scrub a palm across my face. How was that just this morning?

"You—I—it'd be ..." I assumed if she'd had a pregnancy scare, it was with her ex. "But you said ... birth control."

Wren seems to make some sense of my rambling. "There's always a small chance. I was freaked out about it earlier, and I mentioned it to Gia, thinking she'd talk me down. Not say something to you. It's super unlikely, and I'm—*ugh*."

She beelines for the wooded side of the parking area suddenly. I follow, not realizing what's happening until she doubles over.

I walk over, gathering her hair in one hand, twisting it so it stays out of her face.

Wren attempts to shove me away. "Go away," she groans. "This is gross."

"You've looked sexier," I agree.

Her arm flails as she tries to push me again. I grab her wrist, pinning her hand behind her back. She grinds her ass against my crotch, and I growl her name.

She laughs, then vomits again. Gags. "I'm never drinking again."

"Great plan."

Another groan.

"You done?" I ask, releasing her wrists.

Wren wipes her mouth with the back of her hand. "I think so."

"Scale of one to ten, before you get in my truck?"

She thinks. "Four?"

"I'll roll the windows down," I decide.

Wren smiles.

"You'd tell me, right?"

"If I was about to throw up in your truck?" She rolls her eyes. "Yes. And I'd pay to have it detailed, which, honestly, would be an improvement."

"If you got pregnant."

She sobers. Well, sobers as much as she can with who knows how many drinks swimming in her system. "You'd want me to?"

"Yes."

"So, you're the only one allowed to keep secrets?"

"You know all my secrets."

"I don't know what you wrote in those letters."

"Because you didn't bother to tell me you were going to fucking England instead of Los Angeles! Why did you change schools anyway?"

"You know why. I can't stick to a decision, like you said earlier."

"That's not what I said. Or what I meant."

Wren blows out a long breath. "It's down to a two now."

She starts toward my truck, stumbling after only a few steps. The ground here is uneven, but I'm guessing her unsteadiness has more to do with the alcohol lingering in her system.

I scoop her up before she can twist an ankle, ignoring the protests that she smells.

"You're never going to want to have sex with me again," she declares, halfway across the parking lot.

"I always want to have sex with you, Wren. That's how this morning happened."

"I probably wouldn't keep it," she says. Her head is turned away, so I can't read her expression. "Would you still want to know?"

My answer doesn't require any thought. "Yes."

"Okay."

"Okay," I echo.

We reach my truck a few seconds later. Wren slides out of my arms immediately, which I'm a little disappointed by.

I climb into the driver's side. She's beaten me inside, her fingers drumming a steady tap against the door.

"We should have done some of that date stuff you suggested to Gus," I say, sticking the key into the ignition. "I didn't know—I was insecure about everything you could do yourself that I couldn't offer you. Figured it was better to not try at all than to take you to a free concert when you were used to a ten-course meal at a fancy restaurant."

"It's fine. I mostly wanted to have sex that summer anyway."

"I'm serious, Wren."

"So am I. I didn't care what we did, Sawyer. I just wanted to be with you. If we were alone, even better." She yawns. "Besides, that guy I gave my number to earlier looked like he'd play mini golf with me."

"Hundred Bucks Guy? You gave him your number?" I watched and didn't think she'd talked to him again.

"No." She smirks. "That was just payback for the cilantro."

I glare at her, but I'm fighting a smile myself. Mostly of relief. "Good. Your number's worth more like five hundred."

"A hundred was more than *you* offered."

Recalling how I wound up with Wren's number effectively ends our bickering. That photo is no longer my background, but I still look at it often. More frequently than I should.

Wren's quiet on the drive. I turn the music down to a reasonable volume, focusing on the dark road ahead. It's not until we reach her street—what I think is still her street—and I glance over to confirm it is that I realize she's fast asleep.

I pull into the driveway, relaxing when I recognize her convertible parked by the garage.

She doesn't stir when I whisper her name, so I climb out and walk over to her side. Open the door carefully since she's slumped against it and try to wake her up again. Wren groans, this time burrowing her face against my neck. I glance toward the house. There are enough lights on downstairs that it appears someone is awake.

I sigh because this is a terrible first impression with her family, then scoop Wren up for a second time tonight. Rather than wake up and demand to walk in on her own, she just snuggles closer to my chest.

Careful steps lead me to the front door. I have to ring the doorbell with my elbow because Wren is still conked out.

The door opens a few seconds later, a blonde woman wearing matching pajamas and a frantic expression appearing in the doorway.

"Hi, Mrs. Kensington," I say. "I'm Sawyer Bennett. I'm just … dropping Wren off."

Wren's mom glances at her sleeping daughter. She still appears concerned, but there's some mingled frustration and disappointment too. "I see. Thank you for bringing her home, Sawyer."

"Of course. I'll … it's okay if I carry her upstairs?"

Wren stirs at the sound of my voice, murmuring something unintelligible.

Mrs. Kensington nods once. "Thank you."

I nod, passing Wren's mom and continuing upstairs.

Too late, I realize I should have asked which room was Wren's. Needing no directions is essentially advertising the fact that I've been here before.

Her room looks the same as when I was here last. I carry her straight into the bathroom, repeating her name until her eyes blink open. Once she's conscious and squinting, I set her on the counter. I squirt some Crest on her toothbrush, then hand it to her.

"Thanks," she whispers, sticking it in her mouth and starting to brush. She bends over to spit in the sink, and then I take the brush back. "Hand me those?" she asks, pointing to a package labeled as makeup wipes.

I do, and she pulls two out, using them to clear her face and then tossing them in the trash. She tries to slide off the counter but sways, so I pick her up again and carry her into her room. Wren nearly falls, tugging her shirt off, so I help guide it over her head, praying her mom doesn't come upstairs to find me undressing her drunk daughter.

Not that her mom's opinion of me really matters. Odds are, we'll never meet again.

Wren manages to get her bra and jeans off herself while I search through her drawers for something that looks like pajamas. I toss her the first pair I find, keeping my back turned until I hear the sheets rustle.

Once she's in bed, I head back into the bathroom, filling an empty glass on the counter with tap water and carrying it back into her room. Her eyes are closed again, so I just set it within easy reach.

"Sawyer?" she murmurs.

I glance at Wren's face. Her eyes are still closed. "Yeah?"

"I love you."

Then she nestles against her pillow and appears to fall fast asleep.

CHAPTER 43

Wren

When I stumble into the kitchen with a pounding head and dry mouth, both of my parents are waiting for me. I hustle straight for the espresso machine, pressing the necessary buttons. I took two painkillers and downed a glass of water as soon as I woke up, but nothing has kicked in yet.

"Day off, Dad?"

He crosses his arms before answering, always an ominous sign. "I took the day off, Wren, and got up at six a.m. to drive here after your mother texted me in the middle of the night, saying a stranger drove you home and had to carry you inside because you were too drunk to stand."

"He's not a stranger. He's … important."

"Important? We've never even met this boy."

"He's not a *boy* either. He's twenty, the same age as me. I am sorry for staying out so late and for drinking. It won't happen again."

"It's more than last night, Wren," Mom says. "Your behavior has been extremely erratic lately. Everything seemed to be going so well at

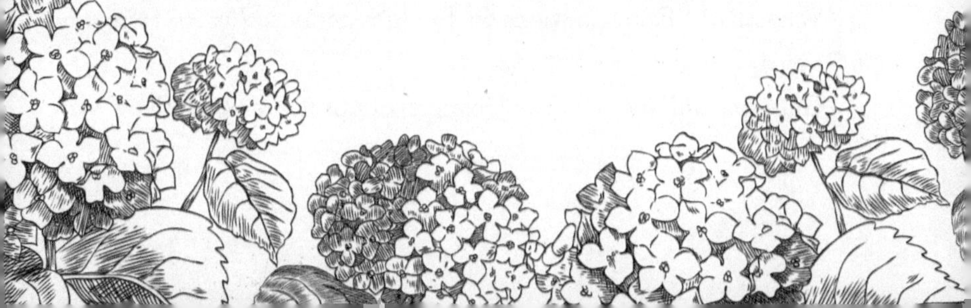

Cambridge, and then you come home and tell us you broke up with Pierre. You resisted coming here at all. Suddenly, you're extending your trip, and now you're out half the night!"

"I'm sorry," I repeat.

"Honey, it's not a matter of you apologizing. It's you telling us what's wrong. All we want to do is help. Do you miss Cambridge? Help us understand what's going on."

I scoff. "I don't miss Cambridge."

"You don't? You seemed … happy there."

"Cambridge is fine. I like it as much as I would any school. I told you and Dad for years that I didn't want to go to college. You never listened. So, I'm getting the super-important degree, okay? I won't be the least educated Kensington."

"You could have gone anywhere," Dad says. "If you're not happy at Cambridge and you want to transfer, we can discuss alternatives."

Mom nods in agreement. "If you're still interested in UCLA, there are—"

"I can't go to UCLA."

Mom's forehead furrows with confusion. "Why not? That's where you were supposed to go."

I exhale a long breath. I'm so tired of keeping this from my parents. And it's not like my grandfather can retroactively let Sawyer drown. "Because it wasn't on Grandpa's list."

My parents exchange one of their patented looks. The sort where they're watching what they say now but will discuss it with each other later.

"What list?" Dad questions in his low, serious, *I'm an important CEO* voice.

"Grandpa did me a favor a couple of summers ago. There were

conditions for his help, and one of them was that I choose a college from his approved list."

"Arthur did *what*?" Mom exclaims.

"Hannah," Dad says quietly, then focuses on me. "What was the favor, Wren?"

I blow out a breath. "There was a bad storm ... Sawyer was out during it. The marina wasn't doing much. I figured Grandpa would know someone important to call, and he did. I couldn't do *nothing*."

"And your grandfather required you to switch colleges in exchange for making a phone call?" Mom sounds pissed. Incredulous.

"I wasn't that enthused about UCLA anyway. I'm probably happier at Cambridge than I would have been in California. Most of my classmates have never heard of Kensington Consolidated."

"Most?" Dad questions.

Mom shoots him an exasperated look. "Really, Oliver?"

"You should have told us, Wren," Dad tells me. "Your grandfather had absolutely no right to insert himself in any part of your life. It was ... reprehensible for him to use your feelings as a pawn to get what he wanted. I will speak to him as soon as I'm back in the city."

"Don't." I lift my chin. "We made a deal. He was clear about his terms. I accepted."

"Terms, plural?"

I should have known Dad had been in too many negotiations to miss that slipup.

"He had me break up with Sawyer too."

"Your *grandfather* knew about this boy?" Mom asks. She sounds stunned. A little hurt too.

The espresso machine shuts off with a gurgle. I reach for the mug, taking an eager sip despite the steaming temperature.

"I told you, he's not a boy. And, yes, Grandpa found out ... accidentally. He didn't approve. And it probably wouldn't have worked out anyway since I was leaving. But, yeah, that was the other condition."

Mom exhales. "I have a meeting I can't miss. We'll talk about this more later, Wren. Drink lots of water today, okay?"

I nod, sipping more coffee. "After I finish this."

She walks over, kissing the top of my head. "I love you."

"Even when I'm a delinquent?"

She huffs a laugh. "Even then."

Mom heads upstairs to get ready for her meeting.

Dad straightens from his pose, leaning against the counter with his arms crossed. "Grab some breakfast and meet me out on the patio. We have a lot more to discuss, including this"—he grimaces—"*important guy*."

For the rest of the day, I attempt to be productive. I clean my room, pack my suitcase, swim a hundred laps, shower, and then spend a ridiculously long time on my appearance. I head back downstairs at quarter of five. Mom is in the living room with Aunt Scarlett, who I haven't seen since Lili's engagement party.

"How are you, Wren?" Scarlett asks, standing to give me a hug.

"Hungover," I admit.

The painkillers eradicated the worst of my headache, but I still feel sluggish. I've never overindulged the way I did last night, and I'm not sure if I should be grateful or resentful that Sawyer showing up made it possible. Worse, I have a vague memory of explaining that to him.

My aunt glances at Mom, who's undoubtedly wearing her disappointed expression.

"I wouldn't have known," Scarlett says, winking at me. "You look beautiful. And very grown up. Are you headed anywhere special?"

"No," Mom answers before I can.

I sigh. "Mom, I promise I'll be home in an hour. Probably less."

"Where are you going?"

"A … residential area."

Scarlett raises her glass of iced tea, but not before I see her smile.

"A residential area," Mom repeats. "Like a boy's house?"

I huff. "I told you, he's not a—"

Mom raises her eyebrows, making me think that's not an argument worth having.

"I just need to talk to him," I state. "It won't take long."

"Did something happen to your phone?" Mom asks mildly.

"You should be happy I prefer face-to-face interactions to relying on technology like most teenagers."

"You're not a teenager anymore, Wren, as you often point out."

I sigh. "I am *really* sorry about last night. But this is *really* important. I need to … thank him." I fix Mom with my most beseeching, pleading expression.

She purses her lips, and I brace myself for another no. But then she glances at the mantel clock.

"One hour, Wren. Not a minute more."

"Deal." I wave goodbye to Aunt Scarlett, then spin toward the doorway.

"Don't think I didn't notice that boy knew which bedroom was yours last night!" Mom calls after me.

I park on the street in front of Sawyer's house, then sit on his front steps again. I check my phone every few minutes, wary of the ticking clock. Last night, he was home from work by five fifteen.

I'm typing a reply to Gia's latest text when I hear my name called. I glance up, seeing the black sedan idling along the curb. Gus is in the driver's seat, waving.

I stand, leaving my phone and walking slowly toward the open window. Facing him isn't as embarrassing as apologizing to Sawyer will be, but it's still plenty humiliating. I like Gus. I care about his (likely low) opinion of me.

"Hey, Gus," I greet, leaning down and resting my elbows on the door. "How's it going?"

"Good," he replies, usual grin on his face. "Big date tonight."

"Oh, that's right! What'd you settle on?"

"Drive-in movie," he answers. "They're showing *Jaws* tonight. Summer classic. I packed blankets and candy, like you suggested. Cap is letting me borrow his truck."

That makes me especially glad I didn't vomit in it last night.

"That sounds perfect," I say.

Gus nods, tapping his fingers against the steering wheel a few times. "You, uh, you doing okay?"

"I've been better. Apologies if I said or did anything incredibly embarrassing in front of you last night."

"Nah, you didn't. Besides, we've all been there."

"Oh, you've vomited repeatedly in front of your ex? Cool club to be a part of."

He laughs, wincing a little. "Uh, not that exact scenario, no. I didn't know … Cap didn't mention, um, details."

I break eye contact, studying the array of baseball caps littering the passenger seat instead. "He has his non-asshole moments, I guess."

"Hey." Gus's voice lowers, compelling me to meet his gaze again. "You were wrong yesterday. I don't hate you, Wren."

"You should."

He shakes his head. "We all tried to get him to come out last night. He didn't show up to Lucky's until I told him you were there. And he had to be at work at seven this morning, but he stayed until closing."

"That was my fault too," I admit. "I guilted him into staying."

"Cap is impossible to manipulate, Wren. What does it say that you were able to guilt him into anything? I could never hate anyone my best friend felt that way about." He clears his throat. "Anyway, I know you didn't come here to talk to me. I just wanted to let you know Cap went to pick his mom up from the base, so he might not be back for a bit. He left work early, but with summer traffic … you never know."

"Oh." *Fuck*. "Okay. Thanks."

"You in town for much longer?"

"Uh, no. I leave tomorrow."

Gus smiles, but this one doesn't reach his eyes. No matter what he says, he must resent me a little. I certainly haven't made Sawyer's life any simpler since I entered it.

"Safe travels."

"Thanks. I hope the date goes well."

"I'll update you … next summer, I guess?"

"Sounds good." I fix a smile on my face, attempting to ignore the implication.

Gus will tell Sawyer how tonight goes, no doubt, and he doesn't seem to think Sawyer and I will be in communication after I depart. Which is probably the correct assumption, but doesn't lend me much confidence, coming from Sawyer's best friend.

"Bye, Wren."

"Bye, Gus."

I step back, and he continues driving down the street.

I didn't think to ask why he was here, but I get my answer when he pulls into a driveway a few houses down, waving once before walking inside the house. I wave back, then return to my same spot on the steps, deliberating my next move.

I have about ten minutes before I need to leave to ensure I get back in time for Mom's deadline. I should have written him a letter earlier or something, but I wasn't sure what to say. I'm still not sure what all to say, so I was sort of relying on winging it once we were face-to-face. Sawyer is hard to read most of the time, but he's impossible to read when I can't see his expression.

A familiar blue truck pulls into the driveway before I've made a decision.

I stand immediately, wiping my damp palms on the skirt of my sundress.

"Wren!" Addison exclaims, climbing out of the cab. "This is a nice surprise. Sawyer didn't mention you were stopping by."

Her warm greeting is wonderful and awful. Obviously, Sawyer didn't share any details about us with her.

"Hi, Addison," I reply. "He didn't know. I just stopped by for a minute."

"Did he tell you about Lancaster?" The pride is overflowing in Addison's voice as she glances at her son.

"He did," I lie rather than admit I heard the college news from Cammie as part of her attempt to prevent me from inflicting more damage. "It's very exciting."

"Where did you end up for school?"

"Uh, Cambridge."

"England?"

I nod.

"That's exciting. One thing I never got to do at the academy was study abroad. What are you studying?"

"Classics. It's not the most practical degree, but … it's more getting the degree that matters to my family." I hide a wince, hearing how privileged and out of touch that sounds. I think Addison likes me. I want her to respect me, too, to see me as someone worthy of her son. "I'll put it to some use," I add.

Addison's smile is kind. "I'm sure you will. You're young. Plenty of time to figure it out."

"Not *that* young," I counter.

She laughs. "I suppose not." She glances at Sawyer again. "Well, I could use some freshening up. It was a long trip. Good to see you, Wren."

"You too, Addison. Welcome home."

"Thank you." She passes me and heads inside.

I shift my weight between my feet, listening to the door open and close behind me.

Sawyer leans back against the hood of his truck, one foot propped on the front fender, staring at me.

I speak first, not that it's anything impressive. "Hey."

"Hey," he echoes.

"I, uh, I can't stay for long. My parents aren't exactly thrilled about my decisions last night, so it took some convincing for my mom to let me come here at all. But I was—I'm flying to California tomorrow to visit my grandparents, and then I'm doing this charity tennis thing in Newport, and Lili found a French designer for the bridesmaids dresses, and once I'm in Paris, it makes sense to stay in Europe until—"

"You're leaving, Wren. I got it. I don't need a full itinerary."

"Right." I swallow. "So, Lancaster, huh?"

Cammie didn't mention which school he was going to. Lancaster is in Connecticut, about three hours from here. A large, sports-centric university.

He nods.

"You playing baseball there?"

"No. Not for the school team at least. I might join intramural or something, if my arm cooperates."

"Cool," is my ironically lame reply. "When do you leave?"

"Few weeks."

He's not being unfriendly, but I'm definitely the one prolonging this conversation. I should just say what I came to and head home. I'm sure I'm over time anyway. I'll call Mom on the drive home, which will hopefully keep her from freaking out too much.

"Well, I just wanted to say ..."

"Goodbye?" he supplies as my voice trails.

"No. I mean, yeah, that too. But mainly, I'm sorry about last night. About storming out of here and about how I acted at Lucky's. I was ... getting drunk seemed like a solution at the time, and I'm sorry you had to ... deal with that."

"You remember it?"

"Mostly, I think," I reply. "More than I'd like to, honestly, like the side-of-the-parking-lot bit."

Mention of me vomiting draws a smile out of him. "I lost count of how many drinks you had. It's impressive you kept that down for as long as you did."

"I'll mention that to my parents. Maybe they'll be less disappointed."

His smile lingers for a few more seconds, then slowly disappears.

"Thank you also. For sticking that extremely unflattering moment out and for driving me home. My mom said you carried me upstairs, and

I doubt I managed to brush my teeth and change into pajamas on my own, so … thanks."

Another nod.

"Okay. Bye." I start to wave, think better of it, and tuck my hair behind my ear in an artless attempt to cover up my uncertainty.

He calls my name once I'm halfway across the yard. I turn quickly, my expression probably far too eager.

"You forgot your phone," Sawyer adds, snagging it off the steps and then walking toward me.

Definitely far too eager.

"Oh. Right." I laugh awkwardly, reaching out to retrieve it from him.

Except Sawyer doesn't let my phone go. He holds my gaze, too, and we're a lot closer than we were before. His smell surrounds me—laundry detergent and salty air and sunscreen and something more musky or masculine that I always assumed was cologne. But I've never seen him put any on, so maybe it's just his body wash or deodorant.

"Be careful in LA and Newport and Paris and Italy and wherever else you're going."

I try to ignore the pounding in my chest as my pulse reacts to his close proximity. And to what sounds suspiciously like concern. "Trust me, I'm off alcohol for *a while*."

One corner of his mouth tilts up, and my heart ricochets against my rib cage in response.

"I didn't mean drinking. Wear a seat belt and a life jacket, that sort of thing."

I frown. "Wouldn't the life jacket get in the way of the seat belt? Sounds like a straitjacket situation."

He rolls his eyes, but his smile has grown a little wider. "You're such a smart-ass."

I grin back. "You too. I mean, be careful. Don't tear your other UCL or go bluffing after dark or anything." At his questioning look, I add, "I found a blog online that mentioned what happened in the league."

Sawyer nods once. "Fucking up my left arm is highly unlikely. Despite my dad's best efforts, I was never much of a switch pitcher."

My phone lights up in his hand. *Mom* is calling.

"Time's up," I say, grimacing.

"I should head in anyway. Someone made a fuck ton of fish tacos in my kitchen last night, and I've been looking forward to eating the rest of them all day."

I smile. "Make sure you heat up the fish and tortillas before you add the slaw and sauce. Otherwise, they'll get gross."

"Yes, chef."

"If they still taste okay, let your mom try one. Maybe she'll hate me a little less, if you ever tell her everything that happened between us."

His expression turns serious. "No one hates you, Wren."

"You do," I whisper. "After how I … left."

"I hate how you left. I don't hate you. I never have."

I suck my lower lip in my mouth. "Can I kiss you?"

He raises one eyebrow. "You've never asked for permission before."

"It was a yes-or-no question."

Sawyer chuckles, then kisses me. When our mouths separate, he says, "You never have to ask, Wren."

Then he turns and heads for his house. I'm pretty sure I see Addison duck away from the front window as he heads across the yard.

This was exactly how it looked when we ended before—me watching him walk away. But this feels different, feels more like a start than an ending, and I really hope it is.

I'm not sure I'll survive the alternative a second time.

CHAPTER 44

Sawyer

"Have you seen much of Wren this summer?"

I glance at the clock on the stove between bites. "Congrats, Mom. You lasted a whole twenty minutes without asking about her."

"She's the only girl you've ever brought home, Sawyer. Of course I'm going to ask. Are you two back together?"

"We were never together."

"Well, you seemed together when I met her before. And just now."

"We're … friends."

"You've never kissed Gus in the front yard."

I aim a disbelieving look her way. "You were spying on us?"

"I glanced out the window."

I scoff, heaping more sauce on my taco. "That's suspicious timing."

"If my opinion matters, I approve. She seems like a sweet girl."

I hum, chewing. If my mouth wasn't full, I might laugh. Not only

because *sweet* is not an adjective I'd use to describe Wren—*dynamic, gorgeous, dazzling* all seem like better descriptors—but because I truly don't get why Wren thinks everyone in my life hates her. Yeah, she left without much of an explanation. But we hadn't been dating. She didn't owe me anything. I owe her, probably, since Gus has always insisted she's the reason the Coast Guard showed up the night Wade and I were caught in that storm. I've never even thanked her for however she pulled that off. I was too busy being bitter about how easily she left me behind.

"You should invite her over for dinner," Mom continues. "I'd like to get to know her better."

I swallow. "She's leaving tomorrow."

"Oh. Will she be back later this summer? I'm home for the next two months."

"No, she won't."

"So, when will you see her again?"

I sigh. "I don't know, Mom. Not for a while, I'm guessing. We don't … we don't really keep in close touch."

"Because …"

I reach for a napkin, dabbing at the sauce that's dribbled on my hand. "Because that's just how it is with us. What's with the twenty questions tonight?"

"I'm proud of you, Sawyer. I was proud when you left to try out and play in that minor league. I was proud how you handled getting injured. I'm proud you applied to college. I know it wasn't easy to return to, then lose baseball or to ask for those recommendations. I've never worried you wouldn't be successful. You're one of the smartest, most driven people I know, and I know a lot of smart, driven people.

"But when it comes to emotions? To honesty and to relationships and to love? I know I set a terrible example for you. Navigating all of that can be confusing for anyone, but it might be especially confusing for you. You can talk to me about any of it, or if you want to talk to someone else, we can set that up too. I just—I would hate to see you give up someone important to you because of choices I made."

"It was Dad's fault, Mom, not yours."

"Not all of it," she replies. "I overlooked things I shouldn't have. I made excuses when I shouldn't have. I put you and-and Skylar in situations that could have been much worse. I can't change any of that. You're an adult; you can—do—make your own decisions. But the two times I've seen you happiest lately were when Wren was here. Don't assume that's a coincidence. Your generation probably thinks it's not cool to get attached or that commitment is—"

"Mom," I groan, "that's not—"

"Let me finish, Sawyer. Letting someone know you care is important. I care about all the parts of your life, and I want you to know that. That's all I'm trying to say."

I nod. "I'm glad you're home, Mom."

"Me too." She picks up a taco. "Your cooking has really improved."

"Oh. Uh, I didn't—Wren made these."

My mom displays no surprise. "Do we need to have a conversation about responsibility when you have girls over to an unsupervised house?"

"Nope," I say quickly.

"I assume health class covered the basics, but if you have questions—"

"No questions here," I interject.

She gives me a fond, slightly exasperated smile. "If that changes ..."

"Mom, no offense, but that is one part of my life you cannot care about."

"As long as you're being safe."

"I *am*." I exhale. "Also, there aren't *girls*. There's—I've only had one over, okay?"

"Okay." She picks up her taco again. "Now, tell me about the marina. How is being manager going?"

After we've caught up on everything that didn't make it into our phone calls over the past few weeks, Gus drops by to pick up the truck keys. Mom is all impressed by Gus's date plan, especially when Gus informs her the drive-in movie was Wren's idea. I almost pull out my phone to text her, telling her so, but something stops me. My pride maybe.

Wren hasn't texted me. She hasn't texted me in two years. How hard would it have been for her to send a short message, letting me know she was going to Cambridge? Or saying she'd be back in the Hamptons this week? Aside from the letters she sent senior year, Wren has never reached out to me when we weren't in the same place.

It fuels all my insecurities about how huge her world is—how small mine must seem by comparison. Aside from trips to see my grandparents in New Hampshire, the only traveling I've done was with the minors team I played with for a partial season until my elbow crapped out. And that was mainly smelly buses and budget motels, hardly the glamour I'm sure is part of the Kensington lifestyle. Wren only seems to want me when it's convenient—when I'm convenient—and that feels like a perilous position to be in.

After Gus leaves on his date, I head into my room. I've started sorting through the years of junk, organizing it into Keep, Bring, or Get Rid of It categories before I move to Lancaster's campus.

Mom pokes her head in my room as I'm flipping through the binder full of old baseball cards. They're probably worth something, but Dad helped me collect most of them. I toss the binder into the box that's headed to the local thrift store.

"I'm headed over to the Griffins' for a glass of wine with Clara."

"Have fun."

"If you fill any donation boxes, stack them in Skylar's room. I'll do a run later this week."

I nod. "Okay."

"I love you."

"Love you too," I reply, reaching for a middle-school jersey and adding it to the same box.

Gus texts just before midnight, letting me know he's outside with my keys. I pull on a hoodie and head into the yard, watching him gather up the blankets in the truck's bed and jump out.

The wide grin on his face basically tells me the answer, but I ask, "How did it go?" anyway.

"It was good. Really good."

"That's awesome, man. I'm happy for you."

"She wants to plan our next date, so I won't have to bug you with ideas for at least a week."

"You weren't bugging me, Gus. I'm sorry if—"

"Hey, I was kidding, Cap. Thanks for letting me borrow the truck. Was way better than the sedan would have been."

He tosses me the keys. I catch them, tucking them in my hoodie pocket.

"I'll see you at work tomorrow," Gus adds.

I nod. "FYI, my mom's over, gossiping with yours, so you've got a double inquisition waiting for you. And my mom tried to give me a 'safe sex' talk earlier, so that might come up too."

Gus laughs. "She walk in on you and Wren?"

"Spied on us kissing."

"Well, if you do it in the front yard …"

"You too? For real?"

"I drove by while she was waiting for you. I was just checking to see if you'd gotten back yet. Bad timing." He hesitates before adding, "She's leaving tomorrow?"

"Yeah." I shove my hands in the pocket of my sweatshirt, fiddling with the keys. "I think maybe—probably—it's for the best. I don't fucking know. It's so confusing with her, and then there are these moments of clarity when it all makes perfect sense. We're like … a roller coaster, and I'm blindfolded, so I never know what part of the ride we're on."

"That sounds … fun and kind of awful."

I laugh once. "Yep. It's pretty much exactly that."

"I'm here whenever you want to talk about it."

"I know. And I am too. You're never bugging me, and feel free to toss something heavier than paper the next time I'm being a shitty friend."

Gus smiles briefly, but then it fades. "You don't give yourself enough credit, Cap. You never do. You've got a lot of people in your corner. Think about why that is sometimes. And remember, we're talking about Wren Kensington. There wasn't a single guy, including me, who wasn't interested when she showed up four summers ago. She picked you. I saw it right away. And it was still there at Lucky's last night. That's special."

I half smile. "You sound like my mom. She's convinced we're some epic love story too."

Gus grins. "Do you want me to grab a banana and demonstrate how to put on a condom next?"

I roll my eyes, spinning around and heading back toward my house. "*Bye*, Gus!"

"Hey, Cap," he calls after me.

"What?" I turn back.

"Are your hands tied?"

"Huh?"

He scoffs, like I'm the one asking weird questions. "On the roller coaster. Are your hands tied?"

"It was a metaphor, dude."

"Obviously. But to, like, visualize, if your hands aren't tied, then you can take the blindfold off. Or ask her to get off it with you. Just … you're not stuck on it, you know?"

I know Gus is trying to help, but he doesn't know everything. Doesn't know I asked her to stay and she left anyway. Where am I supposed to invite her next? Six Flags?

"Yeah. Thanks."

Gus knows me too well. He smiles ruefully. "It was your metaphor, man."

"I know. That helped."

"You're a worse liar than I am."

"I'm definitely not."

"You are!" he calls, jogging away.

I shake my head, then return to my room. Stack the boxes that I filled, then get ready for bed.

Mom still isn't home by the time I shut off the light and climb under the covers. Gus must be getting grilled.

I chuckle, then reach for my phone. Scroll down, down, down, until I find our text exchange. It's only two messages. The photo of us that she sent and the *You should come* text that I sent her a few days later. I'd had lengthier virtual conversations with randomly assigned lab partners in high school.

Gus's date went well, I type, then delete.

She'd care about that since she helped plan their night, but I don't want to send her something about my best friend.

I toss my phone down, then pick it up again.

Hangover gone?

Stupid. She was functioning fine earlier. I erase that message too.

I love you too.

I stare at that text the longest. I've never told anyone I love them before, aside from my family—my mom now.

What would Wren reply if I sent this? I'm fairly certain she has no recollection of the semi-conscious moment last night. She appeared nonplussed earlier, when she thanked me for helping her into bed. If she recalled what she'd mumbled, I don't think that would have been the case.

I don't know if she meant it, and she definitely didn't mean to say it.

This isn't how *I* want to say it, type it, in the second text I've ever sent her.

I'll probably never say it.

So, I delete the four words, tapping the backspace button so it disappears letter by letter.

Sawyer: Send me the taco recipe, please.

CHAPTER 45

SEPTEMBER

Wren: How's college?

Sawyer: 9/10.

Sawyer: How's Florence?

Wren: 9/10.

Wren: What docked a point?

Sawyer: 45 min to the nearest beach. I miss being by the water.

Sawyer: You?

Wren: I'm a little homesick.

Sawyer: You're not that far from Cambridge.

Wren: I wasn't talking about Cambridge.

CHAPTER 46

OCTOBER

Sawyer: Do they celebrate Halloween in Florence?

Wren: Less than at Cambridge.

Wren: Why?

Sawyer: It's a big deal here.

Wren: Duh.

Wren: What are you dressing up as?

Sawyer: I'm not.

Wren: LAME.

Sawyer: IF I dressed up, do you have suggestions?

Wren: *link attached*

Wren: I want photos!!!

CHAPTER 47

NOVEMBER

Wren: Happy Thanksgiving!

Sawyer: You too. You eating pasta instead of turkey this year?

Wren: Pizza.

Wren: And wine.

Sawyer: Your alcohol ban lasted a while, obviously.

Wren: It's glorified grape juice.

Wren: And legal here.

Sawyer: Are your parents there?

Wren: Yeah.

Wren: But Rory isn't, which feels weird.

Wren: We've always spent Thanksgiving as the four of us.

Wren: Is your mom there?

Sawyer: Not this year.

Sawyer: Headed to Gus's soon.

Wren: Say hi to him for me.

Sawyer: I will.

CHAPTER 48

DECEMBER

She's probably not going to answer. *She's probably not going to answer. She's—*

"Hello?"

"Hi. Hey." I tilt my head back, tempted to bang my head against the side of Lucky's, but worried it's quiet enough out here that she'll be able to hear. "You busy?"

It's as silent on her end as it is on mine.

"Nope," she answers. "You?"

"Yeah. I'm talking to you."

She laughs, and my lips curve up in response to the sound. "Where are you?"

"Outside Lucky's. You?"

"Zurich. In Switzerland."

"I might not have a passport, Wren, but I know where Zurich is."

"You don't have a passport?"

"No. I've never been outside the US."

"Now I know what to get you for Christmas next year."

I clear my throat. "I still can't believe what you got me this year."

"It wasn't a big deal," she tells me. "My grandfather's sports agency represents him. It was easy to get."

"It was a big deal to me. How'd you know he was my favorite player?"

"You have a Caleb Winters poster on the back of your bedroom door."

"Oh. Right." I exhale, watching the white cloud of my breath linger in the air for a few moments. It's fucking freezing out here. "I sent your gift to New York. I thought you'd be back there."

"You got me a gift?" She sounds startled. Stunned really.

"You got *me* a gift," I say defensively. "And I didn't get it, so much as, uh, write it. I didn't remember everything I'd put in the letters, but I put as much in them as I could."

"So, it's not just, *Fuck you?*"

I laugh. "I paraphrased. You don't have to read them or reply, but you said you wanted to know, so ..."

The door to Lucky's opens.

Cammie steps outside, an exasperated expression on her face as she marches over, shivering, and says, "Hi, Wren," loudly into the phone speaker. To me, she adds, "Five-minute warning. Everyone's looking for you," before hustling back inside the warm bar.

"That was Cammie," I tell Wren, not wanting her to think some random girl is with me. Not sure how Cammie knew it was Wren on the phone. It's not like I announced what I was doing when I headed out here.

"I figured."

"I should go. Wade has this grand plan of us all taking shots at midnight. He badgered everyone into agreeing, and it's almost twelve."

"Don't drink too much," she cautions.

"I'm standing, like, ten feet from where you threw up," I tell her. "If I'm tempted, I'll just think about that."

Wren groans. "Thank you for that reminder of a moment I'd like to never ever think about again."

I grin. "I'm totally sober right now, and Gus drove tonight. I'll be fine. Happy almost New—" Something else occurs to me. Something that should have occurred to me as soon as she said where she was. "Wait, what time is it there?"

"Almost six."

"Fuck. I'm so sorry. I didn't think—"

"It's fine. Answering a phone is optional, you know."

"So, I didn't wake you up?"

"No. I hadn't gone to sleep yet."

"Must have been some party."

It sounds like she yawns before replying, "It was. I was getting ready for bed when you called. I'd just adjusted to the time change after being in California for Christmas, and this will mess my sleep schedule up all over again."

"Sounds rough."

Silence.

"Sorry," I grumble. "I'm just—sorry. You should get some sleep."

More silence.

"I'm glad you called," she finally says.

"Are you?"

"Yes. I almost called you before midnight here, but I …" She exhales.

"But you didn't." I don't say it harshly, but I do say it, and I hear her pull in a quick breath in response.

"I think I have New Year's Eve PTSD with us. It's the one night a year that's a beginning and an ending. And that's sort of how we've always felt. I'm never sure if it's starting … or about to be over."

"Like a roller coaster?"

"Yeah, sort of. I don't know any roller coasters that last four and a half years though."

"That's how long it's been, huh?"

"Makes us sound old."

I smile. "Do you want to get off the roller coaster?"

"Stop talking, you mean?" Then, "Uh … oh. Hang on one sec."

There's a hum of muffled voices, but I can't make out what's being said. It sounds like she covered the speaker.

Wren returns a minute later, speaking at a normal volume. "Sorry. Tanner forgot to pack toothpaste, so he stopped by to grab some. Somehow, he remembered to bring a giant disco ball, but no toiletries."

I'm very skeptical oral hygiene is the actual reason this guy is skulking around her room, but I ask, "He a friend from Cambridge?" rather than say so.

"From home. We went to high school—and middle school and elementary school—together. Gia invited him."

"He didn't ask Gia for toothpaste."

A pause.

"Are you jealous?"

"I just don't … you with other guys bothers me."

"That's basically the definition of jealousy, Sawyer."

"Then, fine, yeah. I'm jealous."

Wren sighs. "Okay. I'll go ask for the tube back."

I scoff.

"Do you want me to be honest?" Her voice has changed. It's lower. Softer.

"Mmhmm."

"You're the last guy I kissed. So, there's really no one for you to be jealous of."

I tilt my head back, feeling the brick scratch the back of my skull, releasing a long breath that hovers in the air for a while. I'm numbing to the cold because it feels warmer than it did when I walked out here. "We should talk, Wren."

"We're talking right now."

"You know what I mean. Talk for real. Talk … about us."

She's quiet for several seconds. "We've tried that before."

"A lot has changed."

"I know. I'm moving to Milan, and you have a new life at Lancaster."

"Other stuff too."

"Like the year? You only have thirty seconds until your shot, you know."

I figured it was pretty close to midnight by now. "It'll taste the same at 12:01."

I don't have to check the time on my phone. I can hear the eruption of noise inside Lucky's once the clock hits midnight.

She must be able to hear it, too, because she says, "Happy New Year, Sawyer."

"Next—I mean, this year, we should celebrate together."

"I'd like that. More than Zurich."

"So, it's a date?"

"It's a date."

I smile. "Happy New Year, Wren."

We hang up simultaneously.

I watch one final breath linger in the January air, then jog along the salted sidewalk toward Lucky's entrance.

CHAPTER 49

DEAR WREN,

IT'S BEEN TWO WEEKS SINCE YOU LEFT, WHICH WAS PLENTY OF TIME
TO GET USED TO YOU NOT BEING HERE. BUT EVERY TIME I WALK INTO THE
KITCHEN OR PARK IN THE LOT, I LOOK FOR YOU. I EXPECT YOUR CONVERTIBLE
TO BE PARKED BY THE HYDRANGEAS. DID YOU MEAN TO ALWAYS TAKE THAT
SAME SPOT? AARON USED TO TELL PEOPLE WHO TRIED TO PARK THERE
THAT IT WAS YOUR SPOT. YESTERDAY, WADE DID, AND AARON DIDN'T SAY A
WORD. I GUESS HE'S ACCEPTED YOU'RE NOT COMING BACK.

I'M GOING CAR SHOPPING WITH GUS TOMORROW. HE'S BEEN SAVING
UP FOR YEARS, GETTING RIDES WITH ME, BUT HE NEEDS HIS OWN CAR
TO COMMUTE TO COLLEGE THIS FALL. I'M GOING BECAUSE GUESS WHAT. HE
NEEDS A LIFT TO THE DEALERSHIP.

MY DAD BOUGHT ME MY TRUCK. I DON'T THINK I EVER TOLD YOU THAT.
A WEEK BEFORE HE GOT ARRESTED. I FIGURED IT'D GET TAKEN, THAT IT
WAS PART OF HIS OTHER SHADY SHIT, BUT IT NEVER DID. I SHOULD PROBABLY
TRADE IT IN FOR SOMETHING ELSE AT SOME POINT, BUT IT'S GOT GOOD
MEMORIES NOW TOO.

JERRY KING'S SAILBOAT GOT REPAIRED FROM THE STORM DAMAGE. IT
WENT BACK IN THE WATER TODAY. I DIDN'T SAY IT WHEN WE LAST TALKED,

BUT I REALLY WANTED YOU TO STILL BE AT THE MARINA WHEN I GOT BACK THAT NIGHT.

I'M NOT SURE WHEN YOU START SCHOOL OR YOUR EXACT ADDRESS, BUT I FIGURE THIS WILL GET TO YOU EVENTUALLY. THERE'S ONLY ONE WREN KENSINGTON IN THE WORLD.

WRITE BACK.

SAWYER

WREN,

YOU DIDN'T ANSWER MY FIRST LETTER. YOU'RE PROBABLY BUSY WITH CLASSES AND WITH NEW FRIENDS AND WITH ALL THE COLLEGE STUFF. I HOPE YOU LIKE IT MORE THAN YOU THOUGHT YOU WOULD. I HOPE YOU'RE HAPPY.

GUS STARTED COLLEGE LAST WEEK. HE SAYS IT'S BASICALLY LIKE HIGH SCHOOL, WITH MORE COURSE OPTIONS AND NEW PEOPLE. DO YOU AGREE? UCLA IS PROBABLY DIFFERENT FROM COMMUNITY COLLEGE. DO YOU LIVE ON CAMPUS OR IN SOME FANCY BEACH HOUSE? DO YOU SURF? I CAN'T PICTURE YOU SURFING, BUT I ALWAYS HEAR THAT ABOUT CALIFORNIA. DID YOU BRING APOLLO WITH YOU?

WADE AND I ARE THE ONLY ONES WORKING AT THE MARINA STILL. DUSTY SAID WE SHOULD KEEP SHOWING UP UNTIL HE PULLS THE DOCKS IN NOVEMBER. THEN I DON'T KNOW WHAT I'LL DO. ALL THE SUMMER GUYS LEFT. AARON SAID HE DOESN'T THINK HE'LL BE BACK NEXT YEAR. I NEVER LIKED HIM (YOUR FAULT), BUT IT'LL BE A PAIN, HAVING TO TRAIN SOMEONE NEW TO REPLACE HIM.

MY MOM IS ABOUT TO LEAVE FOR THREE MONTHS. SHE'LL BE GONE FOR THANKSGIVING BUT BACK FOR CHRISTMAS. SHE'S WORRIED ABOUT ME, BUT WON'T SAY IT.

SHE FEELS GUILTY, TOO, I THINK, EVEN THOUGH NONE OF IT WAS HER

FAULT. WHEN I TELL HER THAT, SHE NEVER SEEMS TO BELIEVE ME, SO I'VE STOPPED SAYING IT.

I MESSED UP EVERYTHING MY DAD HAD PLANNED FOR ME, AND IT'S NOT THAT SATISFYING. IT'S NOT SATISFYING AT ALL.

SAWYER

WREN,

NOT MUCH TO SHARE ABOUT HERE. IT'S GETTING COLD. I'M ALMOST DONE WORKING AT THE MARINA, AND I HAVE A FEW LEADS FOR OTHER STUFF TO DO UNTIL SUMMER. I'M MEETING WITH MY OLD BASEBALL COACH TOMORROW.

GUS HAS EXAMS NOW, SO I'VE HARDLY SEEN HIM LATELY, EVEN THOUGH HE LIVES RIGHT DOWN THE STREET.

MAYBE YOU'RE BUSY WITH THEM TOO. MORE LIKELY, YOU'RE NOT WRITING BACK FOR OTHER REASONS. SAME ADDRESS, IF YOU EVER DECIDE TO.

SAWYER

WREN,

FUCK YOU.

(SORRY. (THIS WASN'T IN THE ORIGINAL LETTER.))

OBVIOUSLY, I SHOULD HAVE TEXTED YOU ALL THIS SHIT. OR ASKED FOR YOUR COLLEGE ADDRESS. BUT IT ALWAYS FELT DIFFERENT, TELLING YOU STUFF IN LETTERS INSTEAD OF ANY OTHER WAY. I WANTED TO GET BACK TO THAT, I GUESS, TO BEFORE I FUCKED UP REPEATEDLY. TO THAT FALL WHEN WE WERE JUST GETTING TO KNOW EACH OTHER. I NEVER SAID IT, AND I SHOULD'VE I LOVED THAT YOU WROTE ME LETTERS. I KEPT THEM ALL. EVEN BROUGHT THEM WITH ME TO LANCASTER, IN CASE THE HOUSE LIT ON

FIRE OR SOMETHING WHILE I WAS AWAY.

I'M SURE THIS IS THE CHEAPEST, WEIRDEST GIFT YOU'VE EVER GOTTEN. EVEN CALLING IT A GIFT IS PROBABLY A STRETCH. BUT YOU SAID YOU WANTED TO KNOW WHAT I'D WRITTEN YOU, AND THIS IS AS MUCH AS I REMEMBER FROM THEM. IT NEVER REALLY OCCURRED TO ME YOU WEREN'T IGNORING THEM, WHICH IS WHY THE LAST ONE GOT SENT. (I WASN'T TOTALLY KIDDING ABOUT THAT. SORRY AGAIN.)

MERRY CHRISTMAS, WREN. I MISS YOU.

S

CHAPTER 50

JANUARY

Wren: I got your gift.

Sawyer: Better two and a half years late than never?

Wren: Better two and a half years late than never.

Wren: I loved them.

Wren: And I hated them, if that makes any sense.

Sawyer: It does.

Sawyer: I loved and hated writing them.

Wren: What's your address at school?

Sawyer: Faber Hall, Room 219, Lancaster University, 3689 Mansfield St., Lancaster, CT 06264

Wren: I miss you too.

Wren: Happy birthday!

Wren: Are you getting drunk to celebrate?

Sawyer: Nah, that's more your thing.

Wren: You're getting less funny with age.

Sawyer: Thanks for boosting my ego on my big day.

Wren: You're welcome. :)

CHAPTER 51

FEBRUARY

Sawyer,

I visited the Duomo di Milano today with a few other girls in my program. (Postcard included) I tried to sketch the exterior, but I ran out of time. If I ever finish it, maybe I'll send you that too.

It's not that cold in Milan, which is nice. Zurich got about five feet of snow while I was there. Pretty to look at, but it's nice to be able to go outside without putting on ten layers first. There are pigeons everywhere here, and I would hate to see them shivering. There was a gelato place right by the cathedral we stopped at after our tour. We walked up about a thousand stairs to see the roof, so I was starving. But I tossed a small piece of cone to one of the pigeons, and we got swarmed by dozens of them. Maybe hundreds. Lesson learned. We all screamed and ran. You would have laughed, if you'd been there, I think.

Rory and I spent a lot of time together over Christmas,

which was nice. We used to each do our thing, but we made hot chocolate and watched movies and painted each other's nails. I used to feel like she was another mom most of the time, but now we feel more like friends. She only has one semester left of law school, which is crazy to me.

Yes, I always meant to take that spot. If you stand in it, you'll get why.

I'm sorry I wasn't at the marina when you got back.

I agree with Gus—I don't think college felt that different when it came to academics. I never lived on campus at Cambridge, but in different flats near campus. Alone freshman year and with a few friends my second year. I tried surfing once in middle school (my uncle is into it) and swore never again. Thankfully, not a huge hobby in England. Apollo stayed at her usual barn. You're a lot closer to her than I am right now.

Is your mom home? Has she been to Lancaster? You should invite her to visit you, if you haven't. Show her everything you've accomplished.

Tell me about school. How are your new classes? Do you still like your roommate? Are you planning to play any baseball this spring? (Can you play baseball? Don't take that as any encouragement.) Do you go to the beach that's forty-five minutes away a lot? Am I part of any of the good memories in your truck? How is Gus? Are he and Lissa officially dating? And everyone else? Did you see them a lot over Christmas? Will you be working at the marina this summer?

Write back. Please. This is my new address, until May.

—Wren

P.S. I kept all your letters too.

CHAPTER 52

MARCH

Sawyer: Happy birthday, Wren.

Wren: Thanks. It's a little anticlimactic, turning 21 in Europe.

Sawyer: I feel for you. Being stranded in Italy must suck.

Wren: I appreciate your understanding during this difficult time.

Sawyer: Your Duomo sketch arrived yesterday. It's really good.

Wren: Are you going to get it tattooed too?

Sawyer: You noticed that, huh?

Wren: That you had something I drew permanently inked on yourself?

Wren: Yeah, I noticed.

Sawyer: I like boats.

Sawyer: You never said anything.

Wren: I wasn't sure what to say.

Sawyer: I wasn't sure what to get you for your birthday, but I sent something.

Wren: You did?

Sawyer: Yep. You're hard to shop for.

Sawyer: I wanted to get you a gift.

Wren: I'm sure I'll love it.

Wren: But you remembering my birthday was the only gift I really wanted.

CHAPTER 53

Sawyer

"Who's *that*?"

"Damn. You ever seen her before?"

I ignore my friends, typing out a reply to Gus. He's talking about driving up here on Sunday, making up some bullshit about missing the early years of college. You'd think he was a decade out from undergrad, not a junior. We haven't seen each other in person since the holidays—he went to visit Lissa over spring break—and it's the longest stretch we've gone without seeing each other since we met as seven-year-olds.

It sucks, being apart from the people you love. I've had lots of practice, and it still sucks.

"Bennett." Judd elbows my ribs, almost making me drop my phone. "She's staring at you."

I scowl, finishing the message to Gus and hitting Send before glancing up. "I'm not—" *Interested* dies on my tongue.

I can't see her face because some frat guy approached her and she's turned to talk to him. But I recognize the golden curtain of hair. I've seen it splayed across my pillow. Slicked back with salty water. Windswept into a wild halo.

I shove my phone deep into my pocket, walking ahead of my friends without a word. I just checked my messages. She didn't text or call, didn't provide any warning. And I memorized her program's calendar, which was posted on the university website. She was supposed to be in Milan for another week.

Wren turns, missing the disappointment that appears on the face of the guy who was hitting on her, finding me.

She smiles, but it's not the one I'm used to seeing. It's a little tentative, slightly unsure. Not confident or brazen or carefree. Her shoulders lift, then fall in a tiny shrug.

A breeze blows a few strands of hair across her face. She tucks them behind her ear, watching me approach, her bottom lip briefly disappearing inside her mouth. Her blue eyes dart behind me, to where my friends are undoubtedly staring. I don't usually take off like that, and they'd already noticed Wren.

I don't decide to do it.

But I don't really bother to fight the urge either. I keep walking until there's no space left between us, bury my hands in blonde hair, and erase the distance between our mouths too.

She hums when our lips meet. I feel them curve up against mine, a smile fighting to break through. My tongue slips inside, exploring the wet heat. Her arms wrap around my shoulders, hands sliding into my hair while mine find her ass.

This isn't the first time we've kissed. We've kissed so many times that I lost count a long time ago. This feels different. It's lazy, with no purpose or expiration. We're kissing to kiss, which sounds idiotic and obvious, but my brain isn't exactly focused right now. A lot of blood has left my head to pool lower.

When we separate, both breathing heavily, we just stare at each other.

"Hi." Wren smiles. This time, it's bright and full and rivals the sun beaming overhead.

I tug on her hair. "Hey."

Her eyes scan my face, like she's rememorizing my features. "College looks good on you."

"How was Italy?"

"Fun. I ate a lot of bread and pasta. Went to vineyards. Visited old buildings. Studied a little."

"Wrote some letters," I add.

She tilts her head. "A couple."

"Plus fifteen."

"You counted?" Her tone is teasing.

"Yeah," I say seriously. "I did."

The smile fades from Wren's face. "I was—"

"Hey, Bennett! This show still free, or are you going to start charging admission?"

I sigh, spinning to face Wesley. He's grinning wide, his gaze on Wren.

"Wren," I say. "This is my roommate, Wesley. And Judd, Arlo, Eric, and Jeff." I nod to each guy as I introduce them, then pause before adding, "Guys, this is Wren."

I want to add some other descriptor to the introductions, ideally with the word *my* included, but I'm not sure which to use.

"Nice to meet you," Eric says, the other guys adding variations of the same sentiment.

"I gotta head to the train station to pick up Austin," Wesley says. "See you losers later."

"Guess this was your stop anyway," Judd comments, nodding to the entrance of Faber Hall, my dorm.

"Make sure he comes to the party tonight, Wren," Arlo adds before following the other guys. He winks at me, mouthing, *You're welcome.*

Wren glances over as the guys walk away. "They're basically how you described them."

I nod. "So … you're here."

"Yeah. I knew your dorm, so … I was debating if I should text you or just sneak in with someone. Then you showed up."

I nod again. "I more meant, you're in the US."

"Oh. Right. Yeah, I landed … this morning." She hesitated before adding those last two words, like she wasn't sure she should divulge them.

I'm so in love with Wren Kensington that the enormity of it terrifies me, and she's nervous about admitting she came straight here to see me. I hate that, and I hate all the ways I've contributed to it. All the times I've held back because I was scared or sad or simply trying to protect myself from the outcome that always felt inevitable—losing her. I wish we'd been older when we met, that I'd been immediately ready for the commitment. But I also know I wouldn't give up a single second I've known her.

I'm done, I decide. Wren won't leave this campus without knowing exactly what she means to me.

"Want a tour?" I ask, realizing it's been way too long since I said anything.

"Sure."

"Okay, well …" I turn to face the brick building we're standing in front of, and she mimics me. "This is Faber Hall. My, uh, dorm. I can show you my room later."

"Subtle," Wren says.

I laugh. "It's barely more spacious than my truck."

"Well, we made that work."

"I know. It's the reason I'll never get rid of it." I nod left. "Most of the academic buildings are this way."

I hold a hand out. Wren takes it, threading our fingers together as we start walking.

It's weird that she's on campus. I'm accustomed to memories of Wren collected elsewhere—the marina, my house, the beach—but this is one aspect of my life she's never witnessed in person. Equally strange is how little of Wren's life I've witnessed in person. I've never toured her campus. Never visited her in the city. Never seen where she grew up.

"Jeff is from Brooklyn," I comment as we walk.

"Cool." She's distracted, watching a guy skateboard past.

"He wants us all to visit him over the summer."

Now, I have Wren's attention. "Oh, yeah? Are you going to?"

"Probably. There's no real plan. But probably."

She nods. "Rory is finishing law school in a couple of weeks. My parents are hosting a graduation party for her. At our Hamptons house."

"Cool."

Wren's lips twitch before she points at a building ahead. "What's that?"

"Financial aid office," I answer. "Past it, that's the counseling center."

"Oh?"

"Yeah. I, uh … all students have a certain number of sessions allotted each semester. You can request more, if you want, but they don't have the staff for everyone to show up, like, every day."

"Did you go?"

I nod. "A few times. It was nice, talking to someone who didn't know anything about me. I guess she must have had access to my information, but she acted like we were total strangers. I told her about Skylar and about my dad, and it … it wasn't as hard as I'd thought it'd be. I don't know if I'll go back again, but I think it was good that I went."

Wren squeezes my hand. "I talked to a therapist after what happened with Third. His name was Dr. Hurts, ironically."

"Did it help?"

"In some ways. He said the same things my parents had—that it wasn't my fault and that however I was feeling was valid. I think I resented that going to see him meant I couldn't totally pretend it had never happened. Looking back, I needed that so I could … process it. So, yeah, it helped."

This time, I squeeze hers. "Good."

She points at a glass building ahead. "What's that?"

"The giant molecule models hanging from the ceiling didn't give it away? That's the science center."

"I thought those were decorative balls or something."

I snort as we continue toward the sports center.

Showing Wren around campus takes about an hour and a half. We wind up reaching the main dining hall right in the midst of the dinner rush.

"You hungry?" Wren asks, surveying the crowds of chattering students streaming in.

"Yeah," I reply. "But we don't need to eat here. There are places in town—"

"I want to eat here," she insists.

"Okay," I say dubiously.

The dining hall food isn't bad, but it's nothing special either. And it's definitely not up to the standards of someone who's spent most of the past year eating authentic Italian food. But Wren seems set on it, so I follow her inside. She tries to pay for her own meal ticket, and we get into an argument about it.

I win.

"Thanks," Wren says as we walk toward the salad bar.

"You could have said that to start with," I comment dryly.

"Hey." Wren tugs my sleeve.

My steps slow.

"I know you think I'm spoiled and used to people paying my way—"

"I don't think either of those things, Wren. I think that you came here to see me, and the least I can do is buy you dinner. Okay?"

"Okay," she whispers.

I want to kiss her. Right here, in the center of the dining hall, despite being annoyed seeing other couples do the same.

I want to tell her that every aspect of her life I've ever pretended to be annoyed by was me attempting to not lose sight of how incompatible we were.

Before I can do or say anything, someone says my name. My head turns left reluctantly, but I manage a smile when I see Lillian Hale. We share a physics course and wound up in the same study group.

"Hey, Lillian," I greet.

"Hey, Sawyer. I booked a study room for Sunday," Lillian tells me, pausing a few feet away. "I was just about to text the group, then saw you over here." She glances at Wren. "Hey. I don't think we've met before?"

"This is … Wren," I say, placing a palm on Wren's lower back as

I introduce her. Her spine feels stiff under my palm, but maybe I'm imagining the tension. I hope I am. "Wren, this is Lillian. We're co-sufferers in physics together."

"Hostages really," Lillian agrees.

"Nice to meet you." Wren smiles, but her back doesn't relax.

"You too," Lillian replies. She glances at me. "You going to Stewart tonight?"

"Not sure yet," I say.

She nods. "If not, I'll see you Sunday!"

Lillian heads back toward one of the periphery tables.

Wren continues in the direction of the salad bar without saying a word.

I exhale and follow.

A small part of me likes that she's jealous. God knows I've had to watch enough guys lust after her. My phone has been buzzing for the past two hours with messages from the guys, asking if we're dating, how serious it is, if she's coming to the party.

Most of me is exhausted and exasperated. Wren has absolutely no reason to feel threatened by Lillian or anyone else. I haven't given another girl my full attention since I met her, much less kissed or fucked anyone else. Wren has done both, and it's my own damn fault for not admitting how I felt sooner. It's bad enough I have to live with that. I'd rather not waste precious time together with wrong assumptions.

I grab a plate and join her in line. "She's just a friend."

"I didn't ask," Wren says, reaching for a pair of tongs.

"You assumed. I wouldn't have kissed you earlier if I was seeing someone else."

There's a much larger conversation simmering under the surface here. One we need to have soon, one we should have had a while ago.

But this isn't the right place, so that's all I say as I continue down the line, selecting veggies, then follow Wren to the next station.

She picks at her food once we settle at a table, and I'm not sure if it's a commentary on the quality or something else is going on.

"Do you want to go to the party?" I ask. "It's only a few blocks from campus. A few guys on the lacrosse team are hosting."

"Lillian's hoping you'll show up alone," Wren informs me, setting her fork down.

"I'm either going with you or not going at all."

She sighs, finally meeting my gaze. "I should head home. I wasn't planning to spend the night. I didn't bring any stuff with me."

I check the time on my phone. "You've got a two-hour drive back to Manhattan. And aren't you still on Italy time? It's past midnight there."

"I slept on the plane. And I'll stop at a hotel, if I get tired driving."

"I want you to spend the night. Wesley's brother, Austin, is visiting this weekend. His parents got them a hotel room, so I have the dorm room to myself."

"For sex?"

I exhale. "It's been nine months, Wren. Yeah, I want to have sex with you. But that's not the only reason I want you to stay. It hasn't been the only reason for anything since the first time we slept together. Maybe not even then."

She picks up her fork. "I'll stay."

CHAPTER 54
Wren

I'm a coward. I'm a cowardly coward who cowers. Who ducks and avoids and panics at the first sign another girl is interested in the guy I've been in love with for years.

I came to Lancaster with a clear plan. I landed, showered, primped, and drove straight here. I left my program in Milan a week early, submitting all my final papers ahead of deadline and skipping out on the final outing to Lake Como because I was so impatient to be here.

And now that I am? The plan is disintegrating. It's like a bad first date, one where I'm insecure and awkward and self-conscious.

This is Sawyer, I try to remind myself. He's seen me naked. Seen me cry, unfortunately. Seen me vomit, even more unfortunately.

He knows me. Most of the time, I'm more comfortable around him than I am around anyone else.

Except now. Because it *is* Sawyer, and so the stakes could not be higher. At least, in this state of limbo, I've had some of him. The last

time I thought I was about to have all of him, I wound up with none of him. And no matter how many times I tell myself it's different, that he's different and I'm different and we're different, I'm back on that slate floor, chugging champagne, reclined against a washing machine. I've never told Sawyer how much that, "Why?" wrecked me. I attempted the opposite, lying to him outside of clubs and going upstairs with guys who weren't him, in elaborate attempts to ensure he never knew how much he'd hurt me. I'm embarrassed I resorted to that and even more mortified to admit that I did it to him.

So, at almost eleven p.m., I've said none of what I showed up this afternoon to tell him.

"It's Wren, right?"

I glance at the guy who's approached me. He's one of Sawyer's friends who was outside Faber Hall with him earlier. I recognized all their names because Sawyer had mentioned them in his letters, but I haven't connected names with faces yet.

"Right," I reply.

"I'm Jeff," the guy says helpfully.

"Right," I repeat. "Sawyer said you're from Brooklyn? I grew up in New York City too."

Jeff nods. "Yeah, Bennett mentioned that. He talks about you a lot, you know."

"Oh," I say.

"Kinda vague about your relationship status, and he's never shown us any photos. I get why now." Jeff winks.

"Here's your drink." Sawyer reappears beside me.

"Thanks," I say, taking the cup he offers.

"Was just getting to know your girl, Bennett," Jeff says, taking a sip of his beer.

Sawyer doesn't correct him, and a bolt of electricity sizzles through me.

"Where in New York are you from, Wren?" Jeff asks me.

"The Upper East Side."

He whistles. "Fancy. Whereabouts?"

"Fifth Avenue."

"Fuck. Your folks must be loaded. Can I visit?" Jeff glances at Sawyer. "Relax, dude. Totally platonic."

More guys join our group. More of Sawyer's friends. He's popular, which I'm unsurprised by. I noticed the second he stepped into that clearing—he has that rare magnetism that is impossible to learn or imitate. That you naturally gravitate toward.

A few of his friends ask me more questions, but most of the conversation is centered around other Lancaster students I don't know. Mainly, I get curious looks, as everyone silently wonders why I'm here. What my connection to Sawyer is.

I finish my drink and excuse myself to use the bathroom. Predictably, the line is long, snaking around the side of the staircase. I join the end and lean against the paneled wall with a heavy sigh.

I had plenty of opportunities to talk to Sawyer earlier, when it was just the two of us, and I let every one slip by. Wishing we were alone now is ridiculous.

"Is this the bathroom line?" a brunette asks me, craning her neck to see ahead.

"Yep," I reply.

She sighs, mimicking my position against the wall and then glancing over. "I've never seen you before."

"I'm not a student here. I'm just visiting for the weekend."

"From where?"

"I live in New York. Go to college at Cambridge. I just spent my junior year abroad, at Università del Tirreno."

"Oh. Wow. That's really cool—"

"Izzie! He's here, in the kitchen!" A petite girl with a head of brown curls bounces up beside us, shooting me an apologetic look when she realizes she interrupted. "Sorry," she says. "Crush emergency."

"No worries," I tell her, feeling my phone buzz in my pocket and pulling it out to check.

    Rory: You're in Connecticut?!

I sigh.

    Wren: Yes, stalker.

    Rory: Mom checks your phone location too.

    Wren: I'll turn it off.

    Rory: That'll reassure her.

    Wren: I'll be back in NYC tomorrow.

    Rory: You're supposed to be in Italy.

    Wren: Left early. I didn't want to bother Mom and Dad while they were out of town.

Dots appear and disappear as my sister types and stops. I'm sure she's battling the urge to chastise me for leaving Milan early and for telling no one about my change of plans. Both were irresponsible.

    Rory: Say hi to Sawyer from me.

I smile at my phone, liking the message.

"Good news?"

I glance up, straight into Sawyer's green eyes. Belatedly realizing the girls who were whispering next to me have fallen silent. That everyone in this line, everyone in this hallway, is silent and staring this way.

In answer, I flash him my phone screen. One corner of his mouth curves up as he reads the latest text. "Hi back."

My phone buzzes with another message.

    Rory: And text Mom!

I roll my eyes, shutting off my phone before refocusing on Sawyer. "If you need the bathroom, it would probably be faster to walk back to your dorm."

"I don't. I was just checking on you. You've been gone a while."

I've been in line for five minutes. Likely less.

I love you. The words are right there, waiting. Ready. Impatient.

"Yo! Bennett!" His roommate, Wesley, is headed toward us, a younger guy with him.

Wesley pauses to talk to someone else, but the guy with him continues this way.

"Hey," he says, sticking a hand out to Sawyer. "I'm Austin."

"Hey, man," Sawyer replies, shaking it. "Nice to meet you. I'm Sawyer."

Austin nods, smiling, then glances at me.

Sawyer does too. He hesitates, same as he has when introducing me all day.

"I'm Wren," I say, smiling. "Sawyer's girlfriend."

I didn't intend to say it. I'd *wanted* to say it before, to stake some obvious claim. It's socially strange to introduce someone as your first love or your first heartbreak, but simply calling Sawyer a friend doesn't do a great job of encompassing our history. I'm not calling him my boyfriend anyway. I'm asserting he has a claim on me, not the other way around. Also, he was the one who kissed me this afternoon. If he didn't want me getting romantic ideas about us, he should have kept his mouth to himself earlier.

I flip some hair over my shoulder before glancing at Sawyer, striving for some measure of casual. I'm off-balance, searching his face for a reaction, loving and hating that he still manages to make me this nervous. I feel like a seventeen-year-old who just walked up to her crush all over again.

"Nice to meet you, Wren," Austin says, entirely oblivious to the seismic nature of this moment. He glances left. "This is the bathroom line?"

"It is."

"Jeesh," Austin mutters. "Which way is the kitchen?"

"Ahead and to the left," Sawyer answers.

"Cool," Austin says, lifting a hand at me before ambling away.

A group of guys pass by, including Wesley, most of them calling out greetings to Sawyer. He replies, but his eyes remain on me, stepping closer so they have more space to pass. His left hand plants on the wood panel closest to my head.

There's no oxygen in here. I'm breathing too fast. Or maybe I'm not breathing at all.

"You know, there are bathrooms upstairs," Sawyer comments.

I arch an eyebrow. "Are you asking me to go upstairs with you?"

There are whispers around us in the hallway, suggesting at least one person in line is eavesdropping. I couldn't care less that we are not, in fact, alone. It feels like we are.

He smirks. "Went well last time."

"You didn't ask."

"I would have, if I'd stayed downstairs."

I blink rapidly at him. "Really?"

I always assumed if I hadn't followed him, nothing would have happened between us that night.

Sawyer nods. "This thing between us has been a lot of things, Wren, but it's never been one-sided. Not on my end at least."

I'm dangerously close to tears. My nose is stinging, and I'm excessively blinking again.

He leans closer. "We could also go back to my dorm room. It has a bathroom, no line, and a bed."

"Don't you want to stay longer?" I ask. "All your friends—"

"Not even a little bit."

"You sure? I'm not trying to … disrupt your life."

"All you've ever done is disrupt my life, Wren Kensington."

He says it affectionately, not angrily, and I feel the blush burn my cheeks as I push away from the wall, following him outside.

CHAPTER 55

Wren

We talk on the walk back to his dorm, but not about anything important. Mostly about Gus, who's planning to visit before finals. He shares a few updates on Wade and Cammie. Tells me his mom has started dating, which he's pleased and a little grossed out by. We pass a few people once we're inside Faber Hall, two guys who fist-bump him and one girl who gives me an envious look.

And then we're alone. I browse around his room a little bit, even though I was in here earlier, noting the signed baseball on his desk and the Duomo di Milano postcard attached to the bulletin board. Sawyer pulls a bottle of water out of the mini fridge, offering me one too. I accept, mostly so I have something to do with my hands.

"I need to tell you something," I say finally, taking a seat on the edge of his mattress.

His bed is neatly made. I bet, if I pulled up the comforter, the sheet edges would be tightly tucked.

Sawyer sits next to me. "You sound serious."

"I am."

"Okay." He glances at the water bottle he's holding, rolling it between his palms. "I'm listening."

"Okay." I blow out a breath. "Remember when I called you … after New Year's? I was at a club, and I—"

"You were with your boyfriend," he says flatly.

I swallow. "Right. Except I, uh, embellished that bit. There was a guy I met that night that I kissed; he touched me a little, and I … I couldn't get into it. I told him I was going to throw up so he'd leave, and then I went outside. Called you. And also, you were right about Aaron. Nothing happened with him at that party when we went upstairs. I mean, we kissed once. But that was it. And I—" I risk a glance over.

Sawyer's head is down, but he lifts it a little when I stop talking.

I swallow hard, glimpsing his expression. "You're mad."

He tosses the water bottle toward Wesley's bed. It lands upright on the mattress, which is impressive, but I doubt he'd appreciate me complimenting his aim right now.

"Of course I'm fucking mad, Wren! You lied to me!"

"I know. I'm—"

"Earlier, should I have told you I was fucking Lillian? Is that what you want from me? Is this some fucked-up game to you?" He stands, shoving both hands in his hair.

I stand too. "No! That's not—I wasn't trying to—I was hurt, Sawyer. I was hurt after New Year's, and I was trying to get over you, and I thought that was what you wanted from me. I thought you wanted casual, and I thought you wanted me to be unavailable, and I thought you would want me if you thought I'd moved on. I'm not proud of it, okay? Both times, I was planning to go through with it, if that makes it any better. I didn't make it up entirely."

"Better?" He scoffs. "That makes it worse, Wren!"

"I can't change it, Sawyer. I'm trying to be honest—"

"What else have you lied about?"

"Nothing."

"You promise?"

"I mean, nothing major is coming to mind."

He snorts.

"It's not like we met tonight," I say defensively.

"I'm aware," he says tersely. "You've lied for years."

"We weren't even talking for two of them!"

"And whose fault was that?" he shoots back, which shuts me up fast.

Mine. It was my fault.

Silently, I sit back on the edge of his bed.

After a few minutes and a couple of long exhales, Sawyer does too. "Why are you telling me now?" he asks quietly.

"I wanted to be honest with you."

True. But not quite what needed to be said.

I chew on the inside of my cheek a couple of times, then add, "And it felt like it mattered that you knew the truth."

"And it didn't before?"

"It didn't seem like you cared before. Care in the way I wanted you to. And now, I thought … but maybe I was wrong. Maybe it's been too long or too much has happened or …" I sigh. "I just needed to tell you. You deserve to be mad about it. I'd be mad if you lied."

"Figured it was because you're my girlfriend now."

My brain fixates on those last four words, not catching up to his teasing tone for a few seconds.

"You shouldn't kiss girls hello," I say. "Or they'll all get that impression."

"I don't kiss other girls, Wren."

He's not teasing anymore. Sawyer sounds serious. Very serious.

"Since-since when?"

"Since you kissed me, in case you died."

"But I—but that was … I said that … I kissed you the night we met."

He nods.

"That was almost five years ago."

He nods again.

"You … you've done other stuff—I don't want details—right? Like, you've been with other people since we met?"

"No."

I blink at him. "Don't you dare fuck with me, Sawyer. Not about this. If this is your way of getting even because I lied about—"

"*No*, Wren. The answer is no. I haven't kissed, sucked, licked, touched, fucked, done anything with anyone else since we met. If it wasn't with you, nothing happened."

"But …" I start crying. Not delicate tears. Sobs that shake my shoulders and don't stop, even when I press my palms against my eyes.

Sawyer grumbles something I can't hear over my hysteria, then pulls me onto his lap. Right next to my ear, he says, "Wren. Fuck. It's fine. Forget I said anything."

I cry harder, turning my face against his shirt, breathing in his scent and trying to exhale my frustration.

All this time, I was entirely convinced I cared more. That I'd always care more. That something was seriously wrong with me for only wanting one person, especially when that one person didn't share the same mindset. I'm so relieved, so floored, that I was completely wrong.

I snuggle closer, my head nestling naturally against his shoulder, mouth even with his collarbone. I kiss him there first, then higher, working my way up the column of his throat, shifting so I'm straddling him.

"Wren. *Wren.*" His hands are on my cheeks, thumbs swiping away the salty tracks, expression concerned. "We're not—you're upset."

I shake my head. As much as I can with his hands bracketing my face at least. "I'm not upset. I'm happy. Overwhelmed mostly."

"Well, I'm confused."

I exhale. "I spent years thinking I couldn't move on from someone who never got attached to me. Finding out you never moved on either was … a lot."

He scoffs. Grabs my hips, like he's about to lift me off him.

"Stop," I say, planting my hands on his chest. "Tell me what you're thinking."

Sawyer huffs. "Never got attached? I wasn't sure what any of it *meant*, Wren. I kept waiting for you to get bored. To forget about me. To never come back. I was so certain I'd never get to keep you; I never let myself consider the possibility. And the only time I did … you left like it was nothing. You show up here, and I'm—what does it mean, Wren? Are you here because it's almost summer again? Italian guys weren't doing it for you? Fucking Pierre isn't trying to get you back?"

"Has it really—" My voice comes out hoarse, so I try again. "Has it really never occurred to you that I've been in love with you for as long as I've known you? And that I've spent all that time trying to figure out if you'll ever love me back?"

If this was a fairy tale, he'd say it back.

If this was a fantasy, we'd already be naked.

But this is us, so Sawyer barks a low, disbelieving laugh before he says, "You loved me, Wren, when you flirted with my friends? When you left the day after I almost died? When you planned to fuck the guys you told me about and when you actually fucked—"

"I didn't actually fuck anyone." I drop my hands from his chest, sitting straighter. "You want the full truth? I've *never* had sex with anyone else, Sawyer. Every time it could happen, I'd freeze. And not because of what Third did. Because of *you*. Because I'm yours, and you've never ever acted like mine."

I fight the urge to flee. To leave him alone with that knowledge rather than facing his reaction. But we can't continue in this cycle. I need closure, one way or the other. For us to move forward or be final.

All I get is silence.

"I knew that would freak—"

"Remember when you said your degree was just something your family wanted you to get and you had no idea what you'd do after college?"

I scowl. "What does—"

"You said you didn't have a plan after college. Is that still true?"

I nod stiffly, annoyed by him changing the topic.

He nods, too, meeting my gaze. Holding it captive. "Is there room in that non-plan of yours for me?"

The bed tilts beneath me. A flash of vertigo, another moment of falling when I'm certain I'm not. This time, there's no chilly water to center myself.

But there is Sawyer. Under and around, catching me.

"Yes," I whisper. "There's a lot of room. All of it really."

He smiles, a slow, steady one that spreads across his face and stays in place. "I love you, Wren Kensington. I've loved you for a long, long time. I love you so much that it scares me. So much that it took a while to wrap my head around the size of it. And I'm really sorry for not saying it sooner."

I'm crying again, which is embarrassing. At least they're gentler tears this time. I'm probably dehydrated; I never drank any of the water he gave me.

"I'm sorry too. I should've said it—"

"You did."

I stare at him. "What?"

He smirks a little, reaching up to brush my hair off my forehead. "Last summer, the night you got wasted at Lucky's, you said, 'I love you,' after I carried you up to your room."

"Why didn't you tell me?"

"You were drunk, Wren. I didn't know if you meant it, and you never acted like you remembered. But technically, you told me."

"I meant it." I give him a lingering kiss. "I"—kiss—"love"—kiss— "you."

My lips move lower, sucking on the skin of his neck in one spot. Then another.

"I can just tell people I have a girlfriend. You don't have to cover me in hickeys."

"Shut up," I say, smothering his grin with my mouth as I tug at his shirt. He helps me pull it over his head, and I start working on his pants next.

"Wren." His hands cover mine. "I don't have a condom."

"What? Why?"

He gives me an exasperated look. "Why do you think? I haven't needed them. You didn't tell me you were coming. What, did you want me to suggest a trip to the pharmacy as soon as you arrived?"

"Yes!"

Sawyer rolls his eyes. "We can go now."

I groan, collapsing on his bed. "I should have gone on birth control."

"It'll take ten minutes," he says, but he seems as reluctant to leave this room as I am. To rejoin the rest of the world.

He lies down beside me instead. There's barely room for both of us on the twin mattress. Sleeping tonight should be interesting.

I roll my head until his mouth is within reach, kissing him again. He pulls me back onto his lap, sitting up so he can yank off my shirt and unclasp my bra. I start to care a lot less about the lack of condoms, arching my back to allow him better access. When he realizes it, I feel his laugh reverberate against my sensitive skin.

It's better … and worse. Everything we're doing only makes me want more.

I reach for his waistband again, my impatience and his distracting mouth slowing my progress. Once I have his erection free, Sawyer grunts.

"I'm not going to last long *at all*," he tells me.

"So, same as always?"

His teeth scrape my skin, spreading goose bumps everywhere. "Now you know why. You were right; fucking you is better than my hand."

"When did I say that?"

"At Wade's party. You told me I had a high opinion of my hand if I thought jerking off would be like having sex with you."

"I don't remember saying that. I was … nervous that night. Although it does sound like something I'd say."

He laughs. "It does."

I release his cock, needing both hands to work off my pants. I slip my thong down, too, then shove at his chest until he lies back on the mattress.

"Wren …" he says, uncertain, as my hips hover over his erection.

"Relax. I have no interest in getting knocked up."

I shift closer and straddle him, his penis trapped between us. Sawyer realizes what I'm wanting, pulling my ass higher so that my pussy is directly against his dick, pressing it against his stomach. Slowly, I start to move my hips, watching as I work up and down his length.

The burst of pleasure is immediate, a single spark that roars into a bonfire.

"*Fuck*," Sawyer groans, watching us.

I bite my bottom lip so hard that I taste copper, trying to remember he has neighbors on the other side of this wall. I was baiting him before, but I'll likely come first. I can already feel a pending orgasm tingling in my toes. I'm wet—so wet that his cock is shiny from me grinding against it. My hips move faster, chasing more friction. I feel feverish, my entire body flushed with heat and swimming with lust. Fixated on the erotic sight of my pussy coating his cock with my arousal. Conflicted between making this last and a rising desperation to reach the release that's only existed with him.

He looks so perfect under me. Abs flexed. Jaw clenched. Pupils wide. He's tucked an arm behind his head, so I can see the sailboat tattooed on his arm. The two spots I sucked on his neck are bright red too.

Mine.

He's mine.

I've always wanted him, and I never thought I'd really have him. I accepted there might always be some distance between us, that I might never get all of him.

Sawyer's mostly letting me lead, but I can sense his impatience growing. His thighs tense under me, hips jerking like they're fighting the urge to thrust.

My pace quickens, more by instinct than choice. I'm close to losing control too.

His hands land on my thighs, tugging them open even wider. It's almost like he's inside of me, so similar to that second before he pushes in.

"You're so wet. I can feel it." He sounds proud. Possessive.

"It's been just as long for me," I remind him.

"Your hand isn't as good as my cock?"

"I mean, I pretend it's your cock, so …"

Another groan.

It crashes over me a moment later—an immediate, brilliant devastation. I collapse onto his chest, then roll to the two-ish feet of bed on my side, breathing heavily as I watch him come on his stomach. Pass him some tissues to mop up the sticky mess. He does, sitting up to toss them in the trash before lying back down.

"That was really hot," he tells me. "Good idea."

"I'm full of them."

Sawyer chuckles, reaching out and pulling me onto his chest. He kisses my forehead. "I didn't think you'd—I would have understood, I mean, if you'd—we would have been okay if you had wanted to …"

"Did you forget how to finish a sentence?"

He huffs, twirling a loose strand of my hair. "I'm glad you've never had sex with anyone else."

"Really?" I feign shock. "You were so chill about me lending toothpaste to another guy. I figured me fucking someone else would be—*ah*!"

I yelp with surprise as he rolls over me, nearly tumbling us both off the bed in the process. Sawyer kisses me, hard, and I'm certain he'd be doing a lot more than that if he had a condom.

I play with his chain, smiling up at him as we both attempt to catch our breath. "I am also glad you haven't—what was it? Licked, nibbled, sucked—"

"I never mentioned nibbling."

"Oh, you don't like nibbling?" I lift my head, grazing my teeth against his neck.

Sawyer shifts away, groaning. "Why didn't *you* bring condoms?"

"I didn't even pack a toothbrush. I'll have to borrow yours. And toothpaste, even knowing how you feel about sharing it."

He rolls his eyes.

"Also … that felt presumptuous."

"More presumptuous than kissing a random stranger on a cliff? I could have been a serial killer."

"Lucky for me, you're just an asshole."

"I warned you about that. Multiple times." He smirks. "You fell in love with me anyway."

"Yep." I beam back. "I sure did."

CHAPTER 56
Sawyer

I wake up alone. The bed feels too big, even though it's an oversize twin and I've complained the opposite in the past.

For a few frantic seconds, I think it was all a dream. But then I roll over, and something stiff scrapes my cheek. I reach up, grabbing and squinting at the piece of paper. A smile spreads across my face as I scan the familiar handwriting.

She wrote *I love you* on every line except the last one, which reads, *Breakfast run. Be back soon.*

I grin stupidly at the note for a few minutes, then climb out of bed, pull on some shorts, and head toward the bathroom. Not even stubbing a toe on my thick physics textbook—one of the required courses for my naval architecture and marine engineering major—dims my mood.

I'm brushing my teeth when I hear the distinctive beep and click of the door unlocking. Quickly, I spit and stash my toothbrush before walking back into my room.

She's wearing the same jeans from last night with a faded sweatshirt of mine that falls to mid-thigh, blonde hair pulled up in a messy bun. She shuts the door with her hip, hands clutching my ID card, two paper bags, and a cardboard drink tray. She glances at my empty bed, then finds me standing in the doorway.

I grin. "Hey."

Wren scowls, tossing my student ID on my desk. "What are you doing? Get back in bed."

I arch a brow. "Good morning to you too. I can't believe you woke up before me."

"I'm still on Italy time," she replies, walking over to the bed and setting everything she's holding down on the table next to it before yanking the elastic out of her hair. "I wanted to have breakfast together, not at the dining hall."

"I warned you the food wasn't great." I walk up behind her, wrapping my arms around her waist and resting my chin on the top of her head. Just wanting—needing—to touch her.

Wren laughs, reaching into one of the bags. "That's not why I wanted to eat here."

I grin, taking the box of condoms she pulled out and tossing them on the unmade bed. "You went to the pharmacy? How long have you been up?"

"A couple of hours. I talked to my mom too."

I take a seat on the edge of the mattress, reaching for the other bag. It's stuffed with pastries—two muffins, a croissant, a cinnamon bun, and a bagel. "How's your mom?"

"Good. She's in Amsterdam, at a conference."

I nod, unfazed. Wren's parents seem to travel as much as she does. Maybe more.

"You went to Tandem Coffee?" I ask, reading the label on one of the cups.

"Yeah. You've been there before?"

"A couple of times. It's good." I grab a cup, take a sip, then swallow fast, fighting the urge to spit it out.

She grabs the other cup and holds it out to me. "That's mine. I got you black."

"Thanks." I grab it and take a long swig, washing away the other flavors. "What did you get?"

"Lavender latte with oat milk and an extra shot of espresso. Is it good?"

"If you like what lavender and oat milk taste like, probably." I swallow more plain coffee.

"I do. The cashier recommended it. And gave me a free cinnamon bun."

"Let me guess. The cashier was a guy."

Wren sets her drink down, so I do the same. One knee lands left of my thigh, and then she's fully on my lap, arms draped over my shoulders.

"I didn't think you'd get jealous after we were dating," she tells me, a small smirk on her face.

"So, he wasn't flirting with you?"

Wren shrugs one shoulder. "He wrote his number on the bag."

"Cute."

She nods. "It would have been an adorable meet-cute, if I didn't already have a boyfriend."

I manage a smile, but Wren sees straight through it.

"Are you actually jealous? Because I don't even remember his name—"

"No. I'm not. I-I woke up, and you weren't here, and … there was a part of me that was always convinced this would never happen. And ... I'm scared it'll—concerned something will fuck it up. Me, specifically." I rub my palms against her thighs. "I'm not jealous of some random guy, although I'm never going to like it when you get hit on. I'm worried you're going to realize winding up with a guy without a passport isn't what you want."

Wren leans closer, until our foreheads are almost touching. "Do you know why I sent you that first letter?"

"Because you wanted to pass English?"

"Not even a little bit. Because I thought I'd never see you again. And if I didn't, I wanted you to have some reminder of me. Because I wanted you then, and I want you now, and there won't ever be a time when I don't want you. Also, your lack of a passport is, A) irrelevant, and, B) easily fixed. If you want to travel, that is. I've gone to a lot of cool places, and this is my favorite spot—wherever you are. I've never been sure about anything the way I'm sure about you. I don't make up fake hookups for just anyone, you know."

I tighten my hold on her hips. "Not funny."

"Any other response to my romantic speech?"

I smile. "I love you."

"Better." She brushes my hair off my forehead. I'm about to kiss her when she adds, "My mom wants to meet you."

"I've met your mom," I say stupidly.

"Pretty sure she was thinking you'd stay for a meal this time. And that my dad would be there too. And that I would be conscious."

"Right."

"They'll both be in the Hamptons for Rory's graduation party. My mom said you're welcome to come to the party ... and suggested dinner after."

"Right," I repeat. Suddenly, that's the only word in my vocabulary.

Wren studies me. "They'll like you."

"You think so, huh?" I ask dryly.

"I know so. As far as parents go, mine are pretty great. They want me to be happy, and you make me very happy."

"Not just not sad?"

"Not just not sad," she says, playing with my hair. "Also, if you're coming to the party—"

"If you want me there, I'll be there."

She smiles, but then it becomes nervous. "My grandfather will be at Rory's party. And I'll talk to him beforehand, but he might be mad I broke our deal and say something to you anyway, so …"

I frown. "What deal?"

Wren exhales. "A lot of people consider my grandfather to be really important. My dad replaced him as CEO of Kensington Consolidated a long time ago, and now my uncle and cousin are part of the company, but Grandpa's still sort of in charge in a lot of ways."

"Okay …" I say, having no idea where this is going.

"The night you got caught out in that storm, I called my dad to see if he knew anyone who could help. Dusty was trying … but he wasn't getting through to anyone. My dad didn't answer, so I called my grandfather."

I tense. Still confused, but somehow knowing I won't like what comes next.

"He knew about the fight you got into at Lucky's—the lawyer Rory had called told him—and he was never happy about me picking a public university. So, he said he'd make sure you got rescued … if I ended things with you and went to a college he approved of."

I stare at her, stunned. "Like Cambridge?"

"Yeah." She nods. "Exactly like Cambridge."

"What the *fuck*, Wren?"

She shrugs a shoulder. "I didn't know what else to do. If I hadn't agreed and something happened to you, I never would have forgiven myself. I didn't care that much about where I went to college. You know I was unsure about going at all. And us … I knew how hard leaving you at the end of the summer was going to be, no matter where I was headed. I thought me leaving sooner might be for the best. An attempt at a clean break instead of the back-and-forth we'd been in for so long."

"You should have told me. You should have asked me."

"You weren't there!"

"After. The next day, when I came over and you were packing."

"I'd already decided then."

I exhale.

"I don't want to keep rehashing the past, Sawyer. I want to move forward, together. I only told you so you're not blindsided if it ever comes up and because I wanted to be completely honest with you."

"Completely honest? That's everything?"

Wren nods decisively. "That's everything."

"That's what you said last night."

"I hadn't decided if I was going to tell you about it," she confesses.

I'm still shocked. But this revelation answers questions I've wondered about for a while—why she suddenly changed her mind about us, why she swapped schools so close to starting freshman year. I'm not happy she did any of it, but I am touched—flabbergasted—that she was willing to go to such extremes, especially knowing how stubborn she can be. It soothes some of the fear that history might repeat itself. That I'm more invested in us than she is. That we'll always be tenuous and I'll always be waiting for it to fall apart again.

"I'm glad you told me."

"Yeah?" She looks relieved.

"Yeah. I wish you'd told me three years ago, and I can't believe you'd—"

She kisses me.

I kiss her back for a few seconds. Then ask, "What if they don't like me?"

"My parents?"

I nod.

"They will."

"But what if they don't? Didn't your grandfather tell them why I needed a lawyer? If they tell you to break up with me—"

"My parents would *never* do that."

"Your grandfather did."

"And they were furious he'd interfered. I asked them not to get involved, that it was our deal, but Mom told me my dad chewed Grandpa out over it. Told him he'd never be around me or Rory if he ever pulled anything like that again. Trust me, no one will interfere. And even if they did, I'd choose you. What happened was my way of choosing you. I know it didn't seem that way to you, but it was."

Wren kisses me again, biting my lip gently.

"I like nibbling when you do it," I murmur and feel her laugh vibrate against my lips.

Wren lies down first, using my chain to pull my mouth within reach, just like she did the first time we kissed. I remember that precise moment so clearly, like my brain knew, even then, to pay especially close attention to every detail.

In the quiet room, all I can hear is our increasingly rapid breathing, the friction of our lips … and her stomach grumble.

"Hungry?" I murmur.

"No." Her hands are coasting across my back urgently, like she's trying to touch all of me at once. "Don't stop."

I lift most of my weight off her so I can pull her sweatshirt—my sweatshirt—higher. "You never gave the last one back."

"I'm keeping this one too," she informs me.

"Fine by me." I reach into the pastry bag by her head.

Wren's mouth opens in outrage. "Are you seriously ..." Her voice trails when I swipe some frosting from the cinnamon bun, then smear it across her stomach.

She moans when I lick it off her, then unbutton her jeans and tug them down, followed by her underwear, flinging both toward Wesley's side of the room.

I kiss my way back up her thigh, just to tease her a little more. But honestly, I'm more impatient than she is. Not only because it's been nine months or because this will be our first time as an official couple, but because I'm the only one who has ever seen Wren like this. I did a shitty job conveying to her last night how learning that made me feel.

I was stunned she wanted her first time to be with me. The fact that she wanted *all* her times to be with me ... I can't describe how knowing that feels, even to myself.

"Sawyer ..." She wiggles under me, trying to get me to move faster. Shoving at my shorts with her feet.

Maybe we're equally eager.

"What?"

"You know what."

I push the hoodie a little higher. "Do I?"

"*Yes.* Fuck me."

I grin, shoving more fabric up her chest. Then realize, "Are you wearing nothing under this?"

"I couldn't find my bra and was trying to be quiet. Can you critique my fashion choices later?"

"No. Because you'll be naked later and we'll still be in this bed."

She smiles. "Promise?"

I flip the hoodie over her head, tugging it out from under her and letting it slip off the side of the mattress.

Finally, we're both naked, nothing but warm skin pressed against each other. "I'll promise you anything, Wren Kensington. Anything I have, it's yours."

CHAPTER 57

Wren

"We're too old for this," Sawyer tells me.

I scoff. "Speak for yourself."

"I'm only two months older than you."

"And aging like wine. Or cheese."

"It's a teenager spot."

"I'll go alone."

"The water's still cold."

"Again, I'll go alone."

We both know he won't let me. That he'll insist on *supervising*.

Sawyer shakes his head, pulling onto the grassy side of the road and parking. "Hurry up, or we'll be late."

"First, you didn't want to do this, and now *I'm* the one holding things up? Pick a position." I roll my eyes, opening the door and jumping out of the cab.

I abandon my phone on the seat and toss my sandals in the footwell before slamming the truck door shut. Jog across the asphalt to the start of the trail, smiling when I hear his footsteps right behind me.

"Race you!" I shout, then take off.

Sawyer flashes me a cocky smirk as he passes by, reaching the clearing ahead about five seconds before I do.

I have to stop once I do because most of my hair has fallen out of the hasty ponytail I pulled it into on the drive here. I give up on fixing it, snapping the elastic on my wrist and then pulling off my shirt and stepping out of my shorts.

"Got anything to say?" he teases, watching me pile my clothes. His eyes are focused lower than my face, I notice.

"That you're the one slowing us down now. Unless you're planning to jump with your shirt on."

Sawyer scoffs, mumbling something under his breath as he tugs his T-shirt off. My brain immediately short-circuits. This happens occasionally. I'll spot him doing something ordinary, like driving or texting or brushing his teeth, and be seized by the surreal certainty that he's mine. That I never have to wonder where he is or who he's with, that he isn't a what-if who haunts my dreams and nightmares and fantasies.

"C'mon." He takes my hand, the warmth of his palm countering some of the chill in the air.

It's early, and we're not that far into June. The air temperature is probably hovering in the mid-sixties, and I'd guess the water is about the same.

We reach the edge of the rock face. I peer over the edge of the cliff, down at the churning blue water below. It looks cold.

"Ready?"

"Yeah," I say reluctantly.

He laughs. "This was your idea!"

I glance at him. "This is where we met."

"I'm aware," he drawls.

"It's a good memory."

"Agreed."

"Last time we were here … not so great."

Sawyer sobers, glancing down at the ocean once before meeting my gaze again. He swallows once, his Adam's apple bobbing with the motion. "I remember."

"Before we get banished from this 'teenager spot,' I thought we should come here a third time. So, it's two to one. Good outweighs the bad, you know?"

The left corner of his mouth curves up. "I've been here about a hundred times without you, you know."

"Those don't count," I reply airily.

He chuckles, glancing at the water again. "They were a lot less memorable—that's for sure."

"So?"

"Yeah, let's do it. If I beat you back to the shore a third time, is there a prize?"

I sniff. If we weren't literally standing at the edge of a cliff, I'd shove him. "We tied the first time. And you had a head start both times since you took off without waiting for me. But, sure, I will buy you a drink at Lucky's tonight if you beat me back to the shore without cheating."

"You're so generous for a billionaire."

"We *are* going to be late if you keep begging for rewards. And you're not the one who has to do her hair and makeup."

"That was not begging. You were the one begging last night, when—"

"Are we jumping or not?" I interrupt. Because if he starts describing last night, I'm going to wind up kissing him, and there's a good chance we'll end up having sex in the grass instead of swimming.

"We're jumping. We're jumping."

Sawyer grabs my hand. And we leap, plummeting from rock to water.

Falling.

Together.

CHAPTER 58

THREE YEARS LATER

Midway through skimming an email, the phone screen lights up with an incoming call.

"Hey, man," I greet, reclining in the small chair situated on the balcony.

"How is it?" Gus asks eagerly.

"It's …" I glance around, struggling to summon the right adjective. "It's wild. Literally. I feel like I'm on another planet. We're kayaking around some glaciers later. I'll send pics."

Wren and I have traveled together before, but never just her and me. We went to Portugal with her parents two years ago. Visited her cousin Lili at an actual *castle* in England last summer.

When Wren told me she'd booked a trip for us—her graduation present to me—I was excited. When she shared where we were headed, I genuinely thought she was kidding.

Antarctica is not a destination that would have ever occurred to me, but it's, without a doubt, the coolest place I've ever been. Literally. I zipped up my winter coat just to step out here, and the hand holding my phone is steadily growing numb, but also because of what I just told Gus. It feels entirely otherworldly, floating past boulders of ice, coated with a fresh layer of snow. The first I've seen since last winter. It's October, so leaves are falling in Manhattan, not flakes.

I moved into Wren's penthouse in May, right after I graduated from Lancaster, and am still adjusting to aspects of it. The view didn't take any getting used to. Central Park was a green oasis in the summer. But I think I prefer it in autumn, the foliage a dazzling display of burnt orange and bright yellow. Not the eternally blue ocean, but nothing is.

Gus and I chat for a few more minutes, catching up on the past couple of weeks. We talk often, but haven't seen each other in person since summer. Gus wound up in Boston after graduating college. He has one year left of business school there, but I'm guessing he and Lissa will stay in Massachusetts for longer. I'll make a *move to Manhattan* pitch to him at Thanksgiving anyway. Oliver and Hannah are hosting the holiday at their Hamptons house and included my mom and her boyfriend, Derek—still getting used to that, but happy she's happy— along with the entire Griffin clan.

The hiss of the sliding door opening captures my attention.

"I've gotta go."

"Wren?" Gus guesses.

"Can't tell for sure."

He laughs. "What?"

"I'll send some pics," I promise, then hang up. Grin. "You should bundle up more. I can still see your eyes."

The wool scarf lowers, revealing Wren's scowl. "How are you not cold? All you're wearing is a jacket!"

"And a hat." I slip my phone into a pocket and tug the beanie down so it covers more of my ears. "My hands are a little chilly."

She walks to the railing, glancing around at the surrounding sea before turning and taking a seat on my lap. I hug her tight to my chest, resting my chin next to the pom-pom attached to the top of her hat, then slip my hands into her jacket pockets.

Wren yelps as my frozen fingers brush her warm ones. "Where are your gloves?"

"No idea," I admit. "I was looking before I came out here, then gave up."

She shivers. "Why did you come out here?"

"The view. Also, I was checking some emails."

"*Sawyer*." Wren says my name with a decent dose of exasperation. "You're on vacation."

"I know. I just want to keep up with what's happening in the office."

I'm four months into working at the Manhattan office of one of the top naval architecture firms in the country. And the only downside I've discovered to your life including more than you ever dared to dream of? The terror of losing it never disappears. Wren and I have been officially dating for over three years, and I still marvel every morning that she's the person I wake up next to.

I'm not entirely convinced that fear is a bad thing. I think the day I wake up and simply accept how wonderfully my life has turned out would be cause for concern. But, yeah, it also means I'm checking on projects during vacation in the hopes that it means Hudson & Cox will never think they made a mistake, hiring me.

"Were you talking to your mom?"

"Gus."

"How is he?"

"Good." My hands have warmed to a normal temperature, so I twine my fingers with hers. "Busy. Midterms."

"I don't miss that."

"Yeah. Me neither."

"Do you miss other parts?"

"Of Lancaster?"

She nods, pom-pom brushing my cheek.

"No."

I don't have to think about my answer. I liked college. I made great friends. I earned a degree I'm using daily. But I prefer my current life, not least because it includes a lot more Wren.

"You sure?"

"Very sure. I love my job. Your place—"

"Our place," she interjects.

I smile, even though she can't see it. "Our place is way nicer than anywhere I lived at Lancaster. Also, it's a relief to see that student loan number go down instead of up."

Wren hums.

I tighten my hold on her. "Thank you."

"For what?"

"For lots. And for saying nothing just now."

"You came on this trip without asking me how much it cost. Compromise."

I kiss the top of her head. "Compromise."

I'm never going to feel comfortable with how much wealth Wren has. I've accepted that. We've found a middle ground on most things, after arguments on several topics, such as her repeated offers to pay off my student loans. Wren agreed to a maximum amount on gifts—there's no way this trip didn't blow past that number, but it's the first time she has, and I guess I'll only graduate college once, so it can qualify as an exception. Rather than pay all the utilities, like I was planning to, living rent-free since she owns her penthouse, I conceded we could split them.

Not only is the concept of never having to worry about money a foreign one to me, but it's a factor of the question I—and no doubt many other people—have wondered: *What the hell is Wren Kensington doing with me?* But if it's a choice between being perceived as the "breadwinner" in a relationship and a life with Wren? I'll pick her. Every time.

"Do you miss Cambridge?" I ask.

"God, no," she replies faster than I did.

I laugh, watching it turn to white vapor before dissipating entirely. "Too much rain?"

I know it's a stereotype, but it was sunny *once* during the handful of days I spent in England.

"Too little you. I totally preferred skipping class to having to go to work though."

I huff another laugh. I read some of her essays. Wren's a much stronger student than she claims. And I've seen how excited she is, working at her aunt's magazine.

"Also, you're no longer allowed in the *Haute* offices. There's been a suspicious gathering of interns skulking around every time you stop by for lunch, and I think it's unhealthy for me to dislike most of my coworkers."

"Wren." I groan her name, but I'm sort of chuckling too. "That's ridiculous."

"I agree. You're turning into a workaholic, and you're not even that good-looking."

I grin. "Says the girl who told me I was *really hot* on our first date."

"Only so you'd reassure me I *wasn't ugly*." I can practically hear her eyes rolling.

Not my best line, but Wren should take that being the best I could come up with as the biggest compliment of all. My mind still goes blank when I see her mostly or entirely naked.

I squint as the sun glints off a nearby glacier. "Feels like a long time ago."

"It was a long time ago."

Eight years.

"Mmhmm."

"You're going to need gloves for the kayaking trip, you know."

"I know. I'm ninety percent sure they're somewhere under your tiny, neatly folded pile of clothes. I figured I should wait for you to wake up before touching that."

"Wise move."

I smile, then state, "Gus bought a ring."

"Really?" Wren sits up, twisting so she can see my face. "Has he asked Lissa yet?"

I shake my head, shoving my hands into my own pockets before they have a chance to refreeze. "Nope. He'll probably ask for your opinion on the proposal."

"Do you think he'll ask her in Boston?" Wren is clearly already scheming locations.

I shrug, but I'm not sure she can tell under the bulk of my jacket, so I add, "Dunno."

"Is he asking her before Thanksgiving? We should bring them an engagement gift."

"Not sure."

Wren raises an eyebrow. "Okay. To recap, Gus told you he bought a ring, and you said …"

" 'That's cool.' "

"That's it? No follow-up questions?"

"We'd been talking about work, and then he just threw it out there as an update. If he had a plan, he would have told me. We talked two weeks ago, and he didn't mention it. Caught me off guard. I mean, they're young. Our age."

"Yeah." Wren glances at the ocean, profile backlit by the sun.

"Have you thought about it?" I ask.

"Gus and Lissa getting married? Not really. And I don't know Boston very well. I'll have to research places—"

"Not them, Wren. Us."

She looks at me.

I know Wren well. Know her better than anyone maybe. But I can't gauge what she's thinking at all in this moment.

She pulls a gloved hand out of her pocket, running a finger down the tip of my nose. "Weird way to propose. But yes."

I scoff. "I'm being serious."

"So am I. If you asked, I'd say yes. And, yeah, maybe I have this fantasy in my head where I'm walking down the aisle, an absolute vision in white, and you say something super romantic when I reach you, like, *Nice dress,* about my custom couture gown with a five-foot train—"

"I would come up with something better than *that,*" I interject.

She smiles. "But it doesn't need to happen soon. Or ever, honestly. I love our life exactly like it is now. Would a wedding be fun? Yeah. But after, I think it would feel the same. I'd be as much yours then as I am now."

I brave the frigid air to brush away a strand of blonde hair that the wind blew across her cheek. "I love you a lot, Wren Kensington—you know that?"

"No, you've never mentioned it. Also, I woke up alone in a cold, empty bed."

I hide a smile. "How could I possibly make that up to you?"

"Build a time machine, Mr. Engineer."

"That would require me working on the trip, which I thought wasn't allowed."

"We both know you'll check your email again. I guess I'll have to start writing letters or something to communicate with you."

I stand, still holding her, then walk over to the sliding door that leads into our bedroom. Manage to open it with my elbow, which Wren looks mildly impressed by. Shutting it is harder, but I complete that too. Curse after dropping Wren on the bed and immediately unzip my jacket. I rip my beanie off next, running a hasty hand through my hair.

"Why is it a million degrees in here?"

"I told you, I was cold."

I walk over to the thermostat, turn it ten degrees down, and then survey the pile of clothes that has somehow grown since I was last in our room. "And what happened here?"

"I couldn't find any socks." Wren's unwinding the scarf from around her neck, tossing it unceremoniously on the heap.

"Can't imagine why I'm having trouble finding shit," I mutter.

"FYI, complaining about my cute outfits is not *making it up to me*." She glances at the clock on the bedside table. "Shit. We're going to miss breakfast. I'll organize later."

If I want to avoid frostbite, I will be the one organizing before this afternoon's kayak trip. But I don't say that.

I tell her, "We have twenty minutes until breakfast ends."

"I'm a slow eater."

"We have twenty minutes to get food, not twenty minutes to eat. And you'll come in five, max."

"That's rather arrogant of you," Wren drawls, pulling off her hat. Her gloves and jacket get added to the pile next.

"Wanna bet you won't?" I ask, approaching the bed.

"Not really," she allows.

I smirk, reaching for the waistband of the stretchy pants she's wearing. I yank them down, toss them on the mattress, then slip her underwear off next. "So, we have plenty of time."

I lean over, kiss a line up the inside of her thigh. Wren's fingers weave into my hair, tugging before I reach my destination.

"I want your cock."

Like I'm going to argue with that.

I straighten, yanking the sweatpants I'm wearing down just enough to free my erection.

Wren huffs a laugh. "What was your plan for that? Scandalizing the entire dining room?"

"Walking outside," I say, then thrust into her.

Wren moans, fisting the sheets and arching her back. Our neighbors might hate us. Hopefully, they're at breakfast.

I kiss her, muffling some of the sounds with my mouth. Wren's hands slide under my shirt, nails grazing my back roughly enough to leave marks. For the best, really, that she didn't plan a tropical cruise.

I fuck her harder and faster, and it has absolutely nothing to do with the boat's meal hours. I'm already dangerously close to coming, and I need her to get there first.

I feel it happen a few strokes later and relax into my own release with a relieved groan, pulling out and rolling onto my back. Grin at the ceiling as Wren sits up and scoots off the mattress.

"You'd better be ready to go when I'm finished in the bathroom," she warns. "No way am I kayaking in the cold on an empty stomach."

"I'll be ready," I promise between rapid breaths.

Wren moves around the room. Collecting clothes, I'm guessing. She tosses something on my stomach on her way into the bathroom.

It's the pad of paper provided in every room, with the cruise company's logo printed at the top of the page. Beneath it, Wren wrote:

I love you, Sawyer Bennett.

The End

Acknowledgments

Writing Wren's book felt like reuniting with old friends, which was unexpected. Wren didn't appear much in Lili and Kit's books, partly because I was undecided about how to introduce a teenager into what was an adult series. I sat down to start this story thinking I'd likely wind up saving it for last. And then, *Cruel Summer* pretty much poured out of me. The writing process feels like running a marathon—lots of hard work and second-guessing why you ever attempted it, capped off with an exhausted, jubilant finish. *Cruel Summer* was a race I experienced a runner's high for most of. Here's hoping that ever happens in my career again!

Thanks so much to the incredible team who helped shape and polish this book:

Megan, I adore you and am so appreciative of you going *beyond* beyond to provide the most incredible feedback.

Sierra, I am in awe of your instincts for plot improvement and for picking out perfect promo moments!

Sahara, I love how much you love Sawyer and Wren. I am so grateful for your advice, song suggestions, and enthusiasm!

Jovana, you worked your magic yet again. I can't wait to finish this series with you!

Judy, it's always such a pleasure to work with you.

Books and Moods, I am obsessed with this pink cover and the gorgeous formatting!

To my readers: none of this would be possible without you continuing to read and recommend my books. I hope you enjoyed Wren and Sawyer!

Last (but not least), to my family, for their endless patience and support. This was the *last* deadline I set around the holidays, I promise!

About The Author

C.W. Farnsworth is the author of numerous adult and young adult romance novels featuring sports, strong female leads, and happy endings.

Charlotte lives in Rhode Island and when she isn't writing spends her free time reading, at the beach, or snuggling with her Australian Shepherd.

Find her on Facebook (@cwfarnsworth), TikTok (@authorcwfarnsworth), Instagram (@authorcwfarnsworth) and check out her website www.authorcwfarnsworth.com for news about upcoming releases!

Also By C.W. Farnsworth

Standalones

Four Months, Three Words
Come Break My Heart Again
Winning Mr. Wrong
Back Where We Began
Like I Never Said
Fly Bye
Serve
Heartbreak for Two
Pretty Ugly Promises
Six Summers to Fall
King of Country
Left Field Love

Rival Love

Kiss Now, Lie Later
For Now, Not Forever

The Kensingtons Duet

Fake Empire
Real Regrets

Kensingtons: The Second Generation

False God
Anti-Hero

Cruel Summer

Truth & Lies
Friday Night Lies
Tuesday Night Truths

Kluvberg
First Flight, Final Fall
All The Wrong Plays
Love on the Line

Holt Hockey
Famous Last Words
Against All Odds
From Now On

www.ingramcontent.com/pod-product-compliance
Lightning Source LLC
Chambersburg PA
CBHW030727310726
48969CB00005B/1120